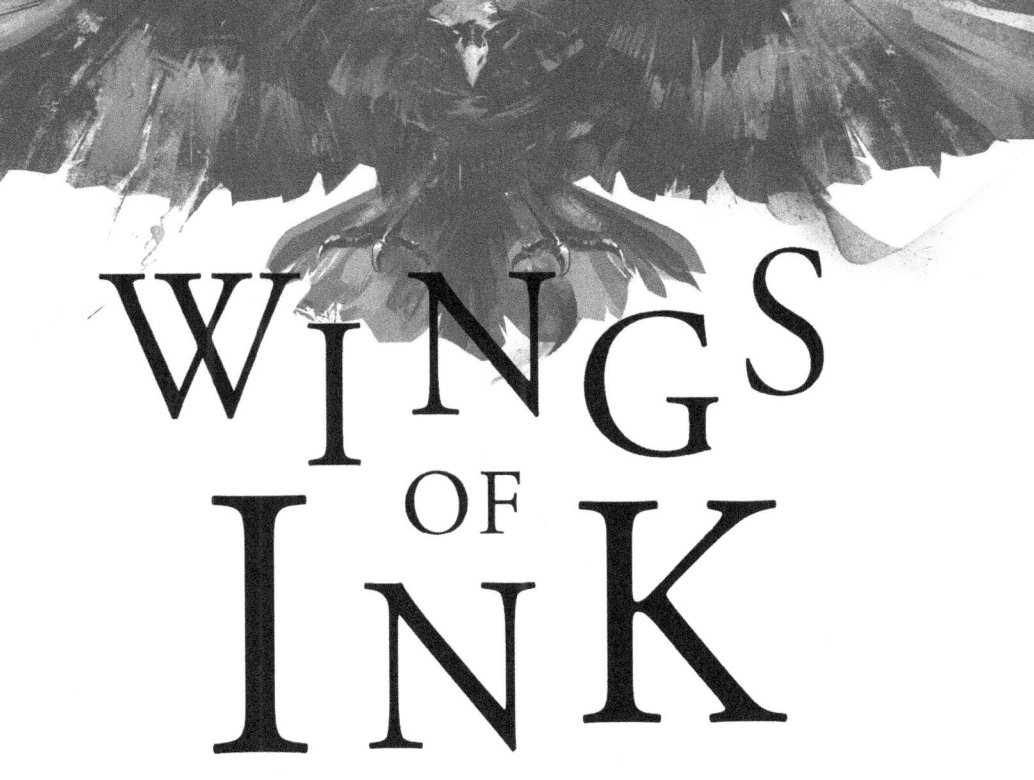

PRAISE FOR

WINGS OF INK

"WINGS OF INK IS AN IRRESISTIBLE ROMANTASY THAT WILL KEEP YOU ON THE EDGE OF YOUR SEAT. A FEISTY HEROINE AND A BROODING CROW KING FIGHT THEIR GROWING ATTRACTION IN THE MIDST OF A DEADLY CURSE, VENGEFUL GODS, AND POLITICAL UNREST. THE SLOW BURN ROMANCE WAS EVERYTHING I WANTED IN AN ENEMIES TO LOVERS FANTASY!"
—*Tessonja Odette, aauthor of the Entangled with Fae series*

"IN THE VEIN OF BEAUTY AND THE BEAST, ANGELINA HAS CREATED A THRILLING AND BEAUTIFUL TALE FILLED WITH EVERYTHING MY FANTASY HEART CRAVES. WITH HANDSOME AND MONSTROUS FAE CROWS, A SIZZLING SLOW-BURN, ENEMIES-TO-LOVERS ROMANCE, MAGIC, SUSPENSE, AND MUCH MORE... THIS STORY IS SURE TO KEEP YOU GLUED TO THE PAGES."
—*Cameo Renae, USA Today Bestselling Author*

"A DELICIOUS BEAUTY AND THE BEAST RETELLING WITH A TWIST! FULL OF SLOW BURN ROMANCE, MYSTERY AND MONSTERS THAT YOU WILL NOT BE ABLE TO PUT DOWN!"
—*Sam Ellen, Haus of Fables*

BOOKS BY ANGELINA J. STEFFORT

THE WINGS OF INK SERIES
Wings of Ink

THE QUARTER MAGE SERIES
The Quarter Mage
The Hour Mage
The Never Mage
The Ever Mage

THE SHATTERED KINGDOM SERIES
Shattered Kingdom
Wicked Crown
Shadow Rule
Lost Towers
Secret Court
Dark Refuge
Reborn Throne
Fatespun

THE TWO WORLDS SERIES
Blood of Two Worlds
Heir of Oblivion
Knight of Redemption
Rule of Dominion

THE BREATH OF FATE SERIES
Torn
Unraveled
Unforgiven
Tethered

THE WINGS SERIES
White
Black
Gray
Spark
Fire
Ashes
Crash

WINGS OF INK

ANGELINA J. STEFFORT

WINGS OF INK

THIS BOOK IS PART OF THE

First published 2024

Copyright © by Angelina J. Steffort 2023

All characters and events in this publication, other than those clearly in the public domain, are fictitious and any resemblance to real persons, living or dead, is purely coincidental.

All rights reserved.
No part of this publication may be reproduced, stored in a retrieval system, or transmitted, in any form or by any means, without prior permission in writing of the publisher, nor be otherwise circulated in any form of binding or cover other than that in which it is published and without a similar condition including this condition being imposed on the subsequent purchaser.

Ebook: ISBN 9783903357747
Print: ISBN 9783903357754

Cover by Fantastical Ink.

www.ajsteffort.com

"If you want to understand love, first learn about freedom."
—Paolo Coelho

ONE

*I**'m not afraid of you.*
   The thought echoes in my tired mind like a splash of icy water in a cave as I stare into the darkness. The same darkness I've been staring at for almost nine months.

Nine months.

I want to cry, but tears have become as rare as the meals they bring to this forgotten part of the prison.

The cells to my left and right are empty. The left one was never populated; the man in the right cell died a few days ago. The stench of decay lacing the dungeons before the guards finally figured out he'd passed away still fills my nose—so I breathe through my mouth and gag on the pleas of the occasional prisoner they take to the gallows I have a view on through the tiny hole in the wall they call a window.

I hate this place. More than I hate the people who put me here, I hate it. Not because it took the only man I've ever loved away from me—or the family I'd watched die the day of our arrival—but because it isn't the open sea. It isn't a swaying ship and endless blue waters. Despite being on an island, the brine doesn't reach my cell, and despite my staring into the darkness of the starless nights, the nightmares don't go away.

I'm not afraid of you.

But I am.

I only keep my eyes open because the occasional flicker of a torch along the walls when a guard makes his rounds reminds me the night hasn't swallowed me up. I'm still alive.

I should be dead.

Boots crunch along the packed dirt floor, and I whirl around, hitting my shoulder on the descending arch of the low ceiling and uttering a curse as I wish I had the dark vision of the fairy night guards. Then, I'm glad I don't because, if I did, their beautiful faces would distract me from what cruel, dangerous bastards they are.

The boots thud closer, making me shrink against the wall. Maybe I'm not afraid of the dark as much as of the creatures hiding within it. I raise my left hand as if that would do anything to protect me from whatever is stopping in front of my door, and pray to the Guardians that they are merely checking on me rather than picking me up for execution. I wouldn't be the first woman to disappear in the middle of the night. They tell the stories of feathered fairies hunting for brides all over Eherea, I have learned in my short twenty years. Even here in prison.

Gritting my teeth, I lean against the wall so I don't sway on my weak legs.

Not eight feet from where I stand, the key squeaks in the rusty lock, and a draft creeps through the small space as the door swings open, allowing in more of the stuffy air from the dark corridors behind my equally dark cell.

"Move," a deep voice orders, and I jerk into motion as if I decided to, even when my limbs were locked in place a moment before. The fairy is using his magic to direct me toward the exit, his power wrapping around my limbs, forcing them along, and there is nothing I can do about it. Even screams won't help because there is no one left in this Guardiansforsaken dungeon but me.

My feet tap over the straw palette I was sitting on in the corner, and I stumble over the edge, catching myself against the wall with my stiff right hand.

The guard's rough chuckle tells me he's still standing by the door, not even bothering to collect me with his hands—and why would he with the magic at his disposal?

I don't care that I stink and frown and my hair hasn't been combed in months with more than the fingers on my good hand. This fairy doesn't have wings—none of the guards at Fort Perenis do. And so, they aren't the ones collecting women at night.

When I am a few steps from the door, a fairy light comes to life, bright enough to take my sight all over again. I grind my teeth and stare through the brightness at the male with the light brown hair in front of whose feet I vomited the day of my arrival. He flicks his fingers at me, a clear summons that I debate ignoring as his magic releases me and his scowl pins me instead.

"You're expected in the general's office." He doesn't look back as he turns on his heels and stalks ahead of me, clearly expecting me to follow. Before I can even think to ask why, he barks, "Move your human ass."

So, I do. I stumble along, careful not to hit my toes on the rocks stuck deep in the dirt of the ground or on the uneven stone steps, which are clearly missing a handrail for feeble prisoners such as me.

Bracing my good hand on the moist wall, I climb one step after the other, eyes trained on the fairy guard's shoulders and shuddering at how little it would take for him to snap my neck. A flick of his fingers, a thought.

Nine months ago, I might have tried to fight him had I run into him on a loot with the Wild Ray. Nine months ago, before Tavrasian soldiers stormed my ship and killed half the crew before taking the rest of us north to this Guardiansforsaken place. Nine months—before they mutilated my hand and threw me in a cell as the only surviving member of the Wild Ray's crew. I don't close my eyes to dwell on the memory, or all I'll see is bloodshed when they slit the throats of the other half of the crew. All but me.

Shame and guilt creep into my bones at the thought that I survived.

And I wonder if it could even be called mercy when the soldier who ordered me locked up had claimed there would be a worse punishment for me than death.

My feet drag like I am wading in water as I make it up the steep stairs, barely keeping up with the strolling pace of the fairy. An orb of light hovers in front of him, illuminating his menacing outline as he fills the narrow door with his broad form.

I don't dare think what other horrors dwell in the fairy realm of Askarea on the mainland. I'll probably never make it off this island that belongs to both the human realms and that of the fairies, even if I ever manage to flee.

A different sort of guilt floods me as I remember the only time I attempted to get out of this place. I still have a long, welded scar running diagonally across my back from when they whipped a magical lash across it as a punishment.

Pressing my lips together in a tight line, I halt, inhaling the stream of fresh air stirring the stale one that has become as familiar as the freedom of the brine on the ship I once called my home.

Late spring, and not one hint of blossoms. If anything, this is proof Fort Perenis is as terrible a place outside the cells as it is inside.

As the guard moves, I step after him into the yard, my gaze darting to the center, to the dais where, nine months ago, I watched the life leave everyone I loved.

"If you think about running, you'll follow them faster than you care to." I hadn't realized he's fallen into step beside me and is now glaring down at me, his cold blue eyes a pale shade of gray in the glow of the magical light.

He jerks his chin the same moment I swallow a retort. Nothing I say will get me out of here. I tried—Guardians, did I try those first weeks after they shoved me in the cell and the door closed behind me. All that got me were mocking hollers. Nobody would tell me what my supposed fate would be either, so, at some point, I stopped shouting into the darkness.

After months of fearing, I stopped guessing. Until, eventually, I gave up hope.

A gust of wind swishes around my shoulders, stirring my dirty braid, and for a moment, I can taste a memory of freedom, but it's gone in a heartbeat, and devastation fills the tiny spot within me that once hoped for a future. I will never see the coasts of the fertile lands of Tavras or the rocky archipelago in the south of Cezux again. Those two human realms are as far from me now as the Wild Ray. And Askarea really isn't a place I dream of entering. Not that I ever will. I'll rot here in this prison, and the beautiful fairy guards will laugh as they watch me slip away.

Shooting a last glance at the dais, I try to remember Ludelle's smile. All I see is the shock on his face when the guard's blade cut into his throat. It is all I ever see—waking or sleeping. I haven't thought his name in twenty-seven days. How I know that? There is a thin groove in the brick stone beneath the window of my cell for each day I manage to keep the pain of thinking his name at bay. I run the fingers of my damaged hand over the fingertips of my good hand where the reminder of those twenty-seven days is also stuck under my nails.

The fairy dips his head at another guard I barely spot in the shadows along the wall, and I could swear I see a flash of white teeth in the darkness where his face should be. His chuckle follows me up the two steps to the double doors, which I assume lead to the general's office.

Warm light eats up the night as I step inside, ushered forward by the guard and greeted by two more inside like I'm a real threat. I might have been once, with a blade in my hands and something to fight for. But where defiance and hope once lived inside my chest, a wasteland spreads as vast as the ocean that once carried my ship on its loving waves.

The fairy pushes me a step forward as I stop behind the threshold, taking in the plain interior of the fortress's hallways. Left and right, simple stone walls frame corridors wide enough for three armed men. Doors are spaced along them in regular intervals the way the cells are underground. Perhaps this is a place for lesser criminals. Then, Fort Perenis doesn't waste its cells on lesser criminals. Nothing but the worst crimes in both the human and the fairy world guarantee a spot in this prison. If humans and fairies agree on nothing else, they agree that some people can't be left with the rest of a functioning society. Apparently, pirates sacking the crown's ships belong among them.

Turning to the narrow set of stairs leading to a torch-lit landing, I force my breath to steady.

"He's getting impatient." One of the guards from inside beckons me forward.

For a moment, I debate the merits of not following, but the fairy guard steps up behind me, and his looming presence terrifies the shit out of me, so I gather what is left of myself and carry it toward the opening door in front of me.

Murmuring voices float from inside like the rustling of leaves in the spring wind. I remember the sound even when I haven't heard it in years. There are no trees in the yard of Fort Perenis, and before, my life as a pirate didn't give me much opportunity to admire wood in any other form than as planks of a ship or a decent bed or table.

The threshold approaches before I am ready, and I brace myself to meet the general who gave the order to kill the rest of my crew—and the man I loved. To kill Ludelle.

I don't know what I expected to find inside, but it isn't the tall, feathered outline against a simmering fireplace by the wall.

ANGELINA J. STEFFORT

TWO

"Ah, there she is." The man in Tavrasian blue and black chimes as if his long-lost daughter just stepped through the door. The sound of his voice drives shivers of purest ice across my back, but it's not him I'm wary of. It's the creature slowly turning at the clear announcement of my arrival.

I stiffen, steps slowing and coming to a halt as I debate making a run for it, but the fairy guard is right beside me, his power shoving me on when my own legs decide they no longer want to cooperate.

"We've been waiting for you."

I pray that by *we* the general means someone other than the winged shadow I try so hard to ignore, but the black leather couch in the corner is unoccupied, as is the chair in front of the desk behind which the general stands with a smirk that brings back memories of the light leaving Ludelle's eyes—so who else could he mean?

The fairy guard walks beside me up to the desk, nodding at the general as he fulfills his duty and delivers me, and I can't help giving him a pleading glance.

He sets his features in stone and faces the general. "The pirate girl as requested," he reports as if the general didn't remember me.

The glimmer of malice in his pale eyes tells me he does. He remembers every scream and every thrashing thrust as I tried to break free when they'd held me down in the courtyard, forced me to watch as my family for the better part of my life bled out in front of me. I want to scream at him now, but the feathered shadow moves by the hearth, and I don't dare speak a word. Instead, I silently seethe at the man in front of me.

"It's been a while since you were brought to this facility." He looks me over like I'm a piece of furniture then looks again with the hungry gaze of a wolf before he wrinkles his nose. "You may leave." He dismisses the fairy, who promptly turns and abandons me. Not that I'd expected any help, but I'd take the male's taunting and his control of my limbs any day over one moment in the presence of the general.

I don't see the Tavrasian man with the mustache when I glare at him over the desk, but the Wild Ray covered in fairy smoke as the soldiers captured us. I see my crew fighting for their lives. I see Ludelle's warm brown eyes as they widen with horror when I'm pushed to my knees beside the other pirates lined up for slaughter, sword at my throat. I see death and destruction and… And my breath catches as a hissed voice sucks all the air from the room.

"Is this the woman?"

My head snaps toward the hearth to find the shadow has unfolded into a male form. I can't make out his face since he has chosen to keep his long brown hair hanging in his features.

Stay-calm-stay-calm-stay-calm.

I'm not calm when the male spreads his arms into long feathered wings as if stretching after a day of having to keep them tucked to his sides.

"The very one." The general nods at me with a cruel smile that transports me once more nine months back when I was locked up as the only surviving member of the Wild Ray's crew. "She's a handful—used to be," he corrects, his glance skimming my thin form, the dirty tunic and pants hanging from my frame like rags. "You might want to feed her a bit before you present her to *him*." He whispers the last word as if anxious he might summon a monster by mere mention.

But I'm too occupied with suppressing any sign of fear at the monster by the hearth that I don't even bother to be offended.

"She will suffice." The hiss runs through me like a whiplash, and I shrink back, knocking the chair over.

The Tavrasian general merely laughs as the winged creature approaches in heavy steps, boots thudding on the stone floor and feathers swishing along the wall as he stops a few paces away.

I try to take in all of him, but my mind is busy wrapping around the beak replacing the creature's mouth and nose, the feathers spreading along his neck, down his shoulders and torso, the wings sprouting from his shoulders instead of arms, and the claws replacing his hands.

"Suffice for what?" My throat is too dry to make my voice carry across the room, but the creature hears me anyway.

"Two weeks until Ret Relah." He drags out the end of the last word as he leans an inch forward into the light, and I gasp as a pair of all-black eyes engulf me with the depths of Eroth's Veil.

Ret Relah, I mouth, things clicking into place.

This isn't a fairytale or a story about the winged nightmares dwelling in the fairylands of Askarea that old women tell little girls to keep them in line. This is a Crow Fairy—I barely even dare think the name—and he has come to take me.

The general's laugh at the horror on my face stirs rage in my body, and for a heartbeat, I am close to reeling around and punching the man in the face. By Eroth, I'm not close. I turn and strike, the old fire flaring in my veins giving me at least the tiniest sense of control.

Before I can pull my fist back to rub my split knuckles where they'd connected with the general's unprepared jaw—right under the ridiculous mustache—an invisible power wraps around my hand, trapping it with the force of steel. My breath comes in gasps, and I wonder if there is a chance I might just hyperventilate myself into oblivion. However, the power grasps faster, and the male steps closer, pinning a raging general in place with all-black eyes that hold the intensity of burning coal.

I don't see the blackness coming as I pass out like I was hit over the head with a magic club.

The general's voice is a faint noise at the back of my mind as I try to blink my eyes open. "Consider Tavras's debt paid." He sounds pissed, ready to kill as he hisses the name of my homeland. But he promised me a punishment worse than death, so I assume I'm not going to die today.

"As agreed upon," the winged male hisses, the sound cutting like little blades, too loud, too close by my ear.

Footsteps thud along the floor, and I wonder if I am lying on the stone or if my body just aches from months in a cell without being able to stretch my legs or do proper exercise. Without sunlight or rain on my skin. Without hope.

"Now, take her and leave." The general's voice is closer this time, as if he's standing right next to me, and there is vengeance in his tone. If the male doesn't take me away, I might die a very ugly death at the hands of the man who had my chosen family executed not even a year ago. But if the Crow were to take me—

Before I can fully open my eyes, I'm swept up and slung over a hard shoulder, head bouncing off a muscled back, making me fling my arms to the sides to brace myself. My hands touch feathers, and I hold in a gasp, swearing to myself I won't make a sound to let them know I am terrified out of my wits.

I fail. My screams echo through the entire fortress as the Crow Fairy drags me into the yard and dumps me into a caged cart drawn by two robust horses. I land with a crack on a wooden crate, which decides not to hold even my diminished weight, and my breath leaves me at the pain spreading across my hip and leg where I hit the floor. A creaking sound tells me the door has been shut, and I can't turn fast enough to see the face of the fairy guard who locks me in before he walks away.

"Let me out of here," I demand, but all I get is a wave of the guard over his shoulder. He doesn't even have the decency to look at me as he dismisses my shouts and angry rattling of the thick wooden bars. "Let me out, you prick!"

This time, my words are meant for the feathered creature by the front of the cart. He doesn't deign to respond, merely climbs onto the wooden bench in front and clicks his tongue—or his beak, I'm not sure—at the horses, and the cart rattles into motion. The gate opens, and we pass through the thick walls that have been holding me captive. Behind me, the feathered fairy steers the horses over the bridge, and in no time, we clear the lake and roll along on a dirt road rather than wooden planks, but my gaze remains locked on the prison.

In the pale moonlight, the fortress looks like the claws of an angry god reaching through a pool of silver for the night sky. Nine months, I've cursed the Guardians, have raged and hoped, and finally despaired about my fate. Yet, I can't find my heart any lighter as the walls disappear under the veil of night and the cart enters the small forest. Perhaps that is because the Guardians no longer pay attention to Eherea. Perhaps they have moved on to a different world whose peoples still seem worthy of redemption. I don't care. It won't change my fate, and if Eroth lets his children wander off, no human or fairy will make them return to aid in something as trivial as the escape of a pirate.

In the front of the cart, the Crow Fairy is quiet, and I am glad he doesn't try to speak to me. That gives me a moment to rub my aching hip and gather my limbs under my body while I take a look around the spring forest—not that I see much in the darkness, but it is better than staring at the stone courtyard of Fort Perenis day and night.

Unlike the day I was brought to the prison, no other guards accompany us this time. Yes, I'm in a cage, and yes, the winged fairy is probably the deadliest creature I've encountered. But I'm also less guarded than I've been in nine months.

A sliver of hope rises in my chest as I scan the bars for weaknesses and the floor for something I could use as a tool or a weapon. If I manage to open the cage, I might be able to escape. The trees would give me cover, and I could sneak to safety. To freedom.

A glance over my shoulder informs me the fairy isn't paying attention. Shiny black feathers define his shoulders and arms, covering his entire torso down to his belt. Where brown hair spilled to his shoulders in the general's office, more black feathers cover his head and the back of his neck. For a moment, I think it is some sort of cloak he keeps draped over himself, but then I notice a patch where a few feathers are missing, leaving behind a white scar. I shudder as I see proof that the feathers are growing directly from his skin. If I had any doubts this was a Crow Fairy before, I am now convinced that is exactly what I'm looking at.

I need to get away before he drags me through the lands to wherever it is the Crow Fairies are hiding and kills me. Everyone knows people taken by the Crows never return. Everyone. Even if most think they're mere fairytales, if they saw what I see, they'd have no doubts that this is my end. Perhaps, not today or tomorrow since the fairy obviously has plans for me or he wouldn't have put me in a cage to cart me off, but eventually, death is coming.

Sweat collects at my neck, trickling into the collar of my tunic.

He hasn't as much as grumbled a word since we've left the fortress, but I don't trust the silence. I watched the fairy guards in the prison long enough to know they always pay attention, even when they seem otherwise occupied. And this is a creature even worse than those handsome prison guards.

If I don't act now, will I get another chance to run?

She will suffice. His hiss slashes through my memory as my eyes snag on the nails on what remains of the crate. Metal nails. I shift my body so my side covers what's left of the splintered wood and I can keep an eye on the fairy while he guides the horses through the near-darkness.

My breathing is too loud as I slide my hand down to the nail closest to my leg and pull, but perhaps that covers up the sound of the metal gradually slipping from the splintered wood until I finally, *finally* hold it between my fingers.

"We will be at the harbor soon," the Crow tells me without turning, and I could swear my heart is about to jump out of my throat as he shifts in his seat two feet in front of where I am cowering. If he decides to reach through the bars and crush my throat with his claws, he'll probably have an easy time.

I try not to think about the hundred ways he could kill me as I focus on inching closer to the back of the cage. Little by little, until I lean my aching side against the door, half covering the lock with my shoulder so I can reach past with my hand unnoticed.

The harbor—

Slowly, I inhale the warm spring air. Brine fills my nose, and my heart leaps into a gallop at the familiar scent of salt and freedom. I haven't seen the ocean since the day I was forced onto this island, and I didn't expect to ever lay eyes on it again.

All I want to do is close my eyes and relish the wind on my face, but not yet. I need to pick that lock with the crooked nail and try to escape before the Crow notices what I'm doing.

"Have you ever been to Askarea?"

I startle as he glances over his shoulder, face more bird than human and feathers covering his skin everywhere except for his mouth and chin.

"You lost your voice?" he asks when I don't respond.

Thank the Guardians, the nail is still wrapped in my palm, which I tuck behind my back on instinct, while the Crow measures me with pitch-black eyes. I wish I could make out more in the darkness, but then, I'm glad I can't. I've seen enough of that monstrous face in the general's office to last a lifetime.

"Not one scream?" he taunts, but there is no humor in his voice.

All I do is shake my head.

I don't know how much longer he stares at me before he turns back to the path, and my heart lowers back into my chest with a deep breath of relief. Keeping my eyes on the fairy, I bring the nail to the lock and feel for a hole. If my hand weren't trembling so much, I could hit the little opening that's meant for a key.

Eleven attempts later, the tip of the nail slides in, and I dare turn enough to grab the lock with my other hand while poking in hopes of making it click open.

Above the trees, the sky is graying, the veil of pale moonlight yielding to the first rays of rosy sun. Under different circumstances, I might have marveled at the way the greens light up in the treetops above me, but right here, right now, all I can do is pray to the Guardians that they'll help me open that lock—or to Eroth that he'll take me quickly should the Crow figure out what I'm up to.

Click. The sound barrels through me like a thunderclap even when it's barely a whisper. My head snaps to the front on instinct while I fumble the lock apart, careful not to push the door open and fall out. That would end my attempt at escape before it's really started.

If the Crow heard the lock, he doesn't show, beaked face turned to the road and shoulders relaxed as he steers the horses with one claw. I don't see what he's doing with the other one, and I honestly don't want to know. All I want is to wait for a narrower part of the path where I can push the door open and bolt into the thicket.

Out the door and into the thicket—but what then? Where will I go when he hunts me down? Where can I run?

As I debate the merits of bolting now and being ended quickly for my boldness versus being dragged to wherever he was taking me, the forest opens into a winding path down a grassy hill, and my chance is over.

Or so I think—until I spot a small village down the end of the road and, behind it, the glistening surface of sunrise-bathed waters. My heart bursts wide open at the view of the sea I'd once called my home, and I know, if I can manage just a little more patience, my chance at freedom waits where the island ends.

THREE

Groups of guards patrolling the pier are the first thing I spot as the cart weaves through the few stone houses that look like they have been standing there for hundreds of years. Perhaps longer. On a low, tiled roof, a ginger cat licks its paw, pausing and ducking as we roll past. I want to duck, too, but I need to act natural, or I'll draw the Crow Fairy's attention, and that is something I cannot afford. The shabby, wooden window blinds are closed on most houses, the village fast asleep except for those in uniform, guarding the world against criminals like me.

I shudder with contained rage at how I was sentenced to be a vessel for the Crows for looting a royal ship or two—well, maybe more than ten. If I were the King of Tavras, I wouldn't be amused as well. Still, would I have the entire crew of pirates killed? Except for the young woman, of course. She is Tavras's tribute for the Crows. Not that I know anything about what the Crows want from me. For a heartbeat, I am tempted to satisfy my curiosity and simply ask the fairy at the front of the cart, but if I do, he'll be paying attention to me, and that's the last thing I need.

The smell of fish intensifies as we roll down the narrow path between houses, and I glance left and right until I spy a corner that looks promising. Two houses stand at an angle with a gap that might be wide enough for me to slip through sideways, but one look at the Crow tells me his massive form won't fit. Perfect.

In my head, I count the rattling clacks that occur with every full turn of the wheels. If this cart makes it back to the prison in one piece, I'll be surprised. One. Two. Three…

Twenty-four turns before we make it to the corner and I have to pit my luck against the fairy's reflexes.

The area is clear of guards, most of them circling at the end of the street where it transforms into a long, wooden pier.

Nail in one hand, I hold my breath as I throw my full weight against the door.

It swings open with little more than a creak, but I make too much noise when I land on the uneven road on my hands and knees. The nail bites into my skin, spearing the flesh of my bad hand, and I gasp, scrambling to the gap between weather-worn stone walls.

"Stop!" The fairy's hiss sends my heart ricocheting into my throat, but I don't look back as I squeeze through the sharp edges. It's a tight fit, but I make it before the Crow can reach the corner.

His hiss bounces off the narrow corridor, multiplying like little whips of sound, commanding me to stop. I push forward, fighting against the magic weaving through the air. It's not as powerful as in the general's office, or maybe I'm not as weak anymore. Maybe the scent of freedom instilled new strength in me.

Little greens cushion the rough edges of the stone where they grow from cracks in the walls, the feel oddly comforting for someone who has spent the past six years either on a ship or in a dungeon where not even a blade of grass sprouted in front of her window.

My hip and leg ache, but the pain is bearable with the rush of adrenaline in my veins. So close. The walls are at a slight angle, allowing me to walk straight instead of sideways, and there is a turn and a cluster of bushes ahead. If I duck into those, I might be able to shake my pursuer.

I make it all of fifteen steps before a shadow blocks out the light at the end of the corridor a few feet ahead, and my heart stops as the Crow lifts his feathered arm and hauls me out of my little escape route by my throat.

"I might try to run, too, if I were you," he hisses, all-black eyes shuttering as he pins me in the spot, claws tightening. "But I will say this only once, and you better listen: There is no escape for you. I don't need a cage to take you to your destination, no chains, not even magic."

And I believe him. The way his claws dig into my windpipe in a controlled squeeze—not hard enough to stop my breathing but enough to only let wheezing gasps through—is all the proof I need.

"Do you understand?"

I can't speak, so I hold that all-black gaze and nod as best as I can with a set of claws locked around my throat.

"Good." His grasp loosens, and I slide down the wall, only now noticing the piercing pain where my back was pressed into the sharp rocks behind me. "Now, get up. We don't have all day, and the king won't be amused if he learns you tried to bolt."

No matter how hard I try to hold them in, tears spring to my eyes as he drags me back to the cart the long way. Tears of fury, of desperation. For a few fearful breaths, I was close to freedom.

My hands curl into fists, and a stinging pain reminds me of the nail in my fist. My tears dry up, and I measure the distance to the next alley before I glance at the feathered neck that would be the best aim for the finger-long piece of iron. I don't hesitate as I ram it into the fairy's flesh right as he tries to push me back into the cage.

The Crow roars, drawing the attention of the guards at the pier, but his grasp slips, and I twist out of his hold, backing out of the cage and running for the dark alley that could be my path to freedom. I don't look back—and I don't need to. The Crow's claws dig into my arms as he catches me right at the corner, his iron hold not budging as I thrash against it.

"One more stunt like that," he hisses as he throws me over his shoulder the way he had at the prison, completely ignoring my fists drumming on his lower back in an attempt at getting him to let me go, "and I will tell the king that, unfortunately, his bride died on the transfer from Fort Perenis." He locks his claws around my knees, preventing me from kicking out with my legs. "Maybe I'll throw you overboard once we're too far out on the waters for you to swim back. I'm sure Tavras will find him another woman before Ret Relah."

Wait. My entire body slackens as his words register. "What?"

He doesn't bother carrying me back to the cart but walks straight to the pier, the guards giving him a wide berth as he steps onto the wooden planks. I don't see much but their fear-filled faces as they stare after the winged menace and the pity in their eyes when their gazes slide to me.

"Help!" I scream, pitting my remaining strength against the fairy's grasp. Yet, there isn't much left with my body exhausted from lack of sleep, lack of nourishment, and lack of a peaceful moment in the past nine months.

The guard closest to us grabs his sword, half-tugging it from its sheath but stopping as if he thinks better of it, and shakes his head.

It dawns on me then that none of them will help me. Not one single armed man will stand up for me as the Crow carries me to the single boat at the end of the pier. This is sanctioned by the King of Tavras. I'm a convicted criminal and was handed over by the king's general. There is no help for me. No freedom. No future.

"Maybe I'll throw you overboard," the Crow repeats as he ungently dumps me in the back of the boat before he steps in behind me. I scramble into a crouch, not daring to stand with my head spinning from being upside down for so long.

He hauls in the rope and pushes the boat away from the pier with one strong motion of his feathered arm.

I'm so nauseous I might puke over the railing for the first time in years.

"Not that." I gesture at the water, wondering if drowning would be a mercy compared to being chosen as the Crow King's—"Bride. You said you'd tell the king that his *bride* died on the transfer from Fort Perenis."

The Crow ducks under the beam of the mainsail, reaching for the halyard.

"That—" His hissed voice still sends shudders of terror through me, but I'm too busy fighting to keep my empty stomach stable to shrink back into the railing. "Last year was Askarea's. Next year is Cezux's turn."

The turn for what? Askarea… The fairylands. And Cezux, the human realm west of my homelands. What did those two realms do?

When I don't react with anything other than a confused blink, he pulls on the halyard, making the sail shoot up, and secures it before bracing his claw on the railing beside him a good five feet away from me. I take my first good look at him, recognizing that his shape is mostly human. Only those winged arms ending in claws, and of course, the beaked face and feathered head and torso. I swallow the bile in my throat.

"The king needs a new bride." He shrugs, and the feathers covering his scalp turn into brown hair and the face more human, except for those all-black eyes and the beak. Those remain. But his voice is less of a hiss when he tells me, "This year, it's Tavras's turn, and Tavras chose you."

Instead of letting me process the meaning of his words, he bends over and picks up a bag I hadn't noticed beside the mast. The boat is already moving, its swaying both soothing and upsetting as memories and fears mingle.

Bride. I am to be his king's *bride*. Not that I understand what that means; only it adds up. The tales and the whispers of women disappearing in the night, taken by feathered fairies. Only women—*brides*.

"You mean the King of Askarea?" I clarify because I need to know where we are going and what level of horror to expect.

The male chuckles as he studies me, bundle in hand as if debating whether or not to hand it over. "We have nothing to do with the King of Askarea. The Crows rule themselves, and our king has his own little kingdom."

Before I can begin to understand what he is saying, he tosses the bundle at me, and I catch it with both hands, wincing at the injury in my stiff one where the nail cut into my palm. "Eat. We have quite a journey ahead of us, and my king doesn't appreciate me bringing back skeletons for brides."

I could swear he is grinning, but the beak makes it difficult to tell any facial expression.

The bundle weighs a thousand pounds in my shaky hands, and I drop it on the wooden boards in front of me, tugging it open as he nods at it.

"Take the hardtack. It might be easier to digest than the news."

He is not wrong.

My stomach grumbles as the smell of dried meat and fruit climbs my nose, but I do as he says and pick up the small bundle of hardtack with my good hand.

The Crow studies me, wind ruffling the feathers along his arms. I want to ask him if he can fly with those, but I'm too busy compartmentalizing the pain in my hand the way I learned over the past months after they'd broken my wrist during the capture of the Wild Ray. My heart aches at the thought of the proud pirate ship I had once called my home. Eroth knows what the Tavrasian soldiers did with it, if they destroyed it as they did with its crew or made it a trophy for their king.

"I can take a look at that." The Crow takes a step closer, making me hit my head as I shrink into the railing behind me. He is staring at my hand, and I am staring at his claws as they point at my bleeding palm.

"No thank you." The words burn in my dry throat, and I yearn for the waterskin I spotted in the bundle at my feet, but I don't dare move under the gaze of the predator before me, too scared that he will pounce if I as much as breathe wrong. Baring my teeth at the pain, I tuck my bad hand behind my back and inhale through my nose to steady myself. The world is swaying, and not only from the waves we're gliding over. Exhaustion and sleep deprivation have made me dizzy.

"Drink and eat." He steps back, glancing out at the ocean as if he can see miles ahead toward our destination. He probably can, but even when his focus is no longer on me, the sight of the monster's outline gilded by the rising morning sun does nothing to put me at ease.

With cautious fingers, I shove a piece of hardtack into my mouth and chew until I start coughing from the dryness in my mouth, so I pick up the waterskin and barely manage to open it with my injured hand. The Crow doesn't offer his help again, and I don't ask even when it takes me several attempts before I finally get the cork out.

The first sip of water is like a dip in the ocean—cool and refreshing, and I want to close my eyes and savor the last of the fresh water as it lingers on my tongue for a heartbeat, two. Not having felt the wind on my skin and seen so much open water in months makes me keep my eyes open, directed at the glistening waves dancing around the boat. I empty half of the contents before setting down the waterskin and resting my back against the railing. My head swims a bit, and I wonder if it is from having hit it earlier or from exhaustion.

Before I come to a conclusion, a comfortable weight spreads through my body, making me smile at the metallic orb rising in the east, and my eyes shut as I drift off into a dreamless sleep.

FOUR

The soothing sway of the ocean's arms has been replaced with a steady, suffocating softness threatening to swallow me up. In my head, a steel hammer is pounding on an anvil, and my eyes are sticky from too much sleep or too many tears, or both. What's really killing me though is my bladder.

With a groan, I roll to my side, anxious that any change in position will be too much and I'll end up wetting myself, but if I remain lying here—wherever *here* is—it will happen for sure.

As I push myself up, I open my eyes ... and need to do a double-take.

Was I worried I'd pee my pants a moment ago? That's the least of my problems.

I'm sitting on a soft mattress, facing a dark stone wall, and by the narrow door a few feet off center of the dimly lit room, a Crow Fairy with a silver spear stands guard, his tall form clad in leather pants and feathers. His face is more bird than human, eyes so black I can see all the way to Eroth's realm in them. He stares at me as if expecting me to attack.

Fear fights the need to relieve myself, and I groan again as pain spreads through my belly.

"Bathing room—" It's all I get out as I leap to my feet and stagger toward the second door on the other end of the room, nearly sighing with relief as I find a toilet.

Nothing has ever felt as good as the moment I sit and let go. Then I remember I fell asleep on a boat and woke up in a foreign room on land. I have no idea where I am and how I got here, or how, by Eroth, I slept through all of it.

The pressure on my bladder is gone when I stand and pull up my pants, but that on my chest is heavy as a boulder. With shaky fingers, I grasp the edge of the basin and brace myself as I sway like my body hasn't figured out I'm on land again.

"Are you coming out any time soon, or should I come in?" The voice startles me to attention, and my heart leaps into my throat as I scan the narrow bathing room for anything I could use as a weapon, finding little besides a bar of soap I could rub into someone's eyes and a folded towel sitting next to the basin. I could use that to smother the Crow if I got it around his face.

My violent thoughts are interrupted by three slow knocks.

I hold my breath, heart racing so loudly I can barely hear the silence as the creature on the other side of the door waits for an answer.

"Are you still alive in there?"

The voice isn't as hissy as the Crow who picked me up from prison. That alone is a riddle I can't solve—especially not by staring at the broken mirror in front of me. One long crack runs through my face, splitting my features in half. Dirt covers my pale skin, my lips jabbed with thin streaks of dried blood running toward the corners of my mouth. My eyes match the gray of the stone walls, not granite dark, but not silver pale either. My cheeks are hollowed out from nine months in prison, and I don't know how long the transfer to wherever I am now took.

"I'm coming in."

It's not a threat, but it might as well have been one by the way his words make me back into the corner beside the basin. I don't have time to flip my greasy, ash-blonde braid over my shoulder before the door swings open with a creak that makes the nails coil off my toes. My hand grabs for the towel a heartbeat before the doorframe fills with the feathered outline of a huge—and I mean *huge*—male.

He's a few inches taller than the one on the boat, and the feathers on his arms and shoulders glimmer in the glow of soft orange peeking through the small window up high in the bathing room wall. My pulse is a gushing river without beat or rhythm as those all-black eyes lock on mine, taking in my fear as if it is air to breathe, and his eyebrow crooks.

Eyebrows. He has eyebrows, just like he has a mouth underneath a bird's beak. Feathers flow from his forehead back to his shoulders and neck, but as I still try to wrap my head around what I'm seeing, they change into a spill of night-dark hair, and along his torso, pale skin covers lean muscle, vanishing in a pair of black leather pants. On his chest, a silver pendant catches my eye before he folds his winged arms over it, effectively blocking out the halo of light framing him from the room behind.

"Alive after all." Were I not scared out of my wits, I might have noticed the amusement in his tone.

I press my back into the hard wall, grabbing for each inch of distance I can bring between the monster and me.

His gaze runs up and down my body with an appraising quality that makes me feel all kinds of sick.

"Well ... mostly," he concludes, nodding at the towel in my hands. "Were you about to wash up, or is this to smother the next person to enter this room?"

"How did you guess?" The words are out before I can bite my tongue.

The Crow spits a laugh, and I realize his voice isn't the same bone-grating hiss as that from the Crow on the boat. It's rich and deep. Almost human. And it makes my hair stand on end.

"Spirited. I like that in a female." He cocks his head, gaze locking with mine as something starts to register in my mind.

Before I can spit a retort, the Crow steps back, light flooding the bathing room, and drops his winged arms to his sides. I catch a glimpse of a bejeweled hand, not a claw, but the Crow walks away so fast I can't be certain.

He turns to the Crow guard by the door, crossing the room in long, graceful strides. "Make sure she washes and changes before you bring her down for dinner."

Something in the way the guard snaps to attention at the Crow's command makes me wonder if *I* am dinner.

I wouldn't be surprised.

The door swings open on a phantom wind as the Crow swishes his hand, and as he disappears from the bedroom, feathers cover his neck and back like on the other Crow Fairies'. I blow out a breath, resting my head against the wall as the door shuts with a click, and wipe the sweat off my brow.

I survived. The prison, the transfer from Fort Perenis to wherever I'm now. I'm still alive. And my heart is beating out of my chest as I understand I must be in the fairy lands. In Crow territory.

My eyes flick to the window, drinking in the view of sunset-gilded trees.

"You heard the king. Get ready for dinner," the guard hisses, shocking me into motion.

My hands grab the towel so hard my palm stings where I injured it with the nail, and I glance down to find a streak of crimson seeping into the brown fabric.

The king. I need to lean on the shelf next to the basin as I slam the door in the Crow's face. The fairy with the black hair was the Crow King.

Gooseflesh spreads over my skin as I try to process that the monster who blocked the threshold a moment ago is my husband-to-be. I pivot just in time to retch into the toilet as my empty stomach rejects the news.

I need to get out of here before they can put me into a magical slumber once more—because by now, I'm certain that's what the Crow on the boat did. It must have been the water or the hardtack. Or both. But if I just met the Crow King, I must be in his palace. And that means I'm in the fairylands of Askarea.

I wish I'd paid attention to the stories my mother told me about the magical creatures in the north of Eherea, but I've never believed in things I can't see or touch. The magic the merchant brought back from the fairy ports, that's something I understand. Fairy smoke, fairy wine, enchanted bracelets that give their bearer stamina or strength. I've seen those things. Touched them—except for the fairy wine. A bottle of that was what had been missing in Ludelle's collection of rare Eherean wines. Something he dreamed of gathering to fill that empty spot on the shelf in the captain's cabin back on the Wild Ray.

The Wild Ray is history though, as is its crew. They are all dead. All, including the man I loved. And I'm the only one left to tell the tale.

Paralyzing desperation creeps through my body, making it hard to breathe.

I'm alone in this Guardiansforsaken world, and what little is left of me has been sold to the Crow King to cover Tavras's duty of providing a new bride.

I don't know what gives out first, my legs or my arms, but when I hit the stone floor, the impact creates a dull pain compared to the sharp ache in my chest.

Sold. Abandoned. Forgotten. I was shipped to Fort Perenis and kept alive in a prison no one returns from for this sole purpose.

I don't know how long I lie there, panting through the pain as I try to figure out a way to reach the window high up in the wall. Unlike the one in the bedroom, all I can see through this one are orange and golden clouds towering in the sky like a fortress of its own.

If I could get the shelf close enough to the wall, I might be able to climb up and smash the glass with my hand. The towel will provide protection against cuts, and if I use my bad hand, I don't risk losing much mobility in case I slice myself open anyway.

Willing strength into my limbs, I shuffle to my feet and grab the edge of the shelf.

It's a small mercy of the Guardians that it isn't hooked into the wall behind, but my damaged hand screams as I use all my strength to pull it away from the stone and in front of the basin.

In prison, I cursed the people who broke my wrist and never bothered to set it and wrap it properly so it could heal, but this was a whole new level of hatred I felt as the uselessness of my right hand hit me in full force. Where I fought with blades in both hands when looting ships with the crew of the Wild Ray, now I can barely bend or move my wrist, let alone shove a massive wooden shelf.

I step around the piece of furniture, bracing my back against the tall board forming the side of the shelf and my feet on the dark stone tiles making up the floor, before I push with all my strength—which isn't much since I haven't eaten or drank for as long as I hadn't gone to a bathing room, not to consider the months in prison where a 'proper' meal consisted of barely enough to feed a toddler.

As the shelf doesn't budge more than half a foot, I take a break and reach for the pitcher beside the basin to take a long drink.

A groan rumbles in my throat at the taste of water. I'm too thirsty to worry if this water is also poisoned. If I get to sleep another few days, at least, I won't need to have dinner with the Crow King.

The thought of the enormous, feathered male instills more fear than I have reason to pit against it, and within moments, I'm back to shoving the shelf under the window.

The wooden structure creaks as I set my foot on the lowest shelf and pull myself up with my good hand on a higher one. It's enough to make my pulse kick back into a gallop, but not enough to stop my pursuit of freedom.

There's a guard right out the bathing room door, and he is expecting me to be clean and presentable the next time I enter the bedroom. Only, I'm not planning on returning there. When I exit this bathing room, it will be through the window, and if I die trying, it will still be a far better fate than marrying the Crow King.

FIVE

I make it all of three boards up before the shelf collapses under my tiny weight. Cursing my bad fortune, I gather my limbs, not bothering to rub any of the sore spots the fall leaves on my body. There are too many by now, and I don't have the time to feel sorry for myself.

The door flies open a heartbeat later, and a hiss fills the room as the Crow guard storms in, claws locking around my upper arms as he sets me back on my feet.

"You haven't learned a thing on our trip from the prison island, have you?" I don't see anything but feathers as he tugs me past the basin, sitting me down on a wooden stool in the corner. "You could have killed yourself."

I manage to find his beaked face above me as he steps back, a clear warning in his all-black eyes. Today, his brown hair falls around his head, feathers covering everything from his neck down to the waistband of his pants. A sword hangs on his belt, the broad blade promising a painful death.

"And you could have the decency not to care." I'm too numb to feel fear, adrenaline blocking out the pain spreading across my body. If I survive the day, I'll count my bruises, but right now, I am face to face with a Crow. A Crow who poisoned me to bring me to this place hidden in the fairylands.

The Crow straightens and steps back, looking me over, and his features change from mostly bird to almost human. I notice a scar running from his cheekbone to the corner of his mouth.

"I don't care about decency. What I care about is that my king is expecting you for dinner, and I am not going to suffer for your defiance." The way he looks at me—similar to that calculating gaze on the boat before I'd drank from the waterskin—makes me shudder with fear.

Not that I should care if a monster got punished by an even worse monster, but there is something in the way his posture shifts, shoulders dipping ever so slightly, that makes me ask, "Am I to be his dinner? Is this why he needs a new bride?" The question of why the Crow King gets a new bride every year has been burning on my tongue since the Crow had brought it up on the journey from prison. But now that I've spoken it, fear of what may be the response locks up my body.

The Crow's laugh hisses through the room, and I shrink against the wall, remembering all the places I was aching.

"It's not Ret Relah yet, little bride." It's all he says before he steps out into the bedroom. "Wash up, or I'll do it for you, and I assure you, you won't like it."

I don't have any doubt he's right. So, I push myself to my shaking legs and pour water into the basin to wash my hands and face while the Crow from the journey stands a few steps outside of the bathing room, eyeing me as if expecting me to try to scale the wall with my bare hands.

"The rest, too," he demands, and it takes me a moment to understand he wants me to strip down and wash the sweat and grime off my entire body.

Before I can retort, I am not going to take off my clothes while he's watching and there is no point cleaning up more if I am only to put on my dirty clothes again, he reaches for a stack of fabric on the foot end of the bed and tosses it at me. It lands at my feet the same moment the door flies shut, and I'm once more alone.

Fear and defiance wage a war in my chest as I debate doing as I was told, but the light filtering in through what should be my escape route tells me night is approaching fast, and there are two Crows right outside the bathing room door. If I want to escape, I need to be smarter about it. Gather some strength. Eat. Rest, if I manage. Learn details about my location and the distance to the next port so I can find a ship and sail east the way Ludelle had always dreamed of doing. I would do many things, but I wouldn't die here.

My injured hand screams as I use it to open my tunic, but I don't care. I endured worse during those first days in my cell at Fort Perenis. The water is cool as I drag a piece of fabric I find on the broken shelf over my pale skin. My stomach is so taut with hunger I barely feel it anymore, and the bruises… I guess it can't wait until tomorrow to count them. Blotches of purple spread along my hip and thigh where I fell on the crate in my cage. On my shoulder, another streak of near black is blooming. I have no idea where I got that one. Maybe the Crow tossed me onto another cart without any regard for which pieces of me would break in the process.

I need to use my left hand to wash up, giving my mangled right one a break. It wouldn't do much good anyway. I've tried grasping forks and spoons with it, and while I can keep ahold of something that fragile, there is no way I can make coordinated use of them.

No one took care of my injury at Fort Perenis, but they tattooed a thin chain around my wrist once the skin had healed, a sign all prisoners at Fort Perenis carry.

I seethe at it as I wipe down my right arm before changing hands to my left, to wash where I otherwise can't reach. Before I wash my hair in the basin, I put on the black cotton pants and tunic the Crow provided so the next creature to barge through the door won't walk in on me naked.

It takes me longer than I hope to rinse the grime out of my tresses, but when I finally do, I'm not ready to face my captors. My fingers get stuck when I comb them through my wet strands, the lengths frizzy and knotted from months without seeing a comb.

I don't give a shit what I look like. What I do care about is the wound on my hand that broke open again and needs binding.

A sweep of the bathing room informs me there's nothing of use for that purpose, so I rinse the washcloth with what's left of the clean water in the pitcher and wrap it around my palm. When I finally muster the courage to enter the bedroom, both Crow guards are waiting for me, the one by the door angling his spear at me and the one who picked me up from prison leaning against the wall across the room, bored gaze on the sunset out the window as if he's been assigned a particularly annoying task and wishes for nothing more than to get back to whatever else he has on his schedule for the night.

I stop on the threshold as his gaze swings to me. "Not what I'd hoped for but better than before." He doesn't explain himself as he gestures at the door, and the Crow with the spear steps aside, pulling the paling wooden gate open.

His hiss creeps down my spine as I cross the room, fear commanding me to get moving, and put as much distance between him and me as I can manage while slipping out into the hallway.

The guard from the journey is at my heels, boots thudding lightly, unlike those of the fairy guards at the prison. I'd ask what makes Crow Fairies so different from other fairies, but my tongue is a tangle of held-back sounds of fear and pain, and I am truly not ready for another piece of bad news tonight.

There's a banister running around the inside of the huge space, blocking out the view on the lower levels. Several doors line the walls between columns of gray stone, and I notice carvings on them—feathers and antlers and ferns, all woven together into intricate patterns climbing the length of the stone pillars.

"This way." The guard catches up with me as I stop on the landing of a wide staircase, and holds out a wing, pointing down the stairs.

He walks beside me as if he isn't something born of nightmares, as talkative as he was on the transfer from the prison—until he poisoned me and put me into a magical slumber.

"Where are we going?" I can't hold my breath for the rest of the path, so I allow my questions to break free, one at a time.

"The dining room," the Crow answers, eyes on what has to be the entrance hall at the bottom of the stairs. "King Myron is expecting you there."

Myron. I search my memory for anything I might have heard about a King with that name and come up blank. The history of Askarea isn't written in human books, and the merchants who try to procure fairy books rarely ever get their hands on anything useful. Fairy poems, perhaps songbooks. Even ancient magic books which humans, supposedly, once used to study magic so they had something to pit against fairies.

But that was all in the past. Askarea was open for trade, and the diplomatic relations between King Recienne and Cezux are good enough. Tavras has closed itself off over the past decades, though, even from our human neighbors in the west. That leaves all things fairy that aren't goods on a merchant ship fables and rumors and stories to scare children into submission. I don't know even half as much as I want to about fairies. Only that the prison guards looked almost human, only taller, more perfect, and had pointed ears. I didn't know what other sorts of fairies existed in Askarea. Perhaps there were the hoofed sort and the horned one the way some tales told; perhaps those were just that—stories.

However, the Crow beside me is real, and so is his king. With his own kingdom as he'd said.

Before I can ask him if dinner is all that is expected of me, we arrive at a tall, carved door framed by two more Crow guards, both in the same leather pants and feathers as the one in my room. They even have the same type of spear. Their faces have more bird features than human ones, and my stomach forgets it is hungry as they click their beaks and caw what sounds like a greeting.

I swallow hard to free my vocal cords, but no sound comes out as they pull open the door, letting us into a large dining room made of the same dark stone as the room where I woke up. At the center, a long table is set with a white tablecloth and gray cloth napkins. The silverware and crystal goblet at the end of the table inform me on which of the eleven empty chairs I will sit.

King Myron sits in the twelfth, his feathered arms angled so his hands are resting in front of him on the table, and he is looking at me with those all-black eyes like I'm a bug under his boot.

"Nice of you to join me." He doesn't sound like he means it, even when his mouth curves up under his beak. I wonder if he can eat through both of them, or if the beak serves as a nose only.

Before I can make up my mind, he angles his head at me, gesturing at the chair across from him at the other end of the table. I'm not upset that there are five seats on each side, separating us. If anything, I can't get enough space between us.

As if reading my mind, the Crow King crooks a brow and leans back in his chair. He lifts a hand, waving it at the Crow who escorted me to this room. "Leave us alone, Royad."

Royad, apparently, inclines his head and—with a quick glance at me—hurries from the room, feathers quivering on his back as he marches out the door.

My nausea from earlier is gone, replaced by a chest-tightening panic that makes me go rigid in my chair.

The sunset kisses the silver on the table, the reflections taking my sight for a heartbeat, and I try to convince myself that I only need to wake up and I'll be back on the Wild Ray, Ludelle's arms around me. That he isn't dead and I'm not Tavras's tribute to the Crows. That this isn't real. But night pushes the merciful sun over the edge of the world, and I find myself staring the Crow King in the eye.

My body goes cold as ice as he shifts in his chair and his features melt into those of a male. A stunningly handsome male, were it not for those eyes with not even a circle of white around the depthless black reminding me of Eroth's Veil. A slightly hooked nose and sharply angled cheekbones complement the full mouth, which is set in a grim curve as he studies me across the table. His wings fold where normal arms would have an elbow as he gestures at the pitcher of wine in front of me, and no matter how eerie, they somehow complement his striking features.

"Please, help yourself."

As if I could even think of drinking wine in the fairylands. What I once hoped to share with Ludelle has become a threat.

I shake my head.

"What? Not thirsty?" King Myron chuckles darkly as if this is his own personal joke. "Or hungry? I could swear I heard your stomach grumble all the way through the palace earlier."

Could he? Guardians beware. If he has hearing like that—

"Don't worry, human bride. I can't hear that." He leans in just enough to make the fairy lights above us throw shadows of his long lashes onto his cheeks. Even from this distance, his eyes seem to swallow the world. "But I can hear your heartbeat right now, and it's telling me you are afraid."

He is not wrong, so I don't say anything. I don't pour myself the luxurious, crimson wine either.

"Are you afraid of my face?" His features shift into those birdlike ones, beak and feathers for hair. "Or are you afraid of my power?" He lifts a hand, and bands of steel snap out of nowhere, locking around my torso and holding me in place as if driven by magic. "Or of what will happen at Ret Relah?" He drags out the last syllable the same way Royad did on the boat, and I can't help but wonder if this is the way the end of spring celebration is to be pronounced and if all humans are doing it wrong.

"You're a quite meager bride," he notes with a sweep of his gaze down my body to where the table is covering up most of me. "So, eat up."

At a flick of his fingers, a feast appears on the table. Roast meats, vegetables, fresh bread. Even a pie sits at the center of the table. I don't take a closer look, or my ravaging hunger will push me to grab a helping of each dish and glut myself. Not that I could with the Crow King's power preventing me from moving.

I seethe at him, and he waves his hand again, the magical bonds falling away like tethers of mist.

"I don't know who told you I was your bride, but they're wrong. I'm not going to marry you." It's the only thing I can think of to say. Not over my dead body am I going to marry that monster.

King Myron laughs, features shifting back into their human form, and the contrast is so startling that, for a heartbeat, I stare with rapt fascination. Then I remember to be afraid, and my pulse skyrockets. "I'm afraid that's not up for debate. I need a new bride, and Tavras sent *you* to my Seeing Forest."

"I wasn't sent," I disagree, clutching my bad hand with my good one to keep them both from grabbing for the food. Guardians, I'm so hungry. "I was taken from Fort Perenis by your ... dog." It's the best term I have for Royad.

King Myron's features freeze, making him somehow even more beautiful—and scary. I don't dare breathe.

"Don't talk of what you know nothing about." He waves a hand in dismissal, feathers shivering across the edge of the table. "Or don't speak at all."

Without another look at me, he loads his plate with food and starts eating.

Naturally, my tongue has its own ideas, loosening at the exact moment he orders my silence. "Seeing Forest... Is that your kingdom?"

He cocks his head at me as if trying to decide how to respond to that, then inclines his head. "For now."

Ice slides down my spine at his gravelly tone, as if this is a question he has been asking himself for hundreds of years and never found a satisfying answer to.

I hold his all-black gaze for as long as I dare. "Why do you need a bride when Askarea provided one last year?" I remember Royad's words vividly. "Do they abandon a monster like you?"

I shouldn't be speaking to him like that. I know it; he knows it. And the glare he gives me tells me I might not live long enough to find out what made his last bride run—other than those feathers and his unquestionable cruelty.

"What's your name, human?" he demands, lowering the chicken leg he was leading to his mouth.

Perhaps if I push him hard enough, he'll change his mind about marrying me. Who am I but a human prisoner? There is no benefit for him other than—

"Your name," he repeats, that deep, cold voice turning lethal.

My body locks up from fear this time. But one more push and I might be either dead or free.

"Knowing you aren't set on keeping me longer than a year, I see no reason to tell you." Bold of me? Perhaps. Reckless? Definitely. Still, it feels so good to show the spark of defiance that will have me doing anything to break free from this new prison I have yet to understand.

And I see it in Myron's eyes that he'll do anything to make sure I don't succeed.

SIX

The sun is up early in this part of the world, or time functions differently, I don't know, but when I wake the next morning, the forest beyond the palace is tinted in bright daylight, bugs and bees buzzing around the yellow-blooming vines crawling up the wall and framing the outside of my window. It takes me a moment to accept that something beautiful, such as the delicate blossoms, exists in this cursed place where cruelty seems to be the main means of communication.

When I made it back to my room the night before, I wasn't nearly satisfied. A slice of meat and a small piece of pie was all I dared eat for fear of being poisoned again. Who knows where I'll wake up the next time the Crows put me under? Of course, I didn't touch the wine. Even with its deep red color, I wasn't certain it wasn't of fairy-making, and if there's one thing I'm trying to avoid at all costs, it's losing my wits in the presence of the enemy.

So, I opted for water back in my room and pulled out the two pieces of bread I managed to sneak into my sleeve when King Myron wasn't looking. That, combined with exhaustion, put me to sleep faster than even the loving waves of the Quiet Sea.

A gaze past the late spring landscape tells me we are far from the ocean. Not even a stripe of the coast is visible between treetops and a clear blue sky. So, this is the Seeing Forest. I don't know where in the fairylands we are or if we have crossed into a different realm altogether. It is something I need to find out so I know where to run to once I escape. Though, at this point, anywhere is better than here. That's probably the reason they didn't show me a map or give me any details about the whereabouts of this *kingdom*.

I rub my good hand over my face and smooth out the tunic and pants I slept in for lack of something else to wear. I surely won't take anything out of the dresser or the armoire. That would mean I'm accepting my situation, and I'm as far from that as from the waters I miss so much.

My hair spills in tangled waves past my shoulders, and I leave it there, not bothering to smooth it or braid it. Who am I going to impress?

At least, I'm alone, no Crows aiming spears at me or forcing me to put on fresh clothes. That gives me a moment to truly take in my room, and I can't help marveling at the detailed carvings on the furniture, the heavy, dark wood, and the silver, ornamented knobs on the armoire and dresser. The bed is a frame of carved stone, though, reminding me of the tombs where they put noble families to rest in Tavrasian graveyards. Were it not for the soft mattress and the plain linen beddings, I would believe this actually was a grave.

Leaning on the wooden windowsill, I glance down the tendrils of green and yellow to measure the distance to the ground. I'm too high up to jump without breaking my neck, and there is no frame to climb down on. The palace is enormous and bone-white on the outside. Towers enclose the expanse of the side where my room is situated, their roofs elevated to accommodate an open space that reminds me of a shelter for birds to slip into, only much, much bigger. The massive stone walls of the palace are cracked in places, I note when I turn my head to take in the dimensions of my prison, but the grooves are too far away for me to reach and use as a foothold—given I'd even make it out the window without tumbling to my death.

I'm great at keeping balance on narrow paths, being a pirate and all. But this is an entirely different challenge. I'm used to climbing masts and nets, not walls. My only chance is to find an exit a level down or two where falling won't mean certain death.

Before I can count the windows lined up beneath me, the door creaks open, and I almost fall on my ass as I jump away from my vantage point, pretending—without much success—I wasn't just scouting for the best escape route.

"I thought they stocked your wardrobe," the Crow King says by way of greeting, sending my heart into a spiral of panic.

"Don't you knock? Is that a discourtesy a king is entitled to?"

He stares at me, features shifting from beak and feathers to human while he tucks his bejeweled hands behind his back, feathers falling along his arms like the sleeves of an eccentric jacket. Indeed, he wears a jacket—sleeveless and with a high collar that hides the silver pendant I spotted on him yesterday. "Bursting into their brides' bedrooms unannounced? Yes, it is." There is no sign of humor in his tone. Not a surprise. Of course, this monster of a king doesn't care about something as trivial as privacy.

"Not yet." I purse my lips as I bring as much distance between us as the room allows—and find myself with the windowsill digging into the small of my back.

"Not until Ret Relah, you mean." He crooks his brow the way he did at dinner, and I'm reminded of how his power locked around my body.

I shiver. "Not if I have anything to say about it."

"Which you don't." Before I can tell him to go cross Eroth's Veil, he continues, "So, spare us both the drama, and pick a dress so I can introduce you to my court."

"To your court," I repeat like I don't have half a brain to spare.

That costs him an uptilted corner of his mouth, and I can't help noticing how painfully attractive that little gesture makes him, despite the all-black eyes. Then, I remember his true face, the feathers and beak and that horrible power of his, and my right hand aches as I wedge it between my back and the wood to protect my spine as I shrink farther into the windowsill.

"It's only a week until Ret Relah." He says it as if that were explanation enough.

Perhaps it is. In his world. But I have no idea what I'm dealing with other than a horde of monsters whose king I'm supposed to marry. No. Fucking. Way.

"I haven't celebrated a Ret Relah in my life." It's the truth.

"Then it's about time you started." His half-smile has disappeared, nose shifting from beak form to human form and back as he waits for I don't know what, standing motionless like a statue of death.

"I'm not planning on starting anytime soon." Just because *he* can't keep a woman happy longer than a year. That reminds me—"Can't you get one of your old brides to return to you?

That would spare both of us the inconvenience, and I promise, I won't tell a soul."

The Crow King turns and stalks to the armoire, throwing the doors open and randomly pulling out a dress. "They're all dead." He turns and tosses the black layers of fabric at me before heading for the door. "Put this on. I'll be waiting in the throne room."

He doesn't look back, leaving me shaking behind the heap of silk and feathers. Before the door closes, I spot two feathered arms ending in claws holding spears, and I know, there is no escape.

Tears stream down my face as I strip out of my tunic and pants and tug on the dress, but I swallow them and wipe my hands over my cheeks to hide the evidence of my despair. A week. The transfer must have taken a few days and this is my second day at the palace. Only one more week before my fate is sealed. One week to flee from this fortress of monsters and make my way to the ocean where freedom beckons and I can follow those dreams of sailing east that Ludelle and I once shared. I bite back the inherent despair that comes with thoughts of the man with whom I've spent years on the Wild Ray, of the memories of brine and wind and the shouts of sailors.

The guards turn to stare at me as I cross the threshold, feathers flowing along my legs in a long, straight skirt. The silver-and-black belt reaches from my waist to just underneath my breasts where it kisses black silk wrapping my décolletage enough to not show cleavage. There are no straps or sleeves, and I have never felt so naked as I do when I walk down the stone hallway, followed by the keen eyes of the guards spaced out along the walls. They don't bother to hide their stares, and I don't bother to pretend I'm not noticing. I seethe back at them, holding my head high as I march toward the stairwell.

I have no idea where the throne room is, but instinct tells me, it must be behind the grandest door on the main floor, so I turn to where I spotted a tall pair of carved double doors. My gaze sweeps along the walls, scanning for doors or a window leading outside. Yet, besides the enormous entrance door, which is guarded by six beaked and clawed Crows, there is nothing.

Halfway down the stairs, a shadow joins me, and I leap to the side, grabbing for the handrail with my bad hand. I wince and curse, earning a questioning glance from Royad, who just scared me out of my wits.

"The king said you may need help," he tells me as he stands there, feathers retreating from his head and torso like a layer that can be peeled off. It takes me a moment to get accustomed to the fully human features revealed in the process. And again, I startle as I take in his features, the way his voice just turned from a hiss to a melodious baritone. "Something wrong with my face?"

I almost laugh at the question because there is so much wrong with his face I can't even begin to tell, and it's not the scar making the corner of his mouth tilt up in what has to be the saddest half-smile of the century. It's the way his human face is as stunning as King Myron's. It's clearly the fairy blood in his veins. No one is as beautiful as fairies—or so the stories say. The fairy guards at Fort Perenis were something to look at, but in comparison to this?

I shake my head. "Nothing."

"Good." Royad holds out his clawed hand, feathers rippling along his wing-arm as he waits for me to take it. "Because you look like you just saw a monster."

The way the unscarred side of his mouth tips up makes me believe he is actually joking.

This is the same male who poisoned me on the boat and brought me to this Guardiansforsaken place. I won't take his hand.

He doesn't seem surprised at my rejection, merely lowers his claw to his side where a long, brutal sword dangles on his belt—as if I need a reminder of the violence contained in that strange hybrid body.

"Is everyone here a Crow Fairy?" I ask because he is the one I need to fear least. He has done his duty and hauled me to King Myron's palace. He's also had every opportunity to kill me, has even threatened to do it, yet, I'm here, alive and breathing. And he is escorting me to the horrible creature whom he claims I am promised to.

"Most are." His head whips left and right as if to check for non-feathered fairies.

I follow his gaze to the Crow guards left and right of the double door. They straighten at his approach as if he is someone important. That makes me think—"Who exactly are you?"

Royad gives me a sideways glance. "The closest thing King Myron has to family." We stop by the doors, and I try not to focus on the huge space they reveal as the guards open them for us. "And you are going to walk in there, bow to the king, and wait for him to introduce you to court, Ayna."

The way he hisses my name gives me pause more than that his features are turning back into those of a bird.

"How do you know my name?" Not that I should be surprised he knows. He was the one to pick me up from prison after all.

"The question should be: Am I the only one who knows." He gestures for me to walk in, gaze landing on the gray fabrics draped from a high canopy at the front of the room. "Since you were such a bad guest during dinner last night, I took the liberty to tell your future husband the name of the woman he'll be married to in a week's time."

Sunlight paints slender rectangles on the floor from where it streams in through the tall windows high up in the wall. The room is so large the entire Wild Ray would fit in it and then some, and every inch is covered in stone, dark and dull like my future. Lined along the sides of the room, Crow guards stand at attention, their spears silver as mist in the glow of fairy lights hovering where the sun doesn't reach.

"Now go." He doesn't need to shove me. My feet start walking on their own as the fluttering of birdsongs catches my attention high up under the ceiling.

A crow—not the fairy type but the actual bird—hovers under the arches near the end of the room, and it isn't the only one. There are dozens of crows filing in through the glassless windows and circling toward the floor. As they descend, their bodies grow until their forms expand into humanoid shapes with claw-tipped wings for arms and beaked and feathered faces. They caw and hiss as they land, wings stirring the air where I stopped at the side of the room to gape at the spectacle. They can shift. They can actually shape-shift from Crow Fairy to bird and back.

I shouldn't be surprised by anything at this point, yet my brain has a hard time keeping up as I take in the shimmering colors where the sunlight hits their feathers. Eerie and beautiful—and monsters.

Shutting my mouth, I make my way through the crowd of Crows, who step out of my path and stare as I approach what has to be the throne, hidden under the canopy at the end of the room. My heart beats so fast it might leap out of my chest as the scrutiny of all-black eyes hits me from all directions, hunger and malice and something more I cannot identify reflecting in their depths.

Royad follows me for a few merciful steps before disappearing between the shuffle of feathered limbs and flurry of shifting crows, leaving me to face the Crow King alone. A guard steps forward, bracing his spear beside him on the stone floor and cocking his head as he watches me walk by with the sort of hunger reminding me of a predator ready to kill.

I shrink to the side, nearly hitting another Crow, and catch myself mere feet from the slightly inclined steps leading up to a throne made of carved stone.

I will never look at birds the same way again.

The figure on the throne leans forward, and I find the Crow King's beautiful human face in the half-light. His eyes sweep down my body, lingering on the feathers of the skirt so long I wonder what is going on behind those all-black eyes—until they snap up to mine, and all I can think is that I need to get out of here before this male can devour my soul.

I retreat one step, but my back hits the sharp end of a spear, and I wince as the tip slices through the fabric of my dress like a needle. At least, my hair covers my back, the welded scar from where the prison guards whipped me for trying to escape. It is bad enough that my left hand is more or less useless.

"Bow to your king." A hissed order I am not ready to obey but don't see a way around if I want to survive the day to figure out a way to flee tomorrow. So, I incline my head enough to hurt my pride, but not enough to show full submission. For that, they'd need to kick me down.

"I said, 'Bow to your king'." The long end of the spear hits the back of my legs, and my knees bark with pain as I am knocked to the floor a moment later.

Gasping, I brace myself on both hands, the pressure too much for my injured one, and try to lift myself again.

"Enough—" King Myron's voice lashes through the room, silencing the whispers and murmurs of his feathered court.

He rises from his throne, a ray of sunlight gilding one winged arm and his profile. A crown of silver feathers and onyx rest upon his raven hair, the jewels drinking up the light. He isn't wearing a jacket now, leaving his chest and stomach bare, and I am not proud to say I am drinking up the view of carved muscle to distract myself from the pain.

"Rise." He is obviously speaking to me, but when I try, my body decides now is a good time to lose balance, and I drop back into a crouch, my good hand cradling my bad one in my lap.

Myron isn't in leather pants today but in black satin that matches the fabric of my dress. And the reason I'm so acutely aware of it is because he steps down from the dais, descending the stairs like the king he is until he stops right in front of me, his thighs filling my view. He owns this palace, these people, and he knows it. And something about the way he looks down at me as I glance up tells me, he thinks he owns me, too.

Before I can spit an insult at him, he holds out a manicured hand in a mockery of an offer to help me up and booms at the room, "Meet Wolayna Milevishja, future Queen of Crows. This year's bride."

Cheers erupt as ice captures my chest. This isn't right. He isn't supposed to know my name. Not even the name everyone called me on the Wild Ray, then in prison. Even Royad only knows me as Ayna.

King Myron crouches before me, his fingers grasping my chin as he leans closer to whisper in my ear. "King Erina Latroy Jelnedyn of Tavras will be glad to know this year's tribute has made it to my home in one piece."

SEVEN

I can't get out a word as he takes my hand in his and pulls me to my feet, throat closed up with terror as the monster is touching me. I don't even feel the pressure of his grasp on my bad hand, that's how paralyzed I am.

"Walk with me, Wolayna." It's not a request, and I'm in too much shock to fight him as he leads me from the throne room through a side door that leads to the familiar dining room, cheers and shouts of the Crow Fairies following us like wolves giving chase.

He doesn't release me until we make it to the door leading *from* the dining room into the hallway. There, Royad is waiting, his features tight as if he is expecting a creature of *his* nightmares to step over the threshold.

"Take her back to her room, and make sure she doesn't run." King Myron says it with such nonchalance that I don't realize what he's saying before Royad ushers me around the corner and up the stairs two floors, 'to the residential part of the palace' as he explains.

My breathing comes the tiniest bit easier as I'm released to my room without being paraded in front of the Crow King's court all evening. The Guardians know the brief introduction was enough for my nerves to all but snap.

The guards who filled the hallway before are gone, probably in the crowd, celebrating with the rest of them the demise of a new bride, and I am not ready to be locked in my room. My knees still ache from where they hit the floor, but I manage to ignore the pain as I calculate the distance from the front door to the stairs. Royad won't let me go; if I'm certain of one thing, it's that. Nonetheless, once he's delivered me to my room, I'll find a way to get out and sneak to the door. As long as the guards are in the throne room, there might be a chance.

It is only when he enters the room with me, sealing the window with a flick of his claws that makes the air ripple before moving on to the bathing room window, that I realize this wasn't a prison before compared to what it is now.

"This is as much for your protection as it is to keep you from running, Ayna, trust me."

"I don't trust you." I don't trust any soul alive. Everyone I once loved or trusted is dead.

"Good." He runs his claws over the door as if searching for something. "Because you shouldn't trust anyone in this palace. You are the new bride, and brides aren't meant to last. There have been ninety-nine brides since Myron ascended the throne, and each of them suffered a horrible death—not all of them after the wedding. So, rest assured that it is in your best interest to stay in this room with all doors and windows sealed."

I try to process his words. *Try.* But all I get is the sense he is mocking me.

"What? Is there a monster out for my blood?" I fold my arms, leaning against the dresser, and glower at him.

"One?" He laughs, and the sound grates along my bones like an instrument of death, and I can't move. Nodding to himself, he steps out the door, questions once more unanswered.

The air ripples around the heavy wood as the lock clicks into place.

I'm sealed in. And I'm never getting out.

It takes three hours before someone thinks to bring me food and fresh water, and when it arrives, I'm not surprised to see Royad himself carrying a tray and a grim face. His beak is on display, as are the feathers down his torso. That means his voice is also more of a hiss laced with the occasional caw as he explains that it is up to me to believe he isn't trying to poison me again.

Yet he doesn't give me answers. Not when I confront him about how Myron knows my full name or what he meant by the brides all 'suffered a horrible death.' All he does is tell me to sit tight and not try to run.

It could be a tactic to keep me from even looking for ways to escape, so I tug on the latch by the window and rattle the doorknob, all to no avail as they don't give an inch. With nothing to do, I start pacing until my feet hurt. Then I sit on the edge of the bed until that becomes uncomfortable, too. Every sound from the hallway startles me back to my feet, be it the soft thuds of boots, the occasional caws and hisses as the guards communicate, or the knock on the door when Royad returns with food every three hours like clockwork.

By the time the sun sets, I'm exhausted from the constant fear and tension, but I'm not done with my room. I open the armoire and pull out a bunch of black dresses I will never wear, and I roam the dresser for a pair of pants and a tunic that will be comfortable enough to sleep in. When I open the first drawer, lacy underthings are all I find, and I want to smack my head for even hoping that this room hasn't been occupied by at least those ninety-nine brides Royad mentioned. I don't know why I even care. I won't be number one hundred.

The dresser shakes as I slam the drawer shut, opening the next one with my good hand. Neatly folded in the corner sits one pair of leather pants. They look entirely too small for my comparatively tall frame, but with the current state of my body, they'll probably fit. One drawer down, I find an assortment of tunics, most of them tight and lace-trimmed, and, naturally, all of them black. All but one.

I reach for the loose shirt and tug it on over my dress before reaching to the side, where the bodice opens—one can never be too careful with how the Crow King likes to make an appearance in this room—before stepping out of the gown and discarding of it in the corner between dresser and armoire.

The shirt is not only long enough to cover me to mid-thigh, but the sleeves are so long I have to roll them up a few times. If I know one thing for certain, it is that none of the brides before me have ever worn it.

I set the pants on top of the dresser for the morning and curl up in bed, struggling to accommodate the sense of the soft mattress when all I am used to is the pallet of straw I slept on in the prison for the past nine months. It reminds me too much of Ludelle's arms, of a time when I woke up in the morning and the world seemed to be smiling at me across the glistening waters around the Wild Ray.

I have nothing now. And what I am will soon cease to exist if Royad is to be believed. If I don't find a way out, in a few days, I'll be bride one hundred, and I'll die a horrible death like the ninety-nine before me.

That night, I cry myself to sleep until the soft waves of the ocean cradle me and the sun kisses my face...

I haven't been this lazy in weeks, but after plundering King Erina's ships, a feast and a few days of rest are more than deserved. Ludelle tells me as much as he reaches across the oil lamp on the nightstand for the bottle of Tavrasian wine he picked from the loot. I blink up at him, kissing his stubbled jaw as he props himself up to take a swig.

"This"—he holds up the bottle, reading the ornately painted label with squinted eyes—"was meant for the king's personal collection."

"Pity." I take the bottle from his long, slender fingers and take a drink. After two gulps, it is empty, but the wine is sweet and heavy, reminding me of summers northwest of Meer where my father took us when he had business in that region. My mother loved that sort of wine. I was too young then to know what wine was exactly, but I recognize the taste of the grapes anyway. Honey and freedom and something wild that I've only experienced in the vineyards of that region.

Ludelle studies me with large brown eyes, pupils blown out as his gaze follows the sliver of skin where my tunic has fallen open. "You are beautiful, Ayna," he whispers. "Precious. And I will always love you."

His arms wrap around mine, and the bottle falls to the floor, forgotten as he covers my mouth with his, our lips finding a familiar, easy rhythm that I will never get tired of. He tastes like sunshine and salt, and my heart is so full it might burst.

"Ayna..." he murmurs my name as I moan his. "Ayna."

"Wolayna!"

I fall out of bed, scrambling to my feet in front of those of Myron, the Crow King. He scowls at me, taking in my disheveled look, my bare legs sticking out from under the shirt, which has ridden up dangerously close to my hips, and something like shock crosses his face. At least, that is what I would have called it had I not known the Crow King was above any emotion other than hatred.

"Get up." He pivots on his heels, facing the wall with the armoire as I tug down the shirt and scramble to my feet.

"What are you doing in here? It's the middle of the night." At least, the sky is dark outside the window. I don't see a moon or stars with the fairy lights bobbing under the ceiling.

Were I not so embarrassed, I might have found a million different curses to send him out the door, but he saw my bruised legs, saw whatever else the shirt exposed of me as I tumbled from the bed.

He takes a stiff step toward the dresser, picks up the leather pants, and tosses them at me without looking over his shoulder. "Put these on."

His aim is impeccable, the pants landing in my arms without me even needing to grab for them. Not that it makes any difference when he let himself into my bedroom in the middle of the night.

"Get dressed first," he orders, back so straight it's almost comical. But this is the king of the Crow Fairies, a monster who has let ninety-nine brides die.

I slip into the pant legs, cursing as I barely get them over my ass, and tie the leather strings in the front before sitting on the edge of the bed.

He whirls around so fast I shrink back half a foot, but he keeps his distance. "You were making noises in your sleep. I thought someone was trying to strangle you."

My eyes dart to the dim fairy lights as I pray to the Guardians they will hide how my cheeks turn crimson. "It was a… A nightmare, that's what it was."

He crooks a brow but doesn't say anything as he marches out the door.

It doesn't matter how often I close my eyes that night; sleep won't find me, and my heart either breaks at the memory of Ludelle's arms around me, or it freezes from fear at the thought of being tied to the feathered king to whom lives mean so little he goes through one bride a year.

Then a small voice reminds me that he came to check on me because he thought someone was trying to kill me, and I don't know how I should feel about that.

Thankfully, the sunrise burns through all thoughts as I am painfully reminded that it doesn't matter what my heart does as I'm summoned yet again to join King Myron in the dining room.

ANGELINA J. STEFFORT

EIGHT

The daily meals with the Crow King are silent and full of tension. Myron doesn't speak other than to tell me the number of days until Ret Relah, and he doesn't look my way more than when I enter the room and when I leave. Sometimes, I try to provoke him into conversation just to relieve the building fear and tension in my chest, but all I get is a glare before he shifts his features into those so similar to a bird that I have a hard time looking at him either.

It is Royad who escorts me around the palace, pointing out all the ways I can't exit and hovering close when we pass the hungry gazes of the Crow guards.

I haven't asked him why he is loyal to a king who lets women die each year, but then, we aren't exactly on good terms. If anything, we are on a *he-dragged-me-across-half-a-continent-to-*

stuff-me-into-an-arranged-marriage-to-a-monster-I-didn't-even-know-existed-and-I-hate-him-for-it basis.

It's more like I ask him why he even bothers to be my bodyguard when I'll likely die within the year anyway. He never responds to that question, so I save it for the next time I'll see Myron—which is tomorrow if he sticks to his usual routines.

Today, Royad picks me up at the dining room door after an especially dire dinner with the Crow King himself, and I don't even bother to be afraid of him as he ushers me past the stairwell, off our usual course, to a long, torch-lit corridor.

"Where are we going?" My slippers thud over the stone tiles as I trudge along beside him.

He gestures at a steep set of stairs that is unguarded, and I go ahead, my hope to escape stirring at the sight of an empty hallway with an open window at the end where it makes a left turn.

"Ret Relah is tomorrow." Royad switches sides, placing himself between me and the window as I slow to get a better look at what's outside. "And you are not going anywhere." He says it like he's scolding me, but something in the way his brows furrow tells me it could be pity just as well.

His claw touches my shoulder, guiding me forward with light pressure, but I flinch away as I feel the sharp points lightly through my tunic. He doesn't speak until we make it to the end of the hallway, and he opens a door to more stairs leading underground.

"Don't say you're smuggling me out of the palace through a secret tunnel." I attempt a joke because my life has become so dire I barely remember what it is like not to live in constant fear, and I need a break, no matter how small.

Shaking his head, Royad points at the bottom of the stairs where a large pool spreads under a low, arched ceiling. "This is all I can offer." He doesn't look back to see if I'm following as he leads the way down to the pool.

For a heartbeat, I stand there, taking in the glow of torches lining the walls, the pattern of rocks making up the walls and ceiling. This is different from the rest of the palace. Steam rises from the water, wafting around Royad as he reaches the end of the stairs, and the scent of herbs and blossoms kisses my senses. The sight is so surprising I need to blink a few times to fit it into my head. "What is this place?"

Royad turns so his wing covers his side as he glances up at me. "The people who built this palace had a great sense of luxury." His claws gesture at the expanse of the pool, the columns carrying the ceiling, the brass bowl filled with fire sitting on the floor by the edge of the pool. "But what's best about them is the everlasting fire." He toes the edge of the bowl with his boot. "Thousands of years, and not one torch has died."

That's—"Magic. Those flames are magical?" I can't help but ask. I've always been curious. It's part of the reason I chose a pirate ship as a refuge when my family was gone. I wanted to see the world, learn new things, make a new home that was nowhere and everywhere. And I wanted to be away from the mainland so I could never fall victim to the winged fairies stealing women at night. Yet, here I am.

A wary smile spreads on Royad's face. "Everything is magical in Askarea, Ayna." He ruffles his wings, a reminder that he is made from magic, too. "So many different sorts of fairies have lived in these lands that it doesn't matter if they have wings or antlers, hooves, or can conjure everlasting flames. In the end, it's all the same magic." The wistful look in his all-black eyes stands in stark contrast to the menace of his form, and I can't help but take a step back.

The door behind me is open, and Royad is at least twenty paces down. If I bolt and slam the door shut behind me, I might make it to the window... And then? Even if no guards are watching, Royad knows the only possible route that would take me to freedom.

Perhaps he can see the wheels turning in my head because he takes a step toward the stairs, then another, slowly approaching. "Please, Ayna, come down here and take a bath. I will wait outside." He means it; I can tell by the way he strides past me, halting on the threshold to check if I am following his request.

A request, not an order. Unlike King Myron, Royad has actually used the word *please*, and I couldn't be more shocked.

"Why?" I mean, *why* doesn't he just shove me underwater to make sure I bathe, but he gives me a half smile and takes a step back from the threshold so he is standing outside the underground spa.

"Because Ret Relah is tomorrow, and Myron won't be pleased if his bride smells."

Before I can retort that, A, I don't smell, and B, if he wants a bride who gives a shit, he might want to find someone who is willing to marry that bastard, Royad closes the door with a wave of his hand, and I am alone in the most luxurious, if ancient, bathing room I've ever seen. The pool is so large I'll actually need to swim to get to the other end.

For a long time, I stand at the head of the stairs, cursing myself for not grabbing the opportunity and run when there was nothing between me and the open window. Then, I remember how easily Royad caught me on the journey from Fort Perenis, and that had been on land he doesn't know like the back of his hand. This palace is his home, and even if I managed to hide in a dark corner, I'm convinced he'd find me. And if not him, then the Crow King's many guards who keep watching my every move like bloodhounds when I meander through the hallways with my bodyguard.

Ret Relah is tomorrow. The ice in my chest is enough to freeze the blood in my entire body, and perhaps this is the last moment I'll get to myself before the wedding ceremony. I don't know what it entails—neither Royad nor Myron have deigned to respond whenever I asked. All I know is that, once a Crow bride, there is no way back. My fate was sealed the moment the Tavrasian general handed me over. Perhaps even before that.

The Crows know my name. My real name. I'm Wolayna Milevishja, daughter of Ivan Milevishja and Elenja Milevishja. My father used to do trade for the Tavrasian Crown. I spent my days as a child in his office and warehouses, surveying the incoming and outgoing goods and riches. That's how I know a good loot from an unworthy one. I saw him handle the gemstone shipments of King Erina's father long before Erina ever got crowned. I'd even seen Erina around the warehouse when the late king graced us with a visit.

Then, one day, it wasn't the king who appraised the jewels, but he sent different men. Ones who took my father to the palace where he was put in the dungeons for treason.

Dark clouds form around my heart at the thought of the months that followed, the interrogations.

"Your name is Wolayna Milevishja?"

I nod at the man leaning over me as I shrink back in my chair. The manacles holding down my hands don't allow for me to shove him away as his face comes so close I can smell his onion breath.

"Answer!" Spittle flies at my cheek.

I nod. It's all I can do, eyes darting to my mother, who is held back by a soldier in blue and black. Her pleas to let me go aren't heard.

"You saw your father load these chests into a carriage." It's not a question because they want me to confirm.

Even if I hadn't seen him, I would be tempted to just nod so they'd leave me alone.

"She's just a child," my mother cries. "Let her go."

The men don't care I'm only ten years old ... or that I have no idea why those chests are so important. But if I have learned one thing from my mother, it is to always tell the truth. So, I close my eyes so I don't see the line of anger on the man's young face and nod.

When I open my eyes again, he is smiling down at me, one hand twirling his mustache. "Good girl."

He steps away, and so do the men holding back my mother. Someone opens the bonds on my wrists, and a moment later, my mother flings her arms around me, pulling me into her shoulder as I cry, cry, cry.

A day later, they make us watch my father's execution.

I blink, and I'm back in the present, steam coiling into my nose as I descend the stairs to the pool.

The general—

The memory of the man interrogating me is blurry, but there is no doubt that horrible man and the general selling me to the Crows are one and the same. He knows who I am. Knew the moment he saw me on the ship, because he wasn't the one petrified by fear that day when I sentenced my father to death with a simple nod. He remembered. Ten years later, and *I'm* the traitor. And in Tavras, traitors pay with their lives.

The ice doesn't leave my body until I slide out of my clothes and wade down the stairs into the water, and it embraces me the way the ocean used to embrace the Wild Ray. I haven't taken a real bath in over a year, and the half-hearted scrub-downs in prison don't count. Yes, I'm clean because I use the washcloth and water in my room at the palace, but it isn't the same as when the water washes over my body, soaking through the paralyzing fear and despair that have been my constant companions since the day the cell door was locked after me in the dungeons of Fort Perenis.

The water is warm as I sink into it up to my shoulders, its scent reminding me of pending summer. I spot flower petals floating in the back of the pool, their colors all blurring into shades of orange and brown in the firelight, but they are crisp and fresh like someone plucked them recently and strew them on the water just before I entered.

The thought makes my gaze dart around the room, checking the shadowy corners for a potential intruder.

There's no one—just the water, the fire, and me. So, I lower myself under the surface, diving the length of the pool. When I come up, my feet barely reach the ground, and I have flower petals all over my hair. It's the first time in ages I feel alive.

I scrub at my scalp, rinsing the petals out of my tresses and watching them float away on a current I didn't notice before. The warm, humid air is glorious to breathe, cleaning my lungs from the lingering ache of my time in prison. This is nothing like the palace of monsters above. This is a sanctuary, and I want time to stop so the sun won't rise tomorrow to announce the end of my life.

I don't know how long I relish the feel of the water carrying me before exhaustion claims my body so thoroughly I am boneless as I climb out of the pool. I'm about to reach for my pants and tunic when I spot they're gone, replaced by a thick towel and a dressing robe made of decadent, black silk.

My head whips around, eyes searching for whoever might have put them there, but the room is empty.

The towel is soft and heavy, soaking up the water dripping from my hair and running down my body, as I wrap it around me and sit on the top of the steps leading into the water so only my feet are in the pool. I stare at the play of light on the ceiling, part from the torches and fire bowl, but part of it is reflections from the dancing waves. They glimmer like brass and amber—like the treasures Ludelle and I used to loot.

A heavy sadness weighs on my heart. One that has nothing to do with my own fate but that of the man I loved with all I have and whose life was ended by a slice into his throat. My tears mingle with the droplets of water on my cheeks, and I can't tell if, maybe, I deserve to end up here after being the only survivor of the Wild Ray's crew. Maybe this is my punishment for getting away when my father betrayed the king, for the few peaceful years with my mother at the coast before she followed my father behind Eroth's Veil. For the blissful years on the Wild Ray. Perhaps, finding love and happiness after being responsible for my father's death angered the Guardians and this is their way of restoring balance. Because, with what lies ahead, there is no way there will be any love in my life ever again. Only death and pain and the constant fear of which moment will be my last, just as I now fear that I won't survive tomorrow.

My face is buried in my palms, a vise clamping on my chest, when something grabs me by the shoulder, throwing my head underwater so fast I can't scream. I struggle for purchase, my feet slipping on the stone underwater as I try to push myself up, but the claws have me in an iron hold, and my air is running out as I thrash in the water. I flail my arms, blindly grasping behind me to where I expect the Crow to be—because who else should attack me in this palace but a Crow Fairy? Perhaps it is King Myron himself who wants to make quick work of his new bride before she can find a way to escape and embarrass him.

My thoughts get more jumbled with each painful heartbeat as I fight, fight to get my head back above the surface. But the claws dig into my shoulder and neck, pushing harder, squeezing so tight I'm sure there'll be a puncture wound on the side of my neck when someone finds my body.

Darkness swims before my eyes, and it would be so easy to give in. Yet, I refuse. I refuse to be bested by these monsters who feel entitled to my life. I stare the darkness in the eye, water burning as I open my lids.

I am not afraid of you, I tell it and reach lower with my good hand, right where I expect the Crow's legs. My fingers curl around leather, and I blindly grasp, throwing my weight forward, straining to keep ahold of whoever's knee I hooked my hand around.

I'm certain the water helps when the monster loses footing and releases my neck to regain balance as he stumbles into the pool.

Air floods my lungs, and I fight a coughing fit as I scramble to my feet just in time to avoid the claws grabbing for me. The male rising from the water is in plain guard uniform, and his face is mostly bird. His hissed caws remind me of curses and insults I'm glad I don't understand. If I don't get my body to move, he'll be on me again so fast I can't even get down a deep breath.

His wings drip with water, giving a better outline of the muscled arm under the feathers. I back away, desperately searching the room for a weapon.

If I make it to the nearest wall, I can pull a torch from a metal hook and set him on fire—at least sear him with the torch if he doesn't catch flames. My own violence doesn't surprise me. I've been cornered for almost ten months, and this creature is going for my throat.

I bolt, not caring about how my towel threatens to slip as I slam my good hand into the wall to stop my face from crashing into it and grab the torch with the bad one.

NINE

Pain traps my breath, but I don't loosen my hold of the handle. If I drop the torch, my life is over. The mean gleam in the Crow's eyes is all the proof I need.

He takes a heavy step closer while I fight for breath at the mere memory of those claws at my throat.

Think, Ayna. Think. I've fought more soldiers than I can count on the loots with the Wild Ray, have killed when necessary. I used to be good with daggers, quick and agile. Now, only one hand remains good enough to wield a weapon of any sort.

"Get back." The threat gives me a heartbeat to switch the torch to my left hand, and I stifle a groan as the pain in my right one recedes.

The Crow laughs a crackled sound that makes the blood in my veins freeze all over again. He isn't here to play games.

I catch his claws with the torch as they lash out toward my arm, the impact drawing a hiss from his beak.

Good. At least, he isn't immune to pain. But, Guardians, is he quick. Before I can bring the torch back to a defensive position, the Crow strikes, claws landing on my forearm, and I scream as he slices down the length from my elbow to my wrist. Warm liquid trickles down my arm, and I know it's more than a shallow cut.

The Crow is shorter than Myron and Royad, but his torso is covered in corded muscle where it's not coated with feathers. His leather pants are stiff from the water, and his wings are sticky, but apart from that, I can't find a weakness. Hopefully, it will be enough.

The Crow cocks his head as if measuring how much fight I have left in me.

I don't wait for him to come to a conclusion but leap forward as if that were a dagger in my hand rather than a piece of ever-burning wood, and surprise hits me hard when I land a blow on the Crow's sternum. I would have stabbed him straight in the heart were that a blade in my hand. Yet, with the torch, I leave a scorch mark between the carpet of feathers running across his shoulders and arms. His hissed scream is almost deafening, and he doubles over, clutching his chest.

This is my chance.

I don't look back as I run for the door, my bare feet slapping the stone floor as the Crow's angry caws follow me.

"Royad!" I'm shouting his name before I reach the door, pushing with my bad hand while trying to keep the other from loosening its grasp on the torch. If I drop that, I am defenseless. There are too many ways in here to kill me, and only one way out.

The door gives, and I stumble into the hallway, almost colliding with Royad, who is staring at me like at a ghost. The caws behind me cease, turning into the beat of wings, and a pair of bird claws rip on my hair as a crow flutters over my head, down the hallway, and out the window that I hoped might be my path to freedom.

"What the fuck happened in there?" Were it not for the shock on Royad's face, I might have accused him of staging the attack himself, but the way his gaze darts down my arm, to the torch in my blood-covered hand, tells me he has no idea.

"The Crow—" I manage to nod in the direction the bird disappeared, and Royad seems to understand.

And just in time for my body to sway as the momentary shock retreats and pain rushes my arm and my throat so badly I can hardly stay on my feet.

Royad looks me over head to toe before he grabs me by the shoulders and leans me against the wall right next to the door. "Don't move," he orders and disappears inside the underground spa for a heartbeat. Two.

It's not nearly enough time for me to wonder where he's going but more than enough to relapse into panic. I grit my teeth at the pain as I tighten my grasp on the torch. I'll be a bloody mess tomorrow. Serves the king well if he forces me to marry him; I won't play the pretty, happy bride—if I survive the day. Guardians, if I survive the *hour*. Which I realize I might not, considering the puddle of blood forming at my feet.

The Crow got me bad, and if there isn't a way to fix me up with magic, this wound might just do the trick and save me from ever being bound to King Myron and his court of monsters.

Royad is back before I can lose consciousness, but I barely make out his face as he returns with a bundle of fabric in his claws. He takes the torch from my hand with what feels like too much ease to make me believe I could have kept it one more moment. He drapes the fabric over my shoulders, slipping my arms into sleeves and loosely binding a belt around my waist before tugging the falling towel from under it and pressing that to my forearm.

"Let's get you fixed up," he says, voice a hiss as his features turn birdlike at the edge of my vision.

Guided by his claws, I take a step forward, but my legs give out, and he catches me around the waist.

A growl tears through the hallway, forcing my fading consciousness to hold on one moment longer. When I turn my head, King Myron is striding toward us, menace in his eyes, and Royad's claws slip from my waist as I slip into darkness.

I don't know if the pain is because I hit the floor as I blacked out or because I nearly drowned in the pool I believed to be lovely, but when I wake at dawn, I can barely take a breath, and even the soft mattress hurts around my ribs. My left arm is bandaged, and so is the side of my throat. Even thinking about moving hurts, so I lie still as I listen to the whispered voices that woke me.

"What were you thinking?" one of the voices asks—King Myron. And Guardians, does he sound furious. "You were supposed to make sure she makes it back to her room and stay there until..." His voice trails away as if he doesn't want to speak the words he was about to say.

"I wanted to do something for once that won't make her think we are *monsters*." Royad emphasizes the last word as if to prove a point.

Myron growls, and I shudder, opening my eyes, but I find neither him nor Royad in my room. The bathing room door is cracked open, though, and I can see shadows moving in the narrow gap filled with fairy light and sunrise.

"That's what we are, Royad." Myron's cold tone makes my breath catch. "We *are* monsters. And we will always stay monsters. Ayna will hate us whether she takes a bath or washes her hair. And she will die like the others. There is nothing you can do about it."

It's a command more than an explanation, and I'm glad I'm not on the receiving end. For, whatever this is about, was I merely doubting the Crow King wants me dead, now I am certain he will personally see to it. He might even have been the one who sent the Crow to kill me.

The rustle of wings sounds in the bathing room, and the door opens, exposing the room is empty. Royad enters the bedroom alone, and I wonder if I merely imagined the conversation. There were days in prison when I was so desperate for Ludelle's company that I dreamed him up. This might be no different. Perhaps, my mind is trying to protect itself by making me hallucinate that someone in this palace might actually care whether I live or die.

My gaze locks with Royad's, and he shakes his head as if answering my thought.

"I will die." It's no longer a question.

Royad doesn't shake his head.

"The attack at the pool…" My voice turns into a croak.

"That was only the beginning." His brows furrow while he studies me as if debating saying more.

"How did the others die?" I must know. I need to know so I can prepare myself; because there is no question I won't leave this palace before the wedding. The morning of Ret Relah has broken, and I am bandaged and recovering from an attack. If I can drag myself to the ceremony on my own feet, that will be a surprise, let alone climb down a wall or run through a forest if I were to ever make it out of here.

Royad considers me for so long I think he's not going to answer. He sucks in a breath, eyes shuttering as if he's looking into a memory. "That's not for me to tell."

I don't know if I should be grateful he is speaking at all or frustrated he isn't being helpful with the information he gives. "Who will tell me?"

He crosses the room, bending down to check the bandage on my arm. "The king. You are his concern, as is your life or death."

Something about the way he says it makes me think there is more, but he probes the white gauze where the cut must start right under my elbow and nods at himself before straightening and walking toward the door.

"I'd send someone to help you get dressed for the wedding, Ayna, but there are only Crows in this palace, and none of them are female. I don't trust them to put a dress on you even when the king trusts them to protect his palace."

There was so much in those few words my head started to spin all over again. "What do you mean, no females?" Were they all dead? All victims of Myron's cruelty?

"There are no female Crows." He pauses, scanning my face, words obviously held back as he purses his lips, directing his eyes at the armoire instead. "Your wedding gown is in there. Be ready at sunset." He leaves it at that, disappearing through the door the air around which ripples as it falls into the lock. Warded or spelled, or simply a magical wall meant to lock the bride in, I don't care as long as the Crow who tried to kill me can't get in here.

I spend the day in thoughts of Ludelle, of what he told me when we were captured.

If we survive this, I'll marry you and take you across the oceans to whatever new world lies hidden in the east, Ayna.

There is no new world for either of us, no getting away. His soul has crossed Eroth's Veil, and mine is trapped in a nightmare. There is no future for either of us. No love. No getting away. If I have no other comfort, I have the thought that he'll be there beyond Eroth's Veil, waiting for me with that soft smile and those warm brown eyes, arms and heart wide open for me.

Or he'll despise me because it was I who caused the slaughter. Ludelle wouldn't have tried to get past the guards if I'd been able to hold my tongue and swallow the wince of pain when they'd poked my shoulder blade with a sharp-pointed sword. He would have been alive—imprisoned like me, but alive.

I try to tell myself that I could have changed the course of his fate—of my own—had I only been stronger. But the truth is that my ending up here has nothing to do with Ludelle or the Wild Ray. This is about my father and his treason.

The sun crosses the sky as I spiral deeper and deeper into despair. I get out of bed only long enough to use the bathing room and glower at myself in the mirror. Naturally, Myron chooses exactly that moment to make an appearance. I'm surprised, though, to hear him knock rather than barrel into my room the way he seems to prefer.

"I'm not dressed," I call over my shoulder, examining the bruise spreading under the bandages on my neck.

Maybe he'll leave me alone if he has the decency not to want to walk in on me naked. Not that I really am naked. I am wearing the oversized tunic from my first night at the palace.

The door creaks open, and I glance at my useless hands that won't allow me to wield a weapon—not that there is any weapon to wield. My heart beats in my throat, making me forget the pain in my chest and arm.

"I'm here to see if you are ready."

I freeze in place, gray eyes wide in shock staring back at me from the mirror. The door is only half open, but I feel his presence as if he were standing right beside me.

Before I can make up my mind whether I should tell him to get lost, King Myron appears in the doorway, tall and clad in black finery so elaborate it almost makes me skip over the feathers on his arms where his jacket is missing sleeves. His face is fully human, no hint of bird or monster—only those all-black eyes that consume me as they track the shirt down my body to where it ends at my thighs.

I lift my chin. I have no way of covering myself, so I might as well own it. "Take a good look, *King*, because this is the last time you'll see this much of me."

He shakes his head as if trying to get rid of an unwelcome thought, but his eyes linger on mine. "Why aren't you in your wedding gown?"

I ignore the way my pulse jolts at his gravelly tone, at the way he pins me with a gaze for the first time in a week. I definitely ignore the strange sense of relief coming with being acknowledged by the monster in whose palace I'm trapped.

"I already told you, I'm not marrying you." The words are out before I can help it, and I brace myself for the strike, for his magic that can bind me or shove me or break me.

It doesn't come. Instead, his lips tip up on one side, and he leans his feathered shoulder on the threshold. "It's not like you have a choice, Wolayna. It's not like either of us has a choice."

What's that supposed to mean?

"What will you do if I don't?"

There is violence in his eyes, and my heart thuds harder, almost racing out of my chest.

"You don't want to test me, Wolayna." The warning is clear, and I don't find my voice to object as he stares me down

His wing rustles as he lifts his hand to point at my hair. "Are you planning to keep it like that?"

"What's wrong with my hair?" Not that it matters. It never mattered on the Wild Ray.

He shakes his head, heading back into the bedroom. I don't dare follow him, tempted to shut the bathing room door to bring some distance between us, but he reappears before I can move. In his arms, he holds a gown of—*surprise!*—feathers and black fabric. I feel like I'm being transformed into a Crow by merely wearing the clothes provided. Maybe that's what will happen after I'm married. Then again, Royad said there are no female Crows.

"Put this on." He gives me a warning look as he sets the dress down on the stool where Royad placed me that first day after I fell from the shelf and leaves the bathing room, closing the door behind him.

I am so stunned I don't think when I reach for the layers of tulle and feathers and lay them out so I can see what I'm about to wear when I stride to my death.

TEN

The fabrics of my skirts hiss against the stone floor as I make my way down the stairs, Crow guard on each side and Royad at my back to oversee the guards' duty. His presence puts me only slightly more at ease. Since King Myron left my room not even half an hour ago, between me putting on a dress that revealed entirely too much of my chest to feel comfortable and Royad picking me up for the ceremony, I have cried gallons of tears and died a million deaths.

Now I'm empty. That leaves too much space for the fear I pushed back so well while I untangled my hair and braided it in an ash-blonde coronet around my head. It's far from fancy, but it allows me to move without my waves getting caught on the feathers climbing from my waist over my breasts where they separate into two thin straps that make me wonder if they might snap if I even breathe wrong. I don't complain though. I haven't worn something this fine in my life, and when I looked at the mirror before leaving the room, the dress allowed me to acknowledge I gained back a few missing pounds. The thought alone makes me feel stronger.

But I'm not at ease. I'm too fucking scared of what the next hours will bring to even consider taking that breath that could eventually destroy my dress.

King Myron's words haven't left my head, hollowing me out little by little as I try to make sense of them.

It's not like you have a choice, Wolayna. It's not like either of us has a choice.

Does he not want to marry me? He is a king, for the Guardians' sake. Can't he just do whatever he pleases? It sure feels that way considering he doesn't seem to care that what he wants will eventually kill me.

"Almost there," Royad narrates from the back, his footsteps louder than usual with the pair of polished boots he's wearing. Even the guards seem to have dressed up, their leather pants somehow smoother and the buckles on their belts and boots shiny like they spent the day polishing them.

"If you don't want me to run again, you better not mention how close I'm getting to being tied to a monster," I murmur. One of the guards caws an angry sound while Royad squeezes in between the Crow and me.

His face is near human today, brown hair spilling in soft waves past his shoulders.

"You combed your hair," I note, earning a grimace.

"Wouldn't want to look like a complete savage on your wedding day." His mouth features a smirk, but his eyes are serious as he tucks a few loose brown strands behind his pointed ear. Yet, it's the absence of malicious glee in his tone that makes me lift my head and listen—really listen—as he tells me, "You would think I'd get used to attending Myron's weddings, but every year anew, it makes me nauseous with anticipation."

I wonder what he's anticipating—the spectacle of my suffering or the festivities themselves. Since there are no female Crows, I wonder what a wedding with the bride the only woman will look like.

Before I can paint a horror scenario in my mind, we reach the end of the hallway, and Royad stops me with a claw to my shoulder. I flinch, but only just. What is one claw compared to the bonds awaiting me in the room behind those enormous double doors?

I glance to the guards left and right of the entrance to the throne room, and my heart sinks as they smirk at me—as far as bird-features can smirk. I feel it, though. Something is changing. Something is expected of me that I don't know if I want to deliver. If it has anything to do with the monsters in these halls, it can't be good.

"Be brave, Ayna," Royad says, claws squeezing gently. "Don't judge by what you see."

He doesn't give me time to panic at his words, waving his hand, and the guards pull the gates open, revealing the view of the throne room I've seen only once thus far.

It's not the sheer size of the hall or the intimidating view of dark stone and sunset flames. It's the crows circling from below the ceiling. They are bigger than normal birds, bodies shifting into those of Crow Fairies as they land. I spot a few beating their winged arms before landing on two feet. They can fly with those wings. My gaze shoots sideways to Royad, down the length of his feathered arms.

"Don't fight him." Royad holds my gaze as if he wills them to have a lasting effect on me, and a flicker of emotion crosses his otherwise impassive features.

I swallow the fear climbing up my throat, all the way past where a thinner bandage is covering the puncture wound from last night. My forearm throbs as if to remind me the neck isn't the only place I'm injured. My voice trembles as I retort, "Isn't it a bit late to give marriage advice?"

Royad shakes his head. "Not for your marriage. If you want a chance to survive, don't fight him tonight."

He marches ahead, not giving me time to respond. I wouldn't have found words anyway, throat clogged with fear as I scan the room for the Crow King.

He's right there, a dark, looming threat at the front of the room where he stands before his throne, features human and beautiful, winged arms at his sides as he stares right back at me between the crowd of monsters that seem to gravitate toward him. They settle in rows along the throne room, forming a corridor that ends by the door, right where I'm standing.

My heartbeat hurts, pounding in my veins like poison, and I wish it were. It would be a quick death then. But the depthless black of Myron's eyes tells me the death he delivers won't be quick. If I fight, it will be over before I can even take a breath to scream.

I don't know what Crow weddings look like, but I know just looking at the hunger in his eyes that I will fight with all I have to keep this creature off me once the ceremony is over. Royad can go stick his advice up his ass.

"It is time." The Crow King's voice rumbles through the room, silencing the caws and hisses of his wedding party, and he holds out a hand toward me as if he has actually been waiting for me to arrive. As if he was looking forward to this occasion. The corner of his lips pulls up, and I can't help but wonder if he is mocking me or if he's just happy he'll get another bride to kill.

Murderer, my mind spits. *Monster. Abomination.*

My guards flank me, their spears directed at my shoulders rather than at the onlookers who seem to be enjoying the view of me in this dress way too much for my taste. I wonder if they even notice the thick scar peeking out from under my dress between my shoulder blades or if they are too busy rejoicing in my downfall to not care about the marks life left on my body. They surely are not distracted by the bandages on my arm and neck.

I try not to care, try not to be afraid. To be brave like Royad said, though he's not even a friend to me. I try to be the Ayna Ludelle would have been proud of as I set one slow foot in front of the other, controlling my shallow breathing and my speeding pulse. I will see this through because, if I don't walk, they'll drag me to the front of the room where King Myron is waiting, and beside him, an ancient man with human arms, back hunched and eyes so milky I can't distinguish a color as I finally come to a halt a few steps from him, wondering if he's the only other human in this palace.

"Ceremonial," the Crow King hisses, and I notice his face has shifted into its beaked version. It's not like I'm seeing him like this for the first time, but my stomach clenches anyway, and I have problems breathing. A monster. Not just by his actions but by his very nature. "Meet Wolayna, my lovely bride."

Nothing about the way he looks at me speaks *lovely*, but I am sure my own eyes are as hard as his as we stare at each other in front of hundreds of Crows.

The man with the hunchback must be a hundred years old at least, but something about the weary expression on his face as he inclines his head at me tells me he has suffered at least a thousand lifetimes. His ears are rounded, human, and that alone is proof to me, he can't be here out of his own free will. No human would.

If I weren't convinced before the Crow court was a death sentence, I would be now.

King Myron flicks his hand at the Ceremonial, who leans on his crooked cane, pulling the gray robes more tightly around his shoulders as he takes a step toward him. "Let's get this over with. We don't have all day."

Both his earlier words and the disdain on his face as he glances around the room with a gaze as cold as ice make me wonder if the Crow King hates standing here in front of his people as much as I do. Yet, he doesn't stop this. He doesn't turn and walk away the way only a king can. He is right here, holding out his hand to me as if he's done it a hundred times.

Ninety-nine times.

I am number one hundred.

Bile collects in my throat at the thought of the blood on King Myron's hands.

I don't take his hand as I step to his side, as far away as I dare and as close as I can tolerate without shuddering, instead staring at the Ceremonial who, apparently, is about to marry us.

If Ludelle could see me now, he'd burn the ocean to get me out of here.

"At the death of spring and dawn of summer, one night exists when we lay our failures to rest and greet a new beginning," the Ceremonial opens, his voice not nearly as weak as I expected, even when he seems to be falling apart at the seams. I don't get to wonder what failures he's referring to when he continues, "In the death of an old bride and the birth of a new one, a new hope settles over our people."

Hope. It's such a big word that I don't even understand the dimensions of it anymore. I used to think hope existed. Not anymore.

"Decay makes way for life in the presence of a revered bride." The Ceremonial glances at me as he speaks, as if he is bestowing me with a task only I can carry out, even if it will cost my life.

The air in the room tastes of wind and forest and pain, and I wonder how I know what pain tastes like. My injured arm reminds me a moment later that pain and fear are all my life now is. King Myron's gaze lingers on the Ceremonial. I don't know how I know, since I don't turn to look at him, but I can feel the absence of his attention, and it is almost a soothing sensation that I get a break from his focus.

The Ceremonial inclines his head first at the Crow King, then me. "It's time for the vows."

"Vows—" I repeat in a murmur. Nobody told me I'd need to recite a vow. I thought I'd merely be declared the Crow King's wife. But vows…

"Repeat after me," Myron hisses, and my blood chills in my veins. "From this day on, I bind myself to this bride. My home shall be her home, my throne shall be her throne."

The Ceremonial shifts his milky eyes to me, and I can't tell if he is bored from performing this ritual for the *I-don't-know-how-manieth* time or if he simply never cared, but something tells me it doesn't matter to him what will happen to me, what role he's playing in this nightmare.

I don't get out a word, tongue like lead and throat all too tight. A glance to the side informs me Royad is standing at the front of the crowd, his winged arms at his sides, hair mingling with feathers where his human features are disappearing in his spreading bird features.

"Speak," Myron demands.

I can't. I just can't.

The Crow King isn't the only one getting impatient; hissed and cawed murmurs rise in the room like fog on a breeze.

"Speak your vow, Wolayna." Myron's hiss jolts my tongue back into action, and I scramble for words.

"I don't remember the words." Because I don't. My mind is too occupied with wondering if I'll die the moment they're spoken. Then there is the one thought I haven't allowed to fill my head but is becoming more and more important with every passing moment I don't die: What happens on the wedding night?

My feet itch to run. Guardians, my entire body is ready to bolt, to fight my way out, but with Crows lingering in every corner of the throne room, there is nowhere I can run.

"*From this day on*," the Crow King hisses, turning his head, an expectant look on his face. His all-black eyes capture mine, and I can't help but wonder if he has a consciousness behind that darkness. Even a hint would be better than this.

"From this day on," I repeat because there is no other option.

"*I bind myself to this groom*," Myron recites, revulsion surfacing on those handsome features as his bird's face slips and I stare at his full lips, the arched, dark brows slanted over his depthless eyes.

"I bind myself to this groom," I murmur, captivated by the contrast of his monster's face and his beauty, which almost brings me to my knees.

"*My home shall be his home, my throne shall be his throne.*"

"I don't have a throne," I say instead of repeating the line he gives me.

The Ceremonial clears his throat. "It's irrelevant."

Myron purses his lips as if keeping himself from speaking.

The Ceremonial explains instead. "It's the line from the last wedding of Carius the Cruel, King of Crows for over two thousand years. It's tradition."

My jaw drops. *Two thousand years.* How old exactly are these creatures?

"Say the line." It's all Myron grits out, his form shaking as if anger is devouring him.

"My home shall be his home, my throne shall be his throne." I rush through the words, not meaning a single one. I no longer have a home. If the Wild Ray hasn't been destroyed, it has probably already drifted across the Eherean oceans to the Guardians know where, so even if that vow is binding, the Crow King will never get his claws on the ship.

As the weight of what I've done settles within it, my chest aches. Wings rustle around me as the Ceremonial lifts a hand, gesturing at Myron and me.

"May this marriage be prosperous and the bride last longer than the ones before her."

If this line is also a tradition, I don't want to know.

Caws fill the throne room, both cheerful and menacing, and I swear the foundations of the palace shake as the marriage is sealed by whatever magic the Ceremonial holds.

ELEVEN

I'm not hungry, but I sit at the long banquet table at the back of the room all the same, poking the steak in front of me while my eyes wander across the feathered crowd. Under shafts of fading sunset light, Crows sit at tables similar to mine, devouring meat with claws and beaks like the monsters they are. Nausea has long decided I won't get a sliver of food down while in the presence of those creatures, and the worst of them is sitting right beside me.

"If you don't enjoy your well-cooked steak, I'm sure one of my people will be happy to share." The way King Myron says it makes the sip of water I'd taken earlier roil in my stomach. Raw meat. On the plates around the room, raw, bloody meat sits, half devoured by hooked beaks.

"No, thank you." I fold my arms over my chest, staring at the plate in front of me, stomach clenching and bile rising instead of words.

Perhaps I should be at least pretending to eat. If he has a shred of decency in him, he'll let me finish my meal before the wedding night. Now I'm nauseous in earnest. What the sight of raw meat hasn't done, the thought of having to spend the night with the Crow King achieves in a heartbeat.

Without another glance at the creatures around me, I cut into my steak and lead a minuscule piece to my mouth. I feel the weight of all-black eyes on me as I chew, but that doesn't stop me from staring at the wall ahead where smooth dark stone shimmers in the moonlight.

"Eat up, little bride." The Crow King's hiss slithers along my neck as he leans closer. "You will need your strength for our wedding night."

My heart lodges in my throat, knife screeching along my silver plate as my hands start shaking.

The cruelty in his tone, the finality… Everything inside my body tenses to run, to fight, and I lift my knife on instinct.

The room responds with hissed gasps and cawing laughter as the Crow King pries the knife from my good hand with a deft one of his and makes it disappear. His gaze scolds me with a set of lips twisted in dark humor, and I tuck my hand under the table out of his reach.

"You think a knife will save you?"

More laughter carries from the rows of tables, filling the air with cold malice and cruel anticipation, and I wish I'd died in Fort Perenis. I wish Ludelle's eyes had been the last thing I saw.

Still, it's the Crow King's all-black ones that hold my horrified stare as he leans even closer, lowering his voice to a whisper so only I can hear, while under the table his hand locks around mine, grasp firm but not brutal. "Hide this in your skirts, Wolayna. Who knows what monster you'll need to fight off tonight." He pushes the familiar handle of the knife back between my fingers, and I don't know what shocks me more, the way his lips twitch as I close my hand on instinct or the way his fingertips graze my wrist as he lets go. "But rest assured, it won't be me. This may be our wedding night, but I'm not going to force myself on you. If I ever bed you, it will be because you beg me to."

For a moment, all I can do is breathe, in and out until I can think again, but no matter how much I try to make sense of his actions, I can't focus long enough to even begin to understand, for the Crows are done eating, and they are getting to their feet, forming a feathered corridor leading all the way from the table where King Myron and I are sitting to the door behind the throne.

"Shall we?" The Crow King heaves himself out of his chair as if reluctant to leave his wedding banquet, but in his eyes, something sparks that I really don't want to see.

He holds out his hand, feathers swishing over the edge of the table as he waits for me to take it. The fact that he even thinks I would ever touch him makes my head explode, but I tuck the knife between the folds of my skirts, grasping onto it in hopes it will remain concealed by the layers of feathers attached to the fabric, and stand. My bad hand, I ball into a fist and lock at my other side.

A room of expectant Crows is watching as I try not to cringe from the man who has taken my future away. One deep breath and another.

I want to run, but I don't want to die badly enough to try.

The Crows' cawed cheers drown out my wild heartbeat as King Myron grasps my bad hand anyway and holds it between us so my palm lays on the back of his, fingers secured so I can't pull away. It's the way a king leads a queen to her throne. Only, I'm not going to a throne. I'm being paraded in front of his people all the way to the end of the room where he pulls me through the open door into a dim hallway.

I pray to the Guardians that this will be the end of it. That he'll let go of me and I can recoil into myself, but the Crows follow us, and Myron holds tight, grasp so hard my fingers go numb. A glance at his face, his unwavering gaze, his set mouth, tells me he is on a mission, as does his deliberate stride. He knows what he's doing, has walked this exact path before—ninety-nine times before with ninety-nine brides. There is no moment of hesitation, not one falter in his graceful movements that would allow for me to hope he'd stop or divert from his path.

"Where are we going?" The caws fill the corridor as the Crows follow us with a few steps distance covers my voice, but the Crow King hears me anyway.

"My chambers." He gives me a flat look that makes me wonder if I'll die tonight after all, and my fingers curl more tightly around the knife.

Instinctively, I stop, digging my heels in and stumbling along as he pulls me on. "Don't fight."

If you want a chance to survive, don't fight him tonight. Royad's words come back, and for a moment, I wonder if this is what he'd referred to. That I should say nothing—do nothing—when I'm being towed away against my will.

"Let me go," I demand, attempting to tug my hand out of his grasp, but he holds fast. "Or take me to my own room, at least." Maybe I can shut the door in his face and push the dresser in front of it to keep him out.

At my words, something lights up in his eyes. A twinkle of amusement that sends a chill down my spine.

"You think you'll be more comfortable having our wedding night in *your* room?" His lips twitch, sensuous and cruel, and I shake my head. Nowhere I'll spend the night with him. Not in my room or any other. When I don't respond, he nods. "I didn't think so."

The walk through the corridor stretches forever under the stare of the Crows, and yet it comes to an end too quickly, too abruptly when the Crow King flicks a finger and a door swings open a few steps ahead, blackened wood making way for the king and his bride. My stomach drops into my knees, and I dig my heels in, debating flipping my good hand with the knife toward the doorframe to lodge the blade there and give me an anchor I can use to rip free from his grasp. And then?

A glance over my shoulder tells me the Crows have followed us all the way, eager black eyes glistening in the light of sparse torches. I spy Royad near the front of the crowd and shoot him a pleading look. *Get me out of here.*

I don't know what makes me think he'd help me. Maybe the fact that he didn't let me die at the spa. Maybe that he didn't kill me on the transfer from prison even when I tried to escape repeatedly. He's not a friend or even an ally, but he is what I'd call the least enemy in this palace. So, I hook my gaze onto his all-black one and pray he won't leave me to my fate.

Don't fight, he mouths, and the last shreds of hope die in my stomach as I am tugged across the threshold and land against the hard chest of the Crow King. The air leaves my lungs at the impact, and I find myself staring at his chest, the smooth fabric of his vest stitching over his muscles as he locks me in place. He clears his throat, and my gaze snaps up to his to find his all-black eyes already on mine. Instead of hunger and cruelty, I find a hint of something else that I have no name for. It's not hesitation. It's not concern either. And I don't get a third guess because his feathered arms wrap around me, as does his magic, and my fear spikes as he grasps my chin with his fingers, leaning in so close I believe he is going to force his mouth onto mine. I'm ready to scream, ready to stick the knife in my hand into his chest or his throat and damn the consequences.

Instead, he veers right at the last moment, lips not even grazing my cheek as he whispers in my ear. "Play along, Wolayna. It's the only chance we'll both get what we want."

My breath stutters, and so do my thoughts. Had my heart been merely galloping before, now it's racing like a wild hunt.

In the corridor, the Crows become impatient, their caws and hisses turning into words.

"Kiss the bride!" a Crow shouts, and the whole crowd starts chanting. "Kiss the bride. Kiss the bride."

Kiss. I'm not going to kiss the monster before me—not before me, but mere inches from me. I can feel his warmth around my shoulders, his hard front where it brushes against mine, even when I lean back into his wings to bring as much space between us as his magic could possibly allow. I'm trapped. I can't get out. Can't breathe.

"Kiss the bride. Kiss the bride."

There is no reason for them to demand Myron kiss me other than that their cruelty must be beyond anything a human could ever comprehend. They want to see me squirm, want to see me humiliated.

Sweat beads my neck at the thought of what they demand, of what I'm expected to do, and I can't help but swallow the small piece of steak that is threatening to come back up. I can't show weakness here, on this threshold of doom where my fate might be decided.

The Crow King hasn't moved an inch. Not away from me, but not toward me either. It almost feels like he's waiting for me, but that can't be right. He is the monster whose brides die within a year. A beaked, winged monster.

Feathers skim my bare skin as I shudder in his deadly embrace. I'm about to die. I'm about to—

"I'm not going to hurt you, Wolayna," King Myron whispers, "but if you don't play along, you won't survive the night. And I really want you to survive." His breath tickles my skin with every word I am struggling to comprehend.

"Kiss the bride. Kiss the bride."

He doesn't flinch at the chants the way I do. Probably because he's heard them ninety-nine times before. And ninety-nine times, his brides have died. The fact that I haven't learned the slightest bit about why and how since I came to this Guardiansforsaken place doesn't make it any better.

Instead of following their demand, he leans a tad closer to my ear, his mouth brushing my hair as he whispers even lower. "They want to see a kiss, so let's give them one. And then I'll close the door and be done with it."

I'm so perplexed that I don't even think of running when he loosens his magic on me and leans back to assess me with a lazy gaze. It's such a vast change from the cold, cruel king of a few moments ago that I have trouble making sense of it.

"Ready?" he asks, and leans in, all traces of Crow gone from his face, leaving behind the handsome features of the male. From the corner of my eye, I see Royad nodding. I don't know if he's answering King Myron's question or if he is answering it for me, but I feel a push of magic against my shoulder that feels lighter. Not as dark as the Crow King's, and before I wonder if it could be Royad's, my mouth collides with my husband's, and the Crows erupt with cheers.

Shock freezes me in place, but before I can panic, the kiss is over and the door swings closed behind me, shutting out all sound and opening the view of what should have been a dance hall, judging by the size of it. But the deep blue silk sofas in front of the hearth below a huge mirror and the broad bed covered in night-blue silk inform me this is actually a bedroom.

I'm so surprised by the view that I don't even notice that the Crow King has moved away from me, and his magic hasn't snaked around me again. When I finally tear my gaze away from the candelabras scattered on the carved dresser, table, the mantle of the hearth, and the nightstand, I find him sitting in a wide armchair on the other end of the room, feathered arms draped over rolled armrests and gaze following me with curiosity.

I go completely still under his stare, under the silence leaking from him until it fills the entire room like a presence of its own. His features are entirely human smooth, fairy-handsome, pointed ears disappearing behind a curtain of black waves. He reaches up with one hand to open the top button of his vest, features turning grim as he leans back in his chair and braces an ankle on his knee.

His stare doesn't lose intensity as I try not to crumble, not to turn back to the door and make a run for it. I can't hear the other Crows for now, but the image of the wall of feathers and menace blocking my escape route hasn't left my thoughts, and there is no way I'll trade the silence in this room for certain death outside.

When the tension is about to tear me apart, heart pounding in my throat so hard it has become a hammering drum in my ears, I grasp the knife in the feathers of my skirts a little harder and face the Crow King. "Can I leave?"

It's a loaded question because, optimally, I mean not only this room, but the palace, the forest, and the fairylands. But, of course, he shakes his head. "For this marriage to be accepted by my people, we need to spend the night together."

Everything inside me recoils as my eyes drop to the feathers along his arms, and he notices, lips twitching downward even more. "Not the way you think. I already told you I won't force myself on you. I have never once forced myself on a bride."

Some of the tension eases from my body—for a heartbeat—because the next, the Crow King gets to his feet, strolling toward me on silent feet, and my muscles remember what it feels like to fight. My hand shoots up in front of me, pointing the knife at the male who stops just out of reach, eyes dark as the night beyond the tall windows and feathers shimmering in the candlelight.

TWELVE

I can't tell if I'm breathing, but my chest hurts from the pressure in my lungs and my ribs from the way my heart keeps throwing itself against them in an attempt to escape.

"Oh, Wolayna," he says with a sigh, fingers curling in the air, and a whole new set of candles flickers to life on the desk in the corner, illuminating his pale features and painting shadows under his eyes. "You've got much to learn."

I wait for him to attack, wait for him to say something more than those cryptic words that don't fit the image of the cruel king I've been readying myself to fight.

His mouth opens as if he is about to say something, but he exhales a shuddering breath instead, squeezing his eyes shut for a long moment that would give me every opportunity to attack.

One leap and I'd have the blade in his heart. I've done it before. Done it multiple times on the loots with Ludelle and the crew of the Wild Ray. However, the moment is gone, and King Myron has locked me in place with his gaze once more.

"Take the bed. You look like you're about to pass out." The way he scans me with wary eyes gives me pause.

Since the day I arrived at this palace, all this male has done is order me around and threaten me. He might not be forcing himself on me right now, but he has forced my hand in marriage. No one has asked me what I think about it. Not even considered it. And now—

"I'm not sleeping in your bed." I keep my knife raised, trying to calm my shaking hand. "I'm not even sleeping in the same room with you." *Monster.* I don't need to say it, the way he averts his eyes tells me he heard me loud and clear. But before I can wonder if there is more to him than the monster he has proven he is over and over again, his features shift into those of a crow, beak and feathers and all, and I shrink a few steps away until my back hits the door. He follows me until the tip of my knife sits on his chest, slicing into the fabric of his vest.

"I'll say this once and only once, Wolayna." The words are hisses and caws, and my heart doesn't beat as he braces one hand on the wood beside my head, fingertips turning into black talons. It's the most birdlike I've seen him and the most terrifying. "I don't care if you think I'm a monster. I don't care what anybody thinks. If you leave this room, you'll die, and I have become rather used to your presence in my halls. So, do us both a favor, and play the good little bride for a few more hours so this marriage is officially sealed and my people stop trying to kill the human bride half of them deem unnecessary."

I don't think to ask what the Crows have against a human woman as a bride if their customs seem to demand a bride from a different kingdom each year. The Crow King's face is so close I can see the blue and purple shimmer on the feathers covering his head instead of hair, and I wish the door would give so I could bring some distance between us. My arm has bent, shoved back by his unrelenting chest. I could easily stick the knife in between his ribs; all I need to do is to shove my hand forward, but I can't move, pinned in place by the horror of his true face. By the fearsome creature that has forced one hundred brides to marry him.

"You're debating killing me." It isn't a question. He doesn't even need to glance down to know I have murder on my mind. So fast I can't see exactly how it happens, the feathers disappear, leaving strands of silken black hair framing his face where his beak retracts, replaced by his slightly hooked nose and full mouth. He gives me a grim smile. "You wouldn't be the first to try. You wouldn't even be the first to actually get a blade lodged between my ribs." He leans in so close I can smell his scent of wind and pine as if he just returned from a flight above his forest. "Do not try, Wolayna. You will not like the consequences."

I don't dare ask what the consequences are. The fact that he's standing here, alive and breathing after being stabbed in the chest before—multiple times if I interpret his words correctly—is enough to make me shudder with fear.

It is when our eyes meet that I remember the other thing he said. "Why are they trying to kill me?" And more importantly. "Why do you care if they succeed?"

King Myron stares me down for a long, silent moment that has my body draining of all warmth, even when he braces his second hand on the other side of my head, leaning in so close I can feel the pressure on the blade. A drop of warm liquid hits my fingers, and I can't help my flinch as I realize my knife cut through his skin.

His features twist as if in pain as he opens his mouth to speak then bites down on his lower lip, nose scrunching as he inhales a sharp breath.

"Let that be my concern," he eventually says, pushing away from the door so hard the wood groans.

My legs are shaking as I watch him stalk toward the couch, where he settles down, picking up a leather-bound book from the low table and directing his gaze to the yellowed pages. The cut on his chest is hidden by the fabric of his vest, but that is definitely blood on my knife. *His* blood.

"You should rest while you can." He gestures at his bed without lifting his gaze from the book. "They'll be checking in with refreshments in an hour." If his wound is hurting, he doesn't show. "They'll be expecting you to be draped in my covers, rosy-cheeked and out of breath."

When my hand tightens around my knife, he glances up, a dark laugh escaping his mouth, and he tilts his head. "How many times do I have to repeat I'm not going to hurt you. I haven't hurt you once since you arrived at my home, have I?" One of his brows arches as he waits for me to respond.

Now that I think about it, he is right. Not once has he hurt me. Even when he pulled me along the hallway to his room, he didn't actually hurt me. Not physically.

"You had me brought here and forced me to marry you. That's its own brand of torture," I inform him, and I could swear he flinches. Then, it could have been the flicker of the candle flame.

"You were sentenced to die." He holds my gaze, features smooth and devoid of all emotion. "This is a much better option than to be butchered by a random Tavrasian soldier on a second-rate pirate ship on the Quiet Sea."

Again… The way he knows so much about my past gives me pause. I swallow the surprise, the fear that comes with realizing how much he truly knows about me while I know nothing. Not even about his people apart from the stories that inspire children's nightmares. It's a challenge in itself to straighten my spine and push away from the door while my legs are shaking and my heart is galloping out of my chest, but I will confidence into my posture, cunning into my expression, and take a step forward.

"How do you know I wouldn't have rather died?" Because with everything I've done, I'd deserve it. All the people who are dead because of me…

The look he gives me is impossible to read, so I take another step forward. "Anything would be better than being here in a forest full of monsters."

This time, he doesn't flinch. He merely holds my gaze as I approach one step at a time. Even when he has been enigmatic and terrifying, the Crow King hasn't lifted a finger against me. No, he has told me twice now that he wants me to survive. Perhaps it is that thought making me bold; perhaps it is the knowledge I have nothing left to lose as I cross the room and sit on the brocade footstool on the other side of the low table, facing the Crow King through a seven-armed candelabra. Shadows dance on his features, reflecting in his eyes like the fires behind Eroth's Veil. But his face yields nothing.

"And you are right to be afraid of them." He lowers his book to his lap, leaning forward an inch as his gaze slides down my feathered dress, snagging on the precarious straps on my shoulders. "You've seen what they are capable of last night by the pools. It would be a shame to lose another bride."

There, again. "Why is it so important I don't die? You don't seem to particularly mourn the ninety-nine other brides," I challenge him, his lack of wrath encouraging me to push harder.

His eyes land on the knife I'm now clutching with both my hands, lingering on my bad one for a breath or two where the chain tattoo that marks me as a Fort Perenis prisoner sits exposed around my wrist, then continues to the tip of the blade where his blood is drying in the warmth of the candle glow. For a long while, he seems to be debating how to answer that. Eventually, he lifts his gaze back to mine, teeth buried in his lower lip again, and shakes his head. "It is not important."

"Then why hand me a knife? Why have Royad play bodyguard? Why force me to stay in this room tonight if you aren't planning on bedding me?" It might be a stupid question, one that might bring his attention back to something I am glad he has excluded from tonight's events. Still, I have to ask, or I'll explode.

"Because I trust Royad, and I don't trust myself." It's all he says before he buries his nose in his book again.

His words hang in the air between us even when he has withdrawn from this conversation, and I can't help but feel a chill crawl through my bones at the meaning of them. *I don't trust myself.*

"How did the others die?" I ask instead of asking what I really want to know—if *he* killed them.

"You're asking the wrong questions, Wolayna." His gaze snaps up, deep and threatening, but instead of fear, something else stirs inside of me. I don't know what he is trying to achieve, but he is pushing me to change course. He *wants* me to keep asking questions, yet he isn't willing to respond in words that make sense.

"What's the right question?" It is my turn to raise a brow and wait in silence as he is fighting for words.

I realize that's exactly what he's doing, mouth opening and closing as if none of those words want to leave his tongue.

"Who killed them?" I offer, but he shakes his head.

Still not the right one.

"What would you like me to ask?" I snap at him, my hands lifting the knife in front of me as if I could carve answers from him with a threat I know he isn't even remotely responsive to. The dried blood on my blade from the cut on his chest proves it.

"Why?" He stares at me with those all-black eyes, and a shiver rolls up my spine.

"*Why* what?" The words fall out of me even when I try to hold onto the fear, the anger, the terror, the despair of the past months in prison, of these past hours of my wedding day.

The Crow King rakes his gaze over me, attention following the gooseflesh rising on my arms and shoulders. "That's the question you should be asking: Why did they die?" Then he points at the bed, shrugging as if we weren't just discussing the hows and whys of ninety-nine deaths, and with a swish, the night-blue covers fold back in silent invitation. "Now rest, Wolayna. I'll wake you when it's time to play the well-satisfied bride."

This time, his words don't allow for any response, not even for me to ask the question he told me to ask. So, I get to my feet and make my way to the bed, knife firmly in my grasp. It won't be much use in case he decides to attack, but the warm silver between my sweaty palms gives me some modicum of safety.

I don't bother to slip under the covers, as his magic suggested by folding them aside, but lie down on top of the luxurious silk, allowing my gaze to glide across the room.

This place is different from the rest of the palace where rough stone and unrefined structures define the halls. In here, a multitude of fabrics and textures mingle, making up the space inhabited by a creature of nightmares. When my eyes land on the Crow King once more, he has sunken back into his book, one feathered arm draped over the armrest of the couch and an ankle crossed over a knee. His hair falls into his face, hiding his eyes while the view on his stone jawline and full mouth remains clear. Something deep inside of me breaks at the sight of the beautiful monster to whom I'm now tied. I want to hate him with all my heart, want to scream and rage at him, want to tell him he is exactly what I expected him to be—the cruel, murderous creature the tales tell of winged fairies—but he's not. I don't know what he is, but as he sits there, motionless in the flickering candlelight, his words of how he doesn't want me to die still hanging in the air even when it feels like a lifetime since he's first spoken them, it is not as difficult as it should be to pretend I might survive the night after all.

And, as I lie there, curled on my side and counting my own heartbeats until the candle stump on the nightstand burns down and snuffs out, the tension of the day finally catches up with me. The warmth and quiet of the room envelop me, and with my knife pressed against my chest the way a child would clutch a toy, I become drowsy.

The occasional hisses of the flames and the dancing shadows paint stories on the walls that I can't decipher as my entire body grows heavy despite my promise to myself to stay awake, stay alert so the Crow King can't sneak up on me.

THIRTEEN

A knock on the door rips me from the momentary lull, kicking my heart back into a gallop and my breath into a ragged mess. I try to sit up, but a pair of hands pushes me back with surprising gentleness.

"Stay here," the Crow King murmurs, gaze unreadable as he scans my face then straightens and turns to the door. "Refreshments have arrived." He takes a step away from the bed then halts, glancing at me over his shoulder, those all-black eyes boring into mine. "I know it's a lot to ask, but for both our sakes, it would be easiest if you pretend I just fucked you into oblivion."

At the shock on my face, his lips twitch into a slight curve of amusement, and I'm grateful for the candlelight, or he might have noticed my blush at his choice of words. Not that Ludelle hadn't done his fair share of doing just that, but I wasn't prepared for those words from the male with the winged arms and impossibly handsome features who surprised me before by shedding a mask the moment the door was closed. Now, I'm not sure what I am looking at—the monster or something entirely else that I yet have to find a name for. But one thing I am certain of... My life depends on how well I convinced the Crows waiting in the hallway that their king had done just that. And I really, really want to live.

So, I push myself up, intending to give my new husband a mock-lascivious glance, but I find myself covered with a thin woolen blanket, and instead, I meet his gaze with bewilderment.

"You were shivering," is all he gives as explanation, and I find myself struggling with hating him as he turns to the door and strolls over, the proud and unbothered king who will hurry for no one. Also, he is no longer wearing his vest, leaving a view on the cords of muscles along his back where his skin isn't covered with feathers. I swallow at the sight of raw strength, at the warrior's body that doesn't need magic to smite his enemies yet has plenty of it at his disposal.

I shiver again as I realize that the creature I'm now tied to is even more dangerous than I initially thought. At least, he's not out for my blood tonight.

He is almost at the door when I realize I am fully dressed and he may have covered me up to hide the fact he hasn't even gotten to take my clothes off. That familiar fear springs to life as he lays his hand on the doorknob and turns, and I don't think as I reach for the straps of my dress and rip them so they dangle off my shoulders. Then I ruffle my hair until it is all tangled strands before I slide up against the headboard, clutching the blanket to my chest so the dress is fully covered and all that's visible are my bare arms and décolletage where the dress dips low enough to make it look like I'm naked underneath the blanket.

Eyes on the opening door, I school my expression into a bland smile and force my lids to lower like I have problems keeping my eyes open.

The moment the door opens, caws and hisses fill the air, and a tension runs through the room like a current in dangerous waters.

Three Crows and the Ceremonial stand on the threshold, cocking their heads to peer past King Myron's broad shoulders.

The Ceremonial holds up a wrinkly hand, and the crowd falls silent while my heart fills the room with its frantic beats. They are out there to pass judgement on what has or hasn't happened in this room, and if I want to live, they need to believe their king performed his matrimonial duties. I can tell by the way one of the Crows peers at me past the king's neck, his gaze drifting from my face to my hair, then down to my bare skin, and a hiss escapes his beak as he takes in the seam of my breasts where the blanket threatens to slip.

"Never seen a naked woman, have you?" I whisper-spit at him and tug the blanket tighter, praying to the Guardians he believes he caught me covering myself up just in time. "Oh … you Crows don't have women, do you?"

I could swear the air stops moving for a heartbeat, and judging by the way the muscles in King Myron's neck bunch, I am certain it is his magic calling the world to silence while I do my best impression of a woman disturbed in her post-pleasure rest.

In the hallway, not one caw or hiss sounds as they all wait for him to speak, and as he glances at me over his shoulder, I glimpse a hint of worry in his eyes that I hadn't expected.

Before I can react, he turns back to the Ceremonial, shoving a hand through his hair and bracing his feet slightly apart. Myron merely nods at the Ceremonial, who inclines his head at the king and raises his voice. "The marriage has been consummated and your new bride will be called Queen of Crows from now on forth."

I don't know if it's the authority of a king that allows him to convince a whole crowd with a nod or if it's the Ceremonial's words that do, but my stomach coils into a spiral of nausea as King Myron steps aside and Royad walks into the room with a tray in his hands, gaze curiously following the length of my body where, from this close, the bunched up skirts of my dress are well visible in the shape of little hills and valleys around my legs. He raises an eyebrow but doesn't say anything as he places the tray on the nightstand.

I brace myself for the wrath of the Guardians to break loose as the lie is discovered, but Royad doesn't say a word as he crosses the threshold either, merely nodding at his king in silent understanding, and vanishes in the crowd.

"Now leave, all of you," the Crow King calls into the hallway, power reverberating in every word. "You already know how little I enjoy being disturbed when I have my new bride to myself for the first time." The cruelty in his tone reminds me of the king dragging me down the corridor to this room, of the male commanding me to speak my vows against my will. Yet, when he shuts the door in their faces and leans against it, head resting back on the wood and gaze on the ceiling, I sense the tension leave his body as I watch him carefully.

No matter that he lied to keep up pretenses, he is still a predator; it is evident in every hard muscle running down the front of his torso, every carved pane and edge of his abdomen. The top button of his leather pants is open, allowing it to sit low on his hips, the V of his muscles disappearing behind dark fabric. I direct my gaze back to his face, finding his already waiting for me.

"Certainly not what I expected." He purses his lips, placing both his hands on the threshold so his feathers spread slightly around his elbows. I've never taken a close enough look to understand how they are attached to his arms, if they are wings he could fly on or mere decoration, but now I'm curious.

"I could say the same." I hold his gaze as he steps out of the doorframe and stalks across the room, each step elegant even when the air of insurmountable power has left him, and he settles on the deep blue couch that is entirely too short for him to stretch out on.

"Drink the wine," he says as he lies back on the silk cushion and closes his eyes. "It will help you sleep."

I'm far from tired, adrenaline coursing through my veins after the view of monsters collecting on the doorstep.

"Why?" I ask into the silence and half expect the Crow King to leap to his feet and attack me. But he doesn't open his eyes, pulling up his legs so his feet are braced on one armrest while his head rests on the other. It's an almost comical view, like an adult folding into a child-sized bed.

"*Why* what, Wolayna?"

His voice is deep and dangerous, implying I need to be careful with what questions I ask even when he's told me the ones that I should be asking.

I ponder that for a moment, allowing myself to study his features in the warm light of the fire.

Why do they want me dead, I think, but out loud, I ask, "Why are you pretending in front of them? Why not take what they believe is yours and ensure there is no lie they could detect?"

At that, his eyes open, finding mine across the room. "Because taking something just because I can doesn't necessarily make me a good king."

I'm so surprised by his answer that I forget to think as I continue. "Then what makes you a good king?" And wish I hadn't because he rolls his head to his side, cutting off that brief connection.

"I'm not a good king, and I never will be. Just as I'm not a good male. Now sleep, Wolayna. We have a lot on our agenda tomorrow."

It's the last thing he says to me, and I don't dare speak another word for fear it will bring back the cold male I feared mere hours ago.

As I settle beneath the woolen blanket, I clutch my knife with both hands again and will myself to calm.

Sleep doesn't find me until the first gray light of dawn creeps into the room through the windows left and right of the bed and my eyes shut from exhaustion.

FOURTEEN

When I open my eyes again, it's bright daylight, and I'm alone in the Crow King's bedroom, bundled up in the woolen blanket I pulled up to my nose the night before. My dress is in place, even with the straps torn, and when I glance to the side, I find my dinner knife neatly set parallel to the edge of the bedside table. Whether it fell during the night or the Crow King merely decided to pry it from my fingers in my sleep, I really don't want to think about it. It's bad enough that I spent the night in his bed and I'm not entirely appalled by the idea. At least, not more than by the thought of going out there and facing the monsters who want me dead.

Why?

With a last glance around the room, I make sure King Myron isn't hiding somewhere in the shadows, ready to strike, but then, I figure, if he hasn't killed me by now, he's not going to do it. Especially since he's voiced numerous times that he wants me to live. Why does he care?

That goes on the list of all the other *why*s I desperately want answers to but don't know where to start digging. I'm still trapped in a palace in a kingdom which seems to consist of one single forest in the middle of the fairylands of Askarea. The only difference is the male I've feared beyond words did a decent deed by allowing me to keep my dignity. Does that make him a good person?

With ninety-nine wives on his conscience, I highly doubt it.

With a groan reserved for the dead rising from their graves, I sit up and drag my legs out of the blanket.

My shoes are gone, too, I realize, as I set my feet on the soft rug in front of the bed. Hues of night blue and gold weave in intricate patterns beneath my toes as I slide them back and forth, digging into the plush material. It's not what I expected. Nothing is. Not the rich colors in a palace that seems otherwise dead, or the wall of books I didn't notice behind the couch last night. I most certainly didn't expect the stationary folded in half with my name scrawled on it in slender, not-so-elegant letters.

Heart pounding, I pick it up and open it, already wondering what the man who told me not a day ago that he doesn't have a choice in this either would have to say this early in the day.

Don't leave the room. Not even with Royad. He will bring you food later. There are plenty of books in here, I'm sure you'll pass your time well until my return.

His words are so hard to decipher I suspect he hasn't written a note to anyone in a while. A year, perhaps, if he treats all his wives the same way.

Much as I hadn't expected a lot of the other things, this doesn't really come as a surprise. It would have been the first time I'd be free to go anywhere in this Godsforsaken palace. Yet, a small voice at the back of my head reminds me of the bloodlust in the Crow's eyes when he'd tried to murder me by the pool. I don't trust the Crow King's words that his people will stop trying to kill me just because the marriage has been sealed. From the way the Crows peeked at me through the door last night, the threat is as real as it was yesterday.

So, I drop the paper on the bedside table and stretch my arms over my head, wincing slightly as I angle my bad hand to the side, swallowing the dryness in my throat. The night before, I didn't touch the wine, and now that I could use it, the tray is gone. Driven by my thirst, I search my way around the room, scanning the walls for a bathing room door. I find it on the wall opposite the bookshelf, almost unnoticeable between a sideboard and a dresser. A simple, narrow door that doesn't seem fit for royal chambers but leads to a bathing room large enough to fit Ludelle's cabin from the Wild Ray. Larger than that. It's enough to fit a lake. And that's exactly what I find there. No toilet, no basin. Instead, the floor is slanted toward the opposite end of the large stone chamber, and from halfway into the room, water laps back and forth like a mockery of the tides at the ocean shore. I can taste the salt in the air, not brine but a cleaner scent than that. Darkness reflects from the surface of the water together with rippling dots of light falling in through the door behind me.

Whether it's the magic of this palace or something unholy, I don't ever want to find out. I approach the water, drawn as if by an invisible rope, bare feet gliding along the slick stone beneath while my heart picks up pace. I inhale the air, inhale the darkness and the silence.

A few more steps and my toes will touch the water. My skin aches for the loving caress of the waves, for the gentle touch that only water can give. The feathers of my dress swish around my feet like a black melody, farther and farther into the room, until they are carried away by the slosh of the next wave. Cool bliss kisses my toes as an endless sadness grasps my chest in a vise.

For a moment, all I can do is stand there and heave one labored breath after the other while the weight of the world settles on my bare shoulders—settles and digs into my skin, into my bones, until the pain is unbearable, until every breath hurts like shards of glass down my throat. Until my chest threatens to implode.

I take another step into the water, eager to ease the sense of hopelessness, the need to lose myself in the waves. This room has seen pain, knows what it means to suffer. It holds myriads of tears. And now, it holds mine, too.

Like rain, they drip from my lashes as I blink and blink and blink them away. But there is no end to them. So, I march farther in, the water up to my calves, and sink to my knees so the water hugs me around the waist. My fingers rake through the ink-dark liquid, coming back guilty of the sorrows spilled into this room. And the pain seems unending. It's eating me up. It's wrapping around me as it soaks my dress, pulls on it, leaden and unyielding.

I cry—I cry the unending tears I thought I no longer had in me. Tears for my father whom I betrayed. Tears for Ludelle, for the family I made on the Wild Ray and lost in a heartbeat. Tears for my own guilt.

And the lake takes and takes and takes. It takes until I'm cold and shivering, until I can barely keep myself upright.

It is then that I dive out of my despair for a deep breath and realize something is very wrong. I remember that I was searching for a bathing room, for a pitcher of water to drink. My heart kicks into a gallop as I feel—really feel—the water around me, not the loving embrace but clawing fingers that are trying to drag me under. I brace my hands on the ground, waves lashing up to my elbows, grasping and reaching higher while I push myself to turn and get out. Crawl if I have to. It doesn't matter as long as I get out of here before the lake drags me under.

The water has other ideas though. Just as I scramble to a half-upright position, a wave lashes against my legs, ripping them out from under me, and my knees hit the stone. Pain explodes in my legs, so powerful it takes my breath away as I strain to keep myself from falling face-first into the water.

I can't breathe. Can't breathe. Can't think.

From a distance, faint voices are calling. *Wolayna.* My name carries on the waves fighting to climb into my lungs. *Wolayna.* Water whips my face, hard and fast and uncompromising.

"Wolayna!"

Hands grab me by the shoulders, yanking me out of the water, and I'm being lifted from the wet trap clutching at me.

"Breathe, Wolayna." His voice is a command surging through me, a calm of thunder tearing the water from my throat as I battle for air. "Breathe."

Only when I'm coughing and panting, water tumbling from my mouth, do I realize I am standing on solid ground once more and the male holding me at feathered-arm's length is the very same who left the note on the bedside table.

"Come on." He gestures to the door and guides me toward the daylight of the bedroom where the nightmarish water can't reach me, and I suck in a deep breath that stings in my raw lungs.

The sunlight hurts my watering eyes, and in my chest, my heart hasn't calmed one bit. When I finally manage to focus on his dark shape, King Myron is fumbling with the handle of the door behind which the dangerous lake is hidden.

"This door isn't supposed to open for you." He doesn't face me, merely continues with whatever he's doing to the wooden rectangle that should be exchanged for a wall of solid rock.

"What ... is that?" My throat hurts as if I swallowed gravel, and my voice doesn't sound any better.

I hold onto the backrest of a nearby chair as I sway on my feet while taking in the frantic movements of the Crow King's hands. His fingertips are black talons again, and I'm beginning to see a pattern. He is losing control over whatever magic is supposed to be at work by that door, or over himself, I'm not certain, but he is losing control.

"This is the dark history of my ancestors. And that is all you need to know about it." He halts, lays both palms against the door, fingers spread and talons digging into the wood. His feathers spread to the sides in half-circles, lean muscles flexing left and right of his spine where he chose to leave out his usual vest. Maybe it's the shock of nearly drowning in what seems to be a conscious lake—inside a room—that makes him appear less frightening even with those wings and talons on full display, but as I watch him, still catching my breath, I can't help but wonder what it would feel like to run my fingers along those feathers.

Before I can become tempted to test it out and face the Crow King's wrath, I sit down in the wooden chair and lean back, ignoring the steady drip of water from my dress. "That lake in there tried to drown me." It's not a gentle conversation starter, but it sure gets a reaction out of him. One that makes me question how I could have believed he didn't appear all that frightening a minute ago.

His black eyes flash as he whirls on me, hands balled into fists at his side as if he is restraining himself from lunging for me. But he doesn't move. "The door shouldn't have opened."

"Why?" I need to know, and it's the one question he told me to ask. So, I'll ask over and over again until I get an answer.

Instead of responding, he leaves his post by the door after one last look to convince himself it's truly closed, and gestures at the table by the couch. "Royad was busy, so I came up myself to bring you lunch."

He crosses the room to open a dresser, his attention lingering on me. The wood creaks as he pulls out drawer after drawer until he finds what he is searching for and turns around, a bundle of black cloth in his hands.

"Because I don't enjoy torturing as much as my father did." A grim smile twists his lips, but his gaze is too serious not to hear the full meaning of his words, and a shudder rakes down my wet body.

"But you do enjoy torturing?" Maybe I shouldn't be asking, but something inside of me tells me I need to know the answer.

He shrugs and bunches the fabric between his fingers. "That depends on who I'm torturing."

I know I should be quaking with fear, but something about the way he says it doesn't make me think he includes me in the faction of people he'd like to see suffer. At least, that's what I hope as I push myself back to my feet and take a step toward him.

"Who?" It's a simple question. As simple as *why*, and maybe I'll get an answer to that.

He holds my gaze for a long time, the distance between us swimming as I keep myself from blinking so I won't miss any hint of emotion. Eventually, he leans back against the dresser, wings rustling as he accommodates his feathers along the carved surfaces of the drawers. "The Crow who tried to kill you in the ancient pools."

I can't be certain I imagined the flicker of shame in his eyes. It's gone so fast it could have been my imagination playing tricks on me.

"You punished him?" I don't know what makes me ask. Perhaps I need to hear that he wasn't involved in the attack.

"He tried to kill my bride." The look he gives me tells me he believes that already explains everything.

Again, I find myself speaking the one question he told me to ask. "Why?"

And this time, he doesn't remain silent. "Because he is a revolutionary bastard who believes we are better off the way things are and that brides only"—he pauses, searching for words until he seems to find one that fits—"*distract* from my kingly duties."

"Which are?" I try to sound casual now that he's finally talking, try to ignore the shivers running through my body as the wet dress hugs my skin with icy fingers.

"Accumulate more power, gain more lands. Become independent from the high fae." He sounds like he's reciting a list someone told him he needed to know by heart, but his eyes are burning with disdain, as if he deems said goals beneath him.

"And what do you think?"

That stops him dead. What little emotion leaked through his facade disappears behind a frown while he eyes me as if he thought he bought a flower and woke up with weeds in his garden. "It doesn't matter what I think."

Before I can figure out what he means by that, he tosses the bundle in his hands at me and heads for the door. "Change, eat. I'll be back soon, and then we'll do our first rounds through the palace as proper husband and wife." He adds a little smirk that doesn't go with the frown from a moment ago, and all I can do is roll my eyes at him before he lets himself out and closes the door behind him, leaving me a dripping, freezing mess.

FIFTEEN

The next time the door opens, it's not the Crow King but Royad, a grin flashing on his face as he looks me up and down with mocking black eyes.

"Must have been quite a night." He gestures at the dressing robe I'm wearing first, then at the feather gown hanging over the chair beside me, still dripping. He picks up one end of a ripped strap and eyes it curiously. "Couldn't wait, could he?"

Since I don't know if Royad knows the truth, I decide to keep up pretenses and absently run a finger along my shoulder. "Patience doesn't seem to be one of my husband's virtues."

Royad's lips stretch into an even broader grin. "Speaking of... Does he have any?"

"Any what?" Royad's gaze wanders to the tray beside me on the table, and he nods at the empty plate.

After changing out of the wet dress, I'd eaten as the Crow King suggested and found myself starved enough to finish the entire meal of mashed potatoes and steamed carrots and peas. Not a meal fit for a king but filling. And most importantly, no raw meat.

"Virtues. Does he have any?" Not that it would make a difference. I'm still his wife by force and would give anything to escape this place. Only, I've learned the hard way that my new husband seems to be the only person able to protect me in his kingdom. I'm not sure how that makes me feel, but not exactly hopeful is a good way to start.

Royad's laugh ends in a hiss as he meets my gaze, finding the honest question there. "I guess that's for you to find out." The smirk he gives me would have been adorable had I been able to call him a friend. Still, this is the male who dragged me through a magical kingdom to this prison of a palace.

"I assume you're not going to help me with it?" The way he didn't help me escape before Ret Relah.

That wipes the grin off his face. He lowers himself onto the couch where the Crow King left the book the night before and gives me a pitiful look. "I wish I could. I truly do. But I'm just a servant."

"A servant he trusts or he wouldn't have sent you to get me from Fort Perenis." Or he wouldn't allow him in this room alone with the bride he claims his people want to murder.

"Maybe." He shrugs, brown waves bouncing over his shoulders.

I pin him with a gaze, leaning over the table and bracing my hands left and right of my tray. My bad hand stings, but I ignore it. "Why do the others want to kill me?" It might not be the best question to ask since I haven't got an answer from the king himself, but it's worth a try.

And the Guardians bless him, Royad speaks. "You mean even after your successful wedding night?" He gives me a pointed glance. "It's a long story, but the quintessence is that half of the Crows are dissatisfied because he keeps taking brides, and the other half is dissatisfied because he can't keep one of them…"

"Alive," I finish for him. "Because he can't keep one of them alive."

Royad merely nods.

"They don't want him to marry? Why?" I mean, I could name a hundred different reasons why a monster like him shouldn't marry someone who didn't choose him, but that's a different story entirely, so I sit back and wait as Royad sorts through his words.

Finally, he brushes his feathers with a claw and nods to himself. "Some believe that the power we possess is all we need to rise to greatness again." The last word comes out a bit strangled, but I am certain it's *again*.

"Again? I thought the Crows were a powerful people in Askarea." It's an assumption I made based on the stories I've heard about them and what I've experienced in this palace. Yet, there is no way to know where they stand in fairy power balance.

"There was a time when we were. Myron's father, King Carius the Cruel was sitting on our throne then, long before the Crow Wars when we were banished to these forests."

It's the most information I've gained since my arrival, and I'm not ready for it to end. "They don't teach us much about Askarea in the human realms."

"Perhaps that's your luck. Askarea's history is bloody, even without the Crow Fairies. And since we've been confined to the Seeing Forest, the Crows have become restless. They don't like that Myron made a trade with King Recienne of Askarea for only *one* bride per year." When I raise an eyebrow in question, he explains, "Before the war, all Crows of noble descent went on a hunt for a new bride each Ret Relah, but not since Carius lost and Myron succeeded him. In the beginning, we didn't get any brides at all—courtesy of the Fairy King—but then our magic started unweaving the wards on our kingdom, and Crows started roaming the fairylands again. Instead of starting another war, Myron made a deal with Recienne. We'd stay in our own little realm in exchange for one bride each year. Now, instead of many chances, we only have one... *Bride*," he corrects. "Instead of many *brides*." I can't be certain, but he seems to be scrambling for words, gaze flitting over the furniture, the ceiling, anywhere but me.

The room falls silent except for my breathing and the almost tangible awkwardness as he is opening and closing his mouth. I've seen King Myron do the same thing, and I'm beginning to think that it isn't because Crows aren't naturally eloquent; quite the opposite. There is something amiss, but as I study him, his human features shift to beak and feathers, and all I get is a hiss as he finally meets my gaze.

I shrink into my chair, instantly regretting that I still cringe from his monstrous appearance when his Crow nature takes over. Or was the shift deliberate so he didn't need to continue the trajectory of the conversation?

The misery in his eyes tells me it's neither. Something more is going on that keeps him from telling me the truth.

Willing my nerves to calm and my heart to slow, I sit up and face him, letting my gaze slide over his face in acknowledgement of everything that is and isn't there: the feathers framing his features where usually his brown hair hangs in loose strands, his scar that hasn't vanished entirely even when his skin has turned grayish around his eyes and beak. The mouth that is still human.

"Tell me about Askarea." It's a simple request and allows for him to tell me practically anything he wants to share.

Royad cocks his head in a very bird-like manner and lifts a claw in front of him, turning it back and forth, flexing it in a display of the sharp weapon it is. "You're not afraid of me, Ayna, are you?" His words are a sharp hiss the way they always are when he shifts into this birdlike creature, and the sound of it grates along my bones.

It's a valid question, and the thundering beat my heart has become once more should tell me that I am beyond afraid. Yet, I shake my head. "If the Crow King trusts you, perhaps it's time I did, too."

His mouth twists into a grim line below his beak. "Trust is a fickle thing. Do you trust Myron? You don't even dare call him by his name, do you?"

It's a good question, one I should be asking myself. I don't have an equally good answer for it, though, so I hold Royad's gaze and fold my arms over the silken dressing robe. "I'm wearing King Myron's clothes. That should be answer enough."

Royad's brow creases, pulling feathers lower on his forehead, and I suppress a shudder at the eerie sight. "He's your husband. You wearing his clothes after your wedding night shouldn't surprise me. However, the fact that you haven't skipped his title makes me wonder how close the two of you really got last night."

If this is a test, he has the best Crow Fairy poker face in history. And I should know. Ludelle and the crew of the Wild Ray taught me the card game, and I've become quite adept over the years.

My chest aches at the mere thought of the people I used to call my family. Of the man in whose arms I used to fall asleep, and the thought of tainting his memory by implying I slept with the Crow King—*Myron*. Royad is right. If I want to convince people enough to make them believe their king made me moan all night, I better use his first name and learn how to blush at command.

"Unlike as a conversational partner, Myron is an exceptional lover." It's the best I can do without outright lying, and Royad's mouth twitches, beak and feathers retreating as he slowly grins.

"Oh the joys of being married to the most powerful Crow in existence," he says, voice back to a comfortable baritone.

It's my turn to frown. I'm still not over the whole near-death experience in the hidden lake-room, not to speak about being offered up by my own homeland as a tribute for the Crows. "Is this a conversation you have with every bride?" With my eyes, I shoot little daggers at him. Just because I trust him doesn't mean I need to like him.

"Only with those who matter."

His words give me pause, but before I can ask what he means by that, he sits up and gestures at the tray between us. "Are you going to finish your tea?"

The half-empty cup is sitting in the corner where the dark wood meets an iron frame, steam no longer rising from the light-green liquid. I shake my head.

"Then let's get you some fresh clothes so Myron can parade you around the palace."

The fact that he laughs as he says it gives me hope that he's only joking, but nothing has been a joke in this new world so far, and hope has gotten me nowhere.

"Let's make a deal." Gesturing at the too-long dressing gown along my body, I get to my feet and stroll behind the chair with the wet dress draped over it.

Royad raises a brow at me.

"You get me some clothes, and I promise to change, no matter what you bring me. And you'll answer a few questions in return."

His lips purse as he considers then shrugs. "I promise I'll try to answer all of your questions if you get dressed first," he makes a counteroffer. "And never suggest that same deal to Myron.

He'll come up with all sorts of ideas of what lacy little nothings to put you in."

Even when I throw him a look of outrage, a part of me is surprisingly curious about what it would be like to have Myron's full predatory attention on me as he sees me in said little nothings. And that thought horrifies me to no end.

"Deal."

Royad's lips curl, and he marches from the room, throwing over his shoulder that he'll be back in a moment. That leaves me with memories of the stories people told me when I was a child. About fairies and bargains, about a time when humans had magic and that magic saved us from the immortal creatures of Askarea.

I replay the bargain I agreed to in my mind and am satisfied that at least I haven't sold my soul. Whatever Royad brings me to wear, I'll get some answers.

When he doesn't return for a few minutes, I walk around the table and pick up the book Myron left there the night before. The heavy leather binding is worn from countless reads, as are the pages, some of them so faded they have become unreadable, I flip through the chapters until something catches my eye.

It's a drawing of a tall stone palace with spires and battlements like an old fortress. The angle is different from when I glance out the window at the bone-white walls, but it is definitely the palace I'm standing in. Curious to find out more about the Crow palace, I start reading; only, there is not one single reference to the Crows. Not one word mentioning winged fairies or annual bridal sacrifices.

Instead, one word keeps coming up over and over again. *Flame*. Eternal Flame. I don't know how Askarea dates its history, but this book is old. I browse ahead to find a hint of the

Crows, but the book doesn't even mention a war. All it does reference is high fae, forest fairies, and *Flames*.

I'm about to start reading in earnest when the door opens, and in strolls Royad, a stack of black fabrics in his hands that makes me think I will never wear a different color again.

"I see you have found a different source of information." He eyes the book while setting down the clothes beside me on the couch. "Anything interesting in there?"

I debate telling him that his king is reading particularly steamy romance novels in his spare time but think better as his feathers brush my arm when he pats the heap of fabric. A shudder works its way through my body, and I'm reminded of all the reasons I should be shying away from these creatures—including the murderous lake Myron is hiding in his closet.

"Did the Crows build this palace?" It's the most diplomatic way I can ask if they conquered their territory from another people without actually saying it.

Royad shakes his head at me. "We agreed you dress first."

Something in his gaze tells me the head shake wasn't entirely to admonish me for expecting answers before I hold up my end of the bargain.

"Can you at least point me toward a bathing room that won't kill me?" I lay on the sarcasm heavily, but it's fear driving me to that bravado. I don't want to find myself again trapped in the element I used to love most in the world.

At that, Royad's gaze flicks to the wet dress on the chair, and he steps around the table to examine it from up close. "Is that what happened?" He is working hard to hide his alarm, but as he bends over the damp feathers, his features tighten, and I could swear that's fear in his all-black eyes.

"Part of it." Laying the book back on the table, I gather the fresh clothes in one arm and start looking around the room. "Now, where can I change?"

Royad's gaze darts to the plain wooden door before it bounces to the other side of the room, and he flicks a hand. A door I hadn't noticed in the elaborate brocade wallpaper swings open, revealing the view on a bathing room double the size of the one in my room, complete with a toilet, a large bathtub with a golden rim, and a stack of fluffy towels sitting beside it on a carved wooden stool.

"Take your time." He motions for me to walk in.

As I do, I throw over my shoulder. "Had I known he had a toilet in here, I wouldn't have needed to pee in the lake. Maybe that's why it tried to drown me."

Not that I did. But my point gets across, and I nearly laugh at his horrified expression. He knows about the room without a doubt, and he knows what it's capable of. Perhaps Myron isn't ready to give the answers I'm seeking, but Royad and I have a bargain. And I'm ready to take advantage of it in any way I can.

I didn't specify how many questions or when I'd ask them. It was he who pushed the asking after I got dressed. That could be in a few minutes or in a few weeks. As long as I can think of something to ask, there is no limit.

This is my first win since I was dragged to this palace, and I allow a half-smile onto my lips as I close the door behind me.

SIXTEEN

My room is as gray and unwelcoming as ever when we step inside after a brisk walk through the hallways. I learned that Myron's room is situated on the same level but on the other side of the balcony-like corridor running around the square cut opening up into the entrance hallway below. Every few paces, guards are stationed by the columns as if the palace has been breached before and those dark alcoves are where thieves and assassins were hiding.

Goosebumps rise on my arms at the mere thought of any creature powerful enough to scare a Crow Fairy. The clothes I'm wearing are comfortable enough to allow me to feel like myself for once instead of a captive bride, thin linen pants and a fitted tunic that might be too tight to fight in, but then, whom would I fight—and with what weapon?

Royad settles on the single chair by the desk in the corner, eyeing me pace between the bed and the bathing room door while I wait for him to answer the one question I asked him before leaving Myron's room.

"Are you going to tell me?" I prompt when he merely follows me with a heavy silence that might be deliberate but somehow feels more like an attempt at forming the right words.

"It's an ancient room for sure. Thousands of years old." He pauses, waiting to know if I'm satisfied, but I'm not.

"Has it always been in the building?" I figure asking about why it tried killing me hasn't brought me any answers, perhaps figuring out what exactly it is and how it got there is a better start. No personal issues involved.

Not that anything about a relationship with a room should be personal—unless it's murderous. Then it's something to consider. It surely hasn't killed off Myron or Royad. So, it's either personal against me or it has something to do with the role I've taken up in this palace.

"Not always." Royad swallows. "Not the way it is now."

"What is that supposed to mean?" It's hard enough to believe there truly is a lake locked in a palace room on this very floor. "Did you put the water in there?"

Royad's gaze locks on mine. "That's something you'll need to ask Myron."

Of course, there's no direct answer. "Is that a fairy thing? Not being able to give a solid answer?"

For a moment, Royad considers me, those all-black eyes not half as hard as I'm used to, and I could swear it's pity I spot there. "All fairies are experts with words. But Crows are not normal fairies. We aren't like the high fae of Askarea. We aren't even like the other fairies of Askarea." He starts saying something else, but his voice cracks on the first sound, and he shakes his head. "And that's all I will say on that matter."

The way his gaze is now pleading for me not to push the topic makes me wonder if there is more to it. If there is a hidden meaning behind his evasions. If he *wants* me to find out on my own.

"Very well…" I settle on the edge of my bed, braiding my damp hair over my shoulder just to have something to do with my hands. "While we wait for Myron, then, tell me a bit more about Carius the Cruel." Before Royad can open his mouth again, I add, "And what do they call Myron?"

A flicker of affection crosses Royad's features as he answers, "The Valiant."

I have nothing to say to that except, "Whoever gave him that name made a mistake." There is nothing gallant or brave about the creature I married. If anything, he is a coward. A *dangerous* coward. A coward who insists on marrying every year when he knows his new bride will die. Who pretends to have had a wedding night rather than putting an end to whatever horrible tradition has been kept alive by his people. "Perhaps *the Cruel* would fit equally."

Royad is on his feet so fast my heart leaps into my throat as he bends over the table, pinning me with a gaze that speaks murder. "Myron is nothing like his father. You have no idea of how *valiant* Myron is. No. Idea." I could swear I hear his teeth grind against each other. With a deep inhale, he straightens and marches to the dresser by the wall where he leans back, hands braced on the edge of the wood on each side of his hips. "Be careful how you speak about him, Ayna. He is your only hope." Blood trickles from the corner of his mouth as his sentence ends in a wince, but the words are out, and all I can do is stare.

"What's happening?" I'm on my feet and rushing across the room before I can think any better, and my fingers fall on the side of his cheek, turning his head so I can take a better look at the blood.

Royad pulls out of my touch, taking a step away and wiping his mouth with his sleeve. "It isn't Myron's fault he is a monster. It isn't his fault any of us are." His breathing is uneven, more blood leaking from his lips as he keeps speaking. "Don't expect any answers, no matter who you ask. But never stop asking." He wipes his mouth again, drawing a crimson streak over his cheek, while I stand there, gaping at the Crow King's loyal servant, who is slowly backing away toward the door. "You were chosen as a bride by Tavras because you are a lost cause, Ayna. But that's not how Myron sees it. It is because you have nothing to lose that you have everything to gain."

He chokes on the last word, hand flying to his throat, but before I can reach him, he shifts, face first, then all the way to his feet, until he is a bird twice the size of a normal crow. He flutters, and the door opens on a phantom wind.

"Wait!" My shout dies in the hallway where the guards turn their heads, pinning me on the threshold with mere stares while Royad's wingbeats disappear to the entrance hall where he dives out of sight.

Fuck that Myron doesn't want me to leave the room alone. Fuck that I am scared to death of the beaked, armed creatures tracking my every movement. Fuck that I might as well run into death's arms as I cross the threshold and bolt down the hallway to the stairs leading to the ground floor. No one attacks me as I rush past, my breathing labored from lack of exercise by the time I make it to the vast space defining the welcome area of the palace—not that anyone would ever want to visit here—so I keep going. Keep running past tall, feathered, muscled males with beaks and all-black eyes, vicious hisses following me at every turn. Ahead, the dark stone floor is lit up by a beam of sunshine, and when I follow the direction it's coming from, I notice the front door is cracked open.

Had it not been already racing, my heart would start at the glimpse of freedom.

It doesn't matter how many times Royad and Myron have warned me. When I taste the fresh air, the floral taste of summer, I turn right and bolt for the door. None of the guards try to stop me as I veer from my original path to follow Royad and approach the door. Perhaps pretending I spent a steamy night with their king was enough to hammer into their heads that I'm untouchable, but the gleaming darkness in their eyes tells me they might never be convinced.

Royad is wrong about Myron the Valiant, about me having everything to gain. But he is right about one thing. I'm a lost cause, and I have nothing to lose. So, I make a mad dash for the gap promising air and freedom.

My shoulder hits the door as one of the guards slams it shut a moment too late to stop me. My shoulder throbs, and I gasp for air as I run blindly, waiting for my eyes to adjust to the glistening sun. But I'm out. My boots pound the pale gravel beneath my feet, and my lungs pump the mild air, songbirds chirp their melody to my escape, and with every step I take, clinging onto hope becomes a tiny bit easier.

It's a good hundred feet to the edge of the forest, and by the time I make it to the first trees, my lungs are burning. My legs are shaking, and my bad hand is clutching my shoulder with all the strength it has, which isn't much, but it's better than letting it dangle freely as I weave between trees and bushes. Each step is torture, the weight of my arm pulling on the joint where it must be dislocated as I jostle it while dodging branches.

Still, I keep going, keep pushing myself to my limits. Without a weapon, and my good hand useless, I have no way to defend myself if they chase me. Bringing as much space as possible between myself and the Crow palace is the only way to save myself. Biting back winces and gasps, I move through the forest as fast as I dare without making too much noise. At least, there aren't layers of fallen leaves covering the ground the way I remember Tavrasian forests. Here, my steps are cushioned by moss and ferns, which at least helps me disguise my heavy, human footfalls.

I have no idea where I'm running or what I'll find on the other end of the forest, but it can't be worse than the prison I was taken from or the palace full of monsters I am running from, so I keep going, each heartbeat painful as I push my limits. Above me, the treetops cover the golden sun, providing cover as I thread through the underbrush.

As I swerve from the bushes into a small clearing, my foot slips on something hard, and I tumble to the ground with a curse and a gasp. My shoulder shrieks with pain, and so does my bad hand when I catch myself on it, only to come face to face with a withered skull—a withered *human* skull.

I scramble back on my haunches, half expecting for the remains of a person to attack me, but they lie silent and forgotten, and I rush on along the edge of the clearing, praying to the Guardians that I won't end up like the last human who crossed this path. I don't even dare imagine how they found their end. If this skull once belonged to a bride.

Bile mixes with the taste of iron in my mouth as I strain against exhaustion, but I don't-stop-don't-stop-don't stop, trees becoming a blur of green and brown around me as tears force their way to my eyes.

If I continue at this pace, I'll collapse, and they'll find me and drag me right back. But if I slow, they'll find me anyway.

Even with Royad's cryptic words that Crows weren't like other fairies, they are still fairies. Bird-shifting, bride-stealing, tribute-demanding fairies who are out for my blood.

Above, a shadow moves beyond the green layers of leaves. I tell myself that it's a songbird even when I don't believe it for a frantic heartbeat.

I duck under a low pine just as the shadow dives through the treetops, landing on a thick branch a few trees ahead. The bark digs into my skin as I press my back against the tree trunk, holding my breath and willing myself to keep still even when my shoulder is a pain-pulsing mess.

From behind me, a hiss calls the attention of the shadow, which hops forward out of the leaves, revealing a large, male form with feathered arms and claws for hands. I don't see his face, and I don't need to. The way he hisses and caws tell me all I'll see are feathers and a beak and soulless eyes. If he spots me down here, I'm dead, and I'm not even thinking about the second Crow behind the tree where I'm hiding.

"Come out, little bride," the one in the treetops hisses, the sound sending shivers of panic down my back while my throat slowly closes up. The feeling is familiar, similar to drowning, minus the pain. It's the fear driving me to stop moving entirely, including breathing, for if they find me, I'm dead. "I haven't tasted human flesh in a while."

I-can't-I-can't-I-can't close my eyes, no matter how much I want to make them disappear with a blink, the way I made my cell at Fort Perenis disappear during those long months in the damp darkness. If I shut my eyes for a heartbeat, I might be disemboweled before I even realize they are upon me. Then, perhaps that's the more merciful way to go. I don't want to think about the myriads of other cruel ways of killing me they might come up with.

They know I'm here, might even have let me escape, only to chase me through the forest. I wouldn't put it past them to want to make a hunt of it.

The Crow on the branch swings his legs over the wood and slides down. The last few feet, he beats his wings to buffer the fall and lands on his boots. My hiding place suddenly doesn't feel so well concealed anymore. Even if he can't see me, he might smell me. I strain my ears for a sign of the second Crow.

There, a swish to my right.

My entire body protesting from my absolute stillness, I inhale a painful breath and inch to the left around the trunk. Searing pain rakes down my arm as my injured shoulder brushes the bark, and I barely balance myself on my toes where I squat under the branches. If they can see me, they haven't given a sign, haven't lunged for me or dragged me out with their magic.

Run, my inner voice commands. *Run fast.*

The Crow whose legs and claws I can see through the underbrush is blocking the path I'd been following away from the palace and the other one…

I need to get out of here, need to make a run for it.

I'm about to tell myself that running will only get me caught faster when something sharp digs into my good shoulder, ripping me to my feet and out of my hiding place. A scream tears from my lungs, hoarse and breathless, but a scream anyway.

"Shut your mouth." A second claw falls around my face, covering my mouth so hard I taste blood. "We don't feel like sharing our meal."

Panic is no longer strong enough a word to describe what happens when he sniffs my hair, pulling me against his feathered chest. His beak clicks right by my ear, nicking the sensitive skin at the top of it, and I start thrashing in his grasp. Forget the pain in my shoulder—it no longer matters. Forget my crippled hand. I claw at the Crow's winglike arm with all that I have, the hissing, cawing laughter of both of them becoming a tapestry of nightmares to my futile efforts to free myself.

"King Myron has made a mistake letting you out of his sight, little bride."

Guardians help me, I can't-breathe-can't-breathe-can't-breathe as I struggle and kick aimlessly.

The Crow holding me caws violently to the other, and I don't need to understand the exact words to know the meaning.

I'm dinner. They're ready to slice me open and feed on my organs.

I've known fear, have fretted for my life before. But never like this. Never have I seen death on my doorstep with a vicious grin on his face like that.

If I don't manage to break free, there won't be enough left of me for Royad or Myron to find once they realize I'm gone—if they even bother to go looking. I'll be another set of bones withering away in the moss and ferns of this Seeing Forest.

The thought hits me like a rock in the head, and I go still in my captor's grasp, wheels spinning in my mind as I try to remember the Ayna who fought alongside pirates, who put their captain on his back in training, who knew how to smile and to laugh. The Ayna who had something to live for.

She's deep down there, somewhere, but as I reach for her, only the bitter, teeth-baring woman who withered in prison for almost a year stares back at me. It doesn't matter. I'll take her help as much as any other's.

I spent months observing how the fairy guards' superior senses and instincts made flight literally impossible for me, am bearing the scars on my back, on my arms, and my hands. Yet I also spent months learning to compartmentalize pain and work around it. And that's what I do.

With a scream, I distract the fairy holding me as I throw my head back into his jaw and kick my heel up between his legs. Claws rip over my cheek and mouth as he lets go, cawing a curse and hissing in pain as he reaches for his crotch. And then I'm running.

I don't look back for what the other Crow is doing. If he's following me or watching his hunting partner writhe in pain. I just bolt, cutting through the lush greenery like a blade. My shoulder is a branding iron, but I pant through the agony, clutching my hand to my chest to keep it from jostling too much while my bad hand shoves aside branches and holds onto tree trunks so I don't slip as I take sharp turns.

I no longer know if I'm running from or to the palace, don't know if I'm being followed or if my followers are already almost upon me. All I know is that, if I stop, I'm dead for real this time. So, I pump my legs, no matter how much they burn, the promise of air and freedom dangling like a spider's silk-thin thread before me. Of a moment of rest if I make it to the edge of the forest where the Crow Fairies cannot reach.

It's all I need to push myself harder, faster, my heart beating like butterfly wings in honey. I don't slow, don't give up because, if I do, it will be the end of me.

A bone-shattering roar rips the air, making me stumble over a root as I lose focus for a breath, and I'm down. My knees hit the moss between the roots—a small mercy I realize—as above me, shadows are closing in, blocking out the sun beyond the canopy of branches. My head is not as lucky.

A crack runs through my skull as I hit the trunk of an ancient oak between a cluster of pines, and the impact takes my breath away. The screaming pain in my shoulder is nothing compared to the fire burning at the back of my head as I slither down the side of the tree, hair being yanked from its roots in places. I don't know if the cry of agony lodged in my throat escapes or if I'm beyond making any sound, but when I slump over roots and ferns, blood on my tongue and death in my veins, I can't bring myself to care. All I can think of is to keep breathing, keep moving.

My whole body is an aching mess as I twist onto my stomach, pulling my legs and arms under me as I begin to crawl forward.

The sky is dark with circling birds, and I don't mean the singing kind. Their shadows block out the summer sun, painting the forest ground in twilight. For a moment, I wonder if Myron has sent his entire people to hunt me down, if he has ordered them to bring me back, dead or alive.

Then, they are diving. One after the other, they fall through the treetops like winged coals, Crows in their bird form. Their wings stir the air in a wind strong enough to lift the few fallen leaves off the ground, and their caws turn to hisses as, one by one, they shift into tall male forms.

This is it. This is how I die.

I scramble a few feet farther toward the thicket to my right, but there is no way I'll make it. No way in Eroth's realm or that of any other god.

Just as I'm ready to resign myself to my fate, another roar echoes through the forest, and all I can do is flatten myself to the ground and cover my ears as I wait for it to be over.

Wings boom, and heavy boots hit the ground hard enough to break the roots they are landing on. Silver buckles glimmer on polished, black leather as the Crows shift back into their bird forms and the shadows disperse above the trees. The ground is shaking as he steps forward into the single beam of light filtering through the gap the Crows tore into the canopy of leaves, or maybe it's that I'm shaking so hard I can no longer tell the difference, and it doesn't matter. Each breath hurts; each heartbeat is like a whip lashing through my body. The moisture in my eyes might be tears … or blood dripping from the cut on my forehead. Whatever it is, I blink it away as I lift my chin an inch to look death in the eye. And they are deep and dark and solid black as they stare back at me from Myron's chiseled face, engulfing me in eons of ire.

SEVENTEEN

Blind panic grasps me in an iron hold, and all feeling leaves my body as he stares me down from a few feet away, shiny black feathers framing his bare, muscled torso, and I force one breath after the other down my throat before I black out.

He cocks his head, gaze darting along my form, and he presses his mouth into a thin line so hard the usually rosy skin turns white. The Crows fled from him like a herd of deer from a predator, like a swarm of tuna races from a shark. And now, this predator with his powerful frame and dangerous magic is towering over me, closing in for the kill.

I've been on the ground by my captors before at the prison when I was held down while I had to watch Ludelle's blood spill at their hands. I've seen ranks and hierarchies and work from the moment I was big enough to march into my father's office.

I observed guards bending to commands for a year at Fort Perenis, watched them bow their heads at the orders of their general and fulfill their duties. But I, sure as Eroth will pull me beyond his veil once Myron gets his fingers on me, have never seen an entire people flee at the arrival of their king. The thought alone is enough to make my entire self go still, my heart to skip a beat, my breath to lodge in my throat.

What power does he hold that makes them fall in line? This isn't about royalty alone. This is something more.

Before I can make up my mind if I'm scared to death or impressed or both, Myron's features smooth into a blankness that is even more terrifying than the fury I found earlier.

I need to get to my feet to get out of this vulnerable position where he can smother me with a boot on my shoulder or break my arm by twisting it. I need a tree behind my back so I don't fall over if I manage to stand at all. I need—

Before I can figure out what I need, Myron crosses the distance between us, a blur of black feathers and contained power, and I forget to be afraid as he crouches down beside me, gaze locked on mine as he keeps holding in that rage I glimpsed earlier.

"I'm not going to ask you if you're hurt because it's obvious that you are." A black talon scrapes over my bicep where blood is trickling from my shoulder. I guess it's more than just dislocated. "The question is where does it hurt most?"

Everywhere, I want to respond, but my lips won't move. Nothing moves under the focus of the beast who now kneels beside me, hands hovering in front of him as if he's debating how to best roll me over to check the rest of my body for injuries.

His anger hasn't evaporated, oh no. On the contrary, I can sense it simmering below the surface like an ocean of embers.

But it isn't directed at me, I realize as his power sweeps along my back, up my neck, a cool breeze that doesn't belong in summer.

"Can you stand up?"

I can't even shake my head.

"Who did this to you?" His words slip through gritted teeth, and the way the ground rumbles beneath me is enough to drive a fresh surge of fear through my system.

Swallowing it down, I force myself to fake strength when all I feel is weak, force steel into my spine when I'm no longer sure I have one. "How should I know? You all look the same in your bird form." My voice is thin, one articulated breath after the other, nothing more, and Myron growls as he watches me push my palm against the ground, cringing as I wince.

"Enough." It's a command, even though I have no idea if he's telling me to stop talking or stop moving—or both. "What were you thinking?" The steel has left his voice, but the ground keeps rumbling, and this time, I'm definitely certain it isn't my shaking.

I press my palms against the moss and roots once more, biting the inside of my cheek as agony almost pushes a scream out through my gritted teeth. But my shoulder isn't stable enough, and my bad hand—I don't even want to begin to feel the multitude of familiar pain as I put weight on my crippled wrist.

Somehow, I manage to roll to the side, and an entirely new universe of agony welcomes me with needle-like clutches.

Shutting my eyes for a moment, I groan, waiting for it to pass. It doesn't.

"Wolayna." Myron's voice is insistent even when he does nothing to urge me to move.

I don't. I can't.

While I'm still debating if he'll watch me fade away right here on the forest ground, a new sort of power wraps around me—not entirely new. I've felt it when he locked me to my chair at dinner, but this time, it isn't the hard restraint of magical bonds but a gentle stroke along my side before it wraps around me, cradling me like a pair of arms.

I only realize the arms are solid and feathered when my cheek is pressed against a silken surface and I open my eyes to a layer of raven-black feathers on Myron's shoulder.

"I've got you," he whispers as I groan again the moment he starts walking. "I'm taking you home."

I know I should object, should struggle and kick and thrash until he loosens his hold on me. But much as my mind is eager to flee, my body is worn out, and the thought alone of falling from his arms and hitting the ground one more time makes new fireworks of pain explode inside my body.

Perhaps it's the head injury throbbing where I hit the tree trunk; perhaps it's exhaustion, but I don't move as he carries me through the forest, his eyes on his path like his life depends on bringing me back safely. It's the first time I see his features from up close, and the angle just emphasizes his strong jawline and brutally sensual mouth. However, it's the all-ink-black of his eyes framed in midnight lashes that I can't seem to look away from.

For a long time, neither of us speaks—he because he's so focused he doesn't seem to perceive the world around him other than that path he cuts through the greenery, and I because I'm busy breathing through the agony of each step that jostles my bones. His wind and pine scent help the slightest bit, as does the way his magic seems to build braces around each place where my muscles are failing to prevent movement. Like his magic can detect each little spike of pain and wraps around it like a bandage.

The trees aren't as dense anymore, and the sun is illuminating the silken black waves falling into his face by the time he glances down at me. The moment our gazes lock, a tingle runs through my body, and I can't help but notice how my heart picks up pace the slightest bit.

Because this is the most dangerous predator of them all, and he is carrying me back to his lair, I tell myself.

As if noticing my flash of fear, he turns away, facing forward again as his hair fades into feathers and his features turn into those of a bird. He hisses softly as he steps out of the trees, assessing the bone-white palace ahead.

Words are collecting on my tongue, questions of how he knew where to find me or why he bothered at all, but I don't voice any of them as he walks up that gravel path, steps never faltering despite my weight, despite holding me so carefully that my injuries are only minimally affected by the rocking movements of his chest against my side, his arms around my shoulders and under my knees.

He strides up the stairs, hissing at the two guards left and right of the door—the ones who watched me run out the door earlier—and they have the decency to cast their gazes downward as their king admonishes them with a single glare.

A few steps up the main staircase, my head slides onto Myron's shoulder, and I get a clear view of the line where his feathers meet the smooth, pale skin stretching over his chest. It's a fascinating detail I've never spent a moment on, but as I stare at the structure of the feathers, the way tiny, fluffy ones cover the area where the first layer of long, slender black feathers begins, a part of me is eager to touch them, feel the soft texture, the contrast between muscle and skin and the airy material coating his arms.

It must be the head injury for sure, or I'd never even notice such a thing.

At the top of the stairs, my eyelids are drooping, and my racing heart is worn out—so is the rest of me—and I almost drift off when Myron jostles me, kicking the door to his bedroom open with his boot.

He doesn't stop and set me down on the threshold, though, or sit me down on the next best chair. No, he continues walking until we are at the bed where I spent our wedding night. My throat is suddenly tight, and the shudder running through my body forces a groan from my lips as it painfully reminds me of my injuries.

Without a word, Myron lays me down on top of deep blue sheets and gently pulls his arms out from under me. I don't fail to notice his wince as some of his feathers are bent the wrong direction when he slides them free of my weight, and I can't help but reach for the patch of shiny black where they stick out in odd angles as he stands there, glancing down at me as if he has no idea what to do with me. They are an inch from my hand, begging for me to smooth them back into place.

"Does that hurt?" About to touch the nearest feather, I lift a fingertip, but Myron cringes away, stepping back a foot so he is out of reach. I have no idea why his rejection stings, but it does, and so does the war in his gaze as he keeps staring down at me, mute like a fish.

"Why?" It's a mere whisper, but it's all I can get out under his scrutiny. His beak and feather-hair recede, bringing back his human features and wavy black strands, and the tight line of his mouth and furrow between his brows make breathing difficult—as do the many injuries on my body.

"Because, no matter how much I wish I didn't care if you live or die, I can't stop now that I've started." He takes another step back as if physical distance will protect him from those words he just spoke, and whatever battle is going on inside of him is coming to an end. If I only knew which side is winning—and what he's been fighting.

He forces down a slow breath, chest expanding and feathers rustling along his arms, and I can't help noticing the strength rippling through his body as he straightens an inch, obviously remembering who he is—who he is supposed to be.

"Where does it hurt most?" His voice is gruff, but his eyes are gentle as he assesses me from a little distance, gaze lingering on my shoulder, my bloodied sleeve, then the side of my head.

Any place is as bad as the other, so I tell him it's the shoulder, which makes him return to the side of the bed and drop to his knees as he probes the side of my shoulder so lightly I am not even sure I feel it. What I do feel is the throbbing pain spreading from my dislocated joint all the way to my neck and down my arm, which has nothing to do with his touch.

"I fear I'll need to set this before I can heal you." The fact that he sounds disgruntled about the idea eases the tight knot of fear and fascination within my stomach the tiniest bit.

"You can heal people?" My voice hitches mid-word as he places his second hand flat on my shoulder as if readying to hold me in place while he pushes the joint back into its socket.

In response, he gives me a rueful smile that makes me wonder if he regrets possessing an ability that can actually help someone. "On occasion. But mostly, I am good at hurting people." The way he says it reminds me of how Ludelle used to speak about not having sailed east yet whenever the topic came up. Regret. But something more... Shame.

A curtain of silken black hair hides his eyes from me as he lowers his head, examining my shoulder with his free hand.

"This might hurt for a moment," he announces as he grips my biceps in a firm yet gentle grasp, and I hold my breath, readying myself for said pain. But before I can panic, he looks up, eyes weary but with a new sort of curiosity that I haven't noticed on him before. "If you could go one place in this world, Ayna, where would that be?"

Images of the Wild Ray flood my mind, brine filling my nose and crashing waves echoing in my memories so hard that I almost miss that he called me Ayna instead of Wolayna.

I'm about to say 'the ocean' when he pushes on my shoulder, and a surge of searing pain rips through my arm as the joint clicks back into place with a pop.

"Brute!" I shout instead, balling my bad hand so hard it distracts from the agony in my shoulder.

Myron's soft, dark chuckle is as unexpected as it is bone-chilling—and beautiful, but I don't acknowledge that. Not when he just shoved my shoulder back into its socket without a warning.

As I finally open my eyes, his all-black ones are already waiting for mine, dancing with amusement and a challenge I don't fully understand.

"Try something else, and maybe you'll land a hit."

It takes me a moment to understand he means names, but my head is clearing up as is the pain in my shoulder as he seems to be sending his power into it.

"Bastard?" I try instead of focusing on the way his grip becomes lighter, almost tender against my arm.

"Not quite there yet." He crooks a brow, encouraging me to continue.

"Wretched ass?" I strain my mind for something more original to call him but find nothing as his features flick back into their bird form. "Monster. Beast." The words are out before I can bite my tongue, and judging by the way he pulls back an inch, I have landed that hit, even when he does his best not to let me see it.

"Perhaps I should leave." He starts pulling his hand away, but I catch it with my bad one, wincing as my fingers wrap around his taloned ones.

Myron's gaze locks on mine, blatant surprise lightening the darkness for a heartbeat, and much as his bird features scare me, if I let him go now, I might never get a single answer. I might not get all healed either, but that doesn't seem as existential right now as making sure he stays to answer all those questions piling up inside my head now that the pulsing ache is retreating to the background.

I can see he's embarrassed about how hideous he is with his beak and those feathers, but he doesn't make them disappear the way he usually does, almost as if he needs them there to protect himself—a mask that will keep me away, will keep anyone away.

I don't know why it matters or why I have the courage to say what I say. Maybe it is the knowledge that he made an entire host of Crow Fairies flee so he could take me to safety—because that's what he did. He doesn't want me to die, and he doesn't want me to know that there's a Myron deep down who might not be the monster he believes he is.

"Perhaps this isn't about those beaks and feathers and talons," I say, clutching his fingers as tightly as my aching hand allows. "Perhaps it's about the fact that there is a part of you who is willing to face the wrath of an entire people in order to save me."

The beak and feathers melt away, and for a heartbeat, he holds my gaze, chest heaving as if he hasn't taken a breath in a million years. That tingling energy runs down my spine again, but before I can wonder what it is, Myron lowers his gaze to examine my wrist.

"What happened here?" He slides his hand out of mine, running one careful fingertip along my mangled wrist an inch above the tattoo where my joints are stiff and unyielding. The pain hasn't receded here as if it were impenetrable by his power.

I shake my head. "It doesn't matter."

But that only seems to bring back the fury from when he picked me up in the forest. His breath shudders as he blows it out once, twice. "Even if things don't matter to you, you're a Crow bride now, and they matter to me. If someone hurts you, they'll need to stand trial before me."

I don't know what it is about his words that touches a long-forgotten part of me deep inside of me, but a strange warmth spreads through my belly, all the way to my chest as his eyes meet mine again.

"Who hurt you, Ayna?"

Because I don't even remember who destroyed my hand—I've locked all those memories deep in my memories so I'll never see Ludelle's agonized face again when he realized we were doomed—I shake my head. "It's an old injury from when I was captured by the Tavrasian soldiers."

"From the Wild Ray."

How he knows about the ship, I don't know. Perhaps the same way he knows about my father, so I simply nod, hoping he won't dig any deeper.

"They never cared to set it in prison, so it healed crooked."

The way his free hand balls into a fist is the only sign of how angry that idea makes him. He is the one to shake his head now, and for a moment, I believe he's not going to continue the conversation, but he gently sets my hand beside my hip on the sheets and gets to his feet, the muscles in his chest and stomach rippling with the motion. "I'm sorry."

Silence stretches between us as he stares out the window, and the need to say something almost overwhelms me, but so does the way the pain is leaving my body even now when he's no longer touching me.

"You just saved my life... and healed my injuries." Even with everything he's done, I can't deny that, without him, I'd be crows' feed by now.

"After forcing you into this marriage neither of us wants." His laugh is bitter, and I'm glad he's facing away, or he'd find the same bitterness in my own features.

"So, why do it?" I'm not sure I'm asking about the marrying or the saving, and it doesn't matter as he whips his head around, locking his gaze on mine with an intensity that makes everything tighten in my stomach

"Because if I don't, I'll lose my throne."

I push myself up, muscles shaking from exhaustion even when the pain has turned into a mild soreness reminding me of a heavy workout rather than having survived a Crow attack. "If you don't save me, you'll lose your throne?"

He stares right into my eyes, black arrows so piercing I sense something come to life deep down inside of me.

"If I can't save you, I'll lose so much more than that."

EIGHTEEN

My breath catches, and my heart suddenly races for a very different reason as we remain locked in place, Myron by the window and me perched on the edge of the bed. The afternoon sun paints shadows on his face, gilding his outline of feathers.

"Why?" The question slips out in a whisper, and I don't expect him to answer, don't expect him to move, even when I wish for nothing more than to understand what I've been pulled into. I know with a certainty ingrained in my bones that I won't survive the next months, but if I have to die, I'd like to know *why*.

The silence stretches taut as Myron opens his mouth and no sound comes out.

I've seen him do that before, have seen Royad struggle the same way.

"What is it? Can't you speak?" It's supposed to be a gentle inquiry, but his eyes flash as if I challenged him.

Instead of flinching away, I get to my feet, making my way across the room one deliberate step after the other under the Crow King's scrutiny. "Why, Myron?"

Something thaws in his gaze as I use his name for the first time, shoulders slumping ever so slightly as he sighs. His feathers rustle as he takes a step toward me so there is only one foot of space between us, and I can see all the details of his human features: the ridiculously long lashes, the glass-cut cheekbones, the shadow of stubble along his jaw, the soft curve of his mouth as it draws into a sad smile.

"Did you know my people have been living in this palace for thousands of years?" He doesn't wait for me to respond. "My father had great plans on how to expand his kingdom and took great risks. He conquered land after land, used the peoples he threw under his power, so much so, one day, someone had to put an end to it."

"The Crow War?" I'm barely aware I'm speaking, too captivated by his deep, calm voice. A voice I could fall asleep listening to if he read me a story.

Myron shakes his head. "Long before the Crow Wars—the first and the second one." He glances at the table by the couch where I'd left his book next to the breakfast tray. "It was a time when there were female Crow Fae... Fairies," he corrects, and I could swear the slightly darker seam where his lips part is crimson. He swipes his tongue over them, and it's gone.

"Female Crows? Royad told me there were no female Crows."

Myron steps around me, striding toward the seating arrangement where he sits down on the night blue armchair beside the couch. His chest heaves as if our conversation is a dead weight on his lungs, so I wait, curious if this time I'll get an actual answer.

"There aren't," he eventually says. "Not anymore."

A shiver runs down my spine at the thought of what horrible event might eradicate all females of a species. Hopefully, not a series of unsuccessful marriages. "Why?"

It's the only thing I allow myself to say as I meet his gaze yet again, and all I get is darkness as he seems to dive into a past invisible to me. "Somebody deemed the Crows unworthy of living but was too cruel to kill us all right away."

My chest tightens with horror. "Who would do something like that?"

Myron gives a bitter laugh that curls around my body like tendrils of darkness. "Don't you want to know what makes us so unworthy?"

I don't dare ask.

Myron says it anyway. "Crows are known for their bloodlust, for their cruelty, for their inability to—" He breaks off, coughing so hard he might not stop again, and for a moment, I debate asking if it is the words he's trying to get out that are suffocating him or if he just choked on a feather. Instead, I swallow my curiosity, waiting for his coughing to cease and his words to continue. He's a powerful immortal who has survived hundreds of years if not thousands, he can survive a coughing fit. But when the seizure doesn't end, I can't stop myself from crossing the distance between us and picking up the half-full water glass from the tray, handing it to him. "Here."

As he finishes drinking, cough ebbing with each gulp, a film of ruby remains on his lips, the color so compelling on his pale features I can't seem to look away.

"Inability to what?" I pick up the napkin from the tray, unfolding it until I have a clean corner between my fingers, and lift it toward his face.

I've never seen Myron freeze like this. Still, like a statue of muscles and feathers, a menace of unearthly beauty who has the blood of ninety-nine brides on his hands—or his lips, I'm still undecided about that.

As I touch the white fabric to the corner of his mouth, his eyes snap to mine, genuinely frightened as if he is scared of what he might do if I get too close.

I have to admit, *I'm* scared of what he might do. Of what *I* might do if I don't figure out what's going on soon. But for now, I don't do anything other than wipe his mouth clean with a brush so light I can barely feel the pressure. A shudder rakes through him, breaking the preternatural stillness, and in his eyes, heat springs to life. Heat and a ravenous hunger that should have served as a warning.

I don't shy away, though. I don't do anything at all, napkin lingering on his bottom lip as slender veins of crimson spread from the point where the fabric connects with his skin.

"You're bleeding." I don't ask why. Not this time, when I feel the intensity of his gaze all the way to my core. Like a phantom touch, his presence wraps around me, wind and pine and devastation. His features are flickering between human and bird as if he's having trouble controlling himself, and I can no longer tell what holds me in place, fear, fascination, or his magic.

Only when my breath hitches from the tension in the air do I lower my hand to my lap, my gaze following the red-streaked napkin.

Myron intercepts it before I can touch my thigh, fingers curling around my bad wrist and talons retreating as he seems to regain control of his shifter body. The irony doesn't fail me that his grip is light like a feather.

"Don't..." His voice trails away as if he isn't quite sure he wants to speak, but he tugs my hand an inch closer toward him. "Don't turn away."

My eyes lock on his waiting ones, and for the first time, I find something more than the Crow King there. Something vulnerable, fathomless that I can't even begin to understand.

"Don't be afraid of me, Ayna. I am more than the monster you see." That speck of blood reappears on his lips, and this time, I don't hold back.

"Why are you bleeding?"

Myron's tongue flicks over his lower lip, wiping away the droplet of blood like before, but his gaze leaves mine. "Because if I say what I want to say, I won't be around much longer to save ... the Crow throne." He slides his hand over mine, fingers wrapping around my palm rather than my wrist. "Because if my bride dies this year, I won't have it in me to try another time."

Try what? I want to ask, but I'm spellbound by the way his features are fighting the feathers climbing up his neck. He's shifting. Guardians, he's shifting, and I've never been more terrified and more intrigued.

As I stare into his eyes, his feathers swim and blur until all I can see are the black voids between his lids. They threaten to swallow me whole if I don't pull away, if I don't save myself.

"I know you don't want to be bound to a monster any more than I want to be bound to a human criminal, and I would let you go if I believed there was a chance for you to survive once you leave this palace." He pauses, pursing his lips and the feathers recede from his head, revealing his black hair once more. It's such a relief to see his face entirely human again that I almost sigh. But Myron is already continuing. "Give me one year, Ayna. If you survive that long, I'll set you free."

It's the first time his words have a clear meaning. "Survive a year." He owes me so many answers I can't even count them, but what I really need to know is if he means what he says. "And then I'll be free to go wherever I want?"

Dipping his chin, he releases my hand and leans back in his chair.

"And I won't be chased by a flock of murderous shifter fairies?"

He swallows but inclines his head. "I will make sure of it."

The tightness in my stomach unfolds with every deep breath I'm taking. This might be the best chance I'll ever get, so I straighten my spine and will strength into my trembling voice. "It seems it's in both our interests that I stay alive. Let me propose a deal." I can't believe I'm doing this, but what choice do I have? No one else in this palace is going to offer me freedom. "You do everything in your power to help me survive your riotous people, and I'll play my part in our marriage. I'll play the happy bride and walk around the palace on your arm. And on Ret Relah next year, you let me go first thing in the morning."

As he lifts said arm to shake my offered hand, his feathers shimmer in subdued hues of dark purple and blue. "Deal." He gives me a smirk that makes me go over every word I've said to make sure I haven't dug my own grave before I shake with him.

I don't know what changed, but as he eyes me over our joined hands, that darkness in his gaze lifts the slightest bit, and I could swear specks of gray frizzle the black of his eye around the edges.

"You're smart, Wolayna. Smarter than I gave you credit for."

If it was meant as an offense, I don't take it as one. The Guardians know, if I want to stay alive, I'll need to work closely with him, and that means understanding the situation so I know what to do and what to avoid.

"So, what do you need me to do to defend your throne?" I'm not referencing the *so much more* part of his earlier statement because, the truth is, it doesn't matter. It doesn't matter what he has to win or to lose, or if he deserves to be on the throne. If keeping him there will guarantee my freedom, I'm all for it.

"Politics." Brows furrowing, he glances at the bookshelf behind the couch. "The Crows meet once a month to discuss strategy."

"Strategy for what?" Answers are something I have come to not take for granted during my time in the Seeing Forest, so I don't expect it when he goes into detail, the serious expression settling on his features making his human face even more handsome. I try not to let it distract me.

"When my father failed to break free from this ... limited kingdom and the crown fell upon my head, my people split into two groups. One who believes that we should continue the path my father had been walking for thousands of years, for whom the annual bride is mere entertainment, and who believes in the power of war."

"And the other?" I ask when he pauses so long I'm not certain he'll continue at all.

The corner of Myron's mouth twitches bitterly. "The other faction believes I should stay the course and hold up peace with King Recienne of Askarea."

His gaze becomes distant as he drifts to a world I cannot see in his mind.

"Royad said all nobles used to get a bride before the war," I remember, earning a frown from the king before me.

"Royad should hold his tongue before he accidentally kills you."

A startled laugh escapes my lips. This is surely a joke and a bad one at that. "I thought you said he can be trusted."

Myron nods. "He can, but even he can make mistakes."

I don't know what to do with this piece of information, so I fold my arms over my chest and start pacing the room. "So, he could accidentally kill me by saying the wrong things?" Not that it makes any sense, but I humor him to get to the core of this.

"Technically any of us could. But it might turn out deadly for themselves. Plus, most of my people would rather take the more direct approach and slice you open with their claws and beaks."

"Well, that's a comfort." I turn on my heels and march back toward the window before facing him again.

He doesn't as much as chuckle at my sarcasm. On the contrary, an echo of the fury from before spreads across his features, and I almost cringe at the power radiating from his body as he stands as if ready for a fight.

"Don't worry, Wolayna. They won't dare openly attack you after what happened today. Not if you don't try to run again, which our bargain demands you don't."

"I never agreed on not trying again," I point out, but all I get is a chuckle.

"You agreed to play the happy bride, and happy brides don't run."

Of course, he found a loophole. Apparently, I'm not the only one who's smart here.

"Happy brides also don't get drowned by a lake stored in a side room." Turning back to the window, I try to sound casual as I stroll away. Not one bone or muscle in my body is hurting now, even when I still have blood on my arm and on my face and neck and my clothes are dirty from crawling over the forest ground. A bath would be a great idea, but I'm too terrified I'll end up in that very room all over again.

Myron doesn't respond until I turn and face him again. "I already told you that door shouldn't have opened for you. It shouldn't open for anyone but the King of Crows. It hasn't opened in a hundred years."

The unease in his tone brings the tightness back to my stomach. "Why did it open for me?"

Gesturing at the shelf behind him, Myron shakes his head. "Perhaps you should do a little reading next time I leave you alone. Find out more about the history of your kingdom, Wolayna."

My jaw drops as, for the first time, he names what my marriage to him implies.

"You'll get used to it soon enough. As for now, let's get you cleaned up and take a stroll through the palace to show everyone you've made it back from your little walk safely."

With a slight bow, he motions for me to enter his bathing room—not the killing sort—and I obey, only because, the sooner we start this, the sooner it will be over. In my mind, I'm already putting together a list of things to ask Royad about next time I see him to get more background information. But for now—

On my way to the bathing room, I stop a foot from Myron, placing my hand on his feathered biceps and swallowing the sense of fear that still rises whenever I'm reminded what he is. "Thank you for saving me today."

Gracefully inclining his head, he places his free hand over mine to hold it there. "It's my honor, my queen." And in that moment, he is more than the male who I was forced to marry. More than the monster who dragged me down the hallway to his bedroom. He is more than the male who told me he'd never force himself on me and more than the king who is fighting to keep stability in his restricted realm. In this moment, he is humble and gentle and genuine.

As I finally pull my hand away and cross the threshold into the bathing room, my mind isn't the only part of me that's confused. Something deep down in my stomach has decided to remain clenched until I can unriddle the male who seems to resent what he has done to me almost as much as what the other Crows were trying to do to me.

NINETEEN

After the escape debacle, I've spent a week hiding in Myron's room whenever he is busy or I am not walking the hallways with him to demonstrate I'm still alive and supposedly happy. I don't know why he cares so much that his people believe I am, but I have been too busy drilling into any book on Crow Fairies and the history of Askarea that I can find. There is little on the Crows in those books, although I have learned that Carius killed an entire dynasty of fire-wielding fairies in order to settle here with his people. That at least explains why the book Myron read that first night keeps referencing Flames.

I also find a brief paragraph about the Ultimate Sacrifice, a ritual performed by thousands of human mages who bled on the borders of the fairylands to seal the wicked immortals in their realm. It's a comfort to think humans were once able to wield magic, and I wonder what it would be like to have some sort of power to match my enemies'. So far, my wits are the only weapon I have, and I am doing whatever I can to hone that weapon.

Myron no longer tells me to stay in his room when he leaves, and he doesn't have to. My experience with his people in the forest is enough to make me want to never leave his artful chambers ever again. However, I do whenever Royad drops by to take me for a walk.

We've rounded the palace a few times over the past days, but I haven't seen much of the *limited realm* as they call it, and today is no different. Royad and I are strolling through what must have once been the back gardens of the palace where now brambles and rocks have overpowered what must have once been roses and other flowers.

"When you said the Crows were sealed into the Seeing Forest, does that mean by magic?"

The gravel crunches beneath our boots as Royad is struggling for an answer he can get past his lips. I've had days to learn when and how both Royad and Myron appear to have trouble responding to my questions, and it seems yes and no questions are the easiest for them. I haven't pushed for why they can't say certain things. It's obvious whatever magic prevents them is eager to make them bleed for every wrong word. Even if I don't consider myself their friend, it would be wrong to make them suffer for my curiosity.

Then there is Myron's hint that too much information might accidentally kill me. I try not to dwell on it as I wait for Royad's reluctant nod. "It's always magic." He gestures around the former gardens to the seam of the forest. "The magic that ended the last Crow War is still stored in these very grounds."

It's more than what I expected, and it brings up more questions—as these conversations usually do. "Whose magic?"

He cocks his head, eyes on the clouds hanging low on the horizon where they kiss the treetops in a bath of orange sunset light.

"That of the Fairy King's mate." He swallows as if readying himself for the punishment his extended responses often get him, and I hate to see him flinch and take a deep breath.

So, I tell him what I've read instead, deciding that, if he has something to add, he'll enlighten me, or if I got something wrong, he'll point it out.

"The Flames…" I start hesitantly, waiting to see if he wants to fill something in right away before I continue. "They are who built this palace."

He doesn't correct me, so I take it as a yes.

"And Myron's father killed their entire bloodline."

"Not the entire line," Royad jumps in, directing his gaze at the bone-white walls that are the Crow palace. "Some say a few Fire Fairies got away."

"Fact or tale?"

Royad shrugs. "One can never know these days. We thought humans couldn't be mated to fairies either until King Recienne had a human mate."

I shoot him a look supposed to tear through his crypticism. "What does that have to do with anything?"

"I don't know, Ayna." The expression on Royad's face isn't what I expected, neither is the way his hand shakes as he reaches out to smooth back a strand of hair that has gotten loose from my braid. "Myron knows more about the entire mate business than any of us do."

Whatever bridge he's crossed in his mind, I can't follow. "What does Myron have to do with mates?"

Royad shakes his head in a clear sign he isn't going to answer, but his words don't disappear from my mind even when the sun settles and I'm getting ready for dinner, slipping into a black, slender satin dress that does little to conceal my curves. If nothing else, the daily meals with the Crow King have helped me gain back my weight, and my hips and chest consist of defined slopes once more.

When Myron knocks and enters his bedroom, I am standing in front of the tall mirror in the corner by the bookshelf, braiding back my hair. He stalks a few steps into the room, dressed in fitted black pants and a tight vest that draws my attention to the muscles I know lie beneath the fabric.

He clears his throat. "Ready?" And our eyes meet in the mirror, his coal-dark and endless, and my breath stutters for a heartbeat as he seems as speechless as I am. A few more strides and he stands behind me, gaze sliding over my hair. "Wear it down."

It isn't an order, but the way he catches a lock of ash blonde between his fingertips and drapes it down my back, in a gesture so tender I can barely conceal a shiver as his knuckles brush my bare shoulder, makes me want to obey. It is then that he freezes, that familiar fury filling his gaze.

I only realize where he's looking when the tip of a talon slides along my skin right next to the welded scar on my back. "Whoever did this to you will not like what I have in store for them if they ever cross my path." He pulls back his hand as if catching himself doing something forbidden, but his gaze remains on my scar.

"Your people have lost two wars against the very creatures who did this." I turn around so I can face him without the mirror in between. "If you face one of them, they might do the same thing to you."

Myron's jaw works as he seems to be searching for words. "Maybe you're right. Maybe you aren't. It doesn't matter." He doesn't step away even when the space between us feels crowded and the room suddenly is five degrees warmer. "That won't keep me from giving them what they deserve."

The menace in his eyes tells me everything about what the fairy guards of Fort Perenis should fear if the Crows ever got loose from their Seeing Forest. He smooths his features with a bland smile, emphasizing the sensuous curve of his mouth, and it takes me a beat to remember that I'm supposed to hate him, that I am here because we have a bargain.

Myron shakes his head and holds out his arm, and I slide my hand into the crook of his elbow, the sensation of silky feathers familiar and exciting on my skin as he leads me toward the door and down the hallway to the dining room. With my free hand, I comb through my hair as best I can with my stiff wrist. With everything Myron has been able to heal after the Crow attack, he hasn't found a way to repair that old injury. A few days of rest, however, have worked wonders, and I no longer flinch with every movement.

The hallways are empty, but I plaster a bland smile on my features anyway. Better to keep up appearances so I hold up my end of the bargain. I have no idea what will happen if I don't—if magic will tear me apart, or Myron, or the Guardians themselves will descend from their realm and nail me to a tree with a strike of lightning—and I don't want to find out. All I can think of is freedom. If I keep this up and survive, I'll be free.

The torches on the walls illuminate Myron's features as I study him from the side while I still can without having the attention of his court on me. If it weren't for the feathers and the occasional shift into his crow face, he'd be more than beautiful. But even the feathers don't disturb me as much as they used to.

When we enter the dining room, the Crows seated by the long, white-clothed table stand and bow the way they do at every dinner I've attended since our little bargain. I no longer cringe under their hungry stares as they glance at me over their plates of raw meat. Surely they'd prefer to tear me limb from limb and devour me for a fresh meal.

Myron doesn't even look at them as he guides me to the head of the table where he waits for me to sit before he seats himself in the chair next to mine.

The Crows hiss and caw as they wait for their king to start eating so they can tear into their own meals, but Myron takes his sweet time, making a show of pouring me a glass of wine before he takes a sip from his own glass. Naturally, I don't touch it. Fairy wine supposedly meddles with humans' minds, and I'm not allowing anything to meddle with mine while I am on display for the Crows.

"I see you have adjusted well to your new life, Wolayna," Royad says with a hint of amusement in his eyes that reminds me of some of the crew members of the Wild Ray whom I'd considered family. Older brothers rather than fellow pirates. Something about the way Royad eyes me triggers those old emotions, and I can't help wondering if I'm starting to soften up against my captors. But the truth is, neither Royad nor Myron have ever hurt me. Myron even stated he is as trapped in this situation as I am. The only question is: Do I believe them?

The way they can't seem to get certain answers to cross their tongues is proof that there is more at work than the mere cruelty of a monstrous people. If I could only get enough out of them to piece things together on my own. However, for now, I have to rely on whatever I can find within books and those cryptic hints both Myron and Royad have been giving me. I don't know what's preventing them, but I'm determined to find out. If it has something to do with those Eternal Flames I've read about in the history book Myron left sitting out for me, or if the Guardians themselves are keeping them from speaking to punish them for their cruelties—

If I believed the Guardians still cared for Eherea and its people, I might have believed that, but then, if they did, I wouldn't have ended up here, a prisoner sentenced to death by marriage.

"Myron has been helping me grow into my new role," I say with a saccharine smile that I hope convinces the predators seated around the table. I don't know how Myron chooses each night's assembly, but I'm pretty certain that by now, we've been through half of his people with the way I never see the same beaked faces twice. And, impossible as it may sound, I have found a way to distinguish the Crow Fairies by traits like a shimmer of color on their feathers, the weapons they carry, and small marks on their beaks and bare skin. Some of them have tattoos of birds or symbols of the sky inked onto their necks and chests while others are recognizable for their height or build.

Myron brushes his taloned finger along my bare forearm in silent response while he turns his gaze on Royad. "It's been quite a few ... enjoyable nights."

I want to stick my tongue out at him, tired of pretending he's the greatest lover in history, but I bat my eyes at him, sliding my hand into his and ignoring the way his fingertips turn into talons as they graze the inside of my palm.

However, I can't ignore the shudder running through my body at the heated look he gives me before he disentangles our fingers and starts eating—roasted meat, thank the Guardians. The thought of him eating like the rest of the Crows makes my stomach turn. Before my mind can come up with horror scenarios of Myron's eating habits, he leans in, nose grazing my cheek as he whispers, "Don't worry, Ayna; I don't feast on my brides."

He pauses, his chuckle running along my skin as he leans in a bit farther. "At least not the way you think."

The fork slips from my grasp as I understand what he implies, and he laughs softly, a sound of genuine amusement that I haven't heard from him before. The melody burrows deep within me like an echo of a life I've never gotten to live. The effect is intoxicating, and I can't help but turn my head so I'm face to face with him, holding that heated gaze as I meet his clear challenge. "Another thing I'll be begging you for?"

The heat in his gaze flares into a wildfire, and by the looks of it, he thinks I'll be begging him for so much more before the end. How that makes me feel, I am not even remotely ready to consider, so I tell myself that he's putting on a good show to protect me the same as I'm playing the happy bride so I won't be slaughtered at the next convenience by one of his court.

As I pick up my fork and spear a slice of well-done meat, the other Crows give hisses of relief at the sign that the meal has officially started. Their beaks tear into the raw meat before them. Even Royad has opted for the bloodier version of dinner this evening. I try not to look as he dissects a piece with his claws—because who needs cutlery when you have razor-sharp claws attached to your arms?

All the while, Myron hasn't turned back to his own plate, curious black eyes following my every movement as if he's fascinated beyond words by his new bride. Ignoring the attention as best I can, I saw off one slice of meat after the other until I finish my meal. But I can feel his eyes like a grazing touch on my skin, can sense his need to be convincing with his act of playing the insatiable husband.

Myron presides over this dinner like an emperor who's forgotten he has a people to rule, his gaze lazy and intrigued as he studies my profile while I try to ignore the monsters nibbling away at bloody meat, watching me lift my glass and take a deep drink.

"Sire," one of the Crows raises his voice in a grumbling hiss that is barely recognizable as words. I set my fork down, and Myron gestures for him to speak with a careless motion of his hand. "I heard rumors from the borders about attacks on a fairy settlement near the Seeing Forest."

The other Crows barely pause their hissed conversations to listen as they face the relatively short Crow with brownish feathers and an orange speck on his beak that I've never seen before. My focus, however, is on Myron, on the way he and Royad exchange a glance that has me concerned about the meaning of said attack.

"That's why I named you spymaster, Ephegos, so you'll bring this news directly to me." The reflections from the silver cutlery on his plate paint patterns on his face as he leans forward and braces his wings on the dining table. "What exactly do those rumors say?"

Royad is scanning the room as if he's expecting an attack right now, and his human features transform into his Crow ones within a heartbeat. I suppress a shudder. No matter how many times I see it, it's still creepy and fascinating both at once.

Ephegos pauses, eyes darting to me as if he'd rather I topple from the chair dead right now. "Can I speak openly in the presence of your bride?"

Great. I don't even have a name in these halls. At least, not in the eyes of anyone but Myron and Royad. I slide a bit deeper into my chair, painfully reminded of my childhood years when my father wanted me to disappear from his offices and warehouses whenever certain clients visited for business. With everything I know about him today, I understand that he might have wanted to protect me from his crimes. But eventually, my knowledge killed him. *I'm* responsible for his death. I'm responsible for the death of everyone I love. Perhaps ending up in a place with creatures incapable of love is a just punishment and the best protection I could ask for so I'll never be the reason someone else dies again.

Myron's responding growl slips under my skin without my permission, making me shudder yet again. "She's the current bride and your *queen*." Black talons grow from his fingertips, digging through the white cloth into the sturdy wood beneath. The table groans in his grasp. "You will do well to remember how much I resent any attacks—in word or action—against *my* bride. So, do yourself a favor and behave, Ephegos, or I'll nail your feathered ass to the wall."

The room falls so silent I can hear my own heart beating, and had it not been for Royad's reassuring glance, I might have considered bolting to my room, or to Myron's, it wouldn't matter. Anywhere out of those all-black, observing eyes that see me as nothing more than a fleeting occurrence in their immortal existences, a meal very much like the one they'd just devoured, leaving gold-rimmed plates bloody.

To his credit, Ephegos doesn't quake with fear at Myron's admonishing, his gaze steady as he holds his king's before he slides it to me. I'm waiting to see disgust there, or the hunger of the other Crows, the bloodlust, but all I find is cool calculation. "We wouldn't want that, would we?"

Whether he's asking me or the room in general, no one responds, so he continues. "My source says that someone set a shed full of fairies on fire. How they managed to lock them inside, they don't know."

"Why?" I can't stop myself before the word slips out, and now, all eyes are on me for real, death shimmering in black depths, and hisses announcing I'll pay for speaking at all when my mere existence is already an offense to most of them. I continue anyway, "Why would someone try to burn fairies?"

All air seems to leave the room as I wait for an answer.

It is Myron who eventually gives it. "The Crows have made a lot of mistakes in the past. Not everyone in Eherea has forgotten."

It's not enough to explain anything but a clear sign that Myron insists I'm not being left out. I take it and seal my lips. Maybe they'll reveal more if I let them speak rather than demanding answers they might not be willing—or able—to give.

Ephegos is about to say something else when caws and hisses erupt at the other end of the table. Royad is on his feet, as is Ephegos and a bunch of other Crows who shift and dash for the glassless windows high up in the room before Royad can caw a command.

"What is it?" I ask Myron, who has gone preternaturally still in his chair, nostrils flaring as he's scenting the room.

I see it before I smell it. Wafts of smoke sneak through the door at the end of the room, and from the threshold, Royad's curse echoes through the stone-walled space as he faces the enemy the rest of the Crows have fled from.

TWENTY

Fire. I slip from my chair, reaching for the water jar a few seats down, and run to Royad's aid. I lived on a ship long enough to see fire for more than a threat. It's the literal death of a sailor if not put out immediately. If fire spreads on a ship, the crew is lost. There is no window to climb out of, no shelter to find. It's either death by burning or death by drowning.

My heart hammers in my chest as I pick up a second jar on my way to the door. My bad hand barks in protest, but I put up with the weight and continue my path. The dress makes big steps difficult, but I don't stop. I can't. It's ingrained in me to fight a fire before it can spread, and if smoke like this is already leaking through the hallways, it must be a massive onslaught of flames raging out there.

"Ayna!" Myron's call is an echo in the background as I reach the threshold, almost bumping into Royad's broad shoulder as I try to catch myself. "Stop!"

The sight in the hallway isn't what I expected, and I don't know why that still surprises me. There are no flames, no people throwing buckets of water at their burning home; no one is running for safety. Instead, the hallway is filled with smoke and nothing but smoke, the origin hard to spot through the density of it, but I can make out the overall direction.

"It's all right, Ayna." Myron is at my side in an instant as I turn back and forth in an attempt at understanding what's happening. "There is no fire." His hand falls between my shoulder blades, and I still at the unexpected touch, the warmth of his palm. This isn't a demonstration for his people to convince them that this is a real marriage, but—I don't have it in me to ponder what else it could be. The air rushes from my lungs as the smoke hits us, and I launch into a coughing fit the likes of which even the strongest of storms never managed to give me when they shoved themselves down my throat on the Wild Ray.

"Breathe, Ayna." Myron's magic is invisible, but the way it pushes the smoke back isn't, and it is all I need to be able to draw a deep breath. My breathing calms, but Myron's hand doesn't slip from my back as he works against the tendrils of haze, which retreat down the hallway until, at the corner, they collect around one single torch.

"Fuck Shaelak," Royad exclaims, his claws balling into a facsimile of fists, his features tightening with both fear and fury.

It is by far not the most important question to ask at that moment, but I'm not ready to ask about the smoke and the torch, so—"What is a Shaelak?"

Myron's hand slides from my spine, and Royad's head whips around, eyes narrowing as he realizes I've been standing there all along. "Shaelak is an ancient god. None who would have followed us to Eherea, so you probably haven't heard of him."

It's the most unfiltered statement I've ever gotten from him, and there's not one single drop of blood appearing on his lips, so this must be a safe topic—or as safe as anything can be in this realm.

Also—"If you pray to a god who isn't native to Eherea … where exactly are you from?"

Both Myron and Royad are still as the rocks lying at the bottom of the ocean as my gaze bounces back and forth between them, and I'm ready to put that topic into the collection of those they are reluctant to talk about when, from behind me, the growl of the spymaster rumbles through the empty dining room.

"It's not as important where we're from as long as we know where we're going." His gaze is waiting for me as I whirl around to face the scary creature who has brought nothing but bad news so far.

"Where *are* you going?" I'm not certain whether he means it metaphorically or if he has an actual location in mind.

Ephegos's eyes are calm as he glances to Myron for permission to speak. The latter gestures at the relatively short Crow—just an inch or two taller than me—and gives a small smile. "Wolayna, meet Ephegos, one of the most skilled ward breakers among the Crows and my spymaster."

Ephegos shudders, and the feathers seem to drop from his features, as does the beak as he shifts in a flash, leaving his claw-tipped winged arms the only sign he's actually a Crow. His slick, rye-blond hair is bound at the nape of his neck, and his chest and abdomen are as impressive as Royad's or Myron's. I keep my eyes on Ephegos, meeting the male's gaze as he dips his chin in a gesture of respect. It's the first time anyone here has done that, so I'll take it.

"Pleasure to meet you, Ephegos." I try my best smile, earning a huff from Myron and throat-clearing from Royad.

To his credit, Ephegos ignores both males, striding over and throwing his arms around me as with a long-lost sister. My heart stops beating until the shock dissolves and I realize he isn't about to tear me to ribbons or hack my eyes out with his beak.

With a chuckle that evokes an innate sense of safety with this fairy, he pulls away, holding me at arms' length, careful to keep his claws from cutting my skin where he wraps them around my shoulders. "If I may say, you're even more beautiful than Myron told me."

The warning hiss shooting from Myron's throat makes me like Ephegos even more.

"Interesting. He hasn't told me a thing about you," I joke, my lips curving in response to the infectious grin he's giving me.

"Myron tends to downplay the truth, and I swear it *is* the truth in your case." Ephegos cocks his head as he looks me over.

"As for you, not so much," Myron cuts in, sounding more annoyed than genuinely upset. "That's probably why I didn't bring you up. Plus, I tend to not advertise the existence of my spies."

Letting go of me, Ephegos saunters to Myron's side, patting the king's feathered shoulder as he laughs. "Are you sure it has nothing to do with not wanting to keep from her the incredibly handsome Crow that I am?" He winks at me, but it's not the sly, hungry way I've had men wink at me as they devoured me with their eyes. It's more like he is sharing an inside joke with me. Which, I have to admit, takes me by surprise even more than the sound of Royad's snort-laugh. I don't know where I ended up, but this is not the fortress of doom I was brought to with the prospect of losing my life as a bride. This is a glimpse at a friendship, one older than my existence. At a bond I hadn't believed possible among beaked and winged monsters.

I need to sit down before my legs give out at what I'm witnessing.

"I'm sure that's why." I give him a wink of my own to conceal how much I'm struggling to come to terms with this entirely new side of the Crow King and his two friends.

"See?" Ephegos gestures at Myron as if to make a point. "Perhaps we should let the brides choose their Crow husbands after all. Perhaps this dazzler would have a healthier color in her pretty cheeks if she got to experience what a Crow lover can do."

"Shut your filthy beak, Eph," Royad snaps, but there isn't any bite behind it. "She'll think we're all savages."

"Aren't you?" I throw into the group, wondering if this time I've gone too far, but Royad bursts out in laughter and Ephegos claps. The only one remaining silent is Myron, whose face has gone even paler.

"The two of them certainly are," he says without as much as a hint of humor. "Besides, my females haven't complained in centuries."

"That's because you haven't had a female in centuries," Ephegos points out with an all-too-cheerful grin. He shakes his head at Myron before wrapping his arm around the king's shoulders and pulling him to his side as if he's about to share a secret, then says loud enough for me to hear, "That's all right, Myron. Perhaps next year's bride will prefer your brooding darkness over my outstandingly sightly self." He gestures down his front as if to emphasize those muscles and tight leather pants. As he catches me watching, he raises a brow at me in mock scandal. "No peeking, Wolayna. Your husband won't like that."

Myron groans with exasperation. "Remind me again why I keep you in my court?"

All Ephegos does is nudge his king's shoulder with a fisted claw. "That's why you made me your spymaster. It keeps me well away most of the time."

I'm not sure if they're joking, but Royad's amused features tell me there is no imminent danger the two of them will tear each other's heads off, so I refrain from worrying unless there's a real reason—like a hallway's worth of smoke originating from one single torch.

"What happened out there? And why did the others all flee?" The table is a mess of abandoned cutlery and knocked-over wine glasses. A few chairs fell when the Crows leaped to their feet and shifted.

"Because they're cowards, that's what they are." Ephegos's nose wrinkles in disgust as he scans the scene. "And because there isn't much any of them can do against a real fire. They have magic, yes, the base version of it. Nothing as powerful as Royad's or mine." He stalks toward the end of the table, bracing his claws on the backrest. "And, of course, like Myron's. As Crow King, his magic is unparalleled. Only the Fairy King and his mate can match his power."

Before I can interject what exactly that *mate* business means, he continues. "Feathers burn easily, Ayna. Any Crow would do well to flee."

"But you didn't." It's a simple observation. "Neither of you three did."

"Because we care." Myron is the one answering this time, and the weight of the world seems to be resting on his shoulders as he sighs. "We still care what happens to these people."

"Even when you've given up on—"

"Shut your beak, Ephegos." This time, a clear threat reverberates in Myron's tone as he cuts Ephegos off. It's not only a symbolic statement since he flicks his fingers and Ephegos's face shifts back into that birdlike mask that I will never get used to.

Shock tightens my chest, making it hard to breathe as the momentary lightness leaves the room, but Ephegos's words linger.

TWENTY-ONE

"What does that mean?" I step into Myron's bedroom where he shuts the door behind us and drops onto the deep blue couch with a groan resembling a frustrated cat rather than an actual crow. I don't relent. "What did he mean? What have you given up on?"

Myron shakes his head, eyes firmly closed as if that will make me go away. "It's nothing that should concern you, and he shouldn't have brought it up."

I don't take the time to examine why his words hurt after seeing such a different side of him down there. "Well, he did. And now I want to know." With a few quick strides, I'm across the room, perching on the armrest on the other end of the couch from where he's half sitting, half lying on the blue fabric.

One eye opens, then the other, as if he's hoping I am a bad dream that would evaporate if he pretends to wake up. "You're asking the wrong questions again, Ayna." His voice is flat. Tired. As if those centuries have crushed a part of him he can never get back. But I saw him smile in the dining hall. Saw that spark of humanity in him that I'm not ready to let go of.

"Talk to me, Myron." I slide onto the cushions of the couch, staring the Crow King down as I wait for him to give me a comprehensive answer. He's been evasive since the moment he dismissed both Royad and Ephegos and insisted we go upstairs before we talk about anything.

Now, we're here, and I'm not backing down even if he bleeds for his response.

"Everything seems to revolve around the fact that you are marrying once a year. And you seem less than happy to do so. You even told me you don't have a choice. Royad's cryptic statements about the Crows *getting only one bride instead of many as before*. What does that mean? How does it change anything for you and your court? Why is it so essential that you marry anyone if you apparently don't care—"

I stop myself as his gaze locks on mine, and I realize I just answered my own question.

"Because you no longer care about marrying. That's what Ephegos was going to say. That you no longer care about marrying. Am I right?"

Myron's features darken dangerously as he slowly sits up, leaning over me until I'm pinned to the armrest between his massive wings. Feathers pull in around his neck, climbing higher until his face shifts into bird form. His all-black eyes lock on mine, silent depths denying me answers. His feathers brush along my bare shoulders, my arms, as he tightens his grip on the backrest on one side of me and the edge of the couch on my other side, and an involuntary shiver chases down my skin.

He's trying to scare me, trying to shut me up by petrifying me with his monster form. And though he's intimidating as Eroth himself, I've glimpsed the real Myron in the dining hall. I am no longer afraid of this monster before me—even when my instincts tell me that death is just a talon swipe away. Because he is still deadly. His beak, his talons, his magic—all of them would mean my end if he decided to dissect me.

For a long while, we stare at each other, his bird face inches from mine. I don't budge. No, I swallow the lump in my throat and lift my bad hand, tracing the feathers on the side of his neck.

Myron holds so still he might have turned into a statue, and I could swear I can hear his heart thumping in his chest—perhaps it's mine, though. When he doesn't cringe from my touch, I gather more courage, something I believed I'd lost the day I'd watched the crew of the Wild Ray slaughtered in the prison yard. It's an emboldening sensation, tingling through my body with an almost-compulsion to slide my fingers along those silken feathers again.

I don't question the feeling, just follow that impulse, raising my finger to his cheek where hues of black, sapphire, and purple shimmer in the soft glow of the fairy lights.

"Am I not disgusting to you? You should be terrified to be so close to a creature like me." Myron's words crack between a hiss and a caw, and I should be repulsed by the sound of it, by the sight of his bird face, the beak that can tear through flesh. But I shake my head.

"I'm not afraid of you."

I can feel his shudder under my fingertip, even in his cheek. And as I keep staring into those depthless eyes, his features are clearing, one feather after the other receding. His beak disappears last, leaving behind that handsome face hidden beyond the nightmare of his Crow form.

There's something about the way he looks at me that reaches deep into my core, and as I hold his stare, heat blazes behind those onyx eyes. His breath is a gust of warmth on my face, and his scent wraps around me in a wave of wind and pine and something more that I can't quite place. I'm acutely aware of where his stomach presses against my thigh and hip as he leans over me, the hardness of his body against mine, and instead of wanting to flee, an ache to explore the solid muscles of his chest builds inside of me.

And that is before his gaze drops to my mouth and his throat bobs as he is clearly holding back words he shouldn't be speaking or simply doesn't want to. I don't care.

I hold my breath as I wait for him to shy away, to slip back into the role of the grumpy king and push me away, but he surprises me with a long inhale that makes me feel more naked than the slightly revealing dress actually is. It's in the way his eyes light up as he seems to scent me, the way he pulls his lower lip between his teeth as his hands wrap even harder around the edges of the couch.

"Tell me to leave you alone, and I will. Tell me that you don't want to be so close to a monster, and I won't even bring up how much I want to kiss you right now." My breath hitches as his voice lowers into a near growl. "One word, Ayna, and I'll be gone from this room until my head clears and I no longer think of what one single touch of your fingertip can do to me. Just tell me to leave, and I won't bother you again. I won't even suggest that you might want to be bothered."

He holds his breath as he waits for my response, but I'm too engulfed in his scent, in his very presence, for me to say anything.

All I do is lift my head and line up my mouth with his until our breath mingles and the tension in my core threatens to tear me apart. When my lips touch his, it's not a gentle kiss. It's the pent-up anger and despair, the hope I've not allowed myself to feel in weeks. It's rough, and Myron's ragged breathing washes onto my tongue, taking all words and thoughts away. He groans as I nip on his lower lip, and I could swear I hear the couch fracture in his grasp. But he doesn't lower his weight onto me, he doesn't push more into my space. His hands remain braced at my sides and his feathers spread with the angle of his arms.

Heat pools in my core as his mouth molds mine into a mind-numbing kiss, and I become weightless and boneless as his tongue glides along my lower lip, requesting entrance.

He tastes like sweet wine and mint, a surprising blend that explodes in little bursts on my own tongue, and I moan as he sweeps through my mouth, taking me deeper and deeper until my breathing is shallow and my head is spinning.

My fingers have made their way to the front of his vest, tracing the contours of those muscles I was aching to explore only minutes ago, and Myron makes a sound deep in his throat that is half pleasure, half exasperation.

"Ayna." He squeezes my name out between kisses. "Stop."

I hear him, but my hands don't. They slide higher to his neck, tangling with the silken strands of his hair, and Guardians, does it feel amazing when his mouth crushes down on mine again.

My lips are burning, and so is the rest of my body as I arch into him, my chest pressing against his hard one as I strain to turn my hips so our bodies line up.

"Stop." When he says it this time, it is a growl of warning similar to the one he gave Ephegos in the dining room. "Stop, or what leash I have on my monster form will snap and—"

He doesn't finish the thought, and he doesn't have to. It's there in his eyes as he pushes himself up just enough to meet my gaze, the fear, the embarrassment, the vulnerability.

So, I don't push him. Not on this. Because there are a whole lot of other things to push him on that will take my mind off what just happened.

"If you hate the idea so much, why marry at all?"

Myron gives a grim chuckle that I've learned to recognize as the harbinger of a new enigma. "I already told you I don't have a choice. Not if I want to keep my court intact. Not if I want to appease the faction who believes the Crows have a better future. Or the others who want to keep the tradition upheld as a demonstration of our cruelty."

He's still leaning over me, wings braced apart, but the heat is gone, even when there's a part of me that keeps demanding I study the mouth I just devoured in detail, that I remember every last sensation of whatever that moment was.

"And what about the attack Ephegos talked about? Why would killing any fairies hurt the Crows?" I hadn't gotten sufficient feedback in the dining room before the smoke assaulted the hallway—another riddle I want an answer to. But one after the other.

Myron sighs and sits up, picking pieces of blue fabric from his fingernails as the talons retreat. I don't dare glimpse left or right to see what happened to the cushions of the couch.

"After my father's death, when we were unweaving the wards King Recienne had placed on my realm, some of my people—the ones who believe everything is righteous the way it is and brides are no longer needed—spent their nights haunting the females of the nearby villages." He gives me a long look that should have explained everything, but I can't bring myself to think what he's implying. I can't go there in my mind because that makes those monsters even more despicable than I initially thought. "Not all of the females survived the night, but some did, and they bore younglings from that one encounter. If what Ephegos says is true, those half-Crows are the only ones someone who hates us might be after."

Horror spreads like a bitter tang in my mouth, eradicating Myron's pleasant taste, and I close my eyes to drive the images out of my mind—images of burning creatures, winged or non-winged, it doesn't matter.

Perhaps the lake in the spare bathing room isn't a curse after all. Considering how violently it tried to smother me, it would do away with a set of flames easily. Of course, I don't mention that to Myron. Instead, I ask the only question I can ask.

"If you can unweave wards and leave this forest, why not do so? Why stay here?"

Myron remains silent for a long while, and I start to believe he won't answer. Yet, before the tension in my stomach destroys me, he nods as if in agreement even when he tells me that the wards aren't the only thing keeping them here.

I try to wrap my mind around his response but can't find a reason why they wouldn't leave when they initially came from somewhere else… But that's a topic for another day. Right now, all I want to know is why they haven't left a long time ago. "So, what does? What keeps a strong and powerful people like the Crows in this tiny forest?" I don't mention that I experienced the forest as anything but tiny when I tried to escape its borders.

"We lost a war, Ayna." Myron's gaze wanders the room until it lands on the door to the murderous lake. "Two wars, actually. My father was too cruel to make a real attempt at saving his people. He relished pain and fear too much to care about what happened to them. Let alone his brides." A long pause fills the space between us, and I can almost hear the whimpering and screaming of the females who've come before me, the thrashing and gasping as they fought for their lives in this very room.

"But you are not like that." Fingers shaking, I place my good hand on his wing where his forearm would be. Myron's head snaps around, and his eyes lock on mine, full of doubt and disgust for the creature he is. But that isn't true. If I've learned anything in the past days, it's that Myron the Valiant is more than a torturing monster. Yes, he might be that to his enemies. But not to me. "You are better than your father."

His chest heaves as I wait for my words to settle, as I count my own heartbeats while I wait for him to say something.

Eventually, he shakes his head. "And still, I'm not enough to save my people."

It's the blunt conviction in his tone that tells me he actually believes it, and despite everything—despite the fear and horror I've gone through since I came to this place—it breaks my heart that he thinks so little of himself.

"I thought everyone was responsible for saving themselves." It's a weak attempt at making him feel better but an attempt worth smiling through as I wait for him to look me in the eye.

As he does, a tingle runs through my body that has nothing to do with the beauty of his face and everything with the devastation on his features.

"Perhaps you can, Ayna. But I no longer can. Neither myself nor my people." That he'd admit to weakness like that... Or is it just a belief? After over a century of ruling and marrying one bride after the other, stuck in this forest with no real prospect of escape, I might believe I can't save anyone as well. Not that I could ever save him. He is a magical creature, powerful and strong and at the top of his species. He doesn't need saving.

Maybe he does, a small voice at the back of my head tells me. *From himself.*

TWENTY-TWO

My boots click along the stone floor as I hurry down the corridor at Royad's side in an ensemble of black pants and a lace-trimmed black tunic that are supposed to make me feel more comfortable as I step under the eyes of Myron's court for my very first political meeting.

Two weeks have passed since the incident with the smoke, and I'm none the wiser, even when Royad and Ephegos spent hours briefing me on the ongoing conflict between the factions. At least, now I understand that some Crows believe that Myron will lead his people to freedom while others believe that freedom is something to be taken and Myron is a fool for negotiating for it in parts.

Ephegos brought me a book about the second Crow War, which I devoured even though my heart bled at the details of how the majority of their people were slaughtered by the fairies before being locked into the Seeing Forest yet again.

It also held a chapter on how the Crow brides used to be tormented by their crown, which supposedly was a cursed item of magical power that made the brides pliant by digging into their minds and rooting in their free will until nothing of the women was left. Not a fun prospect now that I think about it, but Myron hasn't tried to put a crown on my head, so I take it he prefers I have my own opinions. He wouldn't need a manipulating crown to force me to do anything anyway. His magic is enough to direct my body like a human puppet.

Yet, he hasn't as much as touched me with that power since he used it to lift me into his arms in the forest. I'm not sure what to think of that.

"They'll be talking first and drinking later," Royad announces as we head down the stairs. His brown hair is fanning out behind him as on a phantom wind, and I can't help but smile at the male as he glances at me sideways with the usual warning in his eyes.

"I won't touch the fairy wine," I promise.

"At least not until you're back in Myron's room. I don't care what happens there." I'm not sure I like the undercurrent in his words.

Nothing has happened between Myron and me since the night we kissed. He's been the perfect gentleman behind closed doors and the monstrous king before his people. Neither of us has brought up the kiss even when I can't help acknowledging his rock-hard abs every time he walks the halls without a vest. It's my favorite look on him, and I am not proud to admit that sometimes I catch myself imagining what it would feel like to touch him without fabric shielding his skin from my fingers.

"Even if he was high on fairy wine, he'd never take advantage of me like that." I say it under my breath, but Royad catches it anyway.

"I wasn't talking about him."

I roll my eyes at him, pretending to be more annoyed than I actually am because, maybe, it would be nice to lose control for once. Maybe, it would be freeing to forget who I am and where I am and what my outlook for the next few months is. It's bad enough Myron has been sleeping on the couch every single night since our wedding, even when I offered to switch. I'm shorter and I'd sleep comfortably there as well, while Myron's legs fall off the couch every once in a while when he stretches out completely.

Whereas… I'm not certain what would happen if I drank fairy wine. Would the spark that comes to life inside of me every time I catch him looking at me be my doom?

Before I can examine the topic any further in my frayed mind, we make it to the throne room where tables are set up in two rows at the front, long side facing the main door we are entering through. Seated with their backs to us are ten Crows, and at the table running through the room in parallel, ten more sit like there's nothing more comfortable than a hardwood bench in a drafty stone hall.

At our approaching footsteps, they turn their heads from the throne at the head of the room to study us, some with disdain in their all-black eyes, some with curious interest, and some with that hunger that makes me want to turn and run for my life before they can get their claws on me.

But there is one thing overruling my fear more than the thought of another round of chase in the forest: Not all of their faces are all bird. A few of them show hints of human features; others have shed their beaks and feathers in exchange for their human faces—and the ones who show their actual faces are all unearthly beautiful. Even if they are scary beyond comprehension.

Among the human Crows—for lack of a better word for them—I spot Ephegos near the end of the table. Beside him, a seat is empty. He waves and gestures for us to come over, and Royad follows his summons with a grim expression on his face the way I know him, but I can see the twinkle in his eyes he's trying to hide as he walks up to his friend and slides into the seat. Which leaves me the only one standing... Well, not the only one.

Atop the dais, by the throne, King Myron the Valiant stands like a regal statue, his face cast in shadows by the tall canopy of gray and white fabrics falling around the back and sides of his throne. His boots are polished to perfection, as is the silver pendant on the leather necklace that rests on his hard chest—his *bare*, hard chest. I swallow the sudden dryness in my mouth.

He doesn't speak a word, merely holds out his hand in silent invitation, and I don't hesitate as I walk up to him in measured strides that I have a difficult time keeping slow enough not to seem eager and fast enough not to seem reluctant. I don't look over my shoulder to the Crows who are all watching me. My attention is bound by the intensity of Myron's gaze as he lets it slide along my curves like a caress, and I suppress a shiver of awareness at the memory of what his body feels like pressed up against mine.

As if reading my thoughts, his mouth tips up at a corner in a smirk that makes him the cruel king he wants to be seen as but tells me more than anything else that he remembers, too. That he remembers the heat of our mingling breath, the sensation of my touch. I stumble up the final step, almost hitting my knee on the hard stone of the floor, but Myron's talon-tipped hand catches me by the elbow, pulling me back upright so we stand with mere inches between us—and my heart is pounding like a war drum announcing an enemy onslaught.

"Careful, Ayna." Myron leans in, whispering so close by my ear that that shiver finally breaks loose. "Or someone might think you are actually attracted to your husband."

Swallowing the rush of flutters in my stomach, I turn my head a few inches so I'm at his ear, letting my lips graze the sensitive skin of his earlobe, and I could swear the reason he nearly crushes my hand in his grasp is because he is fighting a growl as I whisper, "We wouldn't want anyone to be so wildly misled, would we now?"

Before he can respond, I pull back, circling around him to his throne, and perch on the armrest, leg crossed over a knee to block his path to his seat, and blink up at him innocently.

Someone snickers—Ephegos, perhaps, I don't turn to check—and Myron's mouth stretches into a grin that seriously has me considering what that expression would taste like if I licked it off his face. Before I can get carried away, I reel my thoughts in and gesture for him to sit next to me—on his throne or on the other armrest, whichever he prefers.

Myron does neither. Instead, he strolls around me, boots clicking like a counter-beat to the drum that is my heart, and comes to a halt behind the throne, bracing his hands on the backrest.

"As you all can see"—he glances down at the attentive Crows, and I tell myself I shouldn't be staring at him with outright fascination, but it fits my role as the good little bride, and I can pretend it's just for show—"my beautiful bride is joining us for today's meeting."

Beautiful. I don't know why I blush, but it's not because he called me beautiful. I can't care about what he sees when he looks at me.

"My bride, your queen, has shown interest in the politics of our people, and these meetings are a fitting opportunity to introduce her into the customs of our people."

"Not that she needs introduction into your cruel ways," a female voice states from the other end of the room, and I whip my head around so fast I'm sure I sprain a muscle.

The whole room seems to hold its breath as we collectively stare at the female in the doorway. Her copper hair flowing down her shoulder like burning metal seems to be the only part of her that's moving as she takes in the collective of us and how we're staring at her.

"Am I coming at an inconvenient moment, King Myron?" She tilts her head, and I notice her pointed ears, the angle sharper than that of the Crows' ears. She swaggers forward, a smug grin on her face that seems about as real as the expression of calm I pin on my lips, but then, anyone walking into this lair of monsters needs an armor of their own.

"To what do I owe the pleasure, Princess Cliophera?" Myron doesn't move from his position behind the throne, but the way he bites out the words tells me everything I need to know about how pleased he is to see her.

In the ranks below, the Crows have gotten to their feet, claws at the ready as she marches past them like a female on a mission.

"My brother has urgent business to attend to," she drawls as she makes it to the end of the table where she perches on the edge between a silver goblet and a bottle of fairy wine. Her black leather armor makes her look like anything but a princess, as do the multiple blades sheathed along her hips and ribs. A warrior, and a fearless one at that, or she wouldn't just stride into a room full of Crows like they were pets in cages. "So, I took it upon myself to see if this year's bride is still alive."

Her gaze meets mine across feathered, clawed monsters, fine, crystal goblets, and stacks of paper scattered along the two long tables, and the luminous green of them takes me by surprise so much that I nearly forget to keep my face impassive.

I haven't seen normal eyes—eyes with whites around the irises—in almost two months, and I could cry and scream at the same time to see another female in a home of males. Even if it's just for an hour.

Those eyes shutter as she looks me up and down, and I wonder what it is that makes her react that way, like there is something wrong with me.

"What a beautiful one you've chosen this year, King Myron." She hops off the table, so graceful it's hard to believe she's real as her hair flows behind her like a streak of fire, and swaggers down the center between the long tables, all Crow eyes glued to her every movement.

Whether she intends to bind their attention so all-encompassing, I can't bring myself to care. All I can do is stare at the female myself with her energy rolling through the corridor between males until she stands at the bottom of the dais, inclining her head to me. "Queen of Crows."

Unsure of how to respond to her greeting, or whether she is mocking me with the gesture of respect, I stand and take a step forward.

For now, it doesn't matter if she is friend or foe. She's the first person I've seen in what feels like forever who isn't a Crow and whose interest appears to be in my well-being rather than in my demise. So, I'll take it.

"Princess." I imitate her gesture in what I'm certain is a clumsy dip of my chin rather than the regal motion she performed.

"You're alive and well?" She leans forward a few inches as if that will give us privacy in our conversation, but I'm acutely aware of the way every last male in the room is hanging at my open mouth, waiting for the words about to tumble off my tongue.

I swallow them—that I'm devastated, that I'm beyond scared of what my future holds, that I don't expect to survive the year even with Myron's promise he'll let me go first thing next Ret Relah if I continue to play the good bride. That I nearly died too many times, that internally I've been dead since the day the Tavrasian soldiers slit Ludelle's throat. That the only reason I still stand here is that I might not deserve to die peacefully after all the crimes I committed.

Instead, I blow out a slow breath, keeping my gaze on her sparkling jade ones. "Define well."

Behind me, Myron chuckles, a sound so low I barely hear it, more *sense* it deep in my bones, as if his approval were a living, breathing thing snaking along my limbs, granting me support.

The female laughs a chime-like laugh, and I can't help thinking that it's the most beautiful sound I've ever heard. She's the first female fairy I've come across, and the way her features light up with momentary amusement is almost painful in its beauty.

But instead of responding to my demand, she turns to Myron. "What a spirited one you've chosen this year."

Myron's warning hiss sears through me even though it's not meant for me, and I shudder as his bird voice rustles by my ear. "It's not like I have much of a choice in whom I take as a bride, is it?"

At that, the princess's face sobers. "Be grateful that you're getting one at all. My brother has been way too generous."

From the corner of my eyes, I notice Royad and Ephegos reaching for the swords at their hips. I hadn't thought anything of it when Royad showed up armed to pick me up for the meeting. He carries his blade around the palace whenever he escorts me. But it's the first time I actually see him ready to use it.

"Oh come on, Roy. Keep your little blade where it is. I'm not going to attack you. I know the bargain my brother has made with your king."

It dawns on me then that she—that Princess Cliophera—must be the Fairy King's sister. The Fairy King who waged war against the Crows a little over a hundred years ago.

I can't even begin to describe how mind-boggling it is to stand in a room full of creatures from history books—history books I've only recently begun to read, but still—these were creatures defining the fate of this realm in one way or the other.

Royad's hiss tears through my thoughts. "You're not welcome here, Princess."

My hair stands at the back of my neck as I watch my bodyguard turn into a killing machine ready to slaughter the obviously very dangerous fairy in front of me—who simply shrugs his comment off with a chuckle.

"Perhaps I'm not welcome, but at least, I care about whether your brides live or die, considering I should have once become one of them."

My gaze darts to Myron, who confirms with a nod, his bird features on display like a mask of protection. I didn't see it before, but it is clear to me now that the king behind his throne is wearing an armor of his own when he conjures his feathers and beak and talons—which are digging into the backrest of the stone throne now, leaving little dents between the carvings.

I try not to think about what strength he must hold if his mere fingertips can destroy ancient rocks.

"And what a lucky princess you are that you escaped that fate." Myron's tone is relatively bored even when the rest of him gives away how on edge he is.

"Lucky indeed. Your father wasn't a creature to be wed to. Especially with that horrible crown…" She exaggerates a shudder and winks at me as if to tell me she knows exactly what she's doing by upsetting the Crow King. "As for your current bride… She seems a bit … human."

I can't place whether it's supposed to be an insult or a simple assessment of a fact. Myron, however, steps around the throne, his feathered arm pressing against my shoulder as he stands beside me. I don't flinch at the contact even when a million conflicting sensations are running through my body right now.

"That doesn't make her any less." Much as I want to say they don't, his words surprise me. The fact that he stands up for me does. This is still the cold, uncaring king he wants to display in front of his people, yet he shows weakness by showing that it doesn't matter to him what I am. And I have no idea how to feel about that.

"I never said it did." The Fairy Princess strides to the side of the dais, taking in the rest of the room before she faces Myron once more. "Now that I know your bride is in glowing health, I might as well pass on my brother's message and inform you that, if you don't keep your people to the confinements of the Seeing Forest, there will be repercussions."

A hiss runs through the row of Crows, and I nearly ask what she means by that when Myron's hand wraps around mine in warning, and the contact momentarily distracts me on a level that makes it impossible for me to speak.

"My people *have* been remaining within our borders," the Crow King tells her with such authority that I would have believed him even knowing that it's a lie. Ephegos has been spying on the nearby villages for signs of malignant activities and found burned-down sheds and stories about dead half-crows.

Princess Cliophera's gaze lingers on Myron as if waiting for him to admit to the lie for long moments. When he doesn't speak, she shakes her head. "Consider yourself warned. Recienne isn't in the mood for a third war, and if you can't keep your people in line, he might as well take away all your privileges and see you slaughtered by his armies."

It's a bone-chilling threat. One that I can feel reverberating through Myron's body as he leans half an inch closer, his warmth swallowing me up even when ice slides down my spine at the look the fairy gives us.

"If my people disrespect the bargain, I might as well slaughter them myself." Every last fiber in my body tells me that he means it. He'll kill his own people if they disrespect the agreement he made with the Fairy King for the benefit of peace and that one bride a year—that one *chance* a year, as Royad had called it.

As I stare from him to the princess and back to him, something shifts inside me, and I realize that this one tiny detail is what made him bleed that day when he'd shared it. A chance.

Brides are chances. And this year, the chance is me. If only I knew what for?

I put it on the list of things to ask Myron and hope he won't choke on the answer—while working myself to hold the princess's gaze as it lands on me.

"I hope to find you alive and equally well the next time I check in," she says before she turns on her heels and saunters back to the door without as much as a dip of her chin.

The Crows hiss at her as she marches past, and Royad and Ephegos draw their swords, ready to hurl them at the fairy though she doesn't bother to spare anyone a glance, as if her power exceeds all of theirs. Probably, it does, or this arrangement with the Fairy King would have long ended.

When I turn to gauge Myron's reaction, I find his all-black eyes resting on me, an unease tightening his once more human features that ties a knot around my stomach, and I know that whatever he does or doesn't know about what's going on at the borders of the Seeing Forest, none of it scares him as much as the questions burning in my mind—and that I might actually ask them the moment we're alone.

TWENTY-THREE

My skin is still prickling where his wing pressed against my arm when I sit in one of the chairs he had brought onto the dais after the fairy left. I scan the Crows discussing the most recent developments in hissed and cawed statements while trying to ignore the itch to steal a glimpse at Myron's face while he is focused on the meeting rather than on me. He sits a few feet away from me in the other carved chair instead of his throne, listening patiently to the demands and claims his people make.

While the rest of the Crows broke into a clamor the moment the fairy walked out the door, he explained to me in a murmur that the King of Askarea likes to check in on the Crows every now and then and that he likes to remind them that this bargain is at his convenience. I don't know what sort of king would do anything like that, but then, I'd expected all Crows to be monsters, yet I found myself in the middle of a triangle of friends who seem to not want me dead as much as they want something else from me. What that is exactly, I have yet to find out, but it all seems to have something to do with the way they keep referring to my role as a bride.

Myron's eyes snap to mine, and I realize I failed at keeping them away from him. A small smile lingers on his lips that is slightly out of character for the cruel king he intends to portray, and I can't help noticing how much more regal it makes him look, how good, even with the wings, as if the self-loathing monster he believes himself to be has retreated to give him a break.

Before I lower my gaze back to the conversing Crows, I give him a tiny smile of my own and watch his eyes go wide for a heartbeat as they warily follow the movement of my lips as if he can't believe I'm actually smiling at him.

"It doesn't change a thing," Royad's baritone carries above the hisses, drawing my attention back to the conversation. "If the high fae believe we've broken the bargain, they'll send Shaelak himself after us."

Again—that mention of a foreign god that I have never heard of, a reminder of how little I belong with this species who either need me or hate me or both. Something clenches in my chest at the thought that this is the only reason I'm here. Not because anyone wants me here but because I'm part of a bargain I never agreed to. I'm a tool to be used, a pawn. Nothing more, nothing less.

A bride. A *chance*.

"No one is leaving the Seeing Forest." Myron's smile has disappeared as he rolls over the rising voices. "No one but Ephegos and his spies."

Ephegos inclines his head. "We have more reports of fires in the surrounding villages," the spymaster reports, ignoring the caws of upset from the Crows at the other end of the table.

"We've been locked in here for too long, my king," one of them hisses, and I can tell by the flash of anger in his eyes that he is one of the faction working against Myron. "If we don't get out of here, we will be forgotten by the gods."

Myron's tone is like ice as he answers, "Maybe we should be forgotten by the gods."

Gods. How many gods do they think there are? Eroth and the one they call Shaelak. But the Guardians aren't gods. They are Eroth's children.

Before I can dive deeper into the topic, another Crow caws his anger, and the feathers flare as two of them get into a hissed argument. I don't understand a word as their features and bodies become more and more like those of birds, and eventually feathers are flying through the air as they rip at each other with their claws.

"Silence!" Myron thunders, a streak of silvery power flashing across the table and shattering one of the goblets next to the fighting Crows. They jump apart, shifting back into their more human forms, lowering their heads before their king. Because that is what Myron still is—no matter what they believe they can do to him. And I think I'm starting to understand that the faction against brides is the faction that deems a king unnecessary too. They are savages who want to scour the realm for any advantage they can get and take as they please—riches, land, women.

As I am wrapping my head around how deep the cleft between the two fronts truly is, I can't help but wonder why the other faction would hold on to a king if they obviously strive for freedom. Freedom—it hits me then, how much those creatures and I have in common even when some of them won't hesitate to do whatever they can to see me dead if it means it hurts their king.

Another thing strikes me in that moment, and the room around me vanishes as my gaze snaps to Myron: There is a part of the Crow King who will be devastated if I die, and I am not sure it is because I am just another bride wasting away in his care, another proof of his failure. Or if it is something more.

When I trudge up the stairs next to Ephegos an hour of listening to political hick-hacks later, the Crow is oddly quiet. I'm not complaining that he isn't throwing me smiles the way he usually does when my mind is preoccupied with the nagging sensation that Myron isn't the only one who cares in this marriage neither of us wants. I don't know what to do with that revelation, so I shove it to the lowest depths of my being and tell myself that the warm feeling when I think about how the Crow King might actually care about *me*, not because of what I am but because of *who* I am, is actually only lukewarm at best.

"Those meetings really are a pain." Ephegos finally breaks his silence as we reach the hallway leading to Myron's room. His gaze slides along the carvings on the walls, a pensiveness I haven't noticed before taking over his features.

"What do the Crows hope to win by ridding the world of their king?" It's a simple question, but I already know there's no simple answer.

And that's what Ephegos tells me right before he places a claw on my arm as he stops us both in the middle of the hallway. "I like you, Ayna. You're good for Myron. But most of the Crows don't see it that way. Even if he might have returned to his old self—more than he has been in decades—it's not enough to change anything. We're still stuck in the Seeing Forest by his bargain with the Fairy King, and we are still stuck in these hideous—" He lifts an arm, beating it up and down in a display of his thickly feathered, capable wings.

His breathing has become shallow and his complexion paler than the usual golden. There is no blood on his lips, though, so I assume he hasn't spoken anything that will kill him.

Driven by curiosity as much as fascination as I stare at the feathers lining his arm and neck, unfolding over his features as if to hide them until his nose and mouth turn into a beak with an orange fleck on the side, I whisper, "You can shift into the full shape of a bird." Because I've seen them all do it. "But can you shed those feathers and claws completely?" My hand shakes as I lift it to touch his forearm, sliding down to his wrist where the feathers thin until a set of long, sharp claws emerges from the layer of shimmery black.

I could swear Ephegos isn't breathing as his beak opens and closes, grabbling for words or for air or for something else entirely—courage perhaps.

Eventually, he shakes his head. "Not in millennia." This time, as he speaks in the growly hiss that is his bird voice, a droplet of crimson drips from his beak, and I know I've asked something of substance. And he was willing to suffer to give me the answer I sought.

I don't stop him when he continues walking but follow all the way to Myron's door where he shifts back into his human form long enough to open the door for me and give the two Crow guards left and right a warning glance.

"Stay in here," he tells me before he turns, that pensive look back on his face that makes him appear less like the humorous friend I've gotten to know him as and more like a male pondering a walk to the gallows.

As he turns to leave, I grab his shoulder lightly. Instead of halting, he spins around like he's ready to fight, his reflexes so fast my heart leaps into my throat as a whip of magic cracks in the air right beside my head.

Ephegos's eyes are wide, whether it is because he was genuinely expecting an attack or because he can't believe I so casually touched his monster's arm, I don't know. He blows out a slow breath, eyes shuttering a few times as he reels back his power at the lack of danger.

My heart thunders in my throat, but I swallow it down and give him a small smile as he relaxes. "What can I do to help?"

At first, he doesn't seem to understand that I want to know if there is anything I can do to help them out of whatever this mess that seems to be their people's existence is even if I am still lacking the exact definition of how everything fits together. I know something is wrong. Something that's keeping them from telling me the truth. Like a spell cast upon them to stew in their own misery without the ability to ask for aid.

So, I offer it. No matter what it implies, it must be better than watching these two fronts fighting each other internally—than to see the only three people I have left in my life torn apart by it. Ephegos obviously is, and so is Royad every time he tries to answer my frequent question and bleeds for it. And Myron…

I don't even want to begin thinking about the Crow King. He is an enigma of feathers and beauty, of malice and gentleness. And I'm starting to believe that he could be so much more if only he was set free from that spell.

"Stay in his room," Ephegos says with an unreadable expression on his face. "Stay here and survive. It's the best you can do. Time is what will help." The last word is a wince—which is all the confirmation I need that I am on the right track. But Ephegos is bleeding from the corner of his mouth now, and I don't dare push when I have the distinct feeling that he'll answer whether it'll kill him or not.

So, I squeeze his feathered shoulder then pull my hand back, holding his gaze as his eyelids flutter until the shimmering sheen of wetness leaves his gaze.

There has to be something I can do. Maybe Ephegos can't tell me, but I'll find out anyway.

"Tell Myron to come up soon." I add a smile to what is supposed to be a request from friend to friend, not an order by his queen—I'm still struggling to come to terms with the thought of being the Crow Queen. No one calls me by the title, and I pretend it doesn't exist.

At my change of topic, Ephegos relaxes, and he wipes his mouth with the back of his claw. "I'll tell him you're waiting for him, but he'll be busy for a while."

I don't ask with what, and Ephegos doesn't offer any more explanation. When he finally turns to leave, he stops mid-motion, glancing at me over his shoulder. "I'm sorry you're trapped here with us, Ayna. You deserve better than this."

TWENTY-FOUR

His words follow me into the room as I close the door in the guards' faces. They heard every last bit of the exchange, and judging by how they cock their bird heads, they are as curious about what Ephegos meant as I am. But it's not for them to know, so I retreat into the room and settle on the edge of the bed I've been sleeping in for weeks.

Yet, it's not merely what Ephegos said. It's the entire meeting, the entrance of the female with the copper hair, the way she seemed surprised that I'm still alive. The warning she delivered and the raging discussion it triggered among the Crows. And most of all, Myron.

Since there is no way to stop my circling thoughts, I push back to my feet and start getting ready for bed. Maybe a shower will help clean off the day and rinse away all unclarities as to how I can do anything to help Myron, Royad, and Ephegos.

I'm halfway to the bathing room door when dull screams from the hallway catch my attention, and instead of continuing into the promise of a hot shower and relaxed muscles, I pivot to the door leading from the room. There, I lay my ear on the carved wood.

Outside, pounding footsteps rush along the stone tiles. Is that the clinking of metal against metal?

My pulse picks up speed, matching the pace of the Crow's boots. Not in all the weeks I've spent in this palace have I heard anything like it. Not even when the smoke assaulted the dining room and they all dispersed. They merely turned into birds and fluttered to safety.

This is different. There is fighting going on, I'm sure of it.

Everything inside of me readies for battle even when I haven't done proper exercise since the day I was shoved into the cell on the Tavrasian ship taking the crew of the Wild Ray to Fort Perenis. I don't know if I can even remotely handle a blade with my bad hand—the hand that used to be my dominant one, but now is nothing but a supporting act in everything I do.

It doesn't matter when the sounds draw closer and the shouting gets louder. A crash and a thud make me shrink away from the shuddering door, and I am positive, whatever happened out there, the next time something hits the wood, it will jump off its hinges or simply splinter in my face.

So, I step back, searching the room for one of the daggers Myron sometimes leaves sitting out during the night—to have a weapon at hand to defend himself in case someone breaches his room or to give me the option to slit his throat in his sleep, I don't know. But does it matter when I won't kill the one person who promised me freedom?

A flash of metal catches my attention as I squeeze between the bookshelf and the armchair Myron left pushed back from its usual spot after falling asleep reading there, and sure enough, I find a short dagger tucked between the cushion and the armrest as if Myron put it there when he made himself comfortable. I won't go so far as to think he left it there for me to find.

With a motion so familiar I barely feel the months without combat exercise, I pull it free of its sheath and weigh it in my palm before I return to the door, studying the carved wood while my attention is split between the noise from outside and the feel of an actual weapon in my hand.

A scream splits the air, and even dampened by the material separating the hallway and the bedroom, it makes me jump. I can't go out there if there is an attack—by the king-hating faction of Crows or otherwise. But I can't stay here and wait for them to make it to the door either. If the sounds are anything to go by, my guards are probably already dead, and there is nowhere to hide in here. I'd be easy prey.

As I stare down the door that is both my protection and the barrier keeping me from an escape from whatever is raging out there, something inside me comes back to life. At first, it's a flicker, nothing more than a spark, but I recognize the fire of Pirate Ayna I used to be, the one who swung across railings to hijack a merchant ship—or even the Tavrasian royal fleet. A sense of adventure surges through me, and my body remembers how to fight.

"I can do this," I whisper to myself. I've fought on narrow banisters and in close quarters, have overpowered soldiers with nifty tricks when my own height and weight would have put me at a disadvantage. I'm quick and skilled, and even if my muscles have atrophied without the regular workouts and the malnourishment in prison, I have gained back weight and strength over the past weeks at the Crow palace.

My good hand tightens around the dagger as I listen hard and reach for the door.

It swings open with ease as if any magical locks were ripped off with that last blow—not that Myron ever locked me in. I'd tried several times when he left me alone in here, and never once has he done something as horrific as put me in another prison. But with our new agreement, I would never even dream of sneaking past the guards he put by my door.

Except, now the guards are knocked out left and right of the threshold, and the hallway is filled with a familiar smoke snaking down the length of the stairwell. Featured outlines clash with human shapes in leather armor adorned with pieces of metal, which catch the suspicious orange glow that definitely doesn't originate from the torches spaced out along the walls.

I duck, suppressing a cough as smoke fills my lungs, and press against the wall so I'm half-hidden by one of the thick columns along the side of the hallway. One step after the other, I creep forward, careful not to make a sound. The Crows' have superior senses, and I don't want to be caught by them because I fail to be careful, but the attackers are no Crows, and I have no idea what their senses are like. I don't want to find out for sure.

A few more steps and I'm in the alcove with an improved view on the shadows in the smoke, and I don't like what I see. Blades are being driven into Crow necks as well as into those of the attackers. I haven't made out individual faces, but I don't need to in order to fall into outright panic. Whoever the attackers are, they are strong. Fast. And fucking scary. Each movement is deadly, precise, and each gurgling caw grates along my bones with a flavor of horror.

In return, the Crows bring down as many of the attackers, painting the hallway in eerie crimson in addition to the glaring orange the source of which I haven't made out but need to. Whatever it is, it seems to correlate with the smoke, just as that day in the dining hall. No fire—at least, not yet. Even though my instincts scream at me to find a source of water and prepare for all eventualities, I remain where I am as I glance around for a safe path. If I want to escape with my life, now isn't a good time to draw attention to myself by blindly scrambling through the smoke in search of a water source.

So, I keep my dagger raised at my side while I inch toward the other end of the alcove, eyes on the hallway where the tumult slowly dies down.

Just as I reach the end of the carved columns marking the corner, readying myself to sprint to the next alcove, a hand lands on my shoulder, ripping me out of my vantage point so violently I would have stumbled had the fingers not held me in an iron grasp. The scream in my throat dies as a second hand falls over my face, cutting off my air supply, and I am back in the secret bathing room with the murderous lake where I was struggling for air when the water had other ideas. The familiarity of the panic is as surprising as it is stunning. It doesn't matter how many times one fears suffocating; it never seems to get any better—or easier for that matter.

But what it does is get me thinking. Instead of blindly thrashing the way I did in the lake, I gather my wits and slam the dagger into my captor's forearm with a swift movement. I don't care if it's a Crow or one of the others as long as I get free. The lack of claws, though, tells me it's one of the others, and the suspicion is confirmed a moment later when I'm released and a human voice curses in tongues I'm not familiar with. I wheel around, bringing my dagger to the attacker's throat while they are still bemoaning their injury. But the male has his blade under my chin the same instant, and for a short, heart-pounding moment, we both stare at each other. He has normal eyes—dark irises in a bed of striking white, not all-black like a Crow.

Time seems to stand still as he debates what to do with me, as *I* debate whether to push the tip of the dagger into his flesh and make a run for it. He might be pondering the same question for all that is worth, for his lips curve into a pleasant grin—pleasant and equally deadly—and he moves back so fast I don't have a chance at following through with my attack, his leather armor rugged and the metal pieces on his shoulder blood smeared. His short, black hair is streaked with blood as well, and I wonder how many Crows he's killed on his way to the residential levels of the palace.

"What do you want?" I ask instead of trying to attack, but he shakes his head, lifting his curved blade to strike, and my heart stops as I manage to block the blow an inch from my neck.

I'm not proud to admit I'm outmatched. Even with my years of fighting soldiers and skilled sailors who know how to defend their ships. Whatever this fairy is—and I'm certain it is one with his pointed ears and hauntingly beautiful features—it is as bad as the Crows with their claws and magic. Only, this one will use a wicked blade to destroy me.

With a grin, I kick out, hitting the fairy's knee, and watch him retreat a step with gritted teeth. He hisses a laugh that reminds me no less of the Crows than their bird voices.

I don't wait for him to strike back. Instead, I spin around and run.

TWENTY-FIVE

It's a blind chase through smoke, my feet slithering across blood-slick tiles, hands grappling for walls and columns as I race past a corner. Half of me is grateful I didn't slam right into it while the other half is urging me to go faster, faster, faster. At least the corner will knock me out rather than slit my throat and watch me bleed out slowly. I hope that's the worst the fairy will do.

I'm about halfway down the hallway, the smoke drawing closer and closer around me, when the fairy steps into my path as if it has been waiting for me to show up. How it got there so fast, I don't even want to know. My heart is in my throat, as is everything else—my hope, my soul, my life. About to spill onto the floor with one careless breath.

I hold it in, forcing calm into my veins.

There is none.

And as I ready myself to fend off a new blow, to turn and run, to do anything and everything other than die, the fairy raises his empty hand.

At first, I think it is to gesture for me to come closer, but a streak of fire surges from his fingers, lashing out at me. I'm shoved out of the path by a feathered creature. Blood fills my mouth as I bite my tongue at the impact on the hard stones, at the weight pressing me flush against the surface, and this time, the air leaves my lungs in a gust. I spit and gasp while heat sears past me. Closing my eyes fast, I count my heartbeats. Struggling against the body on top of me won't do me any good right now when it protects me from the fiery assault, and I can barely grasp that whoever is covering me with their chest and limbs might as well go up in flames themselves.

A groan in my ear informs me the Crow is alive—and in pain—so I pray to the Guardians, to Eroth, even to that god, Shaelak, to whom the Crows keep referring, to make the fire stop.

It's not the gods who free us but the fairy who must have bolted after burying us in flames.

The Crow slides off me in the fire-free hallway, and I turn my head to the side, wondering what Crow wouldn't delight in my death.

Ephegos's pained eyes stare back at me, and I realize his feathers have been singed all the way to his skin, leaving a pattern similar to a barren winter forest on his arms. Arms that look more human now that they are lacking the layers of silky black.

"By the Guardians—" I cough into the fading smoke and scramble to my knees, dropping the dagger as I try to figure out how to help him.

"It's nothing," Ephegos grits out, trying to push himself into a sitting position. But his arms are weak, and his breath is shallow as he asks, "Didn't I tell you to stay in Myron's room?"

I don't have a chance to respond or to thank him for saving me, for he collapses in front of me, and a wall of flames surges up from the stairwell, and I finally know why I couldn't see fire in the hallway to begin with: it was confined to the lower levels by whatever magic the attackers possess.

But now it is here, eating up the space and the bodies scattered along the stone.

I tug at Ephegos's claws, urging him to wake up, to run with me, but he isn't moving. Isn't even breathing, and I have a moment to wonder if he is just one more Crow whose life was ended by the fairy attack. To wonder if Myron and Royad are among the fallen Crows, too. Then the fire rushes toward us like a tidal wave, eating up everything in its path, and there is nothing I can do but run.

The fire is fast. Faster than my human legs, the distance a few feet shorter each time I check over my shoulder. I'd like to run for the nearest window, for an unaffected stairwell, a nearby door. Basically, anywhere but back to Myron's room. But it's the only free path, and I really want to live.

I haven't realized how much I want to live until the fire closes in, backing me farther and farther into what used to be the only safe space in this palace.

A glance at the table tells me there isn't enough water in the jar, and there's no vase or other source of water. The basin in the bathing room might be enough to wet my clothes and hair so they don't immediately catch fire.

But if I'm honest, there is only one place in this room where I might not die by fire—I might drown though, and that is almost as horrible a prospect.

Almost.

Especially with the flames licking past the threshold.

It is enough to help me make my choice as I dart across the room, dagger forgotten and begging any deity who would listen to save me.

Only, there is no god interested in my survival. When I tear at the doorknob, it doesn't budge, doesn't move as much as an inch. Neither does the door.

"Come on, come on, come on." I throw my full weight in—which isn't remotely enough to level a solid wooden door—and hope for a miracle.

The flames have reached wooden panels along my side of the wall, but they are spreading toward Myron's personal library—the only source of information that won't bleed to death or suffocate when I ask questions—and I see red. My panic is overpowered by a surge of adrenaline, and as I throw my shoulder against the door once more, the wood gives, and it swings open, granting me entrance into the chamber of death.

But the stone room isn't the only thing waiting for me. As if a creature of sentience, the water is climbing from its dark bed, sneaking toward me in tendrils of crystal liquid. My throat closes up as if I'm drowning, but the water isn't coming for me. As if sensing my rage, it grows taller and taller until it forms a wall behind me that equals the flames in both its fearsomeness and its power.

I ready myself to be eaten up by it as it lashes out.

Not a droplet hits my skin as it parts like a curtain, washing around me and filing through the door into the bedroom where it puts out the fire in a life-taking embrace. Spellbound, I watch as the smoke turns into steam and the steam turns into rain and the rain falls back into the puddles collecting on the hardwood floor. Larger and larger they grow until they marry into one mirror-like surface that covers everything between the burnt wood at the other end of the room and the toes of my boots.

Something at the back of my mind tells me to run, but I don't have another step in me, my abused lungs worn out, my heart near exertion, and my limbs shaking as I wonder if that's the price of the Guardians' mercy, if I'll pay with my own life after all and running has been in vain.

Then the sound of footsteps splashing through the water draws my attention, and my eyes snap to the dark shape tearing through the spilled lake.

It's the last thing I see before the world turns to night.

My eyes barely open when the rustling of feathers wakes me what could be minutes or days later. I assume it's minutes since my bladder isn't killing me this time. The room is dark except for a low-hanging fairy light hovering near the couch where my head is propped up on a pillow and my legs draped over the armrest.

"Good morning." Myron greets me with a half-distressed, half-gentle tone as I peel my eyes open and tip my head up until I find him sitting behind me, one wing draped over the backrest so the feathers fall over the edge and out of view, save for the outline of his long, muscled arm.

The sight brings back images of Ephegos's singed feathers and the way he threw himself into harm's way to protect me from the onslaught of flames—how I left him behind—and shame fills me top to bottom before I can even wonder what happened to him.

It's really nothing to wonder about; he sacrificed himself to save me.

Ice slides down my back, and I shudder even in the toasty warm room, which I recognize as Myron's bedroom.

The Crow King's human features are painted with shadows from the way he angles his head to look down at me. "Are you in pain?" Without moving the wing on the backrest, he brings his other hand to the side of my face, hovering there for a few, long breaths before he grazes them along my cheekbone. "Here?"

It takes me a moment to understand that he is asking me if my face hurts where he touches it, the sensation of his skin against mine so surprising that my mind shuts down momentarily.

"You have a cut right here." His fingers slide up to the corner of my eye, outlining the injury.

I don't know why disappointment fills me as I realize that's all he's doing, that he isn't touching me because he ... wants to. And I shudder again at the bitter taste that fact leaves in my mouth.

"I'm all right." With all the reserves I have left, I push myself into a sitting position, swaying a little, although I'm not even trying to stand up.

Myron's wing slides from the backrest, circling around my waist instead as he stabilizes me before I might slip off the couch like a dead weight.

"Doesn't look like it." I can't help but recognize the modicum of humor snaking into his voice as he looks me over. "You look like you bathed in fire."

I want to object, want to correct him that the last element washing over me was water, but my clothes are dry, and so are my boots—as if I never stood between the murderous lake and the wall of fire going after Myron's library.

"What—" My head bounces back and forth between the soot-stained walls and the immaculate hardwood floor. "What happened?"

When my gaze finally settles on Myron, his all-black eyes are already waiting for me, both pain and fury fighting for the upper hand, and for a moment, I believe he is angry with me. But his gaze softens as our eyes lock, and a crease appears between his raven brows. "You tell me, Ayna."

"Ephegos took me to your room, and then I heard noises outside, in the hallway." I glance at the intact wooden door, closed to protect our privacy in this room where Myron dared to be himself more than anywhere else in the palace. "They were coming closer." The thud at the door springs through my head, drawing me back into the fear of an unknown attacker. "I slipped outside to have at least a chance at running in case they made it through this door. But when I got out, someone captured me. A male, not a Crow. A *high fae* male."

Myron's expression darkens as if I just told him the Guardians themselves had come to snatch me from the palace, but he says nothing even when his mouth twitches with proof he has plenty to say.

At least, at first, he's quiet. Then, he tilts his head, silky hair sliding over his neck as he heaves a breath of determination.

"First—Crow males are *males* as well as any high fae male." He straightens an inch, and I can't help but notice the way his muscles tighten on his stomach, the expanse of his shoulders, feathered or not, and the unmistakable masculinity in his whole appearance. The strong jaw, the sharp cheekbones, the heavy brows—one slanted, one cocked— accentuating his pale features. And that mouth…

"And second—"

I'm suddenly very much aware of the heat of his wing around my waist, the deadly strength keeping me close to his side so gently I wonder if he believes I'm made of glass. Of the way his tongue flicks over his lower lip as he watches me study him.

"Second?" I prompt, but I barely get the word out because he pulls me against him, those sensuous lips hovering an inch from mine. His breath is all mint and fairy wine, and I want to taste him so badly I forget I was just dragged through fire and water.

"Second—" He brings his free hand back to my cheek, thumb grazing down to the corner of my mouth, gliding along my lips. They part in invitation, and I nearly moan at that simple touch. Myron's fingers curl into my hair as he cups my face, gaze glued to where I'm pulling my lower lip between my teeth to stop myself from kissing him. "I don't like when someone touches my wife." His voice is shaking at that last word. *Wife.* He's never called me that, even when we'd been officially married by the Ceremonial. "Someone other than me."

His eyes are black fire, and his skin against mine sizzles like the aftermath of lightning.

But before I can read into it, he pulls back as if remembering something—a role he's playing, a vow he swore, or the self-loathing I've observed creeping up on him so many times. Whatever it is that keeps him from kissing me right now, my body turns cold without his touch, my chest aching at these first signs of rejection.

"No." It isn't more than a whisper, but it gets Myron's attention, as does my hand catching his and leading it back to my face. I don't press it against my cheek, though. Instead, I swipe my mouth along his palm, my eyes never straying from his. "Don't do this."

"What?" He sounds as breathless as I feel as I thread my fingers through his.

"Disappear." For lack of a better word. It's what he always does. Either it's the spell preventing him from speaking freely, or it's him holding in the male who is kind to his friends and who has done nothing to lose my trust. I didn't gift it to him when I was brought to this Godsforsaken palace as a forced bride, but he earned it anyway. And, no matter how much I hated him in the beginning, there is something growing between us, and I can't point my finger if it is just that undeniable attraction overwhelming me or if there is something more. "Don't disappear into that armor you've built around yourself. I'm not afraid of you."

His eyes flare like burning stars as he brings his mouth down on mine, and I don't hesitate to meet him with the same intensity, my lips molding around his firm ones as we move in a dangerous dance of heat and desperation. It's there in every kiss, in every breath, in every touch as his hand knots in my hair, fastening my face to his while the other one brushes down my arm. I remember I should feel pain where the fire singed me earlier, where the fairy pressed his blade against my throat, but all I can feel is the need to sink deeper into him as his hard front crashes against me. All I can do is hold onto him, fingers sliding into his feathers as I grab onto his shoulders, knot my arms behind his neck, anything that will keep him right where he is. Anything to keep the fire burning away that facade he's so expertly built.

Not a monster but a king with a burden so heavy it has split his people. A king with a spell keeping him from naming the curse he's living.

"Ayna—" He moans my name as we come up for breath, but I nip his lower lip, inviting him back into our dance, and he follows with a groan that makes my core tighten. My whole body is on fire, whatever weakness had me swaying replaced by the excitement of being kissed by him, of being touched. My own hand finds its way to his front, contouring his chest, his abs, and his hands fall away from my hair and neck. I want to protest, but he grabs my hips, pulling me onto his lap so I straddle him on the couch, and his fingers slide lower, cupping my ass as he rolls his hips.

My mouth goes desert dry at the hardness straining against his pants, and for a breathless moment, I debate reaching for those leather strings at the front of his pants and unlacing them, but my hands get sidetracked by the ripple of muscle in his chest, and I trace patterns over his bare skin instead, my mouth back on his and my tongue exploring his taste while heat pools between my thighs more with each answering stroke of his tongue.

Until our breathing becomes ragged, and his hold on my flesh near painful.

"Stop," he grinds out between kisses, the way he's devouring me indicating he wants me to do anything but that.

In response, I lower my head to his neck and lick up the side of his throat.

Myron's hips roll again, and he makes a guttural sound, reminding me that I might be playing with fire pushing him.

"If you keep this up, I won't be able to stop, Ayna." He throws back his head, resting it against the couch as I graze my teeth along the soft skin running from his neck to his shoulder—to where feathers form the beginning of his winged arm.

"Maybe I don't want you to stop." I'm not at all sure if I mean what I'm saying, but the way my body reacts to his touch is like a command, like an ancient call that makes it all but impossible to take my hands—or my lips—off him.

Myron's hands slide back up my hips, along my waist, my shoulders, until he is cupping my face between his palms, and gently pulls me away from him. "Please, Ayna, not like this. Not when the Flames just attacked the palace. Not when my *friend* died defending my wife." He clears his throat. "Not when you barely got away with your life."

The torment in his eyes softens the blow of rejection, but I can't help reeling in the heat inch by inch, and with it, the warmth spreading in my stomach at the thought that he might have wanted this just as much as I did a moment ago.

As I climb off his lap, my whole body is shaking as if remembering the exhaustion, and whatever pain I might be lacking on the outside echoes inside my chest like a reminder.

ANGELINA J. STEFFORT

TWENTY-SIX

"The Flames?" My mouth is dry for an entirely different reason now as I settle on the other end of the couch, a good distance between us so I can keep my calm as he points me right back to the horror of devouring flames and Ephegos's shape disappearing in a curtain of fire.

Myron inclines his head, all emotion wiped from his features as he smooths back his hair with his hands. His feathers shimmer in the dim light as if gilded by fairy magic. "Flames. Fire Fairies. The people who used to live in this palace."

"Thousands of years ago," I add. At least, that's what I read in his history books.

"Thousands of years ago, before my people slaughtered them and took their home for themselves." I can't help but notice the bitterness in his tone. "My *father* led the attacks, not me, in case you're wondering."

"I'm not." Because I know by now that Myron would do many things, but he wouldn't slaughter an entire people just to make a new home for himself.

For a few fluttering heartbeats, our eyes lock, and I could swear a shimmer of emotion swirls behind layers of all-black, but he sighs, and it's gone. "The Flames built this palace. Every last torch you find in here is part of their magic—everlasting fire."

As I let that sink in, my gaze snaps to the candle on the table. Not a single flame is dancing in this room.

"Apparently, my father wasn't thorough when extinguishing the Flames forever because, over the past decade, the attacks have increased. And I'm not only speaking about the attacks on the palace. Houses burn—entire villages—where the remaining Flames wander. I don't know if they merely want their home back or if it's a personal vendetta against the Crows…" His words trail away, his gaze intent on mine as he studies my reaction, waiting for the fear to surface in my expression, the horror. But I'd experienced enough horror during those months in prison. I've nearly died too many times to shudder at the mention of an enemy who invaded the only place in the world where I have people I can trust. Only two of them now that Ephegos is gone.

A deep sadness overcomes me instead, and I lower my head, the weight of what happened crashing down on me.

"Ephegos knew," I whisper. "He warned me to stay in your room."

Myron shakes his head in silent denial.

"He warned me, and I didn't listen." The realization clenches my stomach like those razor-sharp claws most Crows fashion at the end of their wings. "He saved me, Myron. If I'd listened to him, he wouldn't have needed to save me, and he'd still be alive." Guilt washes through me, taking the familiar path the months after Ludelle's death have carved out inside of me, the years of shame that were my childhood chiseled from my culpable self. My father is dead because of me. Ludelle and the crew are dead because of me. Ephegos is dead because of me. I might not have known him that long, but he was a smiling soul in the darkness of this realm. Someone who brought information. Someone I trusted.

Myron's gaze weighs on me like rocks dragging me underwater, and no matter how much I want to, I don't dare meet his eyes for fear of finding the same conviction in them that is tying me to the bottom of the ocean. But he leans toward me, hand finding mine in a tender cradle.

"You weren't the one who killed him, Ayna. That was the fire of the Fire Fairies." His voice is soft, soothing—and so full of anguish that I can't help but lift my gaze to meet his as he tells me, "You are blameless."

My heart bleeds as he absolves me of my fault, as I feel it deep in my bones that he means it, too.

"It doesn't change that he's dead." I can't help the tear sliding from my eye.

"Nothing ever changes what the gods will. And it seems the gods will for this torment to become even more brutal." It's an afterthought more, probably not intended to be spoken at all, but the words are out, and his eyes widen with horror as he realizes what he said. Horror—then shame.

Wondering what could have possibly destroyed this strong male's confidence in this world so much that he perceives it as a torment.

A minute ticks by. Two. And we sit with his fingers wrapped around mine in silent companionship. Only when the darkness in the depths of myself threatens to leap from my chest to mingle with the shadows of his past do I pull back my hand and face the unharmed library.

"Will they attack again?" It's easier to focus on the brutality of the assault that decimated his court than on the fact that we seem to have more in common than that unbidden attraction sizzling in the air between us. We both have suffered losses over and over again. I recognize a tortured soul when I see one, and Myron is definitely that. Only, he's learned to disguise it better.

"It's not the question *if* but *when*." Myron's lips are a tight line as he studies the burn marks on the wood panels leading from the door to the bookshelves. "They've come for us before, but never this many and never have gotten so close to—" When he stops himself this time, it isn't because a spell is preventing him from speaking but because he chooses to drop what he was intending to say.

"Close to what?" I hold my breath, exhale slowly as he studies me across the space between us. Inhale the slight taste of soot in the air.

"To losing more than I can bear to."

My heart gives a wild thud. One hammering pulse before launching into a hummingbird flutter. My body is suddenly too long for the pose I'm sitting in, but my legs don't fit well in the space between the edge of the table and Myron's knee when I try to slide them into a more comfortable position. A sheath of sweat covers my palms as I pull away. I wipe them on my thighs, lace my fingers in my lap, and lean back in my seat to bring some distance between us or the words—both spoken and unspoken—will tear me apart with tension.

"I'm sorry about Ephegos." My voice isn't more than a croak.

Myron inclines his head in thanks. "He was one of my best men—and I trusted him with my own life and the safety of my people."

"The same people who want to kill you." It isn't fair. Not when there is so much more to this king than the cold monster ruling with punishing power. If they could see who he really is, see how deeply he can care for one of his own, they might change their minds—

No, they wouldn't. Not those creatures who chased me into the forest. Those who would have feasted on my living flesh. I try not to shudder at the memory of Crow claws digging into my shoulder, of their hissing threats and taunting.

"They deserved safety anyway. Every last Crow does. Even if they seem like terrible monsters to you, they haven't always been like this—" His last word ends in a gasp, and a trickle of blood runs from the corner of his mouth.

"I won't ask what they used to be like because it doesn't matter if they want to kill you now."

He forces a thin smile, understanding that I won't push him on this. But I do address the one topic I haven't dared bring up with either of the three Crows I trust in this palace—two. Ephegos is no longer there to answer and bleed. Grave sadness spreads through me, an echo of the last time I watched one of those I've come to call family slayed.

"You bleed when you speak about certain topics, like the words themselves make you bleed. But that happened before when you tried to talk about the Fire Fairies. And now it doesn't." I don't know how I could have missed that detail before. But it is like every time I learn something, the Crows no longer bleed when they talk about it next time.

Myron clears his throat, tilts his head as if weighing how to phrase his response, then gets to his feet, stepping around the couch to the library behind it. "Because you paid attention. Only things you haven't—" He coughs, bending over, grasping the shelf to support himself, and I'm on my feet, too, placing a soothing hand between his shoulder blades, even when there is nothing I can do to help him—

Nothing other than figuring it out. He just gave me an answer that hurt him and, with it, a tool to make it stop.

There is nothing much other for me to do than to start guessing. "Things I haven't talked about with you?" I try, but the coughing doesn't ease, the heavy panting between frightening me to my core. He shakes his head, and I could swear his breathing rattles the next time he inhales.

Shit. Where are the gods when I need them? Whatever he was trying to tell me, it must be substantial, or the spell wouldn't tear at him like this.

Things… What things could he mean? I've paid attention to a lot since I was brought here, to all the details and answers Royad, Ephegos, and Myron have given me. But the Flames… The Flames are something I figured out on my own. Guessed most of it, at least. And now I know, and whatever he told me about them no longer affected him. But what he's trying to tell me now, I don't know, so he's suffering.

I don't want to make it worse, so I promise myself I will ask only one more time. "You can only talk about things I already know." He gasps a breath of air. "Or things that are irrelevant to the spell."

The words are out before I can think as his all-black eyes lock on mine, black strands shifting over his features as he turns his head to the side with his hand still braced on the shelf. For a moment, I believe he's going to collapse. Drop dead right there, at the foot of the library that has been my savior during lonely hours in this foreign place.

But as I wait, the tension in his shoulders eases, and he breathes more easily. "How do you know about the … spell?" His brittle tone shakes me to my bones, and I slide my hand under his wing, to the side of his waist to offer support, but he's already straightening, a haunted look on his features and a vulnerability in his eyes that pulls on my chest like a length of yarn pulling a leg from a house of cards.

The fact that he can say the word without bleeding and coughing tells me I've been right all along. "There really is a spell." I don't realize how breathless I sound until the rapid movements of my chest become a distraction in the silence between us.

"For thousands of years." Myron smooths a feather on his wing back toward his elbow and turns to rest his back against the shelves.

The information settles in like a rock, and I need to brace myself against the backrest of the couch so as not to stumble under its weight.

A spell. But more than that. "A curse," I whisper.

Myron says nothing, and he doesn't need to.

For a long time, we stare at each other, understanding passing between us in the dim glow of the fairy light. My heart pounds, my palms sweat, my limbs shake, but I hold my ground against the force that is Myron, the Valiant.

A bride. A chance, it echoes in my mind.

I don't repeat the thought but swallow the lump forming in my throat and croak, "Who placed the curse on you?"

It's one question too many, and Myron is already at his limit. Instead of bleeding for my curiosity, he shakes his head before he turns and stalks to the door. "We'll talk about the water later."

My gaze follows his to the door to the murderous bathing room, and I open my mouth to ask what he knows about what happened, but when I turn, his body is covered in feathers and shrinking to the size of a bird. Before I can get out a word, he launches into the air and flutters through the opening door.

TWENTY-SEVEN

Seven days have passed since the Flame attack, but the palace is still in an uproar. The walls are still soot-stained, and the Crows remain on edge. Despite keeping the heavily guarded windows and doors open during the days, the stench of burnt flesh lingers in the air like a ghost of all the Crows who lost their lives in the attack. Some of them were from the pro-Myron faction like Ephegos while others were from the faction against him, Royad explained after the attack, but Myron gives them all a proper memorial anyway.

I haven't talked to anyone but Myron and Royad since the attack, and no one has approached me, even when the Crows stationed at the palace give me curious and sometimes concerned glances as I pass through the hallways at the side of their king or that of their king's confidant. What they see when I pass them, I cannot tell, but it is no longer the little bride they taunted or chased or even attempted to kill. I am not sure if the new creature they see is much better either.

"Ignore them," Myron whispers as he opens a plain wooden door, waiting for me to cross the threshold before he follows on silent feet. No matter how many times I wander the palace with him, I can't get used to his stealth—worse even than Royad's, whose wings at least rustle when he makes a quick movement. But Myron is quiet like a shark in deep waters and equally dangerous. "They'll get used to the fact that this year's bride is stronger than the ones before."

I'm scared to ask the meaning of his statement with the all-black eyes of the Crow guards following us into the corridor. With a swift wave of his hand, Myron makes the door shut before falling into step beside me again.

"It's hard to ignore them when they look at me like they want to roast me for dinner."

Myron's chuckle is as startlingly beautiful as is the humor in his tone as he tells me, "No matter how well they roast you, none of them could devour you as well as I could."

"And by *devour* you mean sucking out my soul before handing me to the Guardians?" I try to make it a joke, but Myron's chuckle fades as he pins me to the wall beside the door, one hand braced beside my head, the other gently curling around my waist so his taloned fingertips graze the small of my back.

"By *devour*, I mean slowly." He lowers his face so it's level with mine. "Deliciously." He leans in until his lips brush my ear, and my breath hitches despite the calm I'm trying to keep. "*Devour.* You."

The way his breath tickles my skin makes it very clear that he isn't talking about the same type of *devouring*, and I press my knees together at the sudden heat between my legs.

We've been dancing around each other since the kiss after the attack, his gazes intense when he studies me across the room and even worse from up close, such hunger dwelling in the depths of those black eyes. And I'm nearly as bad. One glance at his tall form, at the torso he puts on display so often when we spend our days in the room beneath the palace where he's been taking me to work on my fighting skills, and my mind zaps back to the feel of his skin under my palm.

With the Fire Fairies breaking into the palace for the second time within mere weeks, Myron insists I be in top shape, and he sees to it himself, making it harder for me to focus on wielding the dagger he gave me—and which I'm carrying everywhere now—when sweat glistens in the grooves of his muscles and his eyes twinkle whenever he catches me staring.

He hasn't said a word about the curse, and I haven't asked again. Not about that, anyway, instead trying to read up on everything I can to better understand the Flames once populating this region of Askarea.

I shiver as his talons dig into the thin fabric of my tunic—just lightly enough to remind me they're there—and Myron pulls back with a smirk.

"Shouldn't we be training?" I quip, placing one hand on my dagger as he hovers there, breath mingling with mine, inviting me to close the gap and do some *devouring* of my own.

"I'm all for it, depending on what sort of skill you want to practice."

I roll my eyes at him. "Is that the charm you spring on all your brides because, if it is, I assure you they might have died merely to escape that." I mean it as a joke, but Myron's expression darkens, and I swear the stone room does too as his power fills the air between us.

"Believe me, if I wanted to charm you, you'd know." In the depths of his eyes, I spot a spark that sends shudders of the good kind through my body, and I wonder if I'm playing with a different sort of fire. One I won't be able to contain once it tastes the charged air between us.

"Is that a promise, Myron? Or should I say *Moron?* Might be a spelling error." Pushing him when he's this close isn't a smart idea, but it's a better idea than all the hundreds of ways my body is telling me to press against him, to taste him, breathe him.

Myron's guttural growl reverberates through every inch of my body, making the hair stand at the back of my neck. And that is before he braces his second hand on the other side of my head, wings flaring to both sides, blocking out the light of the chandelier high up under the arched ceiling, and he closes his eyes, inhaling long and deep as if memorizing my scent.

When he opens them, the spark is gone. He lowers his wings, shrugging toward the training room. "I'm not making any promises, Ayna. We both know where that could end."

Despite the lighter tone, there is something in his voice that tells me he's fighting as hard as I am to let go of the moment. No matter how tempting, this can't be anything more than the sizzling attraction it's been growing into. I've lost too many people, and so has he. Even considering letting him closer might shatter me if I wake tomorrow and the Flames burn him to cinder the way they did with Ephegos. My heart is still bleeding over the Crow spy, and I can only imagine that Myron is devastated, losing a friend he's been with for more than a thousand years.

I follow him into the stone chamber where we've spent at least an hour every day, wielding blades and words in an attempt to get me back in shape. Today is no different.

Myron picks up a dull training sword from the rack at the side of the fairy-light-drenched room and drags the tip over the rough stone of the floor as he approaches me with a serious expression—the face of Myron the Fighter, I've learned. As I've learned that the Crow is an excellent swordsman. Not that he needs a blade when he has refined, invisible power at his fingertips that can bring down enemies without even touching them.

I have about five heartbeats before he's upon me, and I use them to study his graceful approach, the strength in the lines of his body, the set of his mouth and jaw as he studies his target. A lump forms in my throat at the thought of fighting this creature of magic who I'll never defeat, no matter how much of my human brawn I put into a strike.

"Ready?" he purrs, lips twitching ever so slightly as he gestures at my dagger with the point of his sword.

I draw my weapon, readying myself for the softened blow he's about to deliver. We've been through this multiple times, and every time, Myron adulterates his deadliness to match my human strength, slowing his pace to meet mine. And no matter how much I appreciate it, every time anew, I am reminded of just how weak I am next to him.

Today, apparently, is no different.

Only, Royad chooses to join us halfway into the training session, a grim expression on his features, and picks up a sword to spar with Myron. The Crow King blocks his attack with ease, his gaze on me while I debate whether I should use this moment of him busying himself with barring Royad's sword to land that blow I've been trying to since the moment we started working.

I don't know why I'm surprised that he sees my sneak attack coming, but as he wraps his magic around my wrist and my waist, holding me in place a pace away, his eyes flash a dangerous shade of night, and my breath catches as they lock on mine.

"Careful, Ayna. Attacking a king's flank in an ambush like that might result in that very king pinning you against the wall with his magic." The grasp of his power tightens around my wrist holding my blade well away from his chest, but around my waist, the invisible touch becomes more proprietary, pulling me in an inch or two while I'm still struggling to find my breath. And I can't help reaching deep into my courage, the one always flaring when Myron challenges me with a statement. Curving my lips into a half-smirk, I lean into his hold, tossing my braid over my shoulder with my free hand. "Another promise, Moron?"

Myron's growl rumbles through the room like slow-building thunder, and despite the obvious warning rolling along on the sound, there is more to it than a threat. Almost like an ... invitation?

The sudden awareness of how his gaze slides over my body as he assesses the way I arch around his magic does nothing to ease the tension lingering in the space between us, and I'm surprised the air doesn't combust right there.

Before either of us can say or do something we would regret, Royad clears his throat, pulling back the sword from Myron's block, and the Crow King releases me so fast I nearly fall on my ass. Only my years of living and fighting on swaying ships save me. In response, Myron's mouth twitches with half-amusement.

When I manage to peel my gaze away from Myron, Royad is full-on grinning.

"What's so funny?" It's not fair to take out my annoyance on him since he isn't the one who taunted me, who's pushing my limits. But he's there, and the way his mouth is split into a dashing white line channels the myriads of conflicting emotions in my chest in a way that has nothing to do with me not wanting either of them to realize how captivated I was a moment ago—and I don't just mean the way Myron's power held me captive.

Royad has the good sense to drop his grin as Myron steps to my side. "Nothing. Let's train." He shakes his head and lifts his sword again, announcing an attack while Myron's gaze bounces back and forth between Royad and me.

Our blades meet, and once again, I'm reminded how much stronger and faster the Crows are. Fairies through and through even with their monstrous appearances. After a while of watching us from up close, Myron settles on a low, carved, cubic rock at the edge of the room, his gaze following the interaction with a thoughtful expression on his face. Not that my eyes are drifting to him every other moment because they're not.

At least, that's what I tell myself until Royad has me by the throat with the tip of his sword, and I have to admit that, had I been focused, I'd never have allowed for that to happen. Even with his superior reflexes.

Myron watches the steel beneath my chin with a crease between his brows, apparently trusting his friend to not slice through my skin even when he easily could.

When the Crow lowers the blade, I take a step back, adrenaline coursing through my veins.

"Again," I demand, and Royad attacks so fast I barely get to catch my breath before his sword is at my throat once more. And this time, I wasn't distracted by the Crow King's chiseled features.

"I'm beginning to think you're not putting in all you've got." Royad's remark is a challenge of a different sort. There is no heat in the space between us even when he is so close I can feel his breath on my face as he leans over me. It's the look of a male trying to figure out a puzzle that has nothing to do with this room or the weapons pitted against each other.

He pulls back, pacing for a moment before he spins and faces me again. Myron merely studies his friend, his face as unreadable as that first day I met him.

"Attack." Royad crooks his fingers, sword at the ready, and I don't hesitate to launch myself at him. If I don't try, I will never defeat him. Not that I'm expecting I ever could, but if I want to be better prepared for the next time the Flames attack, I need to use every opportunity to practice. Plus, if the Flames are anything as strong and magical as the Crows, I'd better get used to working with my disadvantage.

It takes another minute before Royad has me unarmed and backed against the wall.

"Come on, Ayna. There's got to be more." I don't know what he means by that.

"In case you've forgotten," I grit out as I shove at his feathered forearm to bring some space between his sword and my shoulder, "I'm human." I slide a step aside, the hard rock of the wall scraping along my shoulders as I turn to the side, marching up to Myron, who summoned a pitcher of water out of thin air.

He holds it out to me, and I drink directly from it, my bad hand trembling from the weight, and try to ignore the way he studies me with fathomless black eyes.

When I'm done, he takes the pitcher back, and it vanishes from his fingers like it never existed in the first place. Gracefully, he rises to his feet, his wings unfolding as he holds his hand out for my weapon. From the corner of my eye, I spot the pitcher rematerializing on the rock where he was sitting a moment ago.

"I think Royad is right." The darkness in his tone settles in my bones like a calling, like a pull summoning me to step into his space and demand what he means.

"About what?" I croak, deliberately turning away to find the other Crow pacing behind me, gaze on the rock. Not on the rock—on the pitcher.

"I think you are holding back, Ayna. There is more that you can do than half heartedly wield a dagger." If it's meant to be an insult, it doesn't hit, for all I can feel is the bubbling sensation that they are onto something even when I can't put my finger on what exactly it could be.

Until Myron turns to face the rock as well—face the *pitcher* as well.

"Water, Ayna."

It takes me a moment to process what he's saying. Then the moment in the murderous bathing room flashes back into my mind, and I can feel in my very essence that they are right.

We haven't talked about what happened in his room since the day of the Fire Fairy attack—neither the kiss nor the way the lake saved his library from burning to the ground—probably saved me, too—and I was content to let both topics rest. I haven't gone back into the murderous bathing room for fear that the lake's wrath would be for me this time and, just like so many other traumatic experiences, compartmentalizing them at the back of my mind seemed so much easier. But both Myron and Royad are eyeing me now, various degrees of curiosity on their handsome features, and my voice turns into a squeak as I ask what exactly they are suggesting I can do with water.

"I don't think it's coincidence the door opened for you that day, Ayna," Myron explains, sharing a look with Royad that suggests they've talked this through even when I've successfully been avoiding the topic. "The lake room has been closed for over a hundred years. It opened for you the first time you laid a hand on the door, and it opened for you again despite the magical wards I placed on it after it nearly drowned you."

A shudder runs through me at the memory of being dragged under by the masses of water that shouldn't fit into a palace bathing room yet somehow do.

"What are you saying?" I need to hear it spelled out so I don't feel like I'm going crazy.

To my surprise, it's Royad who brings the answer. "I've spent half of my days with you since the moment I picked you up at the prison," he says with a grimace that I mirror at the mention of our beginnings.

"Don't remind me." I shake my head at him, and he nods in response, the understanding between us that of two people who have been through the worst even when it's barely two months since we met. Even when he was the one exchanging one cage for another.

A tentative smile spreads on his face, and I can't help noticing how genuine, how serious that gesture is. Royad isn't as cheerful and joking as Ephegos used to be, but he's warm in a different way. He is loyal and caring, a silent, observant presence, Myron's right hand. His moral support and confidant.

My chest aches as I realize how much I've come to care about the male who carted me out of Fort Perenis in a cage—at how that transfer in truth wasn't one from prison to prison but one to a new sort of freedom. A second chance for my broken existence. A chance I am determined to fight for, now that I have people in my life again who I'm willing to fight for. People who I can't lose or what's left of me will shatter for good. The way Ephegos's death still lingers like a leaden anvil on my chest is proof of what it would mean if Royad was taken from me—or Myron.

The thought of Myron's feathers seared from his wing-arms, flesh raw and life fading from his eyes sucks the breath from my lungs, and my essence riots against the image, against the mere possibility. I try not to pay attention, or I'll shatter right there in front of them both.

"Myron and I—or how you like to call him, Moron," Royad laughs, and it's a natural sound, a free one, despite the darkness of the situation, the prospect of another attack that could tear from us what we care for, "have come to the conclusion that there must be an ounce of magic within you, or you wouldn't have been able to command the water."

My jaw drops, and I need to remind myself to close my mouth as I let the idea settle in my mind. "That can't be right."

While I try to wrap my head around what Royad proposed, Myron takes a step closer, one hand raised as if he were going to touch me, then lowers it before he makes contact with my arm. "Think about it, Ayna." He points at the pitcher. "You are the first bride since my father's death who gets access to the sacred chamber."

"Sacred chamber?" I'm not sure I want to know.

"The sacred chamber where my father used to *initiate* his brides." His lips pull into a bitter line as he holds my gaze.

"What do you mean 'initiate'?" Again, I have the distinct feeling that an answer might traumatize me more than it will do me good. But I can't stop myself from asking anyway.

Myron swallows, blows out a breath, swallows again. "Long before I had my first bride, long before you ever set foot in this realm, brides used to be crowned on their wedding night. A crown that connected the new bride to all the other brides past. All the brides who died in my father's care. All the brides who cried eons of tears as they were brought to the sacred chamber and declared a tribute to the gods by Carius, the Cruel. Brides whose tears now make up the lake who aided you as they buckled under the weight of the crown. The crown was a gift from…" He lets his words trail away in a cough, and I spot a fleck of crimson in the corner of his mouth.

He's on dangerous ground, and we all know it. One more word could be deadly for him.

"It's all right." I hold up a hand to stop him, but he shakes his head, gaze wandering to Royad, who nods and sucks in a deep breath as he braces himself for the pain.

"The gods," he finishes Myron's sentence, and my heart is pounding in my chest as I wait for him to start bleeding.

"From the gods," I repeat when both Crows fix me with watchful eyes, expectant eyes filled with both hope and terror I yet have to understand.

Until Royad's words register and I realize the trickle of blood from Royad's mouth stops the moment they do.

I gasp as things fall into place, and all of a sudden, the maze of information they've given me piece by piece smooths out into one landscape of raw horror.

"The gods cursed you?"

Nobody is more surprised than I am when Myron claps his hands and laughs, face lighting up like he's seeing the sun for the first time in a century.

TWENTY-EIGHT

The hair still stands at the back of my neck when Myron's laugh has stopped echoing through the stone room, and Royad has wiped away the blood, settling down on the floor by the wall and breathing heavily.

"I'm all right," he tells us with a lifted hand to keep us from rushing to his aid. "Just a little winded."

From speaking three words. *By the gods.* The Crows were cursed by the gods.

"I won't ask you what gods," I reassure them. Because if they give me any other piece of information, they might as well die on the spot. I can still see the fading hysteria in Myron's eyes and the slow recovery in Royad's.

"I'm not sure that's a good thing." The darkness is back in Myron's tone, and so is the challenge in his eyes as he locks them on mine.

Resisting the sensation of being swallowed by their all-black depths, I turn to the pitcher once more. Because the water is how we got to the topic of the curse. The sacred chamber where the lake is biding its time to kill a new bride. It didn't open for the ninety-nine brides preceding me, but it opened for me. Twice. I haven't given it a proper thought other than that it must be evil, lusting to take my life. But maybe it was testing me that first time, measuring whether I am worthy or if I'd be easily killed off like the brides before me. But I can't deny that the last encounter with the lake was beneficial for my survival. It is not wrong that the lake worked in my favor, dousing the flames forced upon us by the Fire Fairies.

I also remember the sensation when the water washed around me without touching an inch of my skin, almost as if it knew of my fear—of it and of losing the only source of information I have in this place. There's something more to it, and I'm not proud that I haven't pulled up the topic to examine it in detail the way past Ayna would have—before I lost my family, the man I loved, and my freedom. There is something not so human about having sacred lakes working on your behalf, and I barely dare think the word—*magic*.
"You think I have magic?" It sounds as absurd spoken aloud as it did in my head.

Myron and Royad exchange another look, and I start feeling like I'm the only one here who has no clue what's going on—not that it would be a first. It seems like not knowing what's going on has become my new normal.

"I don't know." Myron finally faces me again, his features paler than I'm accustomed to.

With a shaky hand, I sheath my dagger. "What do you mean, you don't know?"

Royad's footsteps are audible for once as he paces around the room, sword in claw and features shifting back and forth in a nervous display of a grim human face and a dark-feathered bird one. I try not to shudder at the sight. No matter how many times I see them shift, it still shakes me to my very core when Royad or Myron do now that I've come to care for them. It's a stark reminder of how different our species truly are. How different I am as a weak human.

"Something happened with the water that day," Myron continues, his gaze never straying from mine. "Something that I've been waiting to happen again so I can be certain before I push this on you. But—"

"But nothing is happening," I finish for him. The bitterness in my tone shouldn't be there, especially when I'm scared shitless by the thought of having magic. But the way he seems certain on the one hand and disappointed on the other kindles an unfamiliar sense of annoyance in my belly. It's not the fuming rage burning deep inside of me for weeks when I first arrived, nor the mild upset that occasionally flares these days at the Crows' glances following me around the palace. It's something different. Something I haven't experienced since the occasional fights with Ludelle.

I'm not ready to examine what exactly that means for my relationship with the Crow King. If I am annoyed he kept me in the dark about his suspicions or that he might be giving up on some magical ability I didn't even know about, which is refusing to resurface after a grand occurrence when fire was threatening my favorite wall in his room.

"Nothing is happening because you haven't actively tried to make it happen," Myron corrects, and the annoyance in my belly coils into something unsure as I try to believe what he implies.

"You really think I have magic." I blow out a breath, absently rubbing my stiff wrist.

"I believe you have something. Not certain if it's magic or an affinity to the former brides' tears—"

"Tears?" I interrupt him, eyes widening with horror at the picture forming in my mind—one of thousands of women crying and crying enough tears to form an entire lake. "I don't have an affinity for tears." Not mine, not his, not anyone's. And most definitely not the poor women who had as little say in their affiliation with the Crows as I did.

Myron's chuckle fuels that uncertainty into beginning fear. What if this is about more than what happened with the lake? What if something is wrong with me that wasn't wrong with all the other brides? What if that's the gods' way of telling Myron I'm not the one who will break their curse? What if that makes me a purposeless accessory that they could dispose of without consequences?

A long inhale, a long exhale. Long inhale, even longer exhale. My heart is pounding, chest straining to keep it contained as it threatens to race up my throat.

"Ayna—" Royad is beside me, claws on my shoulders, all-black eyes piercing through my building panic. "Ayna, listen to me."

He looks better than a few moments ago when he was pale from spilling words he wasn't supposed to, or when his features were shifting uncontrollably. His gaze is steady, his brown hair tucked behind his ears, and there's a kindness to him I rarely get to see when he plays my bodyguard on our paths through the palace.

I bob my head because there is no word I can get out. What if they are going to dispose of me themselves after all?

In reflex, my good hand flips to my dagger, savoring the coolness of the metal hilt when the rest of me is threatening to overheat.

"No one is going to hurt you. Do you hear me?" His baritone carries through the room with a reassurance I haven't heard since the last time my friends from the Wild Ray told me we'd survive the next attack of a merchant ship and would drink ourselves senseless after the loot the way we always had. Only, instead of helping me, the memory of the family I'd found on the pirate ship tips me deep into a pit of despair.

I bob my head anyway. It isn't Royad's fault what happened with the Wild Ray. It isn't his fault what happened in the lake room, either. It isn't anyone's fault, and if I've learned anything over the past weeks, it's that there is a time to sit and wallow, and then there is a time to stand up for yourself, to take action and make the best of things, no matter how absurd or dire.

I'm not alone in this palace even when it started out that way. I have come to trust Royad and Myron, and they have given me no indication they think any differently of me because of what happened with the water from the lake. Plus, Myron's promise is still valid. I'll be free at the next Ret Relah—if I survive long enough to see it. So, these two Crows are the best chance I have.

I blow out another breath and nod again. "The lake is filled with the brides' tears, isn't it?" The question hurts in my throat, and for a moment, I wonder if their curse has spilled over to me, but I can breathe; I don't taste iron and salt on my tongue.

Royad nods. "Their tears. Not yours. Carius's brides' tears. Myron would have never done something as horrible as—" He breaks off, swallowing hard. "I'm sorry, I can't."

"It's all right," I tell him quickly, my gaze darting to Myron whose features have twisted so much the angles of his face are all off.

The Crow King inclines his head at me as if waiting for me to pass judgement, and yet again, I have no idea what to do with it.

There is another thought knocking everything else to the background as I realize what Myron said earlier and what Royad's saying now doesn't add up.

"You said your father *initiated* his brides in the sacred chamber, a chamber that obviously has a role in the whole curse thing. But you never brought any of your brides there. You never *initiated* any of them." I don't care if I sound like I don't consider myself one of said brides. I never chose to marry him in the first place. But I need answers. I need them more than I need air to breathe, because if this sacred chamber somehow decides to send its lake after me again, I want to be prepared.

"I didn't." Myron's tone is grave as he joins us, replacing Royad, who steps aside for his king to let him gently lay his hands on each side of my shoulders. A crease forms on his forehead as he studies me with intent, too-dark eyes. Eyes which I wonder have once shone in hues of blue or green or hazel, or if he was born this way, with not even a fleck of white between his lids.

"Why?" My voice dries up like a drizzle in the desert.

For a moment, I think he's not going to answer, but he stops his head from slowly rolling from side to side in a silent denial of information and says, "Because no one deserves to suffer for a crime my people committed. Especially not the ones who are supposed to save us."

He doesn't bleed or choke, his skin remains the same smooth, pale layer across his sharp cheekbones and defined torso, and I wonder if I somehow knew it. If I knew deep in my soul that Myron would never hurt an innocent if he could prevent it.

His gaze lingers, mouth the same grim line as a minute ago and fingers as gentle as ever, but there is something new to the darkness in his eyes. Where it was deep and unreadable before, myriads of emotions are swirling like threads of yarn in water—

sorrow, guilt, and a flicker of hope I've spotted on occasion. This is a different sort of hope, though, and I wish I could sense a similar feeling beneath the layers of my own guilt.

Guilt for being alive when my father had to die because of one word from me. Guilt for outliving the strong and brave crew of the Wild Ray. Guilt for having kissed someone else when my heart is still in pieces from the loss of the only man I ever loved. Guilt for slowly forgetting the warm brown of Ludelle's eyes, the sound of his laugh, the way my entire being lit up when he touched me. Guilt for the fading pain when I think of him.

Instead of examining all those variations of guilt, I swallow the lump in my throat and close my eyes so Myron won't see the tears burning behind them.

There is nothing I can change about the past. But I might be able to change something about the future. Might be able to save someone when I have failed to save everyone else in my life.

"What do I need to do?" I ask when I reopen my eyes—

And find Myron's gaze even more alive, more intense, like the waves near the rocky shores just south of the Horn of Eroth.

He opens his mouth to speak, grip on my shoulders tightening as he sucks in a steadying breath.

Instead of words, blood spills from his tongue, and his knees buckle, his weight pulling me to the stone floor with him as he loses balance and collapses right in front of me.

ANGELINA J. STEFFORT

TWENTY-NINE

"Myron!" My voice bounces through the room in high, shrill echoes as I grab for him too late to keep him from falling over. But it isn't my human speed keeping me from reacting in time to protect his head from hitting the floor—Royad took care of that, thank the Guardians—it is the vise tightening around my chest as if a lump of glass exploded into thousands of shards between my ribs.

It hurts. Guardians, does it hurt. For a heartbeat, I wonder if some sneaky Crow ran both of us through with a blade and we were too busy to notice it. But my vision fills with black dots; then I sway on my knees, tumbling over a groaning Myron.

Royad is saying something I can't bring myself to make sense of, but as he places a claw on my forearm, I open my eyes and attempt to focus.

"It's all right, Ayna. You'll be all right. Just breathe."

I understand him now, noticing the panic in his voice as he lifts me off Myron's wing and lays me down on the stone. Then he's back by his king's side, brushing back his hair and wiping blood from his chin and mouth. "Hold on, Myron. Think of sunrises in Askarean spring. Think of fairy wine. By Shaelak, think of the last time you fucked a female if it helps, but stop thinking of telling her."

I'm lost. Even if I weren't half unconscious, I would have missed the meaning of what Royad is trying to get Myron to do.

"Sariell was a pretty one," Myron chokes out, and the vise on my chest loosens the slightest bit.

"She was," Royad agrees, his full attention on Myron as if all our lives depend on it.

"A bit bland in her attitude, though," Myron continues in a voice so breathless I want to roll to the side and check on him myself, but my body won't cooperate. Every breath still slices through my chest like little blades. But I don't taste blood, so that's a good sign, I suppose.

"You like your females with more spice, I know." Royad laughs, but it isn't a humorous sound, more one of devastation.

"More spice, more spirit, more…" His words fade as he heaves a breath like it's hard to push even those few through his pale lips.

Air floods my lungs like I haven't breathed in days, and the sensation of shards vanishes with one final assault as I blow out that deep breath. I try to push myself up, manage to brace my weight on my good hand and partly on my bad one as I roll to the side and lift my torso off the floor.

When I dare glance at Myron, his eyes are on me, blood drying on his cheek and chin, and brows slanted as if he's still struggling. At least, he no longer seems to be dying.

As I study his pale features, the serious look in his eyes, I realize that he wasn't the only one in danger. His condition ... that was what took the breath from my lungs, as if there's a direct connection between him and me. Between every Crow in this palace and the bride who might save them.

"That's what you meant when you said that, if any Crow said too much, I might die." Because of the curse that is keeping them from helping themselves by handing out information that might aid the one supposed to aid them. It's not a question, and neither Myron nor Royad feels the need to disagree or confirm. Their silence, actually, is more of a response than I'd hoped for. But eventually, Myron says with a hoarse voice, "We're connected in a way. Whatever someone says could mess with the curse to a degree that threatens the speaker's life as well as the savior's."

If only I knew how to save them.

For a long moment, Royad and Myron share a glance that tells me any further word might start this whole debacle all over again, and neither of us is in the condition to go through it after just getting away with our lives.

"Not all of us want to be saved." Myron's tone is barely more than a whisper, and I have to strain my ears to pick up the meaning.

"What do you mean not all of you want to be saved?" Blood wells on my lip as my teeth cut into the sensitive skin, biting back more questions. I can't push them, or they'll suffer. Can't push them to risk their lives or mine.

But both Myron and Royad have mentioned it before. Not all Crows are happy with the way things are. With the lack of freedom and the prospect of waiting for Myron to provide it. It seems like the faction against the Crow King might be the one not caring to break a curse as well.

I start voicing my conclusions when it hits me—

When I asked if Ephegos meant Myron no longer cared about marrying, I guessed wrong. "You no longer care about breaking the curse."

Exhaustion takes over Myron's features as he closes his eyes, allowing the Crow feathers to take his appearance and the beak to take that sensuous mouth. He doesn't shake his head. Doesn't nod. For a long moment, he just lies there, chest slowly rising and falling as he breathes in and out like that's the only thing he can bear for now.

When I throw Royad a questioning look, he shakes his head—not in response to my assumption, nor in denial of an answer. He seems as preoccupied with the tiredness plastering Myron's form to the floor as I am.

And can I just say, it scares the shit out of me to see him like that? To see both of them like that—like two dogs beaten, at their limits. Resigned.

Resigned.

The word hangs in the air, ripe for the plucking, and I almost reach for it, allowing the heaviness to drag me back to the stone as well. But if there is anything I can do to break the curse, I can't lie back and wait for it to come to me. I need to go searching for it. Turn over every rock in the palace until I find something to lift that monstrosity off their feathered shoulders. Ephegos once hinted that they can't fully shift into a human form. That must be part of the curse. But there is more, I'm sure, or they wouldn't bleed when bringing it up. That alone is a curse in itself.

Whatever gods cursed them must be cruel beyond comprehension.

Then there remains the other question: Why?

Why did the gods punish the Crows? What did Myron's ancestors do in order to deserve a fate like this?

As determination builds beneath the plain training tunic right where my heart hammers between my ribs, I brave a smile and scramble to my knees so I can take a better look at the Crow King.

"Tell me about Sariell," I murmur, my hand wrapping around his as I try not to dwell on the tightness in my stomach at the thought of a female Myron found pretty.

"She is dead." It's all he needs to say to shut me up before I even get started on the questions. But at least, we navigated around a topic that was killing him. Was killing both of us.

The air in the room is heavy, as is Royad's gaze of gratitude when he settles back on his haunches, a quiet sigh moving his chest.

"We'll talk about the water another day." He rubs his claws over his face, the gesture speaking of the exhaustion of centuries rather than of the past dangerous moments.

"We will," Myron agrees as if Royad was talking to him when the Crow's eyes were very clearly communicating that he was addressing me only.

"We will," I echo, but deep down, I decide that I won't involve either of them in my search, for any question I raise might kill them—and me. And I've only started valuing life enough again to care about how that affects me, too.

The room is bigger when I'm alone than with Myron's company, I notice as I stare at the scorch marks on the wood panel by the door where the fire tried to eat up the library. I've been staring at that same spot for days while Myron and Royad dealt with court politics and rebellious Crows, wondering if the lake would save me again should fire burst in through the doors once more. So far, I haven't found an answer.

I've pulled and tugged on the warded door to the sacred chamber, begging it to open so I could throw my life on the line in an attempt at figuring out whether or not I have the abilities Myron and Royad suggested.

Nothing. Not even a creak of the wood. The lake doesn't want to see me—perhaps because I have too many uncomfortable questions.

Is the water truly a collection of former brides' tears? Is it sentient? Are the gods watching in that small room more than anywhere else in Eherea? And most of all: Why did it open for me when it had remained closed for over a century?

I've shouted those questions and more at the wood to no avail. All that got me was a raised feathered brow from one of the guards by the door when Myron picked me up from his room a few hours later. I don't have more than bored gazes for the guards now. None of them came to my aid when I was trapped by fire, so I assume they don't particularly care if I live or die—not that any of them have tried to kill me since the incident in the forest.

I haven't seen the two assailants from my flight attempt since Myron saved me from their midst either.

And most of all, I have been living under a looming death threat for so long it has lost its imminency.

A glance at the ornate clock on the mantle of the fireplace tells me Myron will be arriving shortly to take me to train as every day. I flex my bad hand, savoring the new strength there despite the stiffness. I've used the hours of combat practice to work on the flexibility of my wrist and fingers and gained a few degrees more freedom with my movements. They don't hurt as badly either, now that I'm finally able to properly hold a dagger. I'm nowhere close to being able to run someone through with that hand in a fight, but at least, I have more accuracy when I aim for the heart.

Myron arrives like clockwork, waiting on the threshold for me to join him, a smile on his face that I hadn't believed possible mere weeks ago, but it's there and directed at me. He's been awfully quiet the past three weeks since the incident in the training room. Naturally, he continues to keep his talon-tipped hand on the small of my back in demonstration of propriety the way only a fairy male can when we walk through the hallways. "It's what keeps the other Crows motivated to stay away from you," he tells me when I ask him if he isn't getting tired of pretending, right as we turn the corner into the private corridor leading up to the secluded training area.

"I don't think any of the Crows still intend to lay a hand on me." It's true. None of them have even looked at me wrong since the fire. However, I'm not sure if it is because of the way Myron sticks to my side whenever we walk the palace together or because word has gotten around that I wielded water to save the king's private bedchamber from burning to the ground.

"There, you see how well it works." I don't imagine the smirk on his lips. It's actually more pronounced than I've ever seen on his gorgeous face. I try not to dwell on the fact that this remains a ruse. Yes, there is undeniable chemistry between the Crow King and me, and yes, I have caught myself fantasizing about the moments when he'd run those hands along my skin, when his mouth had devoured mine in what I can only describe as an all-consuming need. But that's about it.

When it comes to Myron, the Valiant, I can't have feelings, because if I do...

My chest tightens at the thought of the last man I loved. The *only* man I've loved.

I don't even know what they did with Ludelle's body at the prison. If they burned it or buried it or fed it to the wild animals roaming the prison island.

He would have wanted to be dumped in the ocean rather than in the ground.

I bite my lip, and Myron's gaze snaps to the place my teeth cut into the sensitive skin. "Ten more months," he reminds me.

Ten more months until I'm free. I can't believe it's been over two months since Royad took me from Fort Perenis.

"King Erina won't be pleased though if he finds out I let this year's tribute go." He cocks one dark brow, studying how all color drains my face.

It's been a long time since the Tavrasian king's name came up, and the shudder at the mention of King Erina Latroy Jelnedyn is no less intense than the last time Myron brought him up.

"You're not intending to tell him of our deal, are you? He doesn't need to know…"

"He doesn't need to know," Myron confirms before panic can take me. "That, however, doesn't mean he won't hear about it from one source or the other."

"Does he have spies in Askarea?" It's the only logical explanation since I'd be surprised if any of the Crows wandered out of the Seeing Forest to inform the Tavrasian king themselves.

"Kings have spies everywhere, Ayna. Just because they are not walking right under our noses doesn't mean there aren't those who carry information out of the Seeing Forest. The Flames aren't the only ones unhappy with our presence in this realm."

I gnaw on the meaning of his words, on the multiple possibilities of who—besides King Recienne and his court—could even know about the Crows in Eherea.

"Word of the next bride who died always makes it out of this palace somehow," he explains. "Why would it be different with a bride who survives?"

"Survive—" I echo, breathless from the hope I'm fighting from welling up. "Let's learn how to fight immortal monsters first." It's a weak attempt at humor, and Myron doesn't buy it—or he's offended by the use of the word *monsters*, for he shoves open the door to the training room, all the openness vanishes from his gaze and the mask of the unbothered king pulled up once more.

It takes me three heartbeats to digest the sudden change and another three to understand that it's not because he is shutting me and my concerns out. It is because of the copper-haired female leaning against the wall beside the weapons rack, arms crossed over her chest and a smirk on her full lips that distracts from the challenging sparkle in her jade eyes. If it weren't for the uniform-like leathers she's wearing, I could have mistaken her for a beautiful fairy bandit, but she's Princess Cliophera, and frost cracks at her fingertips as she drums them along her biceps.

"I was beginning to think you were trying to trick me, Myron," she chirps with saccharine friendliness that is by no means genuine. Quite the contrary. One look at me and her expression shifts to one of professional assessment. "So, it is true? You want me to train her?"

"What?" The word flips out without my permission as I whirl on Myron. "You could have told me." Told me that I am supposed to train with a high fae—one whose brother is holding the Crows' freedom in his hands with the bargain he offered Myron decades ago.

"I wasn't certain she'd show." Myron slides his fingers around the edge of my waist, grip tightening as if he's readying himself to yank me out of the path of a wicked fairy attack.

Cliophera pushes away from the wall, a chime-like laugh bursting from her lips. "You think I'd let down a female trapped in your little realm of torment? You think wrong." She prowls closer, every movement graceful and feline, predatory and deliberate. She is lethal as much as the Crow King beside me.

My heart is in my throat by the time she comes to a halt in front of me, raking her gaze down my body, up again until she finally meets mine.

"Let's have a little fun, Wolayna, shall we?"

THIRTY

What the fairy princess has in mind doesn't even describe *fun* in the loosest of my definitions. Frost is covering her fingers, running up her arms and weapon as she draws her blade to point it at me.

Myron's wing shoots between us like a feathery beacon of defense, but I have my dagger at the ready—both daggers since my bad hand needs the exercise.

"That's not what we agreed upon," he snarls, stepping into the princess's path, death in his eyes.

But the fairy princess vanishes from my view—blatantly disappears like she never existed in the first place. I gape past Myron's shoulder, lowering my center of gravity for faster reaction in case Princess Cliophera decides to return with a vengeance.

"It's not," she chirps from behind me, the sweetness in her tone dripping down my neck as she places the tip of her sword at my nape. "But I'd like to see how skilled your bride is otherwise before I work with her on her magic."

I freeze in place, and it's not because her frost extends along her blade right onto my exposed skin.

Myron has turned to face her over my shoulder, and there's menace in his eyes. Menace and terror. "Don't forget we have a bargain."

I'm not sure if he's speaking to her or to me. Only the way Princess Cliophera's blade slides away from my neck as she gives an unbothered laugh informs me it's her. "How could I forget?" She stalks around me, winking at me as my gaze snaps to hers, my heart still hammering like it would rather gallop to the ends of the horizon, as far as possible from this Guardiansforsaken place.

"You made a bargain with her?" Now it's me who has menace in her voice as I demand from Myron what, by all his cruel gods, he thought by making a bargain with the entities forcing his people to remain restricted to the Seeing Forest.

"I can train you in swordsmanship, Ayna," he says softly, as if it were only the two of us in this room. "But you have magic. Magic I don't understand. And to train that, you'll need someone who understands human magic."

"A fairy?" I don't even try to hide the panicked giggle bubbling up in my throat. "What does a fairy know about being human?"

Cliophera kicks a pebble into the nearby corner and gives me a meaningful look. "I never said I knew anything about humans. Only that there is someone I know who used to be human but has been alive for over a century, and she is wielding some kick-ass magic."

There's nothing I can say to that.

The fairy princess swaggers back to the weapons rack and picks up the pitcher of water at the foot of it while Myron leans in to whisper close by my ear. "I don't trust her, but she might be the only one willing to help us."

"Help us?" I whisper back, awareness of how close our faces are lining up inside of me as his hair slides against my cheek. "This female threatened you last time she marched into your throne room," I remind him. "Why would she help you?"

"*Us*," he corrects, his hands brushing my dagger-clutching one. "I made a bargain they couldn't refuse."

Before I can ask him what he offered, what other piece of him, his freedom, his people's future he bargained away for me, the fairy princess clears her throat, drawing our attention back to her leather-clad form.

"I hate to interrupt your little—I don't know what it is, but it seems rather intimate. Could it be you've found a bride who doesn't despise you after all, Crow King?"

A tremor runs through Myron's body, and his face shifts to bird features as he hisses a warning at her.

"Oh, don't worry. I'm not going to tell a soul," the princess says with a smirk I quickly learn to identify as delighted observance of the Crow King's misery.

What had she said? She'd once been destined to be Carius's bride? However she escaped and lived to see the day is a story I'd love to hear one day. But for now, I'd really like to not feel like the female is about to invite me to a tea party with deadly creatures.

"Hold up your end of the bargain; I'll hold up mine." It's all Myron says before he gently squeezes my bad hand around the hilt of my dagger. "Don't worry. I'll be right here in case she doesn't."

The princess rolls her eyes at him, gesturing impatiently at the carved rock by the weapons rack where he likes to take up residence when he watches Royad and me spar with our blades.

"Yes, yes, what a noble protector you are." She swirls the water in the crystal jar she's picked up like it were a goblet of wine, and it's almost comical.

Only, there's nothing comical about being shoved into a room with a deadly fairy. One who is scrutinizing me with vigilant green eyes I can't seem to escape. I'll bite off Myron's head for it later—if I walk out of here alive.

Princess Cliophera seems to not be as worried about keeping a beating heart and a breath in her lungs, for she flashes a dazzling smile, which momentarily stuns me. "So, here we are." She uses that sweet voice I am certain is a trap.

"Here we are." I am hovering in a half crouch, ready to block an attack—of blades. I have nothing to shield an attack of magic.

"And you look better even than last time I saw you, Wolayna." Is it just me, or does she sound pleased by the fact I haven't fallen prey to a Crow beak?

"Doing what I can. It's getting a bit boring though with just males around. I could do with a female confidante with all that feathery male attitude around here."

Myron chokes on a cough, and the princess laughs, sheathing the sword in her other hand as she approaches on silent feet.

"I like you, Wolayna." With a flick of her hand, she sends the jar floating in front of her, holding out her other hand to me. "Princess Cliophera Clarette Tarie Amaryll Saphalea de Pauvre," she introduces herself. "But you may call me Clio." She gives a wink. "You know, between royalty."

There is something so undeniably charming about her that I almost take her hand and shake it—then I remember that this is a fairy who hates the Crows, one whose family is responsible for locking Myron's people in this forest. I grab my daggers harder and say nothing.

"Oh, don't worry. You'll warm up to me once you see I'm not here to kill you. What Myron here offered is more than enough motivation to train you in magic, cooking, hunting, or even crochet—if I knew how to do that." She laughs at her own joke and manages to somehow make me smile even when it was a really bad joke.

"I like crochet…" I place a finger at my bottom lip without letting go of my dagger, pretending to think. "I could use something to do while I wait around for this one every day of our fateful marriage."

At that, Clio bursts out with a laugh. A real one rather than one crafted to charm her political opponent—because that's what I am. Tied to Myron and damned to be seen as attached to the Crow Court. But in this one moment, something more shimmers in Clio's jade gaze, and I know that, had we met under different circumstances, I may not have been merely part of a bargain the Fairy Court made with the Crow Court but a friend.

The thought hits me right in the chest where the pain of losing all the people I dared call friends before still simmers like burning embers, and I slam down my defenses so hard something cracks deep inside of me.

It seems to be all I ever am these days. Part of bargains. A woman traded for the Crow's confinement to the Seeing Forest. A potential human magic wielder in a Crow-high fae training arrangement. Someone who asks questions to someone who promises answers. A bride for show in exchange for my freedom.

I can't help the bitterness fueling my words as I step back, pointing at the floating jar with the tip of my blade. "What is it you're going to teach me?"

Clio's features sober as she takes in my mood, reads it right from the swirling anger in my gaze, and nods. "How to survive."

Clio wasn't lying, I decide the next day when she's waiting for me in the training chamber an hour before dinner with a few jars of water at her disposal. Myron settles into his spot on the rock by the wall, monitoring how the fairy instructs me about the same basics of magic I didn't grasp the day before.

"It should resonate somewhere within you when you call it. Like a responding thrum," she explains as I dig deep into myself, searching for any awareness of that magical presence. It's gloriously absent, and so is my fear as all of me is too focused on repeating in my head what she's already taught me about how to keep one step ahead of my enemies in battle.

"It's about survival," she said, all that humor and swagger gone as she switched into the role of a general in a field as easily as I step into one of the feather-adorned dresses Myron keeps pulling for me for dinners. "If you manage to sense magic before it strikes, that will give you a heartbeat to block your opponent." She didn't say shield because that, apparently, is an entirely different ability from wielding water.

I stare at her, sweat beading my neck even as she lets ice spark through the air, cooling the room down enough for my breath to fog in front of my face.

Myron rubs his palms together, folding his wings tightly to his sides. Of course, he failed to put on a vest to cover up those sculpted muscles, and the way the cool air sends goosebumps along his skin is proof that—no matter how powerful—his flesh is just as sensitive as my human one.

"Focus on your magic," Clio bites at me. "Not *his*."

Myron's gaze snaps to mine, and for a brief moment, I forget where we are and what I should be doing. All I can see is the heat in his eyes as he catches me staring.

If I ever bed you, it will be because you beg me to.

I don't know why his words from our wedding banquet float into my mind at this very moment, but there is a part of me that wants to beg—for him to kiss me. To touch me. I'm not sure I'm ready for more with the way my stomach flips. That's how it started with Ludelle, and we all know where that landed me.

The sensation in my stomach turns into dripping bitterness, and I tear my gaze away from Myron's to focus on the female with the copper braid.

"On your magic," she repeats and jerks her chin at me as if that would tell me where to look.

"I'm not even sure I have magic." It's the truth, and no matter how much I want to be unbothered by the possibility, it stings. Stings that I am yet again the weak link. I was in my father's house. My childish naivety got him killed. I was on the Wild Ray where the love Ludelle and I shared got him killed. And I am now—the only human among fairies. Crow or otherwise.

"You do." Myron's plain confidence in me is like a stroke of his hand against my cheek and at the same time fear-instilling.

"We've been over this. It might have been the lake, not me."

"It was you." Again, he doesn't even hesitate.

"Does it matter? If there's a kernel of magic within you, I'll find it," Clio interrupts us, the expression of the general yielding to that of exasperation. "Now focus, or the only magic you'll see today is my invisible kick in your ass."

"Not very princessly of you." I grimace a half-felt fake grin at her, and she rolls her eyes, turning to Myron.

"Are you sure you still want the bargain?"

Myron only nods, and Clio faces me with her hands braced on her hips.

"All right. Then we'll need to step it up a bit, or we'll never get to see your pretty magic, Ayna."

Jars of water fly from the weapons rack, halting slightly above us in the air.

I don't get a warning before she dumps their contents over my head.

The only thing flickering to life inside of me is annoyance as I shake out my wet hair with a groan.

From the sidelines, I could swear Myron's chuckle carries through the frosty air as I gasp through the uncomfortable sensation of half-freezing wet in my collar.

"See?" Clio raises a sardonic brow at me. "That wouldn't happen if you actually listened to me instead of making googly eyes at your husband."

I don't deign her assessment with a response, instead spitting the water out and taking the towel Myron produces from thin air as he strides over, handing it to me.

"She's got a point," he whispers as he tucks a strand of wet hair behind my ear, and I can't stop myself from swatting his chest in a playful way that shouldn't feel so comfortable with the creature he is.

Myron flicks his fingers, and the empty jars disappear. "That's enough for today. We continue tomorrow."

Princess Cliophera strides from the room in the same manner she did the day before, and I wonder what she would say if I begged her to take me with her.

THIRTY-ONE

"What did you trade?" I try for what feels like the hundredth time as Myron walks me back from the training room.

He smooths his feathers out on his left wing—the one turned away from me—obviously avoiding meeting my gaze. "It's none of your concern."

It's easy for him to say that. "It's my life. And my potential magic," I snap at him, in a manner that's so very different from the woman who was scared witless by the powerful monarch at my side mere months ago. "I'd say that makes it my concern."

Myron shakes his head in a manner that convinces me he's not going to break, no matter how hard I push. When he doesn't want to talk, there's nothing that will make the Crow King speak. At least, it's not him trying to force information that will get us killed. If he'd traded anything of that sort, he'd have bled striking the bargain—not that I saw him negotiating with Clio, but something tells me it's nothing that will risk his life or mine. Just something he'd rather keep to himself.

And the secrets just keep piling up.

At least, I've dismantled some of them, like the curse and the Flames, and the lake. It's more than I want to know, to be honest, because it makes me feel even more useless when every attempt at figuring out what will save them is a failure. I don't know how many hours I've spent digging through Myron's library or scouring the details of the carvings in the palace walls. Nothing. All I find is more details on the Flames, who apparently are a people as vengeful as they are powerful—not that I needed to know. Them still trying to take back their palace after thousands of years tells me everything.

Shaking my head in defeat, I change the course of my thoughts to something more imminent. "What's for dinner?"

At that, Myron's gaze snaps to mine. "Fig pie."

Holding back a startled laugh, I lay my hand on his wing where his forearm would be if he had normal arms and earn a brow arched in surprise. "What?"

"I thought you only ate meat."

That, however, makes him laugh, and it's a sound so rare, my chest aches for the king trying to save his people, the male isolating himself further and further from his people in whatever misguided guilt for their horrible situation.

I slow to a stop, and Myron takes the cue, halting beside me and angling himself toward me as I glance along the empty corridors to make sure no one overhears our conversation.

"It's not your fault."

His all-black eyes lock on mine as he tries to decipher what I'm trying to say.

"That I don't eat meat?" It's a lax attempt at humor, and I'm not buying it.

"Your people. The curse. This mess—" I gesture around and at the two of us. "It's not your fault you're stuck here."

Myron cuts me off from whatever his gaze might show, eyes fluttering and shutting as he shakes his head. "That's where you're wrong, Ayna." His voice warps around my name like a caress of silk and darkness. "It *is* my fault." He gestures around, between us. "This mess, my people, that we're still stuck here." His chest rises and falls with a deep breath. "I didn't try hard enough, Ayna. And now, it's almost too late."

When his eyes open again, remorse is the only thing filling the fathomless depths that are Myron, the Valiant. And I forget to breathe.

Just when I think I might black out from the lack of air in my lungs, boots thud along the hallways leading toward the end of our corridor, where it ends in the entrance hall, and Myron turns and starts walking again. "We're expected at dinner."

I don't object when he places his hand on the small of my back, tucking me a bit tighter to him than usual as my thoughts still swirl in my mind.

I couldn't save my father or my crew. I couldn't save Ludelle and Ephegos. But I will find a way to save him.

Over the next weeks, Clio shows up every other day, a dangerous smirk on her beautiful fairy face and always a taunt at the ready for Myron, who never fails to sit with us for the training lessons.

Today is no different. I'm in my black pants and tunic, hair braided back and rolled into a bun at the nape of my neck. My daggers are sheathed at my hips, and my mood is the opposite of bright. I've spent the past two weeks trying to reach that supposed magical well inside of me without success, and Myron seems to be the only one convinced it's there. Clio offered to call it a day more than once, and I'd have happily agreed had Myron not insisted we keep trying.

So, here we are, me sitting cross-legged on the stone floor while Clio paces the room in large ovals, her gaze darting back and forth between the Crow King and me.

"Any specific reason you think I'll be able to find my magic sitting down?" I inquire without looking up from the pitcher of water in front of me, from which I've been trying to draw even a drop of water for the past hour.

"None other than that it's easier to pour a jarful of water over your pretty head from up here," Clio informs me with a grin I've learned to read as her making mock threats.

The warning hiss Myron issues across the room, however, is the real deal. He waves a casual wing at the fairy princess, gesturing for her to step as far away from me as the rectangular room allows.

Clio gives the Crow King a saccharine smile. "Come on, Myron. We've worked together for a century now. Don't act like you can't trust me to keep a bargain. The high fae have delivered every third year as the deal with my brother demands. You really think I'm going to mess up an agreement that could save both of us the trouble in the future?"

My mouth opens to ask what she means, but Myron growls, the sound bouncing around the room drowning out all thoughts.

"Too soon?" Clio asks sweetly over her shoulder before she turns her attention back to me.

Myron doesn't respond, only rises from the rock like a walking menace and comes to stand at my side. "Teach her. That's all you're allowed to do in these halls."

Clio has the good sense to look nervous at the cold fury in the Crow King's tone, and even I shudder as his wrath rakes through the air, tangible like the icy wind the fairy princess likes to produce. It's all I can do not to take a casual step away as the two immortal creatures stare each other down.

I roll my shoulders, reaching into the depth of myself, and beg the Guardians to give me a hint where to find that supposed magic of mine so I can throw a cold shower over Myron's head the way Clio did with me, and much to my surprise, I find a weak current in my veins that has little to do with the adrenalin coursing there.

Reach for it, Clio instructed the days before. *Reach for it, and pull it into your palms.*

That's exactly what I do.

Nobody is more surprised than me when power rushes from my hands and a blob of water rises from a nearby jar.

"Stop it!" Myron's command hisses through the air at the princess whose jade gaze is following the water like she is expecting it to explode into a million droplets any moment.

A smirk of understanding spreads on her lips as she realizes it's not Myron directing the water either. She folds her arms over her chest, raising a brow at him for no other reason than to torment him, I'm certain, and drawls, "Or what?"

I swear, Myron is boiling with rage beside me. I don't know what their bargain entails exactly, but I'm sure refraining from killing each other must be part of it, or they'd long have been at each other's throats.

"I might shower not only her but you as well."

I do appreciate the way she antagonizes the Crow King. I would have done the same thing two months ago, before

I learned what a tormented soul he is, how his cruelty has nothing to do with who he wants to be. How he's been fighting for freedom just as hard as I have—and that over a century.

"It's me." My voice comes out breathless as I hold onto my focus.

Myron's head whips to the side, his gaze tangible as he tries to figure out what I mean. The air feels tense to bursting; so does the magic in my veins as it coils along my arms into my palms, across the space to the bubble of water now hovering right in front of my face.

"By Shaelak—"

"I'd say, the Guardians," Clio corrects with that signature smirk. "But by all means, if you believe your gods are more receptive to our pleas, talk to them instead."

Her comment diverts my attention, and the grasp on my magic slips, sending the bubble spraying across the room.

Myron's bulging eyes are almost comical as he stares at me from his dripping face.

"Well, that's a surprise," Clio notes, her gaze on Myron rather than me. "A little human just rendered the powerful Crow King speechless."

But said Crow King ignores her, his gaze on mine, a smile tugging on his lips and a hint of pride gracing his beautiful, pale features. "I knew it," he whispers, and for that one moment, neither the place nor the fairy princess exist. It's just him and me and the absolute faith he's had in my magic even when I myself doubted there was anything to it.

Before the feeling can settle, can make that simmering warmth grow inside my chest, Clio flicks her hand, and another jar appears in the space between us. "Great. Now that you've figured it out, let's have some fun."

I don't know how many times I summon water that day, only that, with each time even a droplet lifts at my command, I become a little stronger, less vulnerable—and perhaps more of a target than I've been before. The mere idea of the defenseless bride suddenly wielding power will certainly earn me more enemies among the Crows who hope for the curse to remain unbroken, and they'll try to get me out of the way before I can do any more harm.

It's hours later when Clio leaves us to return to King Recienne's court with a parting wave at me that reminds me of a complicit rather than the enemy she is for Myron that I get a moment with my husband alone.

"The next political assembly is tomorrow." He holds the door for me, a thoughtful expression on his features.

"I know." He told me a few days ago to prepare me to step in front of the Crow Court in my official capacity again—also to give me time to process that, this time, Ephegos won't be there as his spymaster. My heart does a painful jolt for the friend I lost, for the lighthearted grins and witty comments he made when he escorted me along the hallways.

When I meet Myron's gaze, I could swear he's thinking about Ephegos, too.

"Who took over his role?" I never asked, shooing away from the pain of the conversation, the guilt flooding me at the mere mention of Ephegos.

"I haven't appointed a new spymaster." His tone is flat, his feet quick as he walks me down the corridor toward the stairs leading into the entrance hall. "Some of the attendees are coming in early so I can talk to them individually about the most recent developments."

"What developments?" I've been so focused on figuring out my magic, the curse, my role here in general that I haven't asked enough questions about the looming threat that are the Fire Fairies. "Did they burn down more villages? Any new intrusions into the palace that I don't know of?"

We reach the landing of the stairs, Myron rolling over whatever information he's about to share with me. His hand finds mine, and a smile spreads open his lips as he pulls me to a halt. "It doesn't matter. I'll take care of it."

I don't know what it is in his expression that scares the shit out of me—perhaps the too-soft smile that reminds me of something real rather than the show he and I have been putting on for his court. The hairs stand at the back of my neck, and my pulse quickens. Then, his words register. "What do you mean, you'll *take care of it*? Is there something going on that I should be aware of?" More Flames? Another assault on the palace he's been hiding from me? Did someone else die? I haven't seen Royad all day—

Myron's hand slides up my arm in a careful caress, his eyes watchful on mine as if he's anxious he'll miss something if he as much as blinks. When he reaches my shoulder, he lifts his fingers to my cheek, cupping my face with a touch so tender I almost lean into it on instinct.

"Everything will be all right, Wolayna." He smiles at me, strands of his hair damp from my water explosion framing his face in a way that gives him a less regal appearance and brings out a more primal sort of beauty.

"You can't possibly know that." My heart stutters. "The Flames are still out there, and the factions are still—"

"It doesn't matter." Myron lowers his face an inch, then another until he's whispering, lips brushing the shell of my ear, and I shiver as warmth creeps through my body like a presence of its own. "Everything will be all right because *you* are here."

He slides his mouth along my cheek, his breath hot and tingling on my skin, and I lean into him, even when he has made no move to touch me other than that mouth skimming my cheek.

"Myron—" His name comes out in a whisper as I brace myself for the onslaught of sensations that is the Crow King's kiss.

I turn my head to meet his mouth, and he tenses, a groan rumbling in his throat that tunes out the rest of the room. I'm ready for this kiss. So, so ready, breathing ragged and heart racing.

But the kiss doesn't come. Instead, Myron's hand grasps my shoulder, tugging me behind him as he whirls to the side like a male on a mission, and it takes me a few heartbeats to notice the blood running down the side of his spine in a thick streak originating right at the edge of his feathers. The hilt of a knife is sticking out of his flesh, gleaming in the fairy lights.

"Fuck—" I see them a moment before they strike again, tall, winged forms of the sort that have haunted my nightmares. And these two are definitely not of the faction believing that the Crows need an actual king.

THIRTY-TWO

A scream lodges in my throat as an invisible force rolls down the hall, Myron's magic holding off whatever blow the Crows deliver with powers of their own. But the knife in his back struck deep, and he grunts under the strain of keeping up his shield. Horror flushes my system like a tidal wave. This isn't the Flames trying to take back their palace. This is an attempt on Myron's life—and they've already landed one hit.

"We need to get out of here," I whisper, my hand hovering above the hilt of the knife protruding from the fluffy transition of feathers to skin as I debate whether dislodging the blade will help him or kill him faster.

"*You* need to get out of here," he mutters so low I barely hear him as he turns his head just enough that I can see his profile.

"I'm not leaving without you," I start to protest, but his magic wraps around my face, shutting my mouth before I can raise my voice and bring attention to myself.

"When I tell you to run, you will run, Ayna." He hisses as he blocks yet another attack with that shield of his. "Find Royad. He'll know what to do."

I nod, gaze locked on the danger approaching from the mouth of the corridor ahead. The stairs to the residential level are behind me. I wouldn't even need to cross in front of Myron. It would be easy.

Easy, except for the panic claiming me little by little at the thought of leaving Myron behind while he's weakened. Not that I can do much to help him. I might actually be a bigger liability than an aid.

The realization hits me all over again, how useless I am, how incapable of saving the people I care for. That somewhere between hating the Crow King and kissing him, I've allowed myself to come to care for him.

If I run, I might make it up the stairs and to the hallway where I know Royad's room to be situated, and if I'm lucky, the Crow male is home. He'll come to save Myron when I can't. Getting help is the best hope I have.

Myron sways on his feet as I place my palm between his shoulder blades in a reassuring touch.

"Be quick, Ayna. I don't know how long I can hold them off."

It is then that I see the black veins creeping across his skin from the edges of the wound. *Poison.* The knife is poisoned.

He doesn't respond when I tell him I'll race for both our lives, his focus back on the assassins, and I crouch, ready to sprint.

Every last muscle in Myron's back tenses as he summons his magic for a strike, hurling it across the hall in a thundering blow. My ears ring from the sound, but Myron's voice pierces through as he orders, "Now!" And I run. I run like I've never run before. Not on my escape through the Seeing Forest.

The stairs fly past under my boots, my steps not faltering on the slippery stone even when my entire body is shaking. The carvings in the wall are a blur, as are the columns and statues as I count them to stop losing myself to panic. Myron is fighting two assassins. Myron is injured. Myron wanted me out of the way because he doesn't think he can win against the two Crows in his state. The location of the knife tells me a lung might have been punctured—in addition to whatever poison the assailants added.

My legs burn, my throat is made of sandpaper, my heart races. If I find Royad before the poison develops its full effect, we might save him. I have to make it.

It's only when I knock on the plain wooden door at the end of the hallway that I realize I haven't passed a single guard on my way up. I was too preoccupied with Myron's lips on my skin, the anticipation of what might happen if our mouths connected to notice the hallways had been deserted.

Fuck. The faction against Myron planned this out well. Whatever they did to the guards—or were the guards even loyal? Did they desert their king the way so many other Crows have?

"Royad!" My lungs threaten to rip from my chest as I shout his name with all my strength, praying that their god Shaelak might have mercy.

There is only silence coming from Royad's room. No hasty footsteps, no door opening to reveal a worried friend ready to use his sword. Nothing.

"Help!" I shout, turning and turning as I run from door to door, hammering with my fists until my bad wrist protests, but no one answers, and my stomach plummets.

There is no help to be found.

My hands wander to my daggers on instinct. If there is no one else around to help their king, I will.

I make it all but five steps toward the stairwell when an ear splitting crack runs through the hallway, and I stumble on the shaking ground. Guardians—whatever is going on down there, my blades are not going to cut it. My human strength and speed are not going to cut it.

Royad isn't here, and there is nothing I can do.

Except, there is.

My pulse picks up pace from its already unhealthy speed as I train my gaze on Myron's bedroom door, legs already moving as I sheath one dagger to have a hand free to open it. Thank the Guardians there is no lock keeping me out, holding me back when I storm toward the murderous bathing room.

"I need water," I tell it with conviction. Because it's the only thing I can think of. If my daggers won't help me, maybe whatever magic I have is willing to aid me in saving one of the two people I have left in the world. "Please."

The door doesn't as much as quiver under the force of my full weight as I shove against it.

"Come on." I don't know why I talk to it or what I expect. It's a piece of wood with a history of not responding, but something about voicing my terror, my need to save him keeps me from shattering completely under the panic that has been building until it threatens to take all my logic.

"Open, by the Guardians. By Eroth. By any god in this fucking universe." I heave a breath, putting my full weight into the push as I scream, "By Shaelak!"

The door swings open so easily I have to drop to my hands and knees to catch my momentum so I won't stumble right into the lake. It's open. It's *open*, and in front of me lie the salty waters of past brides' tears. Of their pain and sorrow.

I try not to think about it as I draw upon my magic the way I trained all afternoon. It's sluggish, just as my body would be, exhausted from hours of workout, but I push through the slowness, urging it to stop creeping through my veins like honey instead of a gushing river.

It's not the magic in my body responding to my pleas but the sentient waters of the murderous lake that climb from their bed in long ribbons.

"Don't kill me," I tell the water, trying to keep my hands steady as I gesture toward the door. "I mean no harm. I mean nothing at all other than to save Myron's life."

"*Why?*" The question echoes in my head like through a haze, not male or female, not anything at all other than a command.

I don't care who or what it is as I retreat from the chamber, pulling on my magic in hopes of drawing the ribbons with me. There is only one answer I can give, and I don't hesitate, despite my shaking hands, my trembling voice, the tightness in my chest that tells me I'm already feeling more for Myron, King of Crows, than I ever intended to allow myself. "Because I am his only chance."

In a thunderous cloud, the water washes around me, ribbons weaving into a web of glistening liquid, shoving me through the door on hands and knees. The stone scrapes along my palms, claiming bloody streaks, which the water instantly clears away with each inch it pushes me back, back, back, until I'm out of the chamber, until my shivering form slumps within the wet constraints.

I brace myself to be swallowed up, to be drowned the way the lake tried that first time I came near.

"*Rise,*" the bodiless voice repeats as the water pulls back, allowing me to scramble to my feet, and I do.

With all I have, I pick myself up, my bad hand giving out as I use it to push myself up. My wince dies in a whirl of cool liquid winding around my arm, caressing the sore spot where my stiff wrist is protesting.

The water doesn't soak me, though. Instead, it's climbing all over my body, weaving around me like armor until I'm wrapped in a shiny shield. In my bad hand, I feel the prickling sensation of my magic—of the lake's power—drawing me forward as if telling me to go save the Crow King.

"Thank you," I whisper into the room, the shaking never ceasing as I set one unsure step after the other toward the hallway where Myron's roars of rage are weakening.

I'm running out of time—and so is he.

The water armor slides smoothly along with my strides as I rush down the hallway, heart beating out of my chest as the noise of battle becomes slower, weaker. Then, I'm at the banister, looking down at the entrance hall—and my blood ices over.

The two Crows are crouching on either side of an unconscious Myron, their bird faces hidden in shadows as they lean over him, claws ready to rip him to ribbons.

"Leave him alone." My voice doesn't tremble from fear now that unadulterated rage floods my veins, my thoughts, every last part of myself.

Their heads snap up, all-black eyes finding mine, and the delight on their features—I remember them like it was yesterday that they hunted me down in the forest, and it's obvious they can't wait to take revenge for my escape.

"Lovely, I've been wondering if we'd get the opportunity to kill the both of you today or if we'd need to hunt you down—again," one of them caws, the sound grating along my bones like coarse sandpaper, and I shake my head to maintain my anger. They tried to kill me then, do much worse than kill me if what

Myron told me is to be believed. They attacked their king in his own home. They brought him to the ground, knocked him out, were about to shred him apart.

"No hunting." I palm my dagger in my good hand, raising the bad one with the pulsing magic contained in it, and give them a feral grin I haven't used since the last looting on the Wild Ray. "Not for you, at least."

I don't wait before I hurl the water at them with a scream. It bursts from my body like a gushing river, eating up the stairs as it falls step by step at neck-breaking speed.

The two Crows startle, leaping to their feet and raising their magic to strike. The air ripples in the entrance hall, making it difficult to breathe, and I cough as a thin, silky layer of water wraps back around my torso, protecting me like translucent steel. The rest of the water stays its course, aiming for the Crows, their eyes widening with fear when their power does little to push me off balance.

"Don't touch Myron," I tell the deadly stream and feel the water nod even when all I can see is the spray of the former brides' tears as they disperse, each of them a projectile piercing the Crows' bodies. Their screams tear through the entrance hall like a sinking ship coming up one last time before the ocean takes it. Then, the water rushes their lungs, their own blood lacing the crystal liquid as it fills their lungs, streaming out through the holes the water punctured all the way through their bodies.

All I can do is stare as they collapse into the waves lapping up at them as the lake drags them under. I don't know where it starts and where it ends, only that it's everywhere. Everywhere, except for that narrow spot where Myron is lying on the gray stone floor like on an island in a rocky sea, one wing stuck beneath his body while the other one is draped over his side at an odd angle. A trickle of blood is running from his mouth, and

I can tell it has nothing to do with a truth he shouldn't have spoken. This is the assassins' doing.

And they've stopped struggling, their limbs floating lifelessly in the water.

"Enough," I tell the lake as I rush down the stairs, taking two steps at once. My boots pound the slick stone as I grab onto the handrail with my bad hand, desperate to keep my weapon and my balance at once.

When I make it down to the lake, the water raises a wave as in question, and I nod at it. "Thank you." I don't stop where the liquid slushes over the lowest steps but hop right into the water.

Before my feet touch the floor, the lake retreats, rolling and winding and coiling until it is a thread of glimmering silver climbing to the upper levels. By the time I drop into a crouch by Myron's side, the stone is clean and dry, and the two assassins lay stranded and dead.

THIRTY-THREE

A groan runs through Myron's body then right through my very heart as he stirs under a light touch of my fingers.

"You…" Blood trickles from his mouth in a fresh streak of crimson, covering the old, drying one. "Saved…"

"Shhh—" I place my finger over his lips. "Keep your strength for healing. Because I didn't beg the murderous lake for aid just so you can die on me once the assassins are taken care of."

I'm not surprised when Myron's mouth twitches in half amusement, half disapproval, and it fucking breaks my heart right at the center. How he manages to look breathtaking even at the brink of death, I am not even trying to understand. It's way too late to convince myself that I am not entirely lost when it comes to the king splayed before me. Lost—because if I weren't, I wouldn't just have put everything at risk to protect him. I would have let the Crows be done with him and made a run for it.

I'm fucked. I truly am.

"Can you stand?" I ask as he slowly coils into a sitting position, flexing his wing arms. By the Guardians—

Bruises spread along his chest and abdomen, stretching along his side all the way to his spine.

"What did they do to you?"

Myron's gaze snaps to follow my own, landing on the purple blotch right above his heart. "This"—he coughs, pauses, and takes a deep breath before he continues—"is a minor nuisance." He brushes off the dust from his pants as he gets to his feet like nothing happened. Only my months of studying the Crow King tell me that his injuries are far from a nuisance. It's in the way his hands slightly tremble as he tucks them to his sides, in the way his features tighten as he takes a step. Well, then there is the blood and bruises. Big giveaway.

"Stop being a Guardiansforsaken proud bastard, and let me help you." I don't ask permission as I grab his hand and drape his wing across my shoulder with as much gentleness as my mild annoyance allows. Apparently, fairy males are no different from men when it comes to injuries. Both are too scared to admit to weakness even when it's obvious they just nearly died.

Myron grunts a protest, but I prop him against my side and tug him along toward the stairs. "You can't half-carry me up there."

"You have no idea what I can do." I grit out the words as we make it to the first of the polished steps and I drag him along. "I just summoned a lake to make sure those monsters"—another step—"can't finish their job." And another. "I used to be the one to get away with the least injuries on loots because I'm quicker than most of the crew of the Wild Ray was." Ignoring the ache in my chest at the mention of my former family, I push my own and half of Myron's weight up the next step.

"Right." The bitterness in his tone strikes me as odd, but I attribute it to the pain he's in. "I wouldn't know. Because you never told me anything about your past."

"Not that you ever needed to ask. You already know everything there is to know about me." Another step and another. We're making good progress here with anything but our communication. "Apparently, your spies are effective even far, far away from the borders of your Seeing Forest. Which means I shouldn't need to tell you what I'm capable of."

Myron grunts again as I rush the next step, my shoulder shoving into his side. "Just because I know about your past doesn't mean I know anything about you." His tone is so strained I fear his voice might snap. The pain he must be in—

"Ready to admit they nearly killed you?" I put more force into the next step just to prove a point.

Gritting his teeth, Myron follows my movements. Naturally, I pretend not to notice the little wince escaping his carefully crafted control.

"You know you were unconscious when I brought the lake down on those monsters."

"Monsters," he echoes so low I barely pick up the different sort of pain in his voice as we make it to the top of the stairs. He braces his other hand on the railing, glancing down the entrance hall where a splatter of blood is the only sign of the fight that nearly killed him.

"Let's get you cleaned up and settled so you can use that sublime power of yours to heal yourself."

He doesn't argue when I pull him along, his weight settling against my side more with every step. He's exhausted, and we both know it. If another assassin is lurking in these hallways, neither of us will be able to defend ourselves, so our best chance is to get him into his room where his wards will lock out any assailant who dares try to get to him.

"Where are the guards?" I ask when we're halfway toward his door.

His feathers slide along my neck as he takes a glance around as if he is only noticing now that the hallways are deserted. "The rebel Crows must have taken them out." The simmering anger in his tone is nothing compared to the fury building inside of me. "Or they never were loyal." The thing with never letting me wander the palace on my own suddenly makes a whole lot more sense.

"There's a reason I only trust Royad and E—" He stops mid-word, his free hand aiming at the door as we make it there, and it swings open at the magical command.

"Ephegos," I whisper, my chest clenching at how close I came to losing Myron just the way I lost my friend.

Because Myron is a friend, too, I tell myself. But there's little I can do to convince myself that's all he is. Friends don't stare at each other with eyes full of fire. They don't devour each other in breathtaking kisses, don't make you question with a touch if you've ever felt alive before.

"He was a good Crow." Myron braces his weight on the threshold as he waits for me to cross, and the space between the ancient wooden frame is suddenly too tight not to make awareness flood my entire system.

"He was." I don't even know what a *good* Crow is. If there is a definition of good and bad in his world other than being on his side or the side against him. I've seen how ruthless he can be when it comes to defending what is his, what he believes in, the limits he's willing to push even when it means he needs to destroy himself in order to make sure his people will be released from their curse.

And there it is, like a thread of silver streaming through my chest to envelop my heart in a woven sheath of dread: Myron is *good*. Everything he does is to protect, to save his people. Even those who work against him he is striving to free. He might be willing to make sacrifices when it comes to those who'd rather see him dead, but he isn't out there waging war. He's not torturing his brides, not forcing them to serve him in any way. He's a good male. No matter what he believes.

And he's given up on himself because he thinks he isn't worthy of being saved.

My heart cracks all over again as I find those all-black eyes staring back at me, find my hand resting lightly upon the bruise over his heart—like I can do anything to protect the organ nestled under that silken skin, those solid muscles, the ribs enclosing it like a cage. He is in a prison of his own. One of the mind.

"Ayna—"

I barely register he's spoken my name. It's become second nature to hear it from his lips, to relish the way his deep timbre wraps around it.

Only when he sways do I realize he is trying to tell me to get inside so he can close the door and sit or lie down—or slump right there on the hardwood floor. I rush over the threshold, securing his arm over my shoulder as I help him toward the bed. Behind us, the door slides shut with a soft click as if Myron can barely expend enough power to move the wood.

My shoulders are aching, my legs less and less steady under the strain of his increasing weight as his strength is fading with each pace we make it closer to the bed. When we are a step away, he collapses into a half-sitting position at the edge of the mattress, the feathers quivering on his shaking wings, but his hand slides around mine, holding on for dear life.

"Thank you."

Again, I shush him, freeing my hand to gently push him back onto the bed before helping him bring his legs up onto the mattress. "You need to rest." Not that I know the least bit of what a Crow needs after draining themselves of their power and being physically injured.

Myron smiles, eyes closing as his head rests on the pillow I sleep on every night. "I was serious earlier. I don't know nearly enough about you, Ayna. Tell me something that a spy or a prison guard cannot tell me about you."

I'm still trying to adjust to how his weak tone affects me but gratefully take the moment to study him without having his scrutiny upon me. It's a new feeling, one of vulnerability—his rather than mine—and it has nothing to do with his physical state. This is about him opening a window I've tried so desperately to keep closed and him creeping through even when he's not trying to.

Perhaps it is the fact that he isn't trying to achieve anything other than tuning out the pain while he recovers that makes me respond. "I killed the man I loved."

My hand is shaking as hard as his were before, but he catches it in a talon-tipped one of his own, clutching it tightly as he presses it back to his chest, right over his heart. "A knife killed Captain Ludelle."

I don't know how he knows Ludelle's name or why his words hurt so much when he's basically giving me absolution, and I don't even want to go into what Ludelle's name on his lips does to me.

"I might as well have been the one wielding it." Tears shoot to my eyes without my permission, my chin crumpling as I press my mouth into a tight line against the sob building in my throat.

The kindness in Myron's eyes should no longer surprise me, yet it does as he lifts his head an inch as if trying to sit up. Blowing out a breath, he slumps back into the pillows as if this attempt cost him more even than opening and closing the door. "It was his choice. He tried to save you, Ayna. If nothing else, that should teach you how much he cared for you."

There is no holding back the sob this time because there is a new guilt building in my chest even as the truth of his words settles deep inside of me. I did love Ludelle. I loved him with my whole heart. But there's a part of me that has only recently come to life under the watchful eyes of the Crow King—and even when I can't allow myself to love Myron, I can't deny that I'm falling for him. Slowly, reluctantly, but I'm halfway there.

There is another thing I can't deny: If he won't return to his grumpy, distant self any time soon, I can't guarantee that I won't crash through the second half of that path to heartbreak. Because if there is one thing I know for certain, it is that if I allow myself to love this male and lose him, there will be no recovering.

THIRTY-FOUR

I sit with Myron half the night as he rests on his plush bed, the blue cotton sheets exactly where I draped them over his form when he fell asleep through our conversation. Telling him about pirate life was supposed to take his mind off the pain—that of his physical injuries as much as that of the betrayal.

"I'll talk to Royad as soon as he shows up," I told Myron right before promising I wouldn't wander off alone to find the Crow.

"We can't rely on the lake to follow you everywhere," he joked when I'd explained how the water from the sacred chamber had allowed me to wield it. Whether it was a one-time rescue aid or a permanent partnership remains to be determined.

Now, Myron is sleeping, his midnight lashes two half-moons below his puckered brows. Even when he's drifted off, the pain and signs of exhaustion don't seem to leave his body. Only the purple bruises are slowly retreating beneath my fingers while his hand hasn't released mine from where he's holding it over his heart.

"You know I sailed the seas for years?" he says, almost making me slide off the edge of the bed where I've been perched all night, unable to bring myself to pull away when his grasp is the only way he allowed himself to tell me he needs my support. A soft smile curves his mouth as his eyes open, finding me panting as I bring my pulse back to a reasonable pace. "I didn't mean to startle you."

"I thought you were sleeping." Or I wouldn't have continued to murmur to him long after I assumed he'd drifted off. Wouldn't have whispered how much I love the dirty teal the Quiet Sea turns the morning after a storm or how my heart sings when I look east to where nothing but freedom is calling. How Ludelle had promised me we'd sail there one day. How I hate myself for not having listened to him and just set sail and disappeared. How I no longer hate this place entirely. How there is a part of me that sees beauty in the grayscale of Crow life. How my human heart might be a speck of color even when I bleed more easily than any of the Crows do. How *he* is one of the reasons I no longer hate it here.

"Healing requires more of a sentient stasis."

Hence the not-letting-go of my hand since his fingers release mine pretty quickly now that he's out of said stasis.

"Sentient," I repeat. He heard everything.

A nod confirms he did. "Thank you for keeping watch over my rest, Wolayna." There is no awkwardness as he smiles at me with exhausted eyes. "I'll guard your secrets the same way you guarded me."

"Where did you sail?" I asked instead of one of the fifteen other options coming to my mind—that he doesn't need to thank me. That I was foolish to believe he wouldn't be able to pick up each and every word even when less than a murmur. That he can forget those things right away because they are none of his business. Because the truth is I want him to know how much my heart aches when I glance out the windows each morning, missing the brine and salty wind washing away the sleepiness. How much I wonder if flying feels similar to sailing across smooth, glistening waters. If there is a chance he might tell me where he came from, where he is aching to go if the curse ever gets broken.

Myron's throat bobs before he speaks, black eyes shimmering in the dimmed fairy lights. "Along the coasts of Neredyn in hopes to escape the gods. West toward new hope, new lands, where our people might find peace." He swallows again, gaze darting to the pitcher of water on the nightstand.

I dive into my newfound magic and draw a string of water into the crystal goblet beside it before handing it to him.

The proud smile Myron presents me with makes my heart swell, and I need to press my mouth into a line in order to keep myself from returning it. It would be the beginning of my end.

"I'd say the fairy princess did a great job teaching me," I say instead, gesturing at the goblet he's sipping from.

He shakes his head. "She is a terrifying creature, but she isn't as horrible as one might believe."

I keep to myself that I figured that out on my own about two days into our training.

"She once was an intended bride. My father had a bargain with King Recienne, the First. She slipped through because a human woman valued the lives of all her friends above her own." The look he gives me turns my heart into a puddle—because the question is there, in his eyes, if I'd sacrifice my life for that of my friends. If I would die rather than see one of them die.

"What a lucky female." It's the only response I find, and Myron nods his agreement.

"Lucky indeed. Lucky, because she knows true love."

I don't know why his words send shivers down my spine, why they sound more like an admission to a flaw than an appreciation of someone else's luck to have found and forged such strong bonds.

Instead of responding, I draw more water into his goblet, and he drains it before sitting up to place it back on the nightstand.

He's so close the air tastes of wind and pine, and his eyes—

Two bottomless midnight windows gazing at me as if he's never seen me before even when he's studied me all this time from afar or up close. Heat coils in my stomach, the sensation rolling through my body as he brushes back a loose strand of hair.

"The water didn't soak you," he notes again, even when we've been through the specifics of what happened. This time, his pride raises a tingling awareness deep inside of me. "You're powerful, Ayna."

"Powerful enough to kill two Crows," I whisper.

"To kill a Crow King if you'd wanted to."

It hovers between us for a breath, his statement, offering for me to say I regret not letting him die, not using that new power to rid the world of him.

"To kill a Crow King," I echo, which is beginning to feel like a habit, so I push on. "Who would I fight with if I killed you off?" It's a weak attempt at dispersing the tension building between us, the tension that has always been there in a way.

"Who indeed?" The grin he gives me is nothing short of wicked, and I forget how to breathe altogether as he invades my space until our faces are lined up with mere inches between. His breath heats my lips as I wait, wait, wait with burning anticipation. His hand wanders up the arm I've braced beside his hip, swiping along my shoulder, my neck in a feather-light brush until it comes to a halt under my chin. With pressure so slight I barely feel it as more than a caress, he tips up my face until my eyes lock on his. "But right now, I'd rather kiss you."

He leans another inch closer, his heated gaze blurring as I inhale the honey and mint of his breath, as I ache to close that gap. But his fingers close around my chin, locking me in place as he hovers just out of reach. "You know, I don't waste time to fight with people I don't care for," he murmurs before he finally, finally quenching that ache the distance between us induced, his mouth touching mine ever so slightly—and pulls back, bringing a whole new devastation to well up inside of me. "As I don't kiss people I don't care for."

"Even for show?"

For a beat, he stills like I've hit him right where it hurts, but he recovers fast, his mouth finding mine in a desperate kiss that has my mouth falling open as I gasp for breath as he sucks and nips on my lips until a moan escapes my throat. The slide of his tongue against mine summons heat to my core as he explores my mouth with expert strokes, as I ignite like a torch of eternal fire.

"Not like this," he whispers when my breathing has turned ragged, my fingers digging into the sheets right by his hip so as not to slide it up his side to feel him shiver under my touch. Guardians—I want him. Want to lean into the hardness of his chest, to run my fingertips along the grooves of his muscles.

"Tell me, Myron…" My voice is trembling as he releases my chin to draw his hand down the side of my neck, mouth following to the base of my throat where he draws idle kisses along my collarbone. "How do you kiss a woman you want?"

His lips still, and for a beat, I'm afraid I said something wrong, asked too much of him when this is all a game to him. But the way his mouth crashes back onto mine tells me it's anything but a game. That he feels the fire as much as I do, that he will combust if he can't get his hands on me.

As if my thought summoned them, his wings wrap around my shoulders, one hand delving into my hair, at the nape of my neck where he tugs slightly until the angle allows him to deepen the kiss as he takes full advantage. My skin is on fire. My entire body is one wave of pleasure after the other chasing through me, fueling the heat melting my core. My eyes fall shut, and the world disappears as he groans low in his throat, the sound kindling a pulsing need that I know will hound me if I let him out of my grasp now. So, I lock my arm around his neck, securing him to my face as I suck on his lower lip, his tongue, as I kiss him like my life depends on it—and he kisses me right back, the same desperation in every ragged breath, every nip of his teeth and stroke of his tongue.

And still, it is not enough. Still, I need him closer.

Pulling back an inch, I slide free my hand between us to explore that chiseled chest of his, every ridge and slope of his muscles as they ripple with his movements. He loosens his hold on me, his fingers tracing the neckline of my tunic while his mouth finds that spot behind my ear I didn't know could send shivers of pure pleasure through my system. But it does. More importantly, *he* does. With every inch he grazes down the side of my neck, I arch into his kiss. With every inch his fingers brush closer to my chest, I lean into his touch until his taloned thumb grazes the underside of my breast and, Guardians above, does my flesh heat even with my tunic still between us.

It is only for a few heartbeats, I swear to myself before I release him for the benefit of unbuttoning my tunic to give him better access, but it's enough to notice the way his eyes track my movements while his fingers curl into my waist as if it costs him restraint not to tear the fabric right off me. The hunger there—like he has been starving for a century and I'm the forbidden fruit he is denying himself.

But I don't want to be. I'm craving him like a sail craves the wind.

"Touch me," I whisper, almost afraid he'll pull back from me like those other times before when a kiss was almost too much.

Instead, the darkness in his eyes turns to black fire. There is no hesitation when he lays me back on the bed and leans over me, sliding me up on the mattress with an arm under my waist and one under my shoulders until my head rests on the pillow. He straddles me, peeling the tunic aside as he places a kiss on my lips first, then lowers his mouth over my breast, tongue swiping a slow circle around my nipple. I cry out as he flicks it with the tip of his tongue, sucking before he releases it. More. I need more.

My hands slide through his feathers as I move them up his thighs to his hips, to the front of his pants, and my mouth dries up at the hardness I find pushing against the waistband. I squeeze gently, and his hiss caresses my peaked flesh where he was about to kiss the tip of my breast.

"Stop it or I won't be able to keep control." His growl drives a new sort of shiver through my body, a primal reaction to an instinct I didn't even know existed deep inside of me. One that makes me want to squeeze harder, push him to find the limits of his oh-so-perfect control.

I want to see him when he jumps the leash he's put on himself. Want to watch him come undone. Want to be the reason he lets go of all reason.

Instead of pulling away, I arch my back as I stroke his length, my other hand finding his firm ass. Guardians, if he won't lose control, I certainly will. He grinds into my palm, a groan on his lips, and I grin at the way his fingers tighten on my waist as he seems to be fighting the urge to rip my pants right off.

"I want you, Myron." I don't know what makes me bold enough to demand him. Don't know if there is anything he's willing to give me. But I don't care. The liquid need between my thighs makes me reckless, impulsive, and I want him. I want him more than I've ever wanted anything. "Please." It's a whisper. A plea that seems to snap what restraint he had left, and as he pounces—

His talons shred through my pants without ever touching my skin, and he's smirking at me like I've just made the most reckless choice of my life—and gloriously pleased with himself. "I promised if I ever bedded you it would be because you begged me to." It's a near growl, and the sound makes me ache for the feel of him between my legs.

I remember our wedding banquet, how I'd feared him then. And how those words had made me wonder if there was any woman willing to get close enough to a monster such as him.

There is no fear now as I meet his smirk with one of my own. His sensuous mouth twitches with delight as I run a finger down the center of his stomach, and it's enough to make me want to press my thighs against each other—or spread them wide, I am no longer sure. "You promised something else."

Myron's lips curl into a feral grin as his gaze cuts to my bare flesh, and he shakes his head. "That I can *devour* you better than anyone else in this palace? That wasn't a promise, just a fact."

He doesn't wait for a response as he slides back, lowers his face between my thighs, and licks straight through my center.

A cry escapes my lips as he hovers right over that spot I need him to touch, teasing with gentle scrapes of his teeth and deft strokes of his tongue until I moan my pleasure and frustration as he keeps me right there on the edge.

I need more of him, need him inside of me or I'll implode from the tension in my core.

"You taste like a gift from the gods, Ayna," he murmurs onto my slick flesh, and the gust of air blowing over the apex of my thighs is enough to make me shove my fingers into his silken hair and knot them there as I moan, "Please, Myron."

I more feel than hear his chuckle, but he obliges, sliding a finger into my core, then a second, stretching me so deliciously I almost tumble over the edge. There are no talons at his fingertips now, thank the Guardians, and each glide of his fingers makes me forget a little more that we just escaped with our lives, that this is the Crow I was married to against my will—that I am not exactly sure anymore if I want to leave at the next Ret Relah. And that's before he puts his mouth back on me, *devouring* as he so bluntly described all those weeks back.

Stars explode in my vision as he pushes me into my release, fingers filling me and tongue caressing me as I shudder and tremble beneath him, and when I'm done, he rises, the buttons of his pants open to reveal the full length he's been hiding beneath the leather.

I whimper—genuinely whimper at the sight of him, because if I don't get his cock inside of me right now, I'll forget myself and beg for real.

"You're so beautiful," he tells me as he swipes his gaze along my naked body, catching on my breasts, my mouth, then locking with mine. "Beautiful beyond words."

My breath catches at the way the black of his eyes shimmers in a bluish tint that reminds me of dark ink, but he closes them before I can be sure.

He leans over me, the tip of his cock hovering a few inches from my entrance, that grin back on his face. I buck my hips, pushing myself closer, but he pulls just out of reach, lowering his mouth to mine in a kiss that should not take me by surprise but entirely does for the painstaking slowness of it.

"Please," I whisper as I come up for air, and Myron groans as he settles between my thighs, nudging inside an inch. "*Please-please-please.*"

He thrusts into me to the hilt in one long stroke, and the moan coming from his lips might have been the most beautiful sound I've ever heard. "Ayna," he whispers. "Ayna." Just my name.

Then he's moving, each thrust slow and powerful, bringing me right back to the cliff I've just leaped from. His hands are *everywhere*—caressing my breasts, stroking my neck, my jaw, my waist. It's not enough. I need to be closer still. So, I lock my arms around his neck, pulling him against my arching chest as I capture his mouth in a kiss that has him growling his approval. The sound pierces right to my core where pleasure has been building like a volcano ready to erupt.

"Perfect, Ayna. You're—" He stops mid-word as I start moving my hips in time with his, deepening the fit and increasing the pace. That's when he snaps, his thrusts becoming harder, wilder as he holds me against his body like he's terrified I'll disappear, like he needs to feel me just as desperately as I need to feel him. Pleasure barrels through me like molten lava as he thrusts his tongue into my mouth in time with his cock, and I legitimately wonder if I just splintered into a million stars. It's only his wings holding me together as he drives into me a few more times, his entire body trembling with release.

I don't know how long we lie there, tangled in each other, his wings draped around me as we find our breath, and our hearts slow from the ecstatic high they were riding, but eventually, exhaustion creeps around the edges of my consciousness like a predator ready to take me.

"I'm a lucky male," Myron whispers, lifting his head just enough to study my face.

Something about the way he's looking at me tugs at the center of my heart, and I'm unwilling to dive into the *whys* and *hows* of what he might call luck.

For a few heartbeats, I just breathe in his scent, my skin still tingling with the lingering sensation of release, but there is one word that comes back to me from our earlier conversation.

"Neredyn—" I ask, trying to keep my tone even as I hope to unravel something about him that I didn't know before. "Where is that?"

Myron's gaze is the beginning and the end of the oceans I've dreamed of sailing as he answers, "East."

THIRTY-FIVE

About noon, a knock on the door startles me from a deep slumber, and I almost slide from the mattress as I shoot into a sitting position, covers clasped to my chest.

"Come in." Myron's voice sounds from the general direction of the couch, strong and sure like nothing happened last night and I'm not in his bed, naked and with his scent all over me. But as our gazes collide a heartbeat before the door springs open and Royad strides in, it's all there. The heat, the ecstasy of his touch, the tingle in my flesh, the memory of his body against mine. And the onslaught of sensations nearly steals my breath.

I dive into the pillows, tugging the covers to my chin just in time as the door swings open.

"Fuck the gods if they can't keep those traitors in check," Royad grumbles by way of greeting, aiming right for the chair across from Myron, who hasn't taken his eyes off me, heat echoing in their black depths as if he is having as much trouble as I have to focus on the present when the most recent past is so much more pleasurable.

"Fuck them, indeed," Myron agrees, a mild grin on his lips that makes him look less like a king and more like a male ready to climb back into bed with me.

I smile back at him even when trepidation of Royad's reaction once he realizes I'm here—in Myron's bed, naked—chases the euphoria from my chest.

Royad drops into the chair, back turned toward me out of courtesy or because he really hasn't noticed me, I don't care. What it does is give me the opportunity to scan the floor beside the bed for the tunic that survived last night—as opposed to my pants. Those lie in ribbons all over the floor between my slippers and the nightstand.

I stifle a shiver at the memory of what that led to before throwing a begging glance at Myron, who's still smiling like the moron he is as he watches me squirm.

"We lost about ten Crows to the traitors," Royad reports, tone all business. "I don't know what they were after, but it must have been something important because they didn't even stop at the threat of their life when we followed them into the forest."

Myron's eyes cut to Royad for a heartbeat before finding mine again, and I can't help the warmth spreading through my veins like a magic of its own—especially when that grin turns into a more serious, deeper expression that has my breath catching in my throat.

"It's like the day of the blood sacrifice all over again," Royad rolls on. "They are pushing toward the borders, and they have been convincing more to join their faction. Shaelak knows what they are trying to achieve, but they are becoming more adept at tricking what few loyal guards we have. Are you even listening to me, or are your thoughts halfway back into Ayna's pants?"

I cough, heat staining my cheeks crimson as he lifts a hand to wave at me without turning around. "Good morning, Queen Wolayna."

"Morning," I mumble, reaching for my tunic and slipping it on before I set my feet on the hardwood floor.

Myron's eyes track the length of my bare legs, and they light up in that bluish tint I thought I imagined the night before, but it's definitely there, even from a distance. But he clears his throat and drops his gaze, waving a hand at the foot end of the bed. "Here." A stack of black velvet appears next to one of leather. "Take your pick. Lazy day in bed or training with the fairy princess."

The velvet gown looks comfortable enough to climb right back into bed and snuggle into it, but the shock of last night's assassination attempt resurfaces as the magic of the night with the Crow King slowly dissipates. It's an easy choice when I reach for the black leather pants.

"No peeking," I tell the Crows as I slide into the leathers and tie my hair in a loose bun at the back of my head with one of the stripes of fabric from yesterday's pants.

When I'm done, I join the males by the table with a smile on my face that is supposed to hide every last bit of terror as the other memories from last night return—the flashes of magic in the entrance hall, Myron collapsed on the stone floor, the lake rushing down the stairs in an all-consuming wave. The bloodied water streaming out of the assassins' bodies.

Suddenly, I can't sit down fast enough, my legs turning weak under the weight of the events—of what I prevented.

"They weren't after anything outside the palace," I tell Royad as he watches me sink into the chair next to him, then glances at Myron, who's scooted a few inches to the side to make room for me to sit at the exact same moment. The disappointment flashing in the king's eyes is harder to ignore than the squeamishness in my stomach at the simple fact that even Royad didn't know what truly happened. "They must have lured you out so they could attack him in peace."

I jerk my chin at Myron, who has draped his wing over the armrest of the couch, talons digging into the carved piece where the upholstery coils around the frame.

"An assassination attempt," Myron spells it out for his friend, whose face has turned pale enough to rival Myron's light skin tone.

"Not the fire fairies for once, though," I continue as if it were my place to hand out such information in this court. But this is Royad, and he needs to know. He's the only one who'll be around to protect Myron once my life has ended—by traitors or the Flames, it doesn't matter. I can't sit around and hope that the lake of tears will answer to me again—or that it will if my own life is at stake instead of that of the king.

As I explain what happened to Royad even in more detail than what I shared with Myron the night before, the Crow's eyes become wider and wider, and with any normal set of eyes, I should have been able to see a thick white ring around the irises by now. But Crow eyes are all-black, and so all I see is a night-dark, almond-shaped window into my friend's terror as he listens patiently, not interrupting once until I've unveiled all secrets of how I saved the Crow King from his own people with the help of a murderous lake.

Only when my words dry up does he brace his wings on his knees, leaning slightly over the table as he locks his gaze on

Myron and asks, "She must like you a lot in order to put her life at risk to save yours."

It's the most unexpected thing for him to say, and the most irrelevant one, so I brush a loose strand of hair from my forehead and give him a sideways glance. "I'm sure you'd have done the same, you know, had you not allowed the traitors to draw you away from your duty."

At that, he winces, the sound pulling up instant remorse for my words. "I didn't mean it like that."

But Royad shakes his head like my words aren't what hurt him. "Of course, I would." He exchanges a look with Myron that is loaded with a century of painful history before blowing out a steadying breath. "It doesn't matter how I feel for my king, though."

I don't know if I imagine the droplet of blood on his lower lip as he averts his face, studying the sunny sky through the half-drawn curtains.

"What are the guards saying?" Myron demands, changing the topic so smoothly I almost don't notice the brief flare of upset crossing his features. "They surely can't all have gone after the traitors."

"Some of them were put in a daze and dragged into the dungeons. I would have been around to stop the assassins had those not been eliminated before, and I wouldn't have had to track down the assailants with a fraction of my usual forces." The way Royad speaks makes me wonder if he has more of an official role in this court than I was led to believe. Not just *the new bride's bodyguard.*

"This is bigger than the curse, isn't it? It's not just about whether the Crows want to remain as they are—in their *monster* form"—I phrase it carefully as not to offend either of the two males in front of me—"but about how they don't believe you'll free them." Not from the curse but from this forest.

"I'm still the most powerful fucking Crow in this realm," Myron bites out, and the icy rage I find in his gaze as I glance his direction mutes me. "I don't care what they believe. I made my choice, and that includes the last bargain I made with Cliophera." He opens his mouth to continue but bites down on his lower lip to stop himself.

We're back at that moment when I realized that particular piece of information has nothing to do with putting any of us in danger if he spills it. It's about him not wanting to tell me.

So, I press on as I find my voice again. "What did the bargain say?" I hope I sound as determined as I feel because having slept with him or not, he owes me this honesty when it comes to a bargain he made because of me.

"Tell her, Myron." Royad has regained his color, but his features are lined with exhaustion.

The sound of Myron gritting his teeth runs through me like a screech of metal on rock, and his features are blurring from beautiful fairy to monstrous Crow.

"Tell her, or I will."

I'm not certain what put Royad on my side in this battle, but I'll take it, leaning back in my chair with folded arms as I try not to balk from the monster I'm not certain he's putting on display on purpose or has lost control over.

"It can't be that horrible." It's a weak attempt at encouraging him, but at least, he shakes his head.

"You're the only one who'll see it as not horrible because it benefits you when it damns my people."

There it is. The one line I might have never expected to hear from him. Him who's only ever been scheming and bargaining to save the people trapped in these lands by a curse.

"Damned them how?" My voice is a mere whisper, and even Royad has gone so still I might have forgotten he's there had his claws not dug into the edge of his seat.

Myron's eyes meet mine, feathers receding from his features as he blows out a breath. "We're trapped in these lands, not primarily because of the curse but because I bargained with King Recienne for a bride a year in exchange for remaining in the Seeing Forest, because I hate for my people to hunt females as they please at each Ret Relah. No one should suffer for the Crow's wrongdoings, especially not innocents. But we need the brides for a chance to break the curse, so the original bargain with King Recienne states that I get one bride each year at Ret Relah."

I open my mouth to tell him I already knew that, but he continues with an expression on his features that informs me if he doesn't say this now, he'll never say it. "One woman or female from Fort Perenis. A prisoner charged with unforgivable crimes. Someone who is lost to society in the fairylands or the human realms."

My throat clogs with the simple fact that this is why I'm here, and my eyes cut to the thin tattoo on my wrist that is a permanent reminder of what I am. A prisoner. I'm a traitor to the Tavrasian crown by the simple logic that my father was, plus the numerous royal ships I plundered. Of course, those... We can't forget those.

I shove the bitterness aside, focusing on what's truly important about the original bargain: Myron made sure he protected innocents from being taken by Crows in the middle of the night.

His gaze speaks volumes as he pauses, assessing every detail of my features as if memorizing them in case I'll turn away from him once he delivers the full story.

"What does the new bargain say?" I prompt before I lose all resolution. "The one that made her agree to help with my magic."

Myron's gaze darkens, but he nods. "I bargained for Cliophera's help in exchange for refraining from taking any more brides. All other conditions of the original bargain with King Recienne remain in place."

Horror plunges my stomach into my knees.

No more brides. No more chances.

If what he says is true, he's bargained away their chance at both freedom and breaking the curse. And he's done it for me. To help me become stronger, to learn to wield my magic so I can defend myself when the Flames attack again. How I'm supposed to feel about that, I don't know. All I know is that my mouth has dried up, and my tongue is unwilling to form words, and inside my chest, my heart is being jostled around like a boat in a thunderstorm.

"Fuck—" Royad sums it up pretty well as if he is hearing this for the first time, too, and I almost agree with a laugh. But incredulity overrules the nervous humor threatening to break through.

"You gave up your chance at saving your people to buy me a chance at surviving the next fire fairy attack?" I half-scream, my heart beating so hard I'm sure both males can hear it.

Royad shakes his head beside me as if to say Myron lost his mind while the Crow King merely stares at me with those all-black eyes like I'm a lighthouse on a dark horizon.

"I did it because no one in this forest deserves saving. Except for you."

THIRTY-SIX

The pies Myron keeps sending for dinner are reminding me of the banquets my father sometimes took me to when I was a child. The only difference is that the events held by the nobility in Meer were colorful and crowded while here, I'm eating in solitude, wondering where the residing king wandered off to while I stuff my face with something so delicious it should be forbidden as a main course.

As a child, I had no problems sneaking under a table with a pastry I had snatched off the buffet and hiding away for the rest of the evening while the adults laughed and danced and made trades which would normally not cross the desk of a simple merchant like my father. But Ivan Milevishja had a way of convincing people to do business with him that I never fully grasped. It was also a way that eventually took him to the gallows—not without my portion of fault, of course. Had I not allowed myself to be tricked into confessing I'd seen him that day the King's guards questioned me, he might have never been charged with treason, and King Erina might not have targeted me. Again, pirating the east-Eherea waters did create a pile of crimes that royally offended him and his court.

The last banquet my father took me to, the old Tavrasian King brought his son, and Erina hated crowds as much as I did back then. He told me when he caught me eating a marzipan croissant under the table as he joined me with a grimace.

"You don't get these anywhere else," he assures me, his light brown waves bouncing as he sits back on his heels, ducking his head so as not to hit it on the carved edge of the table where the white cloth falls back into place like a curtain to cut us off from the pompous world our fathers navigate.

Savoring the sweetness of almond and sugar, I take another bite, studying the intruder to my sanctuary with wary eyes. I know him from my father's warehouse. The king sometimes brings him when he comes to appraise the goods my father acquired or traded for him. Erina usually is quiet then. But today, he's chatty the way eleven-year-old boys rarely ever are.

"When I'm king, I'll make sure everyone has access to marzipan croissants. Even merchant daughters."

I refrain from telling him that it's a condescending thing to say. Even I, at my eight years, know that. Instead, I smile at him, offering him half of the croissant.

Erina shakes his head. "Eat all of it. I can have them whenever I want."

Again, he means well, but the way he says it, eyes slightly narrowed as he looks me over like I'm lesser, makes me internally cringe.

"Must be a beautiful life to be a prince." I mean it more to distract him from the topic of the croissant but instantly regret it when he starts rambling.

"You can't imagine the riches we live in. The palace has marble ceilings and crystal windows. We eat from golden plates."

"You sleep in silken sheets and walk on clouds," I continue for him, a grin on my face, and he returns it, catching onto what I'm doing.

Smart boy. Spoiled boy, too. But not unkind at heart.

"Something like that. You should come visit sometime. I'm sure my father could summon yours to the palace for business instead of making the trip to the warehouse."

I don't point out that I've wondered plenty of times why any king would make the effort to visit a merchant's office rather than summoning them to the palace, but who am I to question what the King of Tavras does when apparently my father is his favorite merchant in all of the realm.

"I could show you around. Menia could tailor a dress for you, and we could walk the hallways like we're the pair destined to ascend the throne one day." A smile plays on his lips, his roundish cheeks forming dimples. He's pretty for his age, not overly tall or stretched in awkward proportions like some boys his age. Like from a picture from fairytale books. Even his sepia and gold jacket looks like he stepped right off a miniature version of a throne, no matter if he's hiding under a table with a merchant daughter.

"Wouldn't that be considered treason?" I whisper, the fingers of my free hand half-covering my mouth.

The smile on Erina's face slips. "For you, not me."

He holds out the plum in his hand for me and waits until I pick it up before he slides out from under the table.

I take a last bite of peach pie as I chase the memory away with a swipe of my hand over my face.

That was a different life, one before I unwittingly betrayed my father. One before my mother took me away from Meer so we weren't exposed to the Tavrasian nobility and their judgmental glances when we walked the streets. And then she died on me, leaving me alone in a world where young women are defined by their pedigree or by whom they marry—or are married to.

I got away the day I snuck onto the Wild Ray to escape what Tavras held in store for a parentless adolescent, and Ludelle's mother saved me in more ways than one. She gave me a new home when she took me in rather than kicking me off the planks, allowed me to work for my keep, earn respect and rank among the crew, and finally, she didn't stand in our way when Ludelle and I fell in love. Without them, I would have ended up on the streets, nothing more than a common whore—or worse.

Trying not to cringe at the image of selling myself on Tavrasian market corners, I take another bite of pie to remind myself I got away then, when I was alone and ready to sail to the ends of the world. I survived. And I'll survive now when a couple of Fire Fairies are out for every living being in the Seeing Forest. I'm not even considering that the enemy is in our own home as well. And yes, I've come to call the grayscale palace the Crows inhabit a sort of home, though I'm not honest enough to admit part of it is that Myron is here. And Royad. I put him on the list immediately so I don't need to consider what it means that the place where Myron is feels more like home than my father's office did as a child. Because it doesn't have any meaning. It. Doesn't.

Instead of returning to my epiphany of how many dark moments my past has held, I focus on the distant sense of water in the open bathing room. The past days after the assassination attempt, I've spent mainly on figuring out how far my magical reach extends (a few feet at the most) and if the sacred chamber would open for me again if I asked in a non-life-threatening situation (no). I'm not relying on it enough to wait until one of us is dying again to summon it, preparing to draw a string of liquid from the basin in the normal bathing room instead.

The power in my veins hums slightly at the exercise I keep repeating every other hour just to flex it like a muscle to be trained rather than an abstract ability I have no clue how to maintain control over—not that I've ever had control. From the cracked-open door, a trickle of liquid weaves through the air a few inches above the ground like my power is too weak to keep it properly afloat.

Finishing the pie, I lean back in the armchair and close my eyes as I tug harder until a warm touch brushes against the back of my palm.

"Not what I expected but so much better," I mutter as Myron's scent of wind and pine drifts into my nose. I don't bother opening my eyes, for I know there is little I could do to fend him off if he chose to attack me. So, I'd rather not see death coming if it's him delivering it. But if he's here to kiss me... I'd rather that be a surprise as well since he hasn't made any attempt at following up on the mind-blowing night we shared. Neither have I, other than the heated gazes we share over dinner and the way my body refuses to calm when he winds a proprietary arm around my waist whenever we enter a room of Crows together. He picked up that habit at the speech he gave after the assassination attack—the speech where he threatened half of his people with a slow and painful death if they ever dared attack him in his own home again—or me, for that matter. Given the expressions of utter horror on some of the Crows' feathered faces when we entered the throne room together that day after the attack, it was easy to judge who belonged to which faction.

The guards who'd been dazed and dragged off by the rebels leaped into action at Myron's command, arresting some of the traitors and taking them to the dungeons. Myron has spent too many hours down there since, and I try not to ask what he did whenever he returns to his room, that beautiful mouth drawn into a tight line and eyes narrowed as if, in his mind, he's still interrogating one of those low-lives.

"I can do even better if you deign to open your pretty eyes, Ayna." His voice pours over my face like sugared mint as I lean toward him on instinct, even when my chest tightens at the thought of what allowing him closer to my heart means. He's become a need rather than a nuisance. A wildfire in my veins whenever I watch him enter a room, wings casually at his sides and the lines of that chiseled chest hardened by the shadows the fairy lights cast in the dim rooms of the palace.

It's no different this time. My breath catches in my throat when I open my eyes to find his face inches from mine. Guardians, I want him. I want to pick up right where we left off almost a week ago, want to devour him like he *devoured* me, until we're both sweat-slick and ready to forget there is a past or a future. Until there is only us. I try not to dwell on how much my chest is aching to dive back into that night and damn the consequences.

"Clio sent a message that she'll be early for training today," he says instead of one of the hundreds of things he could say to ignite me like a torch.

When he draws back so I can see all of his face, he delivers a half-wicked, half-apologetic smile that tells me he has plenty of ways in mind to make up for what he can't do right here, right now. As do I.

Naturally, I keep my mouth shut. If I speak even one word of what I feel for him, how far I've fallen into the bottomless depth that is Myron, the Valiant, I'll never come up above the surface again. And I can't go there. Not after the attack.

I shove down the need to wind my arm around his neck and pull him in for a kiss. "Good. I was practicing anyway."

Both our gazes follow the wet trail on the floor to where it disappears behind the bathroom door, and I can't help but flinch as he smiles, all amusement and nothing of the brooding Crow I first met. "Apparently, I'm exceptional at distracting you," he growls, black fire flaring in his eyes, even when he averts his gaze so fast I almost miss it. "Perhaps I should let you train alone with the fairy princess today."

I must have misheard. "You'd trust her not to try to kill me?"

A crooked brow is all the reaction I get from Myron as he takes my hand between his—the one which now wields water when it's too weak to properly wield any other weapon.

"You do?"

"When it comes to your safety, I trust no one, Wolayna," he tells me as if it's a confession. Only when he continues do I understand, "Not even myself."

"You trust Royad," I name the one male whose loyalty he's never questioned.

Myron dips his chin. "I do. But I'd rather be the one to measure my pace to match yours when you walk the hallways. I'd rather be the one wrapped in your scent from staying a step closer at your side than I'm needed, as I'd rather be the one the other Crows envy for the beautiful bride the gods gifted me this year."

The way his voice turns into a near growl, his gaze predatory… It makes a shiver run down my spine. This is no longer the king escorting his bride in a ruse to make his court believe it's an actual marriage. It's a male who expresses a certain claim that I'm not sure I understand.

As if reading the questions from my eyes, he shakes his head. "You alone, Ayna," he whispers, and the shiver turns into a full-on shudder that has nothing to do with the slight draft from the open window. "You alone hold the power to save us or destroy us. And I won't miss a heartbeat of my own demise."

His words follow us into the hallway as he escorts me down the flights of stairs to the level below the throne room, but I don't have a breath in me to ask what he means because I already know. He gave up any new chances of someone breaking the curse. It's me or no one who'll save them. There are no other meanings to it than that, and I don't dare ask how I can actually break that Guardiansforsaken curse because I don't want him on the brink of death all over again. So, our boots and the swish of his wings are the only sounds as we cross into the dim corridor whose carved walls I know by heart by now.

When we arrive at the training room, Clio is already there, skating over a frozen puddle of ice on her boots like it's an art form.

"Hello, Crow Queen," she chirps as she spins at the edge where ice meets stone, and if I could tear my eyes off the surreal picture, I'm sure I'd find Myron rolling his eyes beside me.

"Hello, Fairy Princess." I slide out of Myron's arm, already missing his warmth as I enter the windowless room, calling for my magic to draw upon the frozen water.

Unlike all the other times, Myron doesn't follow me deep into the room but remains by the door he closes with a flick of his fingers. There, he folds his wings over his chest, the feathers streaming down his front and sides in a silken layer of black while his features turn into those of a bird.

I don't know why the image startles me. Perhaps, it's because I haven't seen the monster in him since the day of the attack, or the night that followed. Perhaps, between focusing on my magic and denying that I'm slowly falling for him, my mind has shut out the fact that he is still stuck in his Crow form. I wouldn't be surprised if he took the opportunity to both scare the shit out of the fairy and to remind me that he isn't the good male I'd like to see in him.

But I'm not stupid or naive. I remember the words he spoke to me after our wedding.

I'm not a good king, and I never will be. Just as I'm not a good male.

I remember that he has tortured the Crows who chased me through the Seeing Forest just as I know he's interrogating the suspected traitors in the dungeons every day. He hasn't shared what news he's found, only that Royad is helping to track down what few Crows got away. Apparently, some did, and those weren't exactly on the Crow King's side. Wherever they fled to, it must be a good hideout, or Myron and Royad would have tracked them down.

Perhaps it's even out of the Seeing Forest. It wouldn't be the first time a Crow got out, or the half-Crows wouldn't exist.

I don't get to ponder the whereabouts of traitorous Crows before Clio stops in front of me, her copper braid flying over her shoulder as she whips her head to the side to release the water on the floor from her ice magic. "Show me what you've learned since the last time I saw you," she challenges with a familiar grin.

And I draw upon my magic and let it rise in a wall fueled by the thought of how easily all this could slip away—this palace, the friendships I've forged between shadows, wings, and claws, the sort-of truce I have even with the fairy female before me. But most of all, Myron, whose presence behind me prickles my skin like a physical touch even when he's standing several feet away. Myron, who has come to mean all too much to me, and for whom I'd bleed if I can't get the water to fight for me.

It strikes me like lightning then, what I've read about the magic of humans protecting their realms from fairies of all sorts by bleeding onto Askarean soil to bind them. Blood holds a magic of its own, and if it could trap an entire people once, perhaps it could set another one free.

Clio smirks at me through the thin layer of wet—and, with a wave of her hand, turns it back into ice and shatters it with a flick of her fingers.

THIRTY-SEVEN

"Tell me about human magic," I demand as we sit on the floor of the furniture-less room an hour later, sweat beading my forehead and determination burning in my belly.

Myron is in deep conversation with Royad, who joined us a few minutes ago with a report from the borders.

The way Clio's copper eyebrow rises on her forehead is almost comical, but I keep my grin in. This is about life and death, and if not death, then freedom, which in my definition equals life.

"He didn't already tell you everything there is to know?" She jerks her chin at Myron, and his gaze snaps to her for a moment while he continues speaking to Royad in a hushed tone. "What do you want to know?"

For some reason, I'm not surprised she'd offer what I ask, yet, I'm not prepared. I haven't made a catalogue of things I need to know the way I once did with Royad when he promised he'd try to answer any question I came up with. So, I go with the first thing that comes to my mind. "Are there many humans like me?"

The sadness filling her eyes gives me pause, but she recovers quickly, her fingers smoothing out the sleeves of her plain linen shirt. She took off her leather jacket sometime during training when I managed to dip a string of water behind her collar.

"Not anymore. Thanks to my own people and their ruthless hunting of humans, whatever human mages existed were decimated in an attempt to seal us within the borders of Askarea." She gives me a warning look. "And before you ask, this is a long story. Longer even than the one of how Myron and his feathery menace of a people got themselves locked in this forest. So, don't ask."

"Feathery menace?" Myron asks over his shoulder, and I know there won't be any privacy, so I need to ask my questions carefully.

"What else would you call winged monsters who like to hunt down women and force them into marriage?" she offers without as much as a twitch of her features. That alone tells me she's been around long enough to witness it all.

"He's not a menace," I jump in before we get off topic and I lose my chance at learning something of use.

"Really? He isn't?" Clio's gaze locks on mine as she tries to figure out something I can't even figure out myself. "What would you call what he did to you then?"

"I don't know—" I stop myself before I can ramble all the things coming to my mind—all the things I'm not supposed to even feel. "He's just my husband, for now. I'm better off here than I was at Fort Perenis, so bringing me here saved me in a way."

Myron's eyes find mine, even when I'm determined not to look at him as I admit that small truth, and I can't help the sensation of his caress, even when he's merely staring at me like I've lost my mind. Maybe I have.

"It's true. At least, the food is better here, and I get to bathe and wear decent clothes." It's a weak defense, but at least, it sticks to facts.

Myron's eyes light up. "I wouldn't call the dress you wore last night *decent*."

Beside me, Clio snorts as if she finds the tension between us more amusing than the world's best joke. "Focus on your cousin, Myron," she says, waving off his gaze. "The Guardians know you'll need a stand-in when your court finally comes for you."

There is no affection in the way she's speaking, only the understanding of enemies who've learned to work around each other over centuries of sharing a border—and a couple of wars, as Myron's history books informed me.

"Wait—what?" I don't know why I never asked that particular question, but now that Clio put it out there…

A good look at Royad tells me everything I already know. His tan skin, brown hair, and the scar running down the side of his face, ending at the corner of his mouth. The two of them look as different as two males could down to Royad's broader nose and shorter, sturdier build. "Cousin? He's your cousin?"

"Shocking, I know," Royad responds when Myron is still gaping at the fairy princess as if she just spilled his best-guarded secret. "At least it explains why I'm sticking around the broody king, doesn't it? Anyone but family would have long bolted."

He's joking. The grin on his face suggests he is, as does his tone, but for some reason, I'm too shocked to process.

"Why didn't you tell me?" I don't know who I'm more upset with, Myron or Royad. I trusted both of them after all.

"You never asked," Myron finally finds his composure. "How the fairy princess has heard about it, I'd really like to know, though, since it's a secret that has been kept since the day our mothers were taken by the curse a few weeks after we were born."

Guardians—what sick god would kill all the females of a species? Why? "What did your people do to deserve a fate like this?" The question bursts out without regard for the outsider with copper hair and her curious glances wandering between Myron, Royad, and me.

Apparently, Myron has forgotten she's here, too, since he mentioned the curse. Or… "Does she know?"

My head whips toward the fairy princess, who gives me an innocent shrug. "It was a condition of the bargain. I'd help you in exchange for ceasing the supply of annual brides—and the truth about why they used to hunt them."

Nausea like I haven't felt since the day I first stepped onto the Wild Ray spreads in my stomach, and I have to flap my hand over my mouth to keep it steady.

"But you can't talk about the curse…"

"She's not a bride. I can tell her anything since she can do nothing about it. But she agreed not to share the knowledge as part of the bargain."

A web of half-truths, that's what I'm trapped in. No one wants to keep anything from me, but I can't know things anyway because of who I am—because of *what* I am to them.

I think I'm going to throw up.

"We couldn't risk anyone knowing in case one of the royal line got assassinated in the way Crows like to assassinate their kings when they're unhappy with the rule," Royad supplies, cutting through the rising bile in my throat. "Our mothers made sure I was placed at court with one of the generals as his supposed son so I could be around and learn all about ruling a kingdom in case I was ever needed to ... step in. Which I really don't want to do. I'm content wielding a sword instead of talking politics."

The smile he and Myron share says everything about the friendship they share even when they are blood, how Royad would gladly lay down his life for his king and cousin. I don't know what it is, but the image of Myron the solitary king crumbles just a little with the thought of Royad having been here all his life. Alone, yet not. Sharing a fate, but sharing it knowing they weren't alone.

Clio sighs through her nose. "Where were we? Ah yes, human magic." She takes my hand, and from the corner of my eyes, I make out Myron tense and Royad's fingers wrap around the hilt of his sword. "I won't hurt her," she reassures them with a roll of her eyes. "Just sharing history *you* should have told her about since it's your ancestors responsible for all the human bloodshed in the Seeing Forest."

"I've never raised a finger to harm a human on purpose," Myron grinds out, and I can tell he's about to snap.

I'll have words about that with him later since the last detail I need to piece together the puzzle is how all the brides died—the ones he's wed. I wouldn't be surprised if the ones of his father or other cruel Crows were the victims of their own husbands.

Clio rolls on, "But you were there when your father tried to kill the very human mage who defied all odds and survived a marriage with him." She gives me a meaningful look, which I try very hard to read while I also try not to miss any reaction of Myron's. "Another story better told when there's more time. But the quintessence is that one human mage made a sacrifice by spilling his lifeblood, and by that, ended the second Crow War. You have magic just like those human mages. It runs in your veins. Who knows, maybe you're from one of the ancient Tavrasian mage families who we thought extinct."

"Mage families?" Questions over questions tumble through my mind, making my head hurt as I try to phrase them. At least, my stomach is forgotten for now.

A pitiful expression on her face, she shakes her head. "It doesn't matter anymore now that you're here and have the power to control water." Her gaze wanders to where her hand is resting on my wrist. "Your magic could be solely because you're a Crow bride and the lake took pity on you."

"How much exactly *do* you know?" I can't control my questions as well as I do my magic, and I don't care when my mind is racing with them like there is no beginning and no end to the stream of things I want to know. "You know what? Forget that. I want to know how to break the curse."

Everyone goes so silent I wonder if I just sucked the air from the room with my words, but when I inhale, my lungs fill with cool breath.

"No." Myron steps away from Royad, who's turned so pale the blood relation is suddenly unmistakable—even to me. He's in front of me so fast I almost hit the wall behind me as I shrink away.

"I don't know how to break it," Clio tells me while Myron's icy gaze turns into the sort of storm capable of sinking ships. "And even if I did, it's not my secret to tell."

"It's not anyone's secret to tell," Myron snaps, menace dripping from every word as he keeps his gaze locked on mine. "Now leave."

I scramble to my feet, stunned into submission by the sudden outburst. I've never seen him anything but in calculated control, and this Myron—the one who threatened his own people that he would slay them himself if they snuck out of the Seeing Forest again... This Myron is one whose path I'm eager to get out of because this Myron's ready to bring down whoever stands between him and what he wants.

I make it all of one step to the side when he braces his taloned hands on each side of my face. "Not you," he whispers. "Never you." Then he turns his head to give Clio a withering look. "Consider your side of the bargain fulfilled. Royad, show our royal guest out."

My heart hammers in my chest like a herd of horses racing for an escape while I hold my breath, swallowing the mingle of relief and sudden heat at Myron's admission. Perhaps he hasn't noticed the meaning of his words, but I have—and I'm not sure what to do with the butterflies in my stomach battling away the former nausea. I don't know what to do with my hands as they want to reach for him.

On her way out, Clio waves at me over her shoulder past Royad's broad frame. "If you ever need a girls' night, let me know." She smiles before she turns to speak to the back of Myron's head, for he hasn't moved an inch since he's bracketed me between a shiny black frame of feathers. "Last word of warning, Crow King: The Fire Fairies have been sighted both east and west of *your* forest." The way she says it emphasizes she knows exactly that the Crows stole this palace from the very ones they are fearing now. "Make sure to keep your bride safe before she ends up like the rest of them."

Her words hang in the air as the door snaps shut behind them. I still don't dare breathe for fear Myron's scent will overwhelm me—or the thought of fire fairies breaking in here to burn us all to cinders makes me scream and run.

For now, all that exists are his eyes—all-black, yet in a lighter way than I remember. A sheen of blue is shimmering around the center like the depths of a hidden ocean.

"How did they die?" I know I shouldn't ask if I don't want him to bleed again. I don't want him to suffer, but I need to know what hand he had in those deaths now that Clio brought it up again.

Myron's lids flutter, blocking out my gaze, and he groans in frustration as he tilts back his head, glancing at the ceiling instead. "Some were killed by the rebel Crows," he sighs. "But you already knew that. Some before a wedding, others after. Some died in Fire Fairy attacks. Some found death a preferable option and took whatever opportunity arose to end themselves."

A lump forms in my throat as I remember the moments I pondered exactly that thought—and dismissed it, decided to fight for my freedom instead because no one and nothing should be capable of taking away the will to live.

"Some were smart enough to *pretend* the way you've pretended. The more convincing a bride is when it comes to publicly showing her affections for her husband, the higher the chance that the traitors in this court won't try to take her down. At least, then the attempts would be only on my life."

I don't dare speak a word for fear he'll cease his own, think better, and change the topic like so many times.

"You're *excellent* at pretending, Ayna. Almost impossible to tell the act from reality." His fingers curl beside my face, talon carving into the stone of the wall. "I wish I were as refined an actor as you."

My heart drops to the floor, right into the puddle of water Clio and I were practicing with, and doesn't come up again as his gaze finds mine again, features torn as if he isn't certain he should say what he's about to say.

Before he can tell me something he'll regret, I rush to his aid, handing him a way out. "And the others? How did they die?"

I could swear the ground shudders as he composes himself, blowing out a breath and another. "The curse, Ayna. You're a Crow now—not by blood, but you're their Queen. And the curse demands there are no—" His breath hitches as a speck of blood appears at the corner of his mouth.

"No female Crows," I finish his sentence, my understanding bringing instant relief for him. He didn't tell me. Merely delivered enough of the truth to hook me onto its trail. He's not paying for it this time. "The curse killed them."

Features grave, he nods, and I can't even fathom the cruelty of his gods.

"What did you do to upset your deities so much they killed off your chance to procreate? What makes you so horrible you can't be allowed to continue to live as a people?"

"My ancestors took from the lands of Neredyn whatever they wanted—*who*ever they wanted—and the maker of humans didn't like the way my people brought darkness over hers."

"Shaelak?" My voice is trembling as hard as my hands as I try to keep myself from touching him, from clinging onto him in an attempt at comfort—for him or for me, I don't care; perhaps for the both of us.

"Don't ask what you're not ready to hear, Ayna. Don't ask anything at all unless you're ready to break the curse."

The devastation in his eyes. The fear...

My chest constricts, and my hand lands over his heart out of its own volition, and his shoulders rise and fall in a soul-deep breath.

"Tell me how?"

The shake of his head is a relief because it means he won't risk his own life to help me save them all.

Because if he dies, I'm afraid, I might no longer care for saving any of them.

THIRTY-EIGHT

The knife in my hand reflects like a mirror, the setting sun creeping in through the windows when I lower it over my palm. Blood bound the Crows to the forest. A human mage's blood. I'm not a mage, but I am human, and I have magic, so it's worth a try—not to release them from the Seeing Forest, because they can easily break those wards and go roaming about all of Eherea—and beyond—if they so please. Only the bargain with the high fae is keeping them from leaving. That, and Myron's tight rein on everyone who's been setting a booted toe out of line since the assassination attack. The Fire Fairies haven't invaded the forest again as far as I can tell, but Myron has spent more time away from the palace than I care for, taking a small piece of me with him every time he leaves and weaving it back in whenever he returns with the same grim expression on his features, which only light up once we retreat behind the door to his room.

Today, he's gone back to the dungeons with Royad, and I can't help wondering who of the two plays the nice Crow when they interrogate the traitors, or if it's even traitors they have down there. It's been two weeks since the assassination attack, and everything has been suspiciously quiet.

As I lead the knife to my skin, I don't think about any of it though. All I can think of is that this might be the moment I break the curse and set them free. If Ludelle could see me now, he'd be pleased with my bravery even when he'd hate that it is for another man. And my mother... She wouldn't even bother trying to understand when it won't change anything about me being married to a king. Only, I might die if the curse isn't broken. Myron's promise of freedom means nothing when I'll be taken by the curse. Even if he'd sent me away with Clio to protect me, I'd still be his bride, and the curse would follow me. It sure has followed the Crows across an ocean.

The tip of the knife slices the skin between my thumb and index finger, making me bite my tongue to hold in a gasp of pain as I drag the blade across my palm right in front of the sacred chamber, which didn't design to open even for a noble cause such as me offering my blood to break the curse.

I've been waiting for days for an opportunity when neither Myron nor Royad is around to talk me out of my endeavor, and when they left earlier this evening, I decided that every day I wait is a risk that I'm not willing to take. So, here I am, bleeding onto the polished hardwood floor of Myron's bedroom in hopes that his vengeful gods will listen.

"I don't know what to say in order to catch your attention, Shaelak," I murmur at the locked door, behind which the lake is hopefully listening. "If you're the one who truly cursed the Crows, you've done an incredible job because they are suffering every single day." I leave out that some of them had rather the curse was never broken because, even if he's a Neredynian god, I'm sure he knows the way all gods somehow know what's going on. "But the Crow King has atoned for the horrible acts of his fathers and forefathers long enough. He was an infant when the curse struck, so he couldn't even have conceived the idea of hurting anyone." Unless Crows are born evil, which I entirely and full-heartedly doubt since I've met Myron, Royad, and Ephegos. I hope Shaelak knows it, too.

"I'm offering my blood to break the curse. I'm the last bride Myron will be taking. No female will follow after me, so this is his last chance." And I want to make it count.

Sure enough, the door in front of me rattles like something is trying to break free from the chamber beyond it, and it would be a lie if I said that I'm not quivering with fear.

If Shaelak heard me and stepped into that bathing room, I'm dead. Perhaps, I'm dead anyway if the lake decides I'm a fool for even trying.

But the water has tried to kill me only once while it has aided me twice, so I'll take my chances.

There is nothing that could have prepared me for the moment the door bursts open though—not the plain wood of the sacred chamber but the carved one of Myron's bedroom, and the Crow King storms in, blade in hand and magic spearing through the air toward me to latch onto my hand and mend the fresh cut.

"I don't know what you think you're doing by spilling your human blood onto my freshly cleaned floors, but I assure you, now is not the time."

He doesn't wait for a response as he drags me to my feet, picking the belt with my sheathed daggers from the cupboard near the door and pushing it into my hands. Before I can open my mouth to voice the question, he loses his patience with my fumbling the belt around my hips and takes it back, sheathing his own sword before buckling me in with a few efficient movements of his fingers.

"They're here." It's all he needs to say for my heart to plunge from my chest as fear spreads through my veins where I'd been hoping my magic would pulse instead. He takes my shoulders with a taloned grasp. "Listen carefully, Ayna."

My pulse is a drum in my head as his eyes lock on mine, holding me in place even when his fingers slide down my arms to take my hands in his.

"I need you to get out of here before the Fire Fairies can overrun the palace."

"I'm not—"

"Leaving? Yes, you are." His growl is pure menace as he leans in, grip tightening on my hands. "I didn't sacrifice everything to keep you alive just so you can die now. I didn't fight for you over and over again only to watch you be taken by the fire the Flames will wreak on us. I need you to *live*."

My mouth opens in protest, but before I can form even a thought in my stunned mind, Myron pushes on, "I'll take you to the lower level and sneak you out before they can block all exits." He lets go of one hand only to pull me along toward the door.

"Wait."

He doesn't.

"Wait!" I try again, louder this time, more insistent, and Myron's head whips around right by the door, hand on the doorknob and brows drawn in a sharp V that tells me this is not a whim. This is real, and he *is* trying to get me out of here.

"What do you mean, you haven't fought for me over and over again?" Because I already know what he sacrificed, but I don't know what he fought.

Myron shoves a hand through his hair, blowing out a breath as he faces me, back against the door that could be my path to freedom. *Actual freedom.* Why is my heart not rejoicing at the thought of him finally letting me go?

"I shouldn't spring this on you. I—" He bites down on his lower lip, releases it, and sighs as if words were too heavy—or too dangerous. "It's too early, but it might be the only chance I get—" Again, he stops himself, holds my gaze, and shakes his head. "I've fought for you every day from the moment you set foot in this palace. I've fought my own people, fought Royad when I told him I no longer cared about breaking the curse. Fought to keep you alive because I've seen too many females die." He pauses, throat bobbing and black hair sliding into his face as he eyes the tip of his boots.

"I hadn't planned on trying again, Ayna. I'd made my peace with never breaking free with one day being taken by either the Fire Fairies or the traitors in our own ranks. But then I got to know you."

I'm not sure I'm breathing as his gaze swings back to mine, the black at the corners of his eyes dissolving the slightest bit so I see a fleck of grayish white.

"I got to know you enough to understand why Royad kept pestering me about trying one more time—just *one* more time. But you despised me so much even thinking about"—he heaves a breath, leaving out whatever word he was looking for—"no longer seemed right. It didn't seem right to pretend to be anything other than what I am. I decided, if I tried again, I'd let the gods judge if I'm worthy."

My head spins as I'm grabbling for meaning in his words, but all I see is the white spot in the corner of his eyes. It's so tiny it could be a trick from the light, but it holds my attention in a magical grasp as he rambles on.

"And then you ran, and they tried to kill you, and I—" It's not a growl but a similar sound of fury that follows his words, and I finally look away from the white spot to take in all of his face.

Guardians, he's ... beautiful. Terrifying. Feathers have woven into his hair, fighting to replace the silken strands of black, and his mouth...

Now I understand why the sound wasn't a growl. His voice becomes all hisses and caws, and individual syllables lose all meaning. I'm struggling to piece together what he is trying to tell me, but words get lost more by the heartbeat, and if he's right—if the Flames are on their way—we're losing precious time.

"They are coming," I repeat what he initially said, "and you want me out of here so you can die like a hero while I run like a coward."

The shift in his features stops as abruptly as it started. "They are."

"I'm not running alone." My fingers grab tighter onto his even if he was the one holding my hand. Now I'm the one holding his. "I'm not leaving you to die."

"I'm not abandoning my people." There is no arguing with Myron about this. I don't even need to meet his gaze to know he will stay here until his final breath, trying to right a wrong he never committed.

"I can't leave for the bargain I made with Recienne and Cliophera." Even without the bargain, he'd never run. He might give up the palace to the Flames and leave, but he wouldn't run like a coward. That's me. And all it got me was being nearly killed by two Crows.

"So, we're at an impasse. You won't leave, and I won't leave without you."

The expression on his face drives a dagger into my heart because it reminds me so much of that hope I've spotted so scarcely throughout the past months that I almost believe I've said something he's been waiting for.

But Myron shakes his head. "An impasse I won't accept." His fingers weave through mine. "You have to go. Cliophera will take you in. Head west and cross the river that marks the border of the forest, and you'll find your way to Aceleau."

"What's Aceleau?" I can no longer feel my fingers, that's how hard I'm holding onto him.

"The capital of Askarea, seat of Recienne's power. The best hope for you to survive. Now, let's get you out of here."

I don't correct him when I know he won't allow for any discussions. Even with my water magic, I'm not enough of an asset to make a difference in a battle of raging flames. Not when the sacred lake hasn't responded again. And even with the aid of the lake, I wouldn't be able to do much good.

"So, why all the training? Why bargain away your chance to break the curse next year if I fail? Why bring in the fairy princess to make something less weak?" I'm not proud of the accusation in my tone, but I'd never admit that because, deep down, I know it is born from the sense of rejection. Of being just what I've always believed I am: not good enough.

Not good enough to hold my tongue and save my father. Not good enough to fight my way out on the Wild Ray and save Ludelle and the crew. Not even good enough to break a curse that shouldn't require anything other than my blood.

Myron stops, breathless as he drops my hand to take my face between his palms. "Because I can't bear to watch you die now that I've come to love you, and I couldn't let you go any sooner because—"

Blood wells on his lips as he crashes them onto mine in a fervent kiss, taking my breath, my sanity. His fingers dig into my hair, tilting back my head as he breaks away, his gaze locking on mine, breathing ragged and that hope a near-blue flame where his irises would be had his eyes been normal.

There are no words in my head, only the rolling sound of waves as they crest and tumble. "I tried to break the curse." I don't need to hold up my palm for him to understand, for he drops one hand from my cheek to cradle my fingers in his.

"I know. And I'll be forever grateful that you even considered helping a monster like me."

"You're not a—"

"We don't have time, Ayna. The blood isn't going to break the curse." Crimson drops spill from his lips. He wipes them away with the back of his hand, and I lay a finger over his mouth, preventing him from speaking.

"I'll try again once you've defeated the Flames. I'll come back and—" I'm really doing this. I'm really considering running—and returning to finish what I've started. Past Ayna would warn me not to be foolish, that an enemy like the Flames couldn't be outrun. And that the Crows couldn't be trusted either.

"I don't need you to return, Ayna." He captures my other hand, removing it from his mouth after a soft kiss to my palm, and the shiver running through me has nothing to do with fear of what it might mean to make my way through the forest again. "I need you to live." He brushes his thumb over my knuckles as he leads my hand to his heart, placing it to feel its steady beat.

"The curse will kill me anyway."

Myron shakes his head. "Not when I'm dead, it won't. I need to know that you'll be safe so I can die in peace when the Flames tear us to shreds."

Guardians—"No." My voice is less than a whisper.

When he kisses me this time, it isn't the fiery sensation I'm used to; it's a harbinger of the end—and I can't bring myself to tear away even when he does. My mouth follows his until he's pulled himself up to his full height and his lips are out of reach.

"It's time." He doesn't wait for my response before opening the door with a flick of his fingers.

Outside, the stench of singed flesh fills the air, and caws turn into screams where Crows are burning.

THIRTY-NINE

The last time I've felt fear like this wasn't when I was running from the palace and the traitor Crows hunted me down, or when I'd run for the lake when they attacked Myron. In the former incident, I was only fretting for my own life, and in the latter, I thought Myron could handle himself for a while, even with the poison impacting his ability to wield his power.

This is different. Not unlike in the first Flame attack when wildfire consumed everyone and everything in its path, just more controlled. Where Crows were fighting last time, today what few guards were stationed on this floor have already turned into charred, featherless corpses.

"Too late to get out." I pull my shirt over my mouth and nose to block out the stench of burning flesh as I try to find one Crow—just one—who's still alive and fighting.

There are none.

Myron ducks around the corner, tugging me along into the same alcove where I'd sought shelter the last time—and where I was captured by a Fire Fairy. Goosebumps rise on my arms and neck at the mere thought of such a powerful creature getting ahold of me again. Even Myron is afraid of them. He doesn't show much on that composed face of his, but I know him well enough by now to spot the tiny tells like the tense lines bracketing his mouth and the way his gaze darts back over his shoulder to check on me more often than he should when his fingers are locked around mine and he can feel me right behind him.

Because I can't bear to watch you die now that I've come to love you. His words wrap around me like a blanket of safety, and all I want is to forget the Flames exist. All I want is to have one last moment where I can show him how much he means to me because I can't get myself to tell him in words how far I've fallen for him, or my heart will be wrecked beyond repair if anything happens to him. As long as I don't speak the words, they aren't true, and I don't ... and I don't feel for him what I do.

"How did they get in here so fast?" Myron seems to be asking himself more than me. "They were halfway into the forest the last time I checked."

"And you didn't think to send out an army to stop them?" It's not my place to question his war strategies. The most I know about battle tactics is from the loots with the Wild Ray, and that was on water and the biggest challenge usually was to sneak up on the target ship close enough so we could enter with ropes or planks. This is an entirely different caliber of battle.

"I don't have an army large enough at my disposal to smother them in open grounds. The palace is easier to defend."

We both stare out at the burning banner waving from the opposite wall, my mind racing toward the sacred chamber where a possible ally is slumbering.

"Royad should be arranging defenses at the ground level," Myron explains, his magic racing across the hall where it snuffs out the fires within reach. At least, there are no new ones flaring up. "They must have gotten in through one of the abandoned wings."

He points at the dark corner where the balcony serving as a hallway two levels up from the entrance hall meets one of the alcoves. I've never noticed it as anything other than an extended alcove, but then, I've never had much opportunity to explore the palace.

"Not so easy to defend after all," I utter under my breath.

Myron shakes his head, face grim and violence in his eyes.

"There are a few places in these halls that have been sealed off for good reason after the last Crow War." His magic curls around the top part of the banner and slices it off so only a sliver of burning fabric glides to the ground. "I'd hoped my magic would keep them inaccessible for anyone. Apparently, I made a mistake."

"Apparently." My fingers curl as I shut out the stench and the smoke trying to climb down my nose while Myron swipes clear the upper level for us to cross to the stairs.

"We need to get you out before they send a second wave of fire."

My head whips toward him. "You mean this was only the first attack?"

I haven't spotted a single Fire Fairy, and yet, there is no Crow alive on this level of the palace. The Flames wiped them out with a giant arm of heat. My stomach turns, and I have to swallow the bile to keep myself from emptying my last meal at Myron's feet.

"We need to get down there and help Royad," I argue instead of vomiting because having a task to focus on is always better than to dwell on the unsteadiness of my stomach. I learned that the hard way during my first days on the Wild Ray. "We need to help."

He gives me a sideways glance that makes me question if he just bargained away his chance to break the curse next year for nothing if he sends me away into the dangers of the fairylands.

"I can handle water. Not much but enough to douse some fires and soak some Flames." At least, I'd die trying. Power thrums in my veins as I reach for the lake once more, and I can sense the water as it answers my call. I don't ask him to let me help; it's no longer his choice. I might have run had the Fire Fairies not already breached the palace, but now there is no way I'm going to leave Myron and Royad to their fate.

"You'll stay hidden, and if the situation escalates, you'll run." It's not a request, and I don't bother telling him that I don't take orders from him. The chafing noise of steel on steel is echoing from the level below, and the angry hisses and caws are telling me that Royad has managed to pull together a line of defense.

Without a word, I step out of the alcove, feeling the lake rushing after me as I make my way to the same banister from where I fought the traitorous Crows. I try to ignore the burnt corpses scattered across the floor, not wanting to recognize a face—whatever faction they belong to. All I can think of is that I have a weapon at my disposal that neither of the Crows do: I have water to wield. And our enemy commands fire.

"Ayna," Myron hisses as he follows like a winged shadow, his magic coiling around me in an attempt to protect me. But the water has reached us, and it cuts off his power like a shield of its own, weaving and winding around me like it did last time until I'm layered in an armor of tears.

Myron's magic bounces right off, and I could swear I hear him gasp through the battle noise from below. I don't stop to check his expression—shock or pride, betrayal or fear, it doesn't matter. I'm here, and I'm capable. I'm alive, and all I want is for him to live long enough so I get to break the curse. So, he'd better deal with my decision to fight when the entrance hall is swarming with fire-wielding fairies in leather armor who back up their strikes of fire with stabs of their slender blades.

"Let's have some fun," I say with a wink I don't feel, imitating Clio's bravado as best I can, and let my gaze lock onto the nearest opponent engaged in claw-to-sword combat with a Crow I don't know but who's obviously as eager to defend the palace as I am, so I'm good to help him out.

Myron's magic floats right alongside my strings of water lashing through the hall like whips commanded by the hands of ghosts. His invisible power slices into Fire Fairies, suffocating the spreading fire before it even leaves their hands.

There are fighting pairs everywhere. Crows and Flames seem to be evenly matched in physical strength as long as the devouring force of flames isn't involved. And for now, they seem to have used up most of their resources by razing the upper level of all life—all but ours. And we are coming at them with a vengeance.

The lake slides up and down my arms, striking out of its own volition and reeling itself back in, and every time it does, more streaks of crimson mingle with the otherwise crystal liquid. I haven't spotted Royad yet, but he can't be far. He's organized the defense, so he must be somewhere on the lower level.

As I'm scanning the hall for a sign of the Crow, I spot three Fire Fairies who haven't engaged in combat and are trying to sneak past the two Crows trying to hold back another three of the intruders with claws, swords, and the scraps of magic some of them possess. They are closing in fast, their backs sliding along the wall so as not to be noticed by attentive opponents, and at their fingertips, fire rises, spreading around their blades as one after the other leaps at the Crows locked in battle. The water surges toward them a moment too late, and all I can do is stop the flames from spreading across their feathers as the blades leave their backs. If their ability to heal is as refined as Myron's, they might have stood a chance, but they don't even get a moment to try. The Fire Fairies in front of them shove their own blades into their stunned bodies, and they drop like birds shot from the skies.

And they are not the only ones.

As I reel back the fire, dragging it across the stone tiles in an attempt to push the Flames off balance, I realize that we're overrun. The Fire Fairies killed the guards up here with an assault of fire, but this time, they aren't here to send a message. Today, they are here to end the Crows for good; I can tell by the way they don't stop to taunt their opponents, They go for the quick kill. And they are landing more blows by the minute, even without using their fire now that I've drenched all Crows in water so they won't go up in flames at first contact.

Beside me, Myron is picking out individual Flames and pinning them to the walls as he impales them with his power, and for once, I'm grateful for his ability to strike without hesitation and the insurmountable strength each blow conveys. It's beautiful and terrifying. *He* is beautiful. Wings and feathers and talons ripping through the air as he shreds every last Flame attempting to ascend the stairs to take us out.

Of course, they've noticed us up here, my water rolling through the room in coils and waves thinning their rows as they thin ours with their blades isn't anything to overlook easily.

"Where is Royad?" I shout at Myron over the noise of steel clashing and water roaring, over the cries of dying Crows and Fire Fairies.

He shakes his head. "He must be at the back or in the throne room."

A glance into the back of the hall where the doors to the throne room stand wide open tells me that the battle has spread.

"They won't stop until they kill all of us—or we all of them." It's a fact, not a question, and the way blood of both friend and foe is spreading on the floors is proof that we might get to a point where none of us will be left to tell the tale of how this battle ends.

If only it ended.

By the time the first Flame makes it up the stairs, my neck is beaded with sweat under my braid, and my arms ache from directing the water back and forth. I'm surprised the lake hasn't decided the effort is futile and abandoned us.

Myron is there, ready to rip out the fairy's throat before it comes within striking distance for my own dagger. Blood sprays as his talons rip through the Flame's neck and chest, his horrified expression frozen on his dying face.

Shit! This is what people talk about when they speak of the nightmares in the fairylands. I'm not proud to admit there's no one at whose side I'd rather fight. Somewhere along the way, this has become my home as much as the Crows', and I'm fucking defending it with all I have. So, my new family has a place to stay when their bargain won't allow them to leave.

My magic slices through the next Fire Fairy coming for us before he is even halfway up the stairs, and Myron's smirk of approval fuels me like a secret source of strength I didn't know I had.

But the sensation is short-lived when the doors in the entrance hall burst open, and every chance I've had for a victory plunges from the skies when I lay eyes on the group of fire-wielding fairies stepping over the threshold, and in their midst—

"Ephegos—" Myron beats me to it, and the disbelief and rage in his voice equals the heat in my chest as his spymaster notices us and he nods his head with the word *revenge* written all over his all-black eyes.

FORTY

"Traitor," I whisper as Ephegos meanders between the corpses as if he doesn't have a care in the world. His grin is back, and he's—

Alive. He's alive. And he betrayed us. I don't understand the full degree of what is happening, but I don't need to in order to know he's been working with the Flames all along. The way they flank him like he's a leader to be protected among their kind. Like he's a king.

I fucking cried for him, harbored guilt for his death. By the Guardians and all the gods of this world and the world the Crows fled from, he's alive and walking, and there's not a single feather on his scarred arms where his leather armor leaves them bare.

Myron's hands ball into fists as his power barrels down the stairs, blocking their path between the fighting Crows and Fire Fairies. There is no need to ask if he feels as betrayed as I do. For him, it has to be a million times worse.

"Let me speak to you, and I'll make sure your people survive," Ephegos shouts, raising a brow and glancing around at the melee. "Some of them, at least. I can't promise the ones who keep fighting us will see the sun fully set tonight."

As if to emphasize his words, a Crow drops to the floor with a gurgling scream a few feet from him when a Fire Fairy shoves her burning blade through his chest. He doesn't burn, though. My water washes right over him to keep the flames in check. If there's a chance he'll survive, this should do the job. And no, I don't care if he's of the faction who hates Myron's guts. Right now, we need any Crow who's willing to walk into battle against the Fire Fairies.

"Call them off, Myron, and I'll let live whoever can stand on their own two feet." Ephegos shoves against the wall of magic Myron put up, and his Flame guards pour their power into trying to burn it away. All that does is cost Myron a bitter laugh.

"Well played, Ephegos." I've never seen him so icy, even with the bored smile he's featuring. "I've got to give it to you; you deceived us all." Yes, that's ice as solid as the one Clio conjures with a flick of her fingers, but I still see the hurt in the way the corner of his mouth is fighting to pull downward, in the way his hands shake.

And Guardians, do I want to take those hands into mine and soothe that pain by reminding him that he's not alone. Even without Ephegos, he still has Royad. He still has me.

Instead, I summon my magic and send a tendril of water to unweave from my armor and coil around Myron's fingers in a gentle caress. The shaking doesn't cease, only gets worse as his gaze meets mine for a heartbeat before he takes a step away from the banister.

"Tell me, what did they offer you to switch loyalties? Freedom? Females? I remember you mentioning frequently that you're missing females most." His words drive shivers of anger down my back.

I trusted Ephegos. Befriended him. He was the reason I started seeing Myron and Royad as something different from the monsters I believed them to be—in part at least. Ephegos had sped up the process, broke down some walls I might have maintained a lot longer had he not captured my defenses with humor and wit. And now—

"You're a fool, Myron. A *blind* fool." Ephegos waves a hand, and the fairies firing at the invisible wall stop and turn their focus on the fighting Crows instead. A wildfire washes through the room so fast I have no chance but watch as Crows go up in flames despite the water coating their wings. Steam mingles with smoke, and screams die as the Crows buckle and drop one by one. At least fifteen are down by the time I manage to push the lake over the fire, and the sight it leaves is even worse than what we found upstairs. There's nothing left of them but ashes.

"Stop it!" The command carries over the hall in Myron's deep timbre, and the walls seem to shudder as his power pushes out. He can't both hold the wall blocking Ephegos's path and smother the fires flaring where the lake has passed. My strength is fading, and I can't keep the fires down, not even when the lake is willing to do most of the work.

"You're killing them. They're your people, too," I shout, panic flooding my veins where my magic has become too weak to hold its ground.

By now, the Crows in the entrance hall are no longer fighting, and all I can hope is for Royad to please, please, please have made it out. The room turns eerily quiet when the screaming stops and all that's left is the biting odor of burnt flesh and painful death.

"Good to see you in one piece, Ayna." Ephegos flashes me a toothy grin that I might have once described as charming. Now I see nothing but fake friendliness and malintentions. "I've been wondering if you'd still be around when I finally return." He leans in as much as Myron's wall allows, pretending that he's whispering right in my ear even when there is a whole flight of stairs separating us. "Tell me, has he worked up the courage and carried out the husbandly duties he missed during your wedding night?"

From the corner of my eyes, I see Myron pale a shade until his face is bone white.

"None of your business, is it?" I spit and send the water I'm still able to command to slap him in the face then watch with satisfaction the steaming red imprint spreading there.

"I remember you a bit less *fiery*." Ephegos's eyes flash with glee. "May I just say you'd do well with the Flames. You're welcome to join us."

"*Us?*" Myron barks before I can retort something that will get me killed. "Last time I saw you, you were still a Crow." He rubs his chin with his thumb and forefinger. "Wait... you *are* a Crow. You travelled with us across the oceans. You fought alongside us... You *died* for us."

"You are wondering how I'm alive, aren't you?" Ephegos leans a shoulder against Myron's wall, folding his featherless arms. Now that I take a closer look, they aren't entirely human. The claws are still there, and the limbs are slightly elongated so they don't properly fit the way normal arms would. "Let me give you a hint so you won't make the same mistake twice, Myron." He lowers his voice to a whisper, which carries like a hiss as his features shift to beak and feathers in proof that he's still a Crow even when he's switched loyalties. "Take a close look at the bodies you bury. It's easy to singe the feathers of a dead Crow and plant it for the mourning ceremony. And before you ask why my arms are the only part of me that's scarred, it's because the Flames put a protection spell on me so I'd survive the fire unharmed—more or less." He lifts an elbow, examining it with a casual glance. "The feathers had to burn, or it wouldn't look real. But I feel *good* without them. Have been waiting for the day when they disappear for too long." As if on a command, the bird features disappear, and he looks human again.

"Why?" It's the only question that really matters, and Myron asks it with more harshness in his tone than I'd ever muster had I been betrayed like that.

As if he's been waiting for that question, Ephegos's features light up, and he clicks his tongue.

"I've waited, Myron. I've waited for decades to watch your downfall happen. I've waited for you to find the one bride you would finally care for. One you'd be willing to give everything up for. It's the only thing that could ever hurt you the way you hurt me."

"I never hurt you." Myron sounds convinced, but there has to be something, or Ephegos wouldn't be standing there with gloating Fire Fairies at his sides like they are family.

"You killed my sister."

Shock clenches my chest. "That's impossible," I object. "There are no female Crows."

That only wrings a pitiful chuckle from Ephegos.

My entire body freezes as I watch Myron digest the news. It's the way his eyes shutter as if he's going through all the beings he's ended to find the one Ephegos is talking about. Before he can get there, Ephegos loses his patience.

"You killed her, Myron. You took her as a fucking bride. You didn't even bother to learn her name before you tossed her body into the silver stream by the border."

Myron's chest heaves as realization crosses his features, and it hits me that this is real. This isn't a made-up story to make the Crow King look bad.

As if reading my questions and the astonishment on my face, Ephegos shoots me a grin. "How did I have a sister? I'm glad you asked. You remember the half-Crows the Flames used to burn down by the borders? She wasn't one of those because she wasn't only half-Crow but also half-Flame, and the Flames would never kill their own. She died because of him." The wild accusation in his eyes as they slide to Myron hits me like a dagger.

A Crow-Flame halfling. And Ephegos betrayed his own people to take revenge on the male whom he blames for her death. The pain lining Myron's features informs me this takes him by surprise as much as it does me, but he has a century-old history with the Crow who turned his back on him over a bride he had no choice in taking. Even if she was Ephegos's blood.

I'm not even trying to interpret the meaning of my defending him. He's the king of a cursed people. He even told me that, if the Crows or the Flames don't kill his brides, the curse does.

"You don't remember her, do you?" Ephegos rolls on. In his claw, a long, elegant blade gleams like a promise of pain as he brings his arms to his sides. How he drew it so fast is beyond me. His claws were empty a moment ago. "They all become a blur of faces and guilt."

Beside me, Myron has become lethally still, the quiet before a storm I don't want to get caught in, but I will if I don't find a way to end this. Because none of the others will.

Courage is a fickle thing, which loves to flare at the most inconvenient of moments and then disappear once it's shoved you into a situation impossible to maneuver yourself out of. As it flares in my chest, I'm not ready for it, but that doesn't matter when the remainders of the lake are already collecting at my fingertips, receding from the rest of the room where steam turns to smoke and fresh wafts of burning stench float toward the top of the stairs. They weave around Myron's wall only in thin streaks, but they are enough to show the Flames exactly where we're vulnerable.

It doesn't take a heartbeat for the first strike to sear past our defenses, and I barely manage to splash a wave of tears over the singeing heat to suffocate it before it can reach Myron's chest.

"Hold!" Ephegos's voice thunders through the entrance hall, and all attempts at picking up the battle where it had been left off are eviscerated by that foreboding rumble. There is nothing cheerful or mocking about Ephegos now. No teasing grin or knowing smirk. Nothing of my friend is left as he gestures with his blade at his king.

"I had hopes, Myron. We both had the same ideals. The same goal. To break the godsdamned curse and free our people. But you gave up." His words are full of the sort of anger only desperation can summon in a person. The sense of helplessness brings out sides of people that should remain buried beneath their anguish. And Ephegos is showing us who he truly is: a male who lost the only family he might ever have—and turned on his king and friend.

Myron doesn't lift a finger to stop him in any way other than the invisible wall I feel fortifying as the smoke is blocked out completely from the lower level. The amount of power flowing into that barrier must be draining him. His jaw is set, mouth pressed in a tight line as he listens to his friend's accusations as if they were things he is telling himself every single day. As if the guilt isn't new and the hopelessness is something they share.

"I thought you were different from your father, that you'd end this curse and free us. That you would keep trying to lead those brides on the right track so they had a chance at surviving. But you *gave up*. You gave up on all of us, and you locked us in this forsaken forest with your thoughtless bargains. But that was only the beginning. Then they brought in Sariell, and I begged you to try."

My heart stopped beating. Sariell... The female Royad had brought up to distract Myron from telling me something that could kill us both.

"I remember Sariell." Myron's tone is so quiet and calm I can't even fathom the amount of self-control he possesses in order to keep those emotions swirling in his eyes leashed. At the bottom of the stairs, Ephegos's face twists with surprise and anguish before it sets into a mask of hatred that makes me believe he doesn't care whether Myron knew her name or not. That the fact she's dead is the only one that counts.

"I remember all of them." Ice melts from Myron's tone, but that only makes it more dangerous, and I'm not the only one who feels it. Around the room, Fire Fairies and Crows are cringing. All but Ephegos. Ephegos who's seen it all. Who's seen Myron at his best and at his worst. Who knows how well he can hide his emotions and how he'd never hurt the people he cares about. And he cares about Ephegos. He might not like that he still does, but I can see in the conflict spreading on his features that he does.

My heart bleeds for him—for both of them and the impossible situation they have been stuck in.

"I remember what it's like to watch the light leave their eyes when the curse takes them. I remember the blood on my hands when I try to save them after my own people try to end their lives. I remember every burn on their skin when *you* people take them with swaths of fire." Myron's hands are trembling, and I can imagine he's ready to bring down the entire palace while all I can do is wait with whatever's left of my powers to erase the fires that are surely coming.

"I bemoaned each and every death. I did it when my father was still in charge, and I am doing it now that the burden has fallen on me." His gaze turns lethal as he stares Ephegos down like the king he is. "You never told me she was your sister." There is no apology in his tone, no plea for forgiveness because he's said it all in the way he remembers his deceased brides.

The Flames flanking Ephegos adjust their stances, readying for an attack.

"Because it wouldn't have made any difference. But if you must know… I didn't dare intervene with her out of fear of diminishing her chances to beat the timely way the curse takes your brides' lives and out of hope. You sealed her fate by marrying her. And I'd hoped you'd do better with her. That things would be different with her. That you'd finally fall—"

I'm still trying to figure out why he stopped mid-sentence when I spot the trickle of blood from the corner of his mouth. The curse—and I taste iron on my tongue as if what he was about to say would have killed us both. A shudder runs down my spine as I realize that nothing has changed. My formless spilling of blood hasn't done a thing to lift the curse.

"Thank the curse for tying your tongue, or I'd tear it out with my bare hands." Myron means it. I can tell by the panicked glance he shoots my way.

"Fall?" I whisper, earning a head shake while the taste of blood remains a bitter reminder of how tied all our fates have become. Ephegos doesn't need to stab me in order to kill me, and judging by the death in his eyes, that's exactly what he wants to do.

"Why didn't you come to *me?*" Myron demands, turning back to Ephegos, who seems to both wither and bloom under the king's stare. As if he's been waiting for exactly that question.

A determined expression spreads on the Crow's face, and I know that whatever comes next will determine if there is a peaceful solution or if this is the end of all of us.

"Your father was a mad man, Myron, and wrong about so many things. But he was right about one thing."

"And what is that?" Myron asks the question his friend has set him up for, playing along as if there is nothing else he can do. Because there are too many Flames in the room and not enough Crows on our side to stand a chance at defeating them.

"We are strong. With or without the curse broken. We are a new species for a new era, and we deserve to be free. You never saw that. All you saw was the guilt of our ancestors. But we are not them. We deserve a fresh start. And you're not willing to let go.

"I've always defended you when it came to whether or not you are the right king for our people or whether we don't need a king at all. But after what happened with Sariell, I realized they were right. You didn't only give up. You sentenced us all to eternal punishment. Trapped and solitary. There is no future for us in this cursed forest. And the Flames offered me the perspective I've found you lacking for the past decades.

"I managed to hide her for centuries, fostering the hope that this was the beginning of something better for all of us. A new family we could build. But your bargains with the high fae led me to believe you no longer cared about a future for his people. So, someone had to build a revolution to bring you down. Someone had to send assassins and let the Flames in so they could send retribution for what our people did to them."

I realize only now that the way Ephegos speaks, the way he's dressed, the weapon clutched in his claw... He no longer sees himself as part of the Crows. He's found a new family with the Flames. One that Myron couldn't give him.

"You failed us all, but more than that, you failed to save Sariell." Malice enters his gaze, and I can sense the lake stir around me as if readying to defend. "I've waited for you to become vulnerable. I've waited for decades. And now I can finally take from you what you hold dearest."

A personal vendetta and retaliation for the lost future of a people. My blood chills with every new revelation.

"No." Myron's voice rips through me like a whip as he slides in front of me, blocking me from Ephegos, who merely chuckles at what he believes is confirmation he's right, and in my chest, an arresting sensation spreads as I comprehend what just happened.

What you hold dearest.

I could swear Myron isn't breathing. Neither am I. He told me earlier that he loved me, but I dismissed it as something he couldn't mean. Because the cruel Crow King certainly cannot love.

Yet, here he is, putting his life between Ephegos and me.

The bitter sweetness on my tongue has nothing to do with the aftertaste of blood as I realize what Ephegos had been about to say when the curse forbade him from speaking. Fall in love. That he'd finally *fall* in love.

"It's not like you can keep her safe." Ephegos raises a challenging brow when I peek past Myron's shoulder, my heart in my throat and the armor of water tightening as my entire being understands that blood has nothing to do with breaking this curse.

Love does.

All those moments when he'd gazed at me, studying me as if I were something to devour, it hadn't been because he'd intended to murder me or because he was upset. He'd been desperately trying to fall in love with me.

Yet, they are all still winged and black-eyed. The curse is still in place.

Maybe he hasn't succeeded. Maybe declaring feelings he doesn't truly have was his last effort to break the curse.

I'm not sure if the sickness in my stomach is from my own blindness or from the way the lake is tying my ribs so hard it hurts.

Despite everything, he's standing in front of me like a shield of wrath and fury, and I'd be blind not to notice he cares. If he doesn't love me, he cares enough to not want to see me die. Because that's the sort of fairy he is. Not a Crow or a Flame, not good or bad, not monster or knight in shining armor. He's just. And he would hate watching me be slaughtered by Crow or Flame or by the curse the same way he hated to see Sariell die.

"Prepare for a new era, Myron, the Valiant." Ephegos gives a tiny wave with his free hand—

And the wall Myron has been maintaining with all his focus goes up in flames. The fire pours from every direction below the balcony where we're standing. The hallways, the throne room, the front gate. Crows go up in smoke and sparks as the fire magic hits them, consuming them in punishing heat and devouring death. Myron's hands are already directing his power to swish across the hall below, snuffing out embers before they can start burning again, but he's already wasted too much of his power to hold off Ephegos after draining so much of his cache to fight the Flames before.

The lake coils around me, refusing to return to the battle, but I command it with my magic, shoving on and on until I meet one streak of fire after the other with lashes of liquid. My hands shake, and my breathing is uneven, but I push on. Thundering explosions splinter stone from the throne room threshold, scattering debris across the melee of feathers and fire, and I scream as a heatwave whooshes over us. Myron's wing covers me before it can touch my face, but the way he quivers and spasms under the force of it sends panic through my veins.

Protect him! I command the water, wrapping my tear armor around his inflammable feathers then his entire body until he's soaked. When the assault is over, he winces, but he doesn't seem to be hurt other than a small burn on his back, which he turns to me to face down the enemy approaching with every breath we take. Ephegos and a cluster of Flames have made it up the first few steps, and the glee in their eyes as they find both Myron and me vulnerable makes me wish I'd never left Tavras as a youth.

Myron's magic whips through the air, knocking back two Flames who tumble down the stairs with screams and curses, but Ephegos doesn't stop to see if they're alive or if yet more lives have been sacrificed in this endless bloodbath.

Below in the entrance hall, the moaning and crying caws of injured Crows are a tapestry to the slaughter by blade and fire.

"We're outnumbered." I stand beside Myron, forcing my water back into battle even if it costs me double the strength from when it's willingly participating in my efforts. I can't let them die, no matter whether they were on Myron's side or on the side of the traitors. This isn't just or right or anything other than a massacre initiated by one traitorous Crow with a taste for revenge. One Crow who had the king's trust and pretended so he could sneak in our enemies when the time was right—when he thought he could hurt Myron the most.

But Myron isn't the only one who was betrayed. "Royad," I mouth at him when another explosion rains rocks and glass over the battle below. If he's still in the throne room, there can't be much of him left.

Horror of a different sort clutches me in a tight grasp.

"Royad can handle himself." Myron focuses on blocking Ephegos and the Flames approaching. They are a quarter up the stairs even when Myron's power is shoving against them with everything he has. The fire is draining too much from him, and if he keeps this up, he won't have anything left to fight with when Ephegos makes it up the stairs.

I reach into my magic and draw upon the lake, urging it to attack Ephegos, to at least slip his blade from his claw. All the water does is retreat even farther, weaving around my body more tightly as it strengthens my armor.

Please, I beg it. *Help me.*

It's not the water answering my call but a flash of silvery-blue that streaks through the halls, leaving icy crystals on walls and corpses in its wake.

FORTY-ONE

My head whips around to find Clio's copper head emerging from the smoke of the throne room. And beside her, Royad's menacing form hovers with a broadsword in one claw and magic in the other.

Hope surges in my chest, loosening the layer of water to let me breathe more freely at the sight of Royad alive. He hasn't betrayed us like Ephegos; instead, he's gotten help. It's only one fairy princess, but if there is anything I've learned about Princess Cliophera, it is that she is a force of nature. And if I didn't know, the ice on the walls speaks for itself.

Royad gives a dip of his chin before he swings his sword at the nearest Fire Fairy, slicing off the head before moving on to the next one while Clio sends splinters of ice flying across the room, making new fires blow up in steam before they can spread and take lives. Myron's magic rushes back to him, focusing on only Ephegos as he takes one slow step after the other. New Flames have rushed to his side, fostering a circle of fire around the three of them that melts Clio's attempts at stopping the Crow.

Everyone seems to be fighting, useful. Everyone but me, whose magic is failing as the lake is collecting around me, its glistening texture making it hard to hide and its density making it hard to move. I'm a living, breathing target, held in place by my own magic—or the lack of it as my strength leaves me little by little.

"Get out of here," Myron shouts, glancing over his shoulder with wide eyes. Bruises of exhaustion mar the pale skin beneath. He's fighting, but he's coming to his limits as well.

And Ephegos hasn't even truly attacked. All he's done is march up a set of stairs.

I want to tell Myron that I can't leave, that my lake won't let me, but I remember that the lake isn't the only water I can wield. Clio is creating ice out of thin air, however she does it. But I don't need to. The chips of ice have turned into steam in the air and puddles on the stone, ready for the taking. So, I take. I take with all the force of a vengeful bride as I summon the water to my fingertips. No one heeds it a look as it rises from the floor to weave into strings and spheres, which wander through the gaps of the battle until it reaches the balcony where it rolls and coils in front of me, building, larger and stronger, until it becomes a cluster of waves at my disposal.

With boneless arms, I shape and build the water into weapons, but wielding this water doesn't cost me half as much strength as the murderous lake does. It might not be as deadly either, but I don't care as long as I get to douse those flames protecting Ephegos. Once he makes it to the top of the stairs, Myron will have to fight with a blade to protect himself, and the fire will put him at a disadvantage.

My stomach is so tight I could throw up, and my heart is no longer contained in my chest. It's beating in my throat, pounding in my ears, pulsing in my palms, a constant reminder of how close to outmatched we are even with Royad and Clio's aid. I'm vaguely aware of the group of Crows that has followed them into the room, their feathers not yet singed and their strikes fresher and more forceful than those of the left-over Crows who've been dodging fire and swords from the beginning. It has to be enough. Please, let it be enough.

The first wave of my magic breaks a clean gap into the flames surrounding Ephegos while I collect more water to strike again. By the way the lake quivers around me, I can tell it's not amused that I've taken initiative and am fighting without it.

It had better get used to it because I'm here, and I won't stand idly while I still have a spark left in me.

"I can't hold him off much longer," Myron tells me as Ephegos and the Flames push up another two steps. He's noticed the segment of the fire circle I've extinguished—of course, he has—but he also notices my struggle. "Leave before it's too late."

I don't know where he imagines I'd be going even if I agreed to leave. There is no way out of here. The stairs are blocked by the approaching traitor of a resurrected Crow, and we're too far up to escape through the windows. I've never had enough freedom in this palace to explore for secret passages or servant corridors or hidden stairwells. He might be able to simply shift and soar from a windowsill, but I'd plunge to my death.

His gaze meets mine for a moment before it shifts to the dark corner at the end of the hall. Horror fills his features, and

I think I see a flicker of orange and red in the dark mirrors that are his eyes.

"No!" His voice tears through me like thunder and lightning a moment before a surge of heat hits my back, shoving me to the ground.

With a gasp, I crash into the slate gray rock, the impact knocking the breath out of me despite the way the lake cushions my fall. A cloud of steam rises from my back where the fire is trying to eat at my form, but my armor of water is thick enough to protect me—at least until it becomes hot enough to reach boiling temperature, and I scream.

The sound hangs in the air for a heartbeat during which all I can do is lift my eyes at Myron for aid.

He's right there, one taloned hand reaching for me while the other is warding off Ephegos and the Flames.

"Get up, Ayna." The command in his voice has me fighting the ache in my flesh. All I can think is that, if I survive this, I'll say a long and thorough prayer to Eroth and the Guardians. If Myron survives it, too, I'll even make a sacrifice to those horrible gods of Myron's homeland.

With a groan, I slide my hand toward his. My palm is slick with sweat, not water. The water has been retreating from around my body, the armor unweaving like it realized it had become a conduit for the punishing heat. Instead, it's formed a wall behind me, blocking out the Fire Fairy who dared sneak up on me.

A glance over my shoulder tells me that there is no one left to block out. The fairy's body lies twisted on the floor, and judging by the look in Myron's eyes when I turn back to him, I know his power broke the creature's neck.

"Royad and the princess can hold them off only so long, Ayna—"

"I'm not leaving without you," I cut him off, but we both know neither of us is leaving this palace alive. Down in the entrance hall, the battle has slowed, and even Clio's ice magic has become sluggish against the fires, which keep flaring at every angle as if they have a life of their own. For every Flame we take down, a new one seems to appear from the shadows and alcoves beyond where the light can reach.

I allow him to pull me to my feet while my free hand is already reaching for the water I whipped through the hallways. It answers my call, but the lake remains a solid wall behind us, blocking out any attacker coming up from above us.

But the danger is no longer there. It's in front of us.

So quick I barely see it, Ephegos breaks free from the formation, darting past Myron as he bends to pull me up. It happens so fast that all I can do is shout my warning and throw myself at Myron to shove him out of harm's way as Ephegos's slender blade stabs at Myron. The pain is sharp and brief before shock sets in and I lose my grasp on my magic. Water drops around me like shattering stars where it's released from my hold, and as I meet Ephegos's all-black eyes, a twinge of pain mirrors there as if it hurts him to see me tumble back to the ground, one hand clutching my side where he slashed me with his blade while my other hand still clutches Myron's winged arm.

"Ayna!" His voice is full of fury and agony; I can't tell which one supersedes the other as he flips back to his feet then drops to his knees at my side.

"I hate to see you die, Ayna," Ephegos says with a smirk that makes it hard to believe he isn't enjoying every last moment of my suffering. "I quite liked you, to be honest. What a pity. You would have made for a great bride had Myron died first."

The ire on Myron's face is nothing compared to the searing pain in my side. It spreads along my ribs all the way to my chest as if the wound isn't merely superficial but deep enough to have speared organs.

In Myron's eyes, darkness so intense is gleaming that I swear I can see the outline of stars sparkling in their vengeful depths as he turns his gaze on Ephegos.

"What have you done?" The low and cold tone is even worse than the burning hot rage rolling off him.

Ephegos stumbles back a step. It's all I see before my vision starts going blurry.

Don't die, a voice at the edge of my consciousness tells me. *You're not done. You haven't saved him. Save him, Ayna. Save him to save yourself.*

Perhaps I'm delirious from the blood spilling rapidly through the fingers I'm pressing over my wound. Perhaps the voice is really there. Perhaps it's the lake urging me to fulfill a task neither of the brides whose tears it contains were able to, and it wants to see me succeed. It doesn't matter when all I can focus on is Myron, who has stepped in between Ephegos and me, his magic making the ground shudder as he hauls it at the male with one furious blow after the other. In his hand, he's holding a sword. In my blurry vision, it looks like it's bursting into flames the way the Fire Fairies' blades did. But then I notice the wall of flames storming for him—for *us*. My heart stutters—from my injury or from fear, I no longer care. All I can see is Myron and the fire rushing for him like bloodhounds on a trail.

No!

I struggle to move so I can protect him from the fiery inferno with my dying body. It's all I can think of as I throw my arms wide, and all the water in the perimeter surges to my aid—the droplets suspended midair, the puddles on the floor, the melting ice on walls and corpses. All of it swirls and rages around us in a blur as I scream. I'm not fast enough to cover Myron with my body, but I'm fast enough to enclose us in a wall of crimson-stained liquid right as the fire is about to send us behind Eroth's Veil.

It hurts—Guardians, does it hurt. Ignoring the agony spreading along my skin as steam crawls through my clothes, nipping at my skin, I maintain the barrier of water, pouring my everything into it. Myron is there, in front of me, like a shield, but his power is near-depleted, his sword clatters to the ground as it heats like in a forge, tendrils of smoke and haze swishing along his talons as he lifts his arm, ready to block whatever is coming our way with his bare hands.

Yet the fog of water and fire consuming each other obscures everything but the tiny space I'm protecting, and when a slender blade of silver and fire slashes through the wall around us, I don't see it coming. Neither does he.

And all I can do is cry out as the sharp tip buries itself in Myron's bare chest.

Myron's talons rake across my arm as he collapses at my feet, trying to hold on, and I'm too weak to catch him. Blood pulses from the wound in my side, but I don't feel it. I don't feel the pain or the strength draining from me with each thud of my heart because there's only one thing I can focus on, and that's the river of crimson gushing from Myron's chest, right where his heart is buried beneath skin, muscle, and bone.

"Myron." Dropping to my knees beside him, I clutch his hand with my free one while the other keeps up the wall of water, willing it to reform where it dissipates from the heat the Flames are pitting against it. How I still have any strength left to maintain this shield, I can't even begin to understand. All I know is that, if I don't, we're both dead.

We can't rely on Royad and Clio and whatever few Crows are still standing to defeat the Fire Fairies and save us. If my magic slips, we'll be exposed, and Ephegos can finish what he started. I can hear his cruel laugh somewhere on the other side of the wall that won't allow them to break through and finish us, but it's only a matter of time now.

"Get up." I tug on Myron's wing as I plead with him to fight the pain and drowsiness coming with severe blood loss.

All he does is give me a weak smile. It's then that I know he won't be getting up. He won't be doing anything at all. Blood wells on his lips as he opens them to speak, and a cough escapes instead.

"Save your strength." I brush back his hair from his forehead, sliding my hand over the wound in delusional hope that my magic might become of the healing sort the way the lake responded when I most needed it. But nothing happens. No miraculous light sealing the gash in his flesh, no tingling in my palm that would tell me that I have the power to save him. "It will be all right." It's a lie, and we both know it, although the smile he gives me tells me he wants to believe it as desperately as I do.

"I dream of flying with you, Ayna." His voice is hoarse and unsteady from pain, but he fights for each word as if his life depends on it.

"Don't speak. Use the energy to heal yourself." It's more a plea than a command even when I'm desperately trying to order him to draw upon the magic that used to save him from all cuts and bruises.

He shakes his head an inch, just once, but it's confirmation he doesn't have any reserves left to save himself or me. We're dying. Both of us.

If Eroth is merciful, he'll take me first so I won't need to watch Myron take his final breath, so I won't need to see him suffer.

The wound in my side is preventing me from doing anything but crouch at his side, bent low enough to watch his face contort in pain with each labored breath he's taking.

"I dream of flying with you, Ayna," he begins again, and this time, I'm not stopping him. "I dream of holding you in my arms as we soar across the ocean. I dream of finding a new life for the both of us." His breath hitches as his body spasms. Fresh blood trickles from the corner of his mouth, but this time, it has nothing to do with him speaking words he shouldn't. It's not the curse making him bleed. "I dream of never letting you go. But you're not mine. Even if I love you with all that I am. I'll die with the curse unbroken, and Royad will shoulder the burden..." His voice trails away as I place a finger on his lips, stopping him before he can break my heart with words of love and death. With a future we can never have.

"I tried," I tell him instead. "I tried to break it. I'd do it with my dying breath if I knew how." As if in response, it becomes hard to breathe at all. My lungs won't take in enough air to form a sentence.

"It's all right—"

There is no battle noise in our small bubble of heat and steam and death; it's him and me and all the words spoken and unspoken that I want to cling to. I want that future. I want it so badly that my chest aches more than the wound that's slowly killing me.

"You'll live, Wolayna. Promise me you'll live." His voice is fading. It's so weak I need to lean in to catch those precious words.

"You'll live, too." I try to phrase it like a promise, but I have nothing left of the hope once dwelling in the chambers of my heart.

Because Myron's gaze locks on mine, those all-black eyes glazed with tears as he slides his palm to my ribs just above the cut that's bleeding and aching—but not as badly as my heart. "Live, my Ayna," he whispers three little words I barely catch, and before I understand what he's doing, a streak of warmth flows from his palm into my injured flesh, bringing instant relief to the pulsing pain.

"Stop." I try to slide out from under his touch, but I'm too weak to move more than a few inches. His hand drops from my waist to the blood-soaked floor, and the thud slaps me with a finality almost as if he'd hit me in the face.

"No!" My wail bounces through the room like a piercing spear of rusty metal. "You can't do this." I shake his shoulder, but Myron's lashes flutter, gaze going unfocused as his head lolls to the side. "You can't leave me behind." *Don't die. Don't die. Don't die.*

Tears burn in my eyes, dripping down my cheeks onto Myron's stilling features. His chest rises slowly, as if in a last effort to beat death.

"Please," I whisper. "Please don't die. Please don't leave me." Because I have nothing and no one in this world if he dies. Because for everything he's done to save me, he doesn't deserve to die like that.

The steam around us has cooled, replaced by a wall of salty water as the lake encloses us like a shield of its own, taking the place of my magic when I'm failing.

I have a faint moment of wondering why it's still here, if it has a mission of its own, and how I play into that mission.

Because you're the last of us. And it's time to end. The voice lingers at the edge of my thoughts, almost drowned out by my sobs and my racing heart, but I hear it. I hear it like a silver thread through the darkness that my future has become.

My fingers clutch Myron's hand as if I can keep him with me by sheer force of will. Instead of saving himself, he saved me with the last of his strength, and I failed him.

I'm the last bride. The final one. And I failed to break the curse Myron has given up on breaking. He sacrificed himself for me because he knew that, if I couldn't break the curse, his death would set me free.

It didn't help him, I tell the water, wondering if the ethereal sound is the immortalized wailing brides or that of the gods of

Neredyn who won't set Myron and his people free. *In the end, I couldn't save him.*

It's all I can think. That I wasn't enough. Even when I was willing to die for him, I wasn't enough.

Feathers spread over Myron's face, his neck, his chest. His mouth and nose turn into a beak, taking away the last of his human features, and those eyes, all-black and depthless, become unseeing.

I don't shy away from his monster form even when he will no longer be offended or hurt if I do. I'm not repulsed by what I see because what I see is his heart—the glorious, kind, and valiant heart that I've known for a while I'd do anything to protect. Because, deep down, I've known for a while that what I feel for this male will ruin me if I ever lose him.

"I love you." My words pour over his Crow face as I place a shaking palm to his cheek and kiss his feathery forehead. "I'm sorry I couldn't save you."

Around me, the lake crashes to the floor like a string holding up a curtain has been cut. Cool wet liquid splashes my face, washing around my legs where I kneel beside the king who'll take my heart to his grave. And I taste the salt of the past brides' tears in the water, taste their pain and their suffering, their hope and their comfort as slowly, slowly my tears mingle with theirs.

Beneath my palm, Myron's heart does a final thud.

Then there's only silence.

ANGELINA J. STEFFORT

FORTY-TWO

"Ayna."

A pair of hands is tugging on my arm, pulling me away from Myron's still, cold body as I cry and cry, my tears soaking his feathers.

"We need to leave, Ayna."

The voice is familiar, but I don't have the strength to think of the name attached to it while I fight with all I have left against the hands trying to tear me away from my husband.

"Give her a moment," another voice speaks, and the pressure vanishes from my arm, allowing me to slump back over Myron's body.

He can't be dead. He can't. Not after everything we've been through. He *can't*.

My chest is so tight I can't breathe, but what does breathing matter now?

"Ayna, look at me." This time, I recognize the first voice and the small hand reaching for my cheek as I shake my head.

Clio.

How she's kneeling on Myron's other side when she was just battling Fire Fairies in the entrance hall, I cannot begin to understand. It hurts too much just thinking about what happened up here on the residential level.

Myron is dead. I don't know whom I'm sending this thought to. Perhaps the lake, which no longer seems to respond to my words or my magic, as if it's fulfilled its task. Instead, it seems to collect closer and closer to Myron's dead body like a mirror carrying him when he no longer can. Perhaps I'm thinking it to myself, forcing myself to acknowledge what my heart refuses to.

It's like a stab to the gut either way.

"Ayna." Royad kneels beside me, his arm wrapping around my shoulders as he gently pulls me to his chest.

I don't want to leave Myron. I don't want to, but Royad is too strong, and his fingers curl around my neck, gently bringing my head to his shoulder.

"He's dead," I sob into his feathers, withering like a delicate petal in the unforgiving cold of winter. "He's dead." *And it's my fault.*

I feel Royad shake his head. "It's nobody's fault but the traitor's."

"Ephegos—"

I don't have the strength to lift my head to assess what happened to the rest of the battle, if we lost or won. Royad and Clio are alive, and there is no sound of combat, no whining and crying and grunting of the wounded.

"Fled when the curse broke. The whole battle dispersed when he bolted." It takes a moment for Royad's words to register, but as they do, I realize it's not his feathers I've been sobbing into but the soft length of his brown hair. I blink against his chest and find nothing but smooth, tan skin stretching the expanse of his shoulders, and the arm that's wrapped around me—it's a real arm. No feathers, no elongated limbs like with Ephegos's seared-off feathers.

The shock numbs the pain clutching my heart for a moment as I lean away to take him in—

Royad has eyes as blue as the ocean, and his features are both pained and relieved as he studies me with a weariness that reminds me of an older brother examining his sister. His arms slide off my shoulders as he holds them out to his sides for me to take a closer look. But all I can do is stare at his eyes. The all-black is gone, clear white surrounding his irises before thick, dark lashes shutter in a blink.

"You look—"

"Different," Royad supplies.

"Human," I correct. Except for the ears—they are still clearly fairy ears, but apart from that and his unearthly beauty, he looks human. No bird trait is left, not a single feather on his skin.

"The curse is broken, Ayna." Royad's arms fold back around me as he crushes me against his chest once more. "You broke it."

Over his shoulder, I glimpse the entrance hall behind us, and what few Crows are still standing are all turning over their hands and arms, staring at the smooth skin and lack of claws with wonder.

"How?" I try not to think or feel as I wait for Royad to confirm what I already know happened.

"You fell in love with him, too."

There is no stopping the onslaught of agony as it hits me how deep my failure truly was. I didn't just fail to save his life; I failed to realize that there is only one power strong enough to end all curses.

Love.

I'd known I was falling for him, had pushed the feelings away like they were a curse of their own for fear I might break if I allowed myself to love him and then lost him. And my selfish fear cost me my one chance at happiness.

Fresh sobs rake through me as I turn around out of Royad's embrace to find Clio's hands on Myron's chest, right over the wound that has long stopped bleeding—when his heart stopped beating.

Sparks of magic pour from her fingers, and even though I know on instinct she's trying to heal him, his chest doesn't rise in a life-giving breath. He's dead.

But Guardians, does it hurt to see him like this. Like a dream taunting me with a future I might have had, had I been strong enough to admit my feelings.

The feathers have receded from his arms, exposing smooth, pale skin over hard cords of muscle. His shoulders are broad in a way that makes me want to curl into them just to remember how well I fit, and his face—

His face is the most beautiful I've ever seen. All hardness and traces of anguish have been smoothed away by death. His lips are still rosy like he might wake from a deep slumber any moment and open his eyes.

Something inside me tells me to try to lift his lids to spy what his eyes are like now that the all-black of the curse has been erased, but Clio shakes her head as I reach for his face.

"We need to leave, Ayna." She has lifted her hands from his chest and is once more reaching for me. This time, I allow her to take my hand and lead it away from the male who looks more beautiful in death than anyone should have the right to.

"I can't leave him." I don't bother asking her where I'd go or why if all that's tethering me to this world is right in front of me. Because, by sacrificing himself to give me a chance at living, Myron has cut that tether, and all I can feel is the pain of where he ripped out my heart and took it with him behind Eroth's Veil.

"He'd want it that way." It's Royad who places his warm hand on my shoulder. "He'd want you to be safe, and I can't provide safety when the Flames could return any moment."

"I thought they fled." My voice doesn't sound like my own as my gaze remains on Myron's perfect form, on the arms I wished would wrap around me one last time. And there is nothing but emptiness.

"They did. After they killed as many Crows as we killed Flames. There was only a small group left, but if they choose to return, they might bring reinforcements," Clio responds, slowly guiding me to my feet as she steps around Myron's body.

I refuse to leave him. I can't. Not yet. "Just a moment." It's all I need. One more moment of his lingering warmth. One last look at him.

Sobs are still shaking me, and what was left of my magic has dissipated, as has the water the lake spilled over us. Only a trickle remains around the edges of Myron's form when I fall back to my knees and press my lips to his.

"I love you," I whisper. But my words get swept away by the sound of an explosion filling my ears, and a sharp pain stings my head before darkness overtakes me. As the room fades from my vision, I'm ready to embrace Eroth's Veil should he offer his hand to pull me through. I'm ready to follow Myron wherever he goes.

Only, when I wake up, I'm not in a place where pain no longer exists or where I might be reunited with all the people I've failed so I could beg their forgiveness. I'm in a plush room of cream and russet ornamentations and lily-scented warmth.

Soft blankets embrace me instead of Myron's strong, feathered wings, and where I once had a heart, a throbbing lump of remorse and agony lives with a vengeance that brings fresh tears to my eyes.

"It's all right, little bride," a voice sounds from the corner of the room, and my heart seizes.

I don't need to turn my head to recognize the male, but I need to make sure I'm not stuck in a nightmare.

Warm brown eyes stare back at me as I sit up to find him in a brown, upholstered brocade chair, one leg crossed over a knee and marred arms folded over his chest. But there is nothing warm in Ephegos's expression as he flashes his teeth in a mocking smile. "Let's see how Myron's ghost will like it when I watch his bride wither away just like he watched my sister fade and die."

FORTY-THREE

MYRON

A bitter gust of wind caresses my skin like mocking blades calling me back from the beckoning darkness.

All those centuries, all those heartbeats of hope and resentment I imagined that, if the curse was finally broken, I'd feel something. Something other than pain and despair. Those two sensations have been my constant companion anyway. But back then, the pain was dull, an ache easily ignored under the prospect of it lasting a lifetime or longer. But this is new.

The needles in my chest, the razorblades running along my shoulders, my arms, are nothing as gentle as I'd imagined death to be.

My eyes snap open, light assaulting me with a new intensity now that the layer of darkness that used to linger on my vision has been lifted like a veil, and from the gaps between sheep-shaped clouds in the azure skies above, the sun burns me with a vengeance. Leaves and branches rustle in the breeze, and somewhere nearby, a stream cheerfully gurgles by.

With a groan, I ball my hand into a fist, testing my strength before I even consider getting up from the soft ground I've been placed on. That, at least, is a small mercy, the cushion of moss carrying my weight. I could have found myself scraped over a set of sharp rocks instead. No idea how my body would have handled that with all my fae senses rushing back in. Where there used to be the moderate perception of a Crow, the sensitivity is increased by a multitude, each sound, each touch, each scent so intense I nearly black out all over again by the force of it. It's exactly as the older Crows used to describe the ones who were matured before the curse fell upon us. I can't remember, but my body thrums with heightened instincts the way that of a predator does.

The tang of salt and iron staining the otherwise clean forest air is all I taste.

I faintly remember the sound of a female's voice as she tells me she loves me, remember the devastation in her beautiful silver-gray eyes as she realized I was healing her instead of healing myself. Remember dying on the floor of my palace in the Seeing Forest. It feels like a lifetime ago, and I am not quite sure how I've gotten from the inferno of fire to the summer-scented clearing where I'm sprawled between ferns and little pink blossoms.

Ayna—

My limbs are filled with lead, but I pit my fae strength against the weight as a sense of urgency spreads through me.

"Ayna." This time, her name spills into the clearing like a prayer as I wait for her face to appear in front of me. But there is nothing but the evergreen branches around me.

"Myron." My cousin's voice sounds from the edge of the clearing where ferns are so high I barely see past them in my sitting position. I should be relieved to spot him standing there, but something tells me all of this is wrong. That I am missing details, moments, maybe hours or days. My fae mind should remember everything like it's been engraved into stone for all eternity, but instead, there is a gap of blackness from the moment Ayna told me she loved me to this torturous moment of waking to the bleak beauty of the Seeing Forest.

"By Shaelak, you're alive." Royad rushes to my side, his hands falling around my shoulders as he pulls me into an embrace the way only brothers can—even when he's only my cousin, he's the closest person I have in this world.

Except for Ayna, who is my heart—the organ now beating in my chest like a slow and steady drum of dread when I scan the seam of the forest for her delicate, human form.

"What happened?" I barely recognize my voice hoarse with terror as I don't find my wife among the cover of branches and blossoms. "How am I alive?" I remember dying. I remember the darkness of Hel's realm as he opened the gates for me to slip through.

Royad's arms slip away, but he keeps clutching my shoulders as if he can't believe I'm real unless he feels my warm, living body in his grasp.

The light in Royad's eyes dims as he looks me over as if expecting I'd remember something. And I do. All of the horrible battles that cost so many their lives to save Ayna—cost my own life.

"Something happened. Ephegos stabbed you, and you lay there on the stone floor in your own blood and the tears of the brides past until your heart had stopped beating. By the time we got you out of the palace, your body was turning cold. You died, Myron. And you came back from the dead. How is that even possible?"

I remember the sensation of Ayna's touch slipping away, Ayna's voice. I also remember the slick and cool liquid of the sacred lake soaking into my clothes, into my skin like a kiss of the gods as I hovered above the darkness on Hel's threshold. Perhaps like an absolution as the curse broke. It doesn't matter. None of it matters if Ayna isn't at my side. If I returned from Hel's realm only to find Ayna went there without me, I won't care if being alive is a mercy gifted by the gods or a curse all over again. I'll follow her there in a heartbeat.

"Where is she?"

Royad's body is shaking, or perhaps it's me who cannot control himself enough to keep my preternatural fae stillness. In my mind, scenes of blood and fire replay as I watch her kneel beside me, her tears dripping to my burning skin. Agony is a raging beast inside my chest as I hear her words echo in my head. *I'm sorry I couldn't save you.*

Because she couldn't save me from dying... But she did save me from the curse.

"Where is she?" I don't bother to acknowledge how good it is to see Royad without his wings, beak, or claws. How everything about him is high fae rather than monster. Even his eyes, so clear like the water around the islands our kind used to inhabit. "Where is Wolayna?"

A tear slides down Royad's cheek, leaving a wet trail along his scar until it meets the corner of his mouth. "I couldn't save her." It's a plea for forgiveness, and my entire being recoils from the meaning of his words.

"What do you mean you couldn't save her?" My body is shaking for real now, the tendons in my forearms standing out as I try to will my hands to still. I've never seen my arms since the curse befell my people when I was still an infant, and I've never been able to shift fully into my human form. Under different circumstances, I might have marveled at how exquisite the pale skin that has never been exposed to sunlight truly is, how much stronger the sensation of the elements on it as another brisk breeze rushes through the corridor of trees to ruffle the ferns and stir my hair. But today is not that day. Today is the day I learn that the bride who finally saved us all has paid a steep price—and if Royad won't tell me soon what exactly that price was, I'm tempted to knock the words out of him because there is nothing kind about me when it comes to Ayna's safety. When it comes to her, there is no sense or reason. There is only the abyss of emotions enveloping me with unknown force.

I've gone out of my way for the past months since she arrived at my palace to make certain none of my people as much as touched her. Again and again, I've threatened lives and ripped out feathers to demonstrate just how willing to kill I am when Ayna's life is in danger.

I don't know when I stopped giving up on breaking the curse, on freedom or on love, and started caring for her instead, but it must have happened sometime between our very chaste wedding night and her first attempt at escape.

The day she called me a moron, I'd already fallen from a cliff with my wings bound behind my back. The smile tugging on my lips at that particular memory is a momentary flicker before my face settles back into grim lines. I can see the mirror of my features in Royad's gaze as he studies me with those unfamiliar blue eyes yet the most familiar expression I've known for centuries.

"Ephegos took her."

In an instant, ire slides through my veins like mercury. Power rises in my blood as I try to calm it down by telling myself I need to know all the facts before I set the world on fire. "Where did he take her?" It comes out as a growl, and I'm surprised my features don't sprout feathers and my voice doesn't turn into a caw.

No more. The curse no longer dictates how and when I shift or how much of me turns into a monster. I'm no longer frozen in a half-state, unable to transform fully into my human form. The curse no longer tries to disguise anything remotely attractive about me into the face of a monster whenever a female is likely to look at me with anything more than disdain in her eyes. The gods know I've done all I could to keep the feathers and talons off my body whenever I was around Ayna, just to give her a chance to see something more than a blood-lusting bird.

No, I'm no longer a slave to that curse, but I can't deny that I'm a slave to my instincts. And my instinct is to find Ephegos and rip out his throat before asking questions.

"Don't keep me waiting, Royad." I'm barely in control of the need to lay waste to the clearing with my returning power when it is surging through my body like a tidal wave slipping its leash. If I don't know where she is right now, I might actually lose my mind and do exactly that.

"I don't know." His tone is cautious, his posture that of a warrior ready to fight, and he's right to be wary of me. I'm not stable, and Ayna's absence is only a small part of it. I was the carrier of an ancient curse for over a century, the responsibility binding everything I am, including the full extent of my fae magic. And now, that power is let loose, and I've never learned to control it. If I'm not careful, I might actually hurt my cousin by accident.

Smart as he is, Royad takes a step back, lowering his hands in a placating gesture, and the look of him afraid of me drives a bolt into my heart—a heart that was dead until recently and only started beating the day Ayna touched me without flinching away. I remember every time she ever touched me, every place her fingers trailed my skin, my feathers. A shudder rakes through me at the mere thought of her hands—so beautiful and powerful, so delicate and gentle. They might be shattered already under the force of Ephegos's vengeance. Because that's the only reason he'd take Ayna away—even when he believes I'm dead. Because that's the sort of Crow he is.

My chest aches all over again at the betrayal of my oldest friend. Not my family the way Royad is and always has been but something just as close. For a solid century, he's been my confidant and spymaster. He knew every thought, every plan regarding my kingdom. Every time I doubted that breaking the curse was even possible, he was the one encouraging me to keep trying. To try just one more time. Had I known that Sariell was his sister…

"I need to find Ayna." It's a fact, and Royad doesn't object. He's known me all my life, and even before the curse, he'd seen me lose my mind the day Ayna sprinted from the palace and nearly got herself killed by two of the traitor Crows. The fine hair on my arms stands up at the mere memory of it, and the sensation is so new it almost distracts me from the fact that Ephegos betrayed us all. He watched closely how I fell for my wife, urged me to pull out my charming self even though all Ayna ever triggered was to brutally be myself. No masks, no filters. I never pretended to be anything other than the monster I am. And she loves me anyway.

The thought alone boggles my mind in a way few things can boggle an ancient mind such as mine. But the curse is broken, and Ephegos knew I was in love. He faked his own death to join the people he chose as his new allies. Seeing him there at the palace, returned from the dead at the side of the Flames, it fucking hurt to the very core of my being. I trusted him with my life and my safety, with the safety of my people and with Ayna's safety.

Now he took her away to take revenge for Sariell's death.

Had he only told me that she was his sister, things might have gone differently. I might have tried harder. Then, there is no *trying* to fall in love. Either one does or one doesn't. And Sariell, smart and pretty as she was, could never have captured the heart of a resigned king ready to spend the rest of all eternity in isolation for all the crimes his people committed. For the slaughter of entire species, for the abuse of land and resources, for the warfare and torment they brought upon an entire continent. Sariell would have never been the answer to the curse even if I'd known who she was to Ephegos.

Perhaps the curse forbade Ephegos from telling me and influencing my perception of the female—not that it would take any blame off him.

The female's pretty brown face and hazel eyes flash before me as I think of the day she married me with half as much reluctance as all the other brides before her. It makes sense now that she wouldn't be as afraid of me as the others. That she'd be prepared for what she'd find when she was wed to a monstrous king whose brides died year after year because he couldn't fall in love. Because he couldn't make anyone fall in love with him.

Not worthy.

For so many decades, I wasn't worthy. But Ayna made me worthy. Whether I believed I was or not, she saw something in me that wasn't Crow and monster, that wasn't cruel and dangerous. She saw something that no one else could see, and it cost her freedom—it almost cost her life.

My chest tightens with terror at the memory of the moment she pushed me out of harm's way, taking the blow of Ephegos's sword. The blood spilling from her side is something that will haunt my sleep until the end of my days.

She was ready to sacrifice herself for me. And I couldn't let her die. I couldn't let the only woman I've ever loved die before my eyes. I couldn't have lived with seeing hers close forever. So, when the time came to make a choice, I chose her life over mine.

"We need to find her." My tone is back to flat and cold the way it used to be before Ayna, because if I don't find her, this new well of emotion inside of me can never reach the surface, or I'll combust. I shove it down as I meet my cousin's gaze.

Royad nods once, but there are thoughts swirling in his eyes that I can't read as anything other than concern we won't find her, no matter how far we go.

"Spit it out," I order in the voice of his king, not his family, and Royad obeys because he knows me better than to believe this mask. He sees behind it where agony is fighting fury, where love is the only thing keeping me holding on by a thread so I don't unleash my power on this forest and destroy everything in my path as I set out to find the woman I just died to save.

"It's been days since the battle." The lump in his throat bobs as he swallows, probably wondering how much of the unfiltered truth I can bear to hear then deciding he'd rather give me all of it than have me find out later he held something back. Smart him. "It's been days since the battle. We thought you were dead. Princess Cliophera was about to take Ayna to the palace in Aceleau the way you asked her to do if anything happened to you."

I flinch at the memory of the day I struck the bargain with the fairy princess. She'd help Ayna master her water magic, and in return, I'd never again demand a bride. I'd keep my people in the Seeing Forest where we'd be forgotten as the unwanted history of Eherea, a continent where the Crows never belonged anyway. But she agreed to something else: If Ayna survived until Ret Relah, she'd take my wife in and protect her when I no longer could. Because I knew back then that she'd never be safe here with me even if I managed to keep her alive for a full year before I let her go as part of the deal Ayna struck with me.

For weeks, I believed that was all it was, that she looked at me the way she did because of that deal, that the heat in her gaze was all an act. But the night she kissed me for the first time—

My heart gives a wild thud that could have been the sound of her name or that of thunder by the way it shakes me awake.

With a quick dip of my chin, I prompt Royad to continue his story.

"We thought Ephegos and the Flames had fled and the rebellious Crows were all dead. The princess was about to sweep Ayna into her arms and return to Aceleau. But we were wrong." The way his features contort does the opposite of giving me hope. "The combination of Crow power and Flame fire creates explosions of the sort that can take down an entire palace." He shudders at a memory I don't share even if I was there that day. "The palace started to collapse. I grabbed your body, unwilling to leave you behind, even if you had fallen in battle. And Clio took Ayna, and together we ran from the palace—at least, I thought she was right behind me.

"When I made it out the main gate, the palace came down. Cliophera and Ayna weren't behind me. A Flame was. And she handed me this."

Royad reaches into the pocket of his leather pants, drawing my attention to the new scar running down the front of his abdomen. He must have earned it while defending our home—a home now lying in rubble.

With shaking hands, he produces a folded piece of wrinkled parchment, which he holds out to me with an expression resembling death on his usually so well-schooled features.

I take it with equally unsteady fingers, opening the grimy paper, which holds one single smear of blood on the outside, and I hope it's not Ayna's.

The Crows are free, but I have their queen.

I recognize Ephegos's handwriting in an instant, and the power surging through me threatens to destroy me piece by piece. There is no threat added to the note, nothing other than a fact stated like a promise of torture. If Ephegos knows I'm alive, I can't tell from those few words he scribbled.

"I'm going to destroy him." My entire body is shaking again, and this time, I don't even try to pretend I'm in control.

Royad merely places a hand on my shoulder, the touch tearing straight through my chest as I sense his support, his love, his loyalty to both me and my wife.

"I'll be right there with you." From the outskirts of the clearing, males in leather pants and boots step into view, their gazes all shades of brown to blue, and their mostly dark hair longish and bound with leather strings. Their chests are naked, as are their arms where once feathers spread over wings ending in sharp and deadly claws. "As will they."

They bow their heads as I look upon the remains of my people. These twenty beings right here are the last of my species left in this world. The gods nearly reached their goal of letting us come to extinction. They cursed us, tortured us with each new bride we lost, each time we gained hope and lost it so bitterly. With the divide the curse created in my people. But Ayna saved us, and we're finally free.

Now, we're going to free her.

I close my eyes, sending my fae power into the world in a silent call for Ayna's presence—

And wait with my thundering heart for a sign that Ephegos hasn't taken her life as well.

*The story continues in Heart of Night.
Coming May 2024...*

MORE BOOKS IN THE ALCUNAIRE

THE WINGS OF INK SERIES
Wings of Ink
Fall of the Wild Ray: A Wings of Ink Prequel

THE QUARTER MAGE SERIES
The Quarter Mage
The Hour Mage
The Never Mage
The Ever Mage

THE SHATTERED KINGDOM SERIES
Shattered Kingdom
Wicked Crown
Shadow Rule
Lost Towers
Secret Court
Dark Refuge
Reborn Throne
Fatespun

ACKNOWLEDGEMENTS

I have to admit that even after writing over thirty books, every new first in a series is daunting. No matter how exciting it is to begin something new, the fear of getting lost on that journey is real.

Writing a story like this wouldn't be possible without the support of my family. Thank you Mark and Rafael for being understanding and patient when my head is stuck in Eherea all over again.

Every writer needs a team behind them. Mine is incredible and tireless when it comes to diving into my stories and finding all the little things I'd usually miss. Thank you Kath for being there basically 24/7 for my writing emergencies. Emily, you know I appreciate your perspective on the worlds I'm building. I know I wrote the right plot twists once you start yelling at me. Thank you for finding those little details where things don't line up, Beba. You're like a bloodhound ploughing through my manuscript. Margot, for always asking the right questions, and for those little gifs representing your reactions while reading. Thank you all for coming along on this new journey long before anyone else ever read a word of it. Dawn, you're a source of inspiration when it comes to my comma drama. Belle, for the countless times I message you to quickly ask which version a sentence sounds better.

Thank you Barbara for our regular working breakfasts. Your persistence during the most difficult of times has been an inspiration to me. I want to be like you when I grow up. Kathi, for voice memos and coffees in bookshops while we relish the presence of the written word.

To the amazing Royals Guards. Thank you for being on my team. You are the core of lovelies that are my readers. When I write, you are in my thoughts. Your enthusiasm and support is what keeps me going when I'm exhausted or can't see the end of the tunnel. I can't thank you enough for making my book releases something to celebrate.

There are so many people I should be thanking at this point that it would take another four hundred pages, so in order to keep it simple: Thank you everyone who ever touched my life with a good word, a kind gesture, or a moment of peace when everything turned into a cacophony.

Last but not least, to my readers: My work is nothing without your imagination. With your amazing minds, you bring my stories to life. Thank you for taking a chance on me and my books.

CAN'T GET ENOUGH OF
ANGELINA'S WORLDS?

SCAN THIS CODE TO FIND MORE BOOKS
BY ANGELINA J. STEFFORT:

About the Author

"Chocolate fanatic, milk-foam enthusiast and huge friend of the southern sting-ray. Writing is an unexpected career-path for me."

Angelina J. Steffort is a bestselling, award-winning Austrian novelist, best known for her Wings series and her Shattered Kingdom series. With over twenty YA and adult fantasy and paranormal romance books under her belt, Angelina is far from done with inventing and exploring new worlds. That might have something to do with her passion for following the narrative of new characters and getting surprised by the twists they spin on her stories. Angelina has multiple educational backgrounds including engineering, business, music, and acting.

Currently, Angelina lives in Vienna, Austria, with her husband and her son.

Find Angelina on social media as @ajsteffort.

Scan this code to subscribe to Angelina's newsletter:

PRONUNCIATION GUIDE

Character Names

Cliophera Clarette Tarie Amaryll Saphalea de Pauvre (Clio): Clee-oh-phee-rah Clah-rett Tah-rie Ah-mah-ryll Sah-PHAH-lee-ah deh POH-vreh (Clee-oh)
Ephegos: Eh-phee-gus
Erina Latroy Jelnedyn: EH-ree-nah LA-troy Yel-neh-dyn
Myron: My-ran
Recienne Oilvier Gustine Univér Emestradassus de Pauvre: Reh-Syen Ol-liv-yeh Gü-Stin Oo-Nee-Vehr Eh-Mehs-trah-Dahs-sus deh POH-vreh
Royad: Roy-ad
Sariell: Sah-ree-elle
Sejen: See-jen
Wolayna (Ayna) Milevishja: Woh-LI-nah (I-nah) Mee-leh-veesh-jah

World

Aceleau: Ah-Seh-Loh
Ansoli: Un-soh-lee
Askarea: Us-KAH-reh-ah
Brolli: Brol-ly
Cezux: Dje-Zush
Cliffs of Ansoli: Cliffs of Un-soh-lee
Dunai: Doo-NAY
Eherea: Ee-HEE-ree-ah
Eroth: Eh-roth
Fort Perenis: Fort Peh-reh-niss
Horn of Eroth: Horn of Eh-roth
Jezuin: Jeh-Zoo-in ("J" as in "jelly")
Ledrynx: Led-rynx
Leeneae: Lee-nee-ae
Meer: Meer
Plithian Plains: Pli-thee-un Plains
Ret Relah: Reht Reh-luh
Tavras: TUH-vrahs

www.ingramcontent.com/pod-product-compliance
Lightning Source LLC
Chambersburg PA
CBHW031602100925
32277CB00028B/269/J